THE HOUSE OF THE RED DUKE

A PHOENIX RISING

A Phoenix Rising is the first in a series set in the candlelit courts of sixteenth century Europe. Rich in detail, it offers a sensual feast: a glimpse of life as we once lived it. Vivienne has a degree in medieval history and a lifelong passion for the Tudors. For her research, she visited most of the places in the book, using it as an opportunity to step back in time....

Visit her website:
www.viviennebrereton.com

VIVIENNE BRERETON

THE HOUSE OF THE RED DUKE

Passion and power at the Tudor court.

Book One

A PHOENIX RISING

YULETIDE
PRESS

Published by Yuletide Press 2019

Paperback ISBN 978-2-9566531-1-0

A CIP catalogue record for this book is available from the British Library.

Cover design by Sasha Frost

Photo credit: Lee Avison/Arcangel

Inside illustrations: Codex Manesse.

∽

As a point of interest, a glossary of sixteenth century words and terms (as well as foreign expressions) may be found at the end of the novel.

For my parents

With love.

HISTORICAL BACKGROUND

The action in '*A Phoenix Rising*' sweeps across four European courts: English, Scottish, French and Habsburg. The 'House' within the series title refers to the House of Howard, perhaps most famously linked with Catherine, Henry VIII's ill-fated fifth wife. Anne Boleyn's mother was also a Howard. The family's power has endured unabated into present day, unlike the charismatic Tudors who dazzled and disappeared in just over a hundred years.

A glance at a map of the British Isles and Europe in around 1500 might surprise the modern reader. It would be familiar…and yet not. Scotland is a separate kingdom, ruled by the incomparable James IV; there is an uneasy peace in Wales, even under the so-called 'Welsh king', Henry Tudor. Ireland, essentially governed by its chieftains, apart from a small area around Dublin, known as the English Pale, is chafing at the bit Henry VII is trying to place upon it.

As for England, on 22nd August 1485, Bosworth Field, just south of Market Bosworth in Leicestershire (the site of the last significant battle of the Wars of the Roses), finds the Yorkist king, Richard (the supposed murderous uncle of his two nephews, Edward and Richard, in the Tower), pitted against the Lancastrian, Henry Tudor. King Richard is slain and Henry Tudor (now Henry VII) immediately dates the beginning of his reign from 21st August, the day before the battle, making traitors of many a family, including the powerful Howards. The head of the House, John Howard, Duke of Norfolk, has perished with his master, King Richard, at Bosworth, and his son, Thomas Howard, Earl of Surrey, loses his title and is thrown into the Tower.

Across the English Channel, or the Narrow Sea, as it is known, Europe is dominated by two major powers: Valois France and the Habsburg Empire. France is much smaller than the country we know today. For example, England still has one remaining foothold in France: the area around Calais, known as the English Pale.

Other European countries play a smaller, but not insignificant role in politics. Even the far-reaching power of the Pope (God's representative on earth, residing in the Papal States) is dwarfed by the mighty Holy Roman Empire which (during this time frame) includes Germany, Austria, the Low Countries, eastern Burgundy, Savoy, Spain, and most of northern Italy, as well as Naples. If Henry VIII has his sights set on the throne of France, restoring England to its former glory of Henry V's Agincourt, greedy Valois and Habsburg eyes are focussed on Italy, comprised of Venice, Milan, Florence, the Papal States, and Naples. In this race for the spoils of war, Italy is often turned into a bloody battlefield.

'A Phoenix Rising' is a timely novel, resonating with current politics in our time. Henry VIII uses the French expression in one of the opening chapters: *'Plus ça change, plus c'est la même chose.'* {'The more things change, the more they stay the same.'}

* In 1520, there's a magnificent Festival just outside Calais known as 'The Field of Cloth of Gold'. (At the time of going to print, we are a mere one year away from its five hundredth year anniversary.)
* Although small geographically, England is a major player within Europe, where allegiances shift all the time. In 1520, the two great Houses of Valois and Habsburg are courting England.
* The question of Scotland (already an independent country), wishing to be taken seriously within Europe as a separate entity from England, looms large in the novel.
* As does the suspicion against foreigners in London, culminating in the 'Evil May Day' riot in 1517.
* Calais is depicted as a hot spot for both conflict and cooperation, being the last remaining English outpost in Europe.
* The 'Ottoman Turk' is seen as a real threat and a cause for Christian crusaders, ruthlessly determined that they are in the right.

Author's note: Maps featured are not drawn to scale but intended for reference only. The map of Western Europe (although described as circa 1500) reflects the constant readjustment of territories, and includes the previous twenty to thirty years. A map drawn up thirty years later would look very different.

HOUSES OF EUROPE
From February, 1497 to June, 1509

TUDOR

February, 1497

Henry VII, King of England (*'Goose'*)
Elizabeth of York, Queen of England
Arthur, Prince of Wales
Princess Margaret
Henry, Duke of York
Princess Mary
Margaret Beaufort, the King's mother

June, 1509

Henry VIII, King of England
Katherine of Aragon, Queen of England
Margaret (Stewart, Queen of Scotland)
Princess Mary
Margaret Beaufort, the King's mother (died June 29th, 1509)

Howard Family

February, 1497

Thomas, Earl of Surrey
Elizabeth (née Tilney), Countess of Surrey
Lord Thomas Howard
Lord Edward Howard
Lord Edmund Howard
Lady Elizabeth Howard
Lady Muriel Howard

June, 1509

Thomas, Earl of Surrey
Agnes (née Tilney), Countess of Surrey
Sir Thomas Howard
Sir Edward Howard

Lord Edmund Howard
Lady Elizabeth Bullen (Howard)
Lady Muriel Knyvett (Howard)

Bullen (Boleyn) Family

June, 1509

Sir Thomas
Lady Elizabeth (née Howard)
Thomas
Mary
Anne
George

Stafford Family

June, 1509

Edward, third Duke of Buckingham
Eleanor (née Percy), Duchess of Buckingham
Henry
Elizabeth
Katherine
Mary
Ralph Neville (the Duke's ward)

Thomas Wolsey. Royal chaplain and almoner ('*Snake*').
Sir Charles Brandon. Future Marshal of the King's Household, and Master of the Horse

STEWART

February, 1497

James IV, King of Scotland

June, 1509

James IV, King of Scotland
Margaret (née Tudor), Queen of Scotland

VALOIS

February, 1497

Charles VIII, King of France
Anne of Brittany, Queen of France
Louis, Duke of Orléans, (second cousin of the King)
Jeanne, Duchess of Orléans (King Charles's sister)

June, 1509

King Louis XII of France
Anne of Brittany, Queen of France
Princess Claude
(Princess Renée, born 1510)
Louise of Savoy, widow. Countess of Angoulême
François, son. Count of Angoulême. Duc de Valois (heir apparent)

Guillaume Gouffier, seigneur de Bonnivet
Robert de La Marck, seigneur de Florange
Anne de Montmorency

HABSBURG

Maximilian I, Holy Roman Emperor
Archduchess Margaret of Austria (daughter)
Prince Charles of Castile (grandson, born 1500)

Changes in rulers since the birth of Thomas Howard, April, 1443—

England	Scotland	France
Henry VI (Lancastrian)	James II (Stewart)	Charles VII (Valois)
Edward IV (Yorkist)	James III (")	Louis XI (")
Edward V (")	James IV (")	Charles VIII (")
Richard III (")		Louis XII (")
Henry VII (Tudor)		François I (")
Henry VIII (")		

Western Europe circa 1500

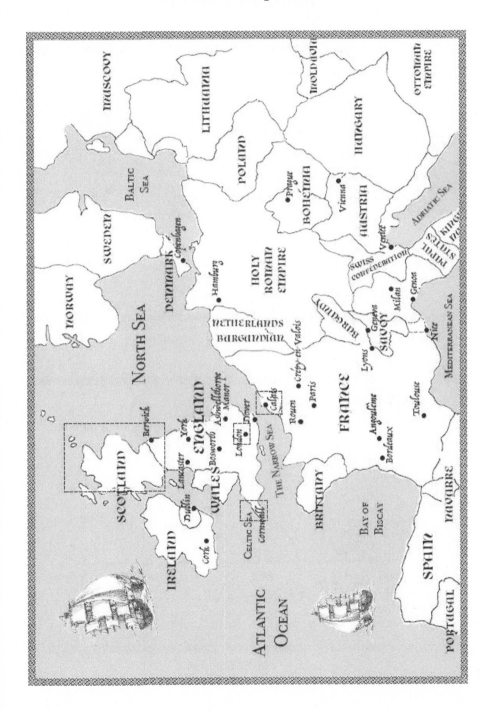

British Isles circa 1500

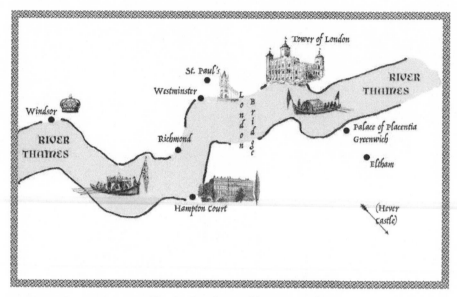

Fig. 1 - London and its surroundings

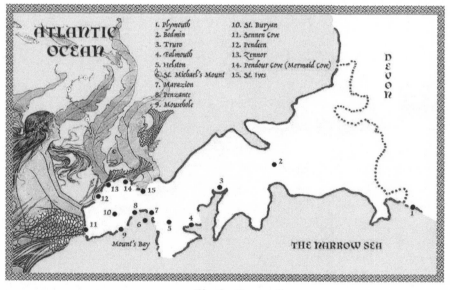

1. Plymouth
2. Bodmin
3. Truro
4. Falmouth
5. Helston
6. St. Michael's Mount
7. Marazion
8. Penzance
9. Mousehole
10. St. Buryan
11. Sennen Cove
12. Pendeen
13. Zennor
14. Pendour Cove (Mermaid Cove)
15. St. Ives

Fig. 2 - Cornwall

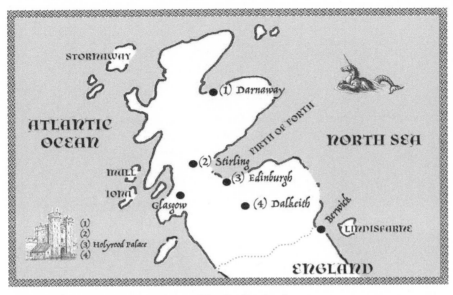

Fig. 3 - Scotland

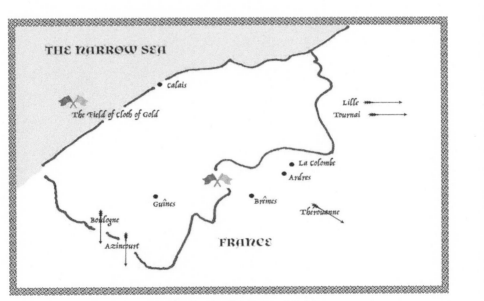

Fig. 4 - English Pale of Calais

Sir Gilbert Talbot to Sir Thomas Howard (Earl of Surrey).
Bosworth Field, August 22nd 1485:

*'Pray tell, Tom, why you supported the tyrant, Richard of the
House of York, the pretender to the throne, who seized it from his
nephew, Edward. Before he and the other royal boy vanished in the
Tower....'*

... *'Because Richard was my crowned King, and if the
Parliamentary authority of England sets the crown upon a stock, I
will fight for that stock. You know me better than anyone, Gilbert.
As I fought for Richard, so I will fight for Henry Tudor, when he is
established by the said authority.'*

PROLOGUE

Twelfth Night, 1497. Zennor Castle, Cornwall, England.

o you think the King and Queen will like me?'
There was trepidation in the girl's voice and she gave an
involuntary shiver.

Aware of a sudden chill in the bedchamber, the boy glanced over at the charred embers in the fireplace - all that remained of the hearty blaze that had greeted them before. Planting a tender kiss on his companion's bare shoulder, he reached for the embroidered green and gold coverlet, lined with ermine. 'Of course they will. You're going to take the court by storm.' Giving her a reassuring smile, he gave the material a little shake.

'Truly?'

He watched the coverlet briefly billow in mid-air before coming to rest over their bodies, in the manner of a sail unfurling on a mast of one of Henry Tudor's fine new ships. 'Truly.'

'What about your father? The thought of meeting him makes me feel faint-hearted.'

The boy sat up. 'You. *"Faint-hearted"*? Never.' But taking note of the expression of uncertainty on her face, his voice softened. 'Father likes pretty women. And you're the fairest maid the length and breadth of Cornwall.'

The girl's fingers fluttered down the outline of her body and fingered the tiny roses and love knots crisscrossing the silk draped over her soft white belly. 'But what if a child should come from this nigh—'

'Hush, sweetheart.' He pressed two fingers to her lips. 'We've done nothing wrong. Besides, we'll be wed soon.' Leaping out of bed, he tossed a glistening black beaver pelt over his shoulders.

'You haven't spoken to your parents yet.'

'I'll speak to them the moment I arrive home.' He strode across the room to throw some more logs on the fire, using a brass poker to split the wood. He

1

watched while the timber spluttered, crackled, and spat out little sparks, before bursting into satisfying flames. Then he grabbed a pair of flickering candles, perched on the mantelpiece, and returned to her side. Placing the candles on the table next to the bed, he lifted a pitcher and poured some golden liquid into a goblet. Raising the cup to his lips, he drank deeply.

'Delicious! Mead fit for a king…or a queen,' he grinned, holding it out to her. 'What a clever idea of yours for such a special night. Wherever did you find it?'

She gave a shy smile. 'From the monastery…over at Saint Buryan. My friend, Alys, says it's an elixir made by fairies, not monks. Or, at least, that's what her mother told her. Mistress Matilda's always sworn that the monks toil by day and the fairy folk by night.'

'A fairy potion?' The boy's hazel eyes were full of mirth as he stretched out his long limbs. 'Then we must have it at our wedding feast. And drink it each day thereafter until the next full moon. Like other lovers do. To bring us luck.'

She pointed at a silver pewter plate on the table upon which lay a dozen pale brown squares, with a sprig of marjoram and a clove in the centre of each one. 'Would you like some gingerbread? Our cook made it for my birthday.'

'Gladly. Have you noticed that lovemaking increases the appetite?' he teased, taking a piece and breaking it in two, popping one half in his mouth while feeding her the other. His shapely lips widened into a smile. 'Mmm. Sinfully sweet and spicy. Just like you.'

The girl blushed. 'The cook got the recipe from a peddler at the fair at Marazion this past spring.'

'The fair where you were crowned Queen of the May? I wish I'd been there. I would have wed you on the spot.'

She reached out to touch his cheek. 'If only we'd known each other then, matters would be so much simpler now.'

Noticing a tiny frown on the girl's smooth brow, he took the goblet from between her fingers and set it down. 'Don't fret, Grace. Father won't refuse me. I'm his favourite son.'

'What of my father?'

'He'll be pleased you've made such a good match.'

'Better than—'

'Yes! Far better than *him*.'

❧

They fell silent for a few moments, the air between them thick with unspoken words; from the great hall below, came the faint sound of drums and the strains of a hurdy gurdy, interspersed with gales of laughter from the revellers.

The boy nodded towards the door, a thick swathe of dark chestnut hair falling across his face. '"*The Horses' Brawl*". Your brother seems to be leading everyone a merry dance in his role of Lord of Misrule. What luck he managed to find the bean in the Twelfth Night cake.'

His companion gave a mischievous giggle. 'I confess luck has very little to do with it. Will and I long ago decided that finding the bean should be a matter of family honour.'

'I see. Then we're very well matched. Your family and mine. A Tredavoe and a Howard. I'd love to see you as the Lady of Misrule.'

'You will,' she said, stroking his hair, 'but not tonight.'

He grasped her fingers in his and kissed them one by one. 'No, not tonight. I only hope we haven't been missed in the great hall.'

'Oh, Ned, why can't we just run away and find a priest?'

The girl gave another shiver and the boy pulled her closer to his chest. 'My love, a Howard never runs away, I've learned that from my father. He's never run away from anything in his whole life. And he always gets up to fight another day. I've told him he reminds me of a phoenix rising from the ashes.'

'Here, let me prove my love for you.' He bent over her and grazed her lips with his own, a laugh catching in his throat. 'My sweeting tastes of honey, cinnamon and ginger, with a hint of saffron.' He placed one hand on his heart: '"*Her mouth was as sweet as any mead whatever.*" So wrote that clever poet, Geoffrey Chaucer.' He drew her to him again. 'With this kiss I plight my troth.'

Entwining her arms around his neck, the girl returned his long embrace with equal passion.

❧

At length, when they were both left gasping for breath, he broke away. Picking up a strand of her long flaxen hair, he wound it tightly around the fourth finger of her left hand. 'Some say this finger has a vein that leads straight to the heart.'

The girl's green eyes flashed. Wiggling her finger, she traced a path downwards from her chin to her chest. 'See. Mine has.'

'Soon you'll be one of us.'

'A Howard?'

'Yes. My wife. Grace Tredavoe no more.'

She let out a long sigh of contentment. 'I can almost hear the King's herald announcing our arrival in the great hall at Westminster for the Christmas celebrations.' Pretending to hold up a trumpet, she adopted a suitably deferential tone: '"Your Majesties, may I present Lord Edward Howard—"'

He laughed. '"And Lady Grace How—"'

'We'll be dressed in such finery and look so happy that the King will—'

'Immediately send me to the Tower for my impudence. Henry Tudor abhors any attempt to outdo him.'

The girl let out a gasp. 'Don't ever say that again, Ned. Not even in jest. Promise me.'

'I promise. But Father has taught us never to be afraid of anything or anyone. Certainly not of the King. He calls him "*Goose*" behind his back.'

'"*Goose*". Why?'

The boy made a clucking noise and flapped his arms against his sides, intending to make her smile again. 'To poke fun at him. For all the harm he's done our family.'

He hugged her tight. 'My love, I only want to please you. That's why I came bearing a gift for the day of your birth. But you have to close your eyes first.'

The boy climbed out of bed and walked over to the window where he reached into a pocket of his green jerkin, draped over a chest. 'Don't open them until I tell you,' he said, reclaiming his place next to her. Grabbing her finger again, he gently unwound the strand of hair and eased a gold ring onto it. 'Not yet. Not yet. *Now*. You can open them now.'

The girl's eyes flew open and she gave a squeal of delight. 'A posy ring! It's so pretty. I love it. And a perfect fit, you clever thing.'

'I had it engraved especially for you. That's why there are sixteen stars on the band: one for each week we've known each other. And for each year you've been on earth. There's something written on the inside too. Take it off so you can read it.'

Biting her lip in excitement, the girl slipped the ring off her finger and read the words in black. Then she gazed into her lover's eyes and slowly repeated them:

'"*My brightest star, my one true love. N.*"'

She gave a sigh of contentment. 'I had no idea it was possible to be this happy.'

'Nor I.'

'Or that a ring could give such pleasure.'

'Nothing less will do for my betrothed. Wait and see. Father is going to make the Howards great again. Second to none…but the Tudors. He's always told us to reach for the stars.'

The girl lay her head down on his chest again and held up her ring, twisting it around in the air. 'Look! I'm reaching for them.'

Closing his fingers over hers, the boy spoke softly. 'We'll reach for them together, sweeting.'

'I do hope you're right about everything.'

'I am. Trust me, as surely as those snowflakes dusting the window pane outside your bedchamber, the fire blazing in the hearth, and the wind howling above Zennor Quoit…all will be well.…'

Spring, 1497.
Ardres Castle, Picardy, France.

William had never seen his sister look so captivating. Or pale. Seated upon a dappled grey mare next to him, her gaze was fixed upon the blue and silver towers and turrets of the imposing castle beyond. The two of them, with their father some way ahead, and several servants bringing up the rear, were crossing the wooden bridge over the moat, on the final part of their journey.

He wondered what was going through her mind as she looked at the unfamiliar castle, so different from their own at Zennor. Was she missing the Celtic sea foaming far beneath their home, at the furthermost tip of Cornwall? Savage and unforgiving when the winter evenings drew in, with enormous waves that made a thunderous sound as they came crashing down upon the dark rugged rocks; yet warm and welcoming as the sun rose in the summer skies, playing host to the friendly dolphins that came to sport there.

He noticed her slender fingers reach down and brush across the flat stomacher of her pale blue gown, with a stroke as light as a feather against gossamer. All of a sudden, he knew exactly what was going through her mind. She looked up at him and her lips curled in a small smile so filled with love and trust it made him feel more rotten than a maggot-pie.

Not long now, she mouthed at him.

Knowing he didn't deserve either her affection or her loyalty, it was as if a knife was being twisted in his gut. He was no more than a Judas. A dissembling canker-blossom. A waterfly who didn't even have the courage to face up to what he'd done. He couldn't bear the thought of the shock and pain in those luminous green eyes of hers, were she to discover the truth. By the Mass! If his terrible secret ever came to light, he feared he'd lose her forever.

PART ONE

FIELD OF GOLD

*' If my head would win him
a castle in France,
when there was war between us,
it should not fail to go. '*

Sir Thomas More (1478-1535).

HOUSE OF HOWARD

Chapter One

Twenty-three years later. 26th April, 1520. London.

I'faith!' burst out John, from the other end of the wherry. 'Listening to the pair of you, I sometimes think the river's the only place on earth we can't be harmed by intrigue.'

'Unless your Uncle Thomas and I are the ones doing the intriguing,' laughed his father, dipping his oar into the Thames and winking at me. Although there was nearly a score and ten years between us, Robert's craggy face (the same hue as a sugar-candied walnut) narrowed the gap and was evidence of a life lived outside, in all weathers.

'True,' I said, glancing over at the formidable Tower of London on my right, and pulling my red and gold velvet blanket more tightly around my knees. Even though the sun was shining, there was a fresh breeze quite capable of stirring up discomfort in my tiresome joints. I pitied the poor souls imprisoned within, listening to the distant sound of church bells, wondering whether they'd ever get any closer than the four walls of their grim dank cells.

'The courts of Europe seem as complex as a spider's web,' said John. 'Alack! Danger lurking around every corner—'

''Fore God!' exclaimed Robert, leaning down on his oar. 'We've got intrigue enough to contend with here in England, without crossing the Narrow Sea for some motley-minded festival that'll empty our coffers and put nothing back on the table. Three weeks of hogwash, if you ask me. Your Uncle Thomas knows what I mean.'

'I do,' I said. 'About both. The Festival and the intrigue. I've seen enough courtiers pitted against each another, hoping to bring down a rival faction with the right whisper in the royal ear. Posing as men of wisdom and culture, some of them are no better than a common tittle-tattler, their tongues as sharp as any fishwife's on Billingsgate Wharf.'

9

John's oar threw up an arc of water next to me. 'Sounds like a fair smattering of our passengers, spinning tales to make the hairs on the back of a man's neck stand on en—'

'Zounds!' puffed his father. 'Idle prating by lords, ladies, the occasional rich cutpurse, bawd or pimp. Not to mention, envoys, carping priests—'

'A lone passenger is likely to confide in us…up to a point,' interrupted John. 'But a group may forget we're there. Hey-ho! Those are always the best titbits.'

I blinked some drops of water from my eyes. 'I've lost count of how many times your "titbits" have helped me at court. This wherry would be a match for any confessional on land.'

'We took Mary to Westminster last week,' said Robert.

'Your granddaughter grows prettier every day, Uncle Thomas. That fine new husband of hers was eyeing up your throne, but we soon put him right.'

I laughed, well able to picture the scene. My '*throne*' had appeared one day a few years ago: a carved chair - complete with a thick leather belt - carefully crafted onto the middle bench. It was named thus to spare my feelings; growing older was never easy.

"*Only a Howard will ever be able to use it,*" the two wherrymen had told me. It amused me how rigidly they kept to the rule.

We were fast approaching London Bridge, a place where many a faint-hearted wherry passenger jumped out at '*The Three Canes*' before rejoining the boat downstream at Billingsgate. The foundations of the bridge created perilous rapids at high or low tide, but for me '*shooting the bridge*' was as exciting a ride as any I'd ever had on horseback - or with the comeliest wench, for that matter. I was not afraid. Like a clucking mother hen, Robert had already ensured my belt was in place; it was a running joke between us that I unstrapped myself whenever he wasn't looking. I also knew that the two of them were the best wherrymen in London and I would trust them with my life. I'd already trusted Robert with all my secrets….

When we were alone in the wherry ('*The Thames Rose*', the grandest on the river, I'd seen to that, demanding an ornate, gilded wooden canopy to shield the passengers from the ever-changing elements), titles were of no import; we were merely Robert, John, and Uncle Thomas: as close as any family related by blood. We Howards had been using the Warner family of wherrymen for as far back as I could remember; indeed, John was named for my father. Many a time had the pair of them acted as my spies, discovering on water - through loose tongues - what was about to take place on land. And many a time had I gone to Greenwich and happily supped at their table in Turnpin Lane, warmly drawn into the bosom of their big riotous family. I think King Henry suspected Robert's value to me judging by the number of times he'd mentioned how much he enjoyed meeting him that icy winter's day, long ago.

<<*Fortunately, like the slippiest eel in the river below, I'm not so easily caught*>> I thought.

Above our heads, I could see daily life carrying on in all the buildings on the bridge. It was almost high tide so the river was particularly ferocious today, making further conversation impossible. As we drew nearer, all I could hear was the booming sound of rushing water, every bit as menacing as any intrigue at the Tudor court.

'Here we go!' I yelled, clinging onto the armrests of my throne as the boat hit the rapids and plunged headfirst into the raging waters—

'God's Death! That was a good one,' gasped Robert, wiping rivulets of water from his cheeks as we left the bridge behind us.

'It certainly was.' I said, pleased I'd managed to escape a total soaking - even though I had a change of clothes with me.

In front of us, the Thames snaked onwards in the direction of our destination. In the far distance, I could see the outline of the soaring wooden spire of Saint Paul's Cathedral. Beneath us, the sunlight was creating as many intricate patterns on the icy waters as on one of the King's Turkey carpets. Once again, the river put me in mind of the court: normally, it was more congested, with smaller boats edging around the bigger ones as best they could, leaving the magnificent barges to sally forth with all the confidence of Henry striding through his presence chamber....

HOUSE OF HOWARD

Chapter Two

The same day. Hampton Court Palace, Surrey.

I've lived through the reigns of six kings. And served four of them to the best of my ability>> I thought. Robert and John had left me seated in a small panelled chamber on a high-backed wooden chair (made bearable for my old bones by a red velvet cushion), my trusty wooden cane by my side.

As I twiddled my thumbs and tapped my foot, waiting to be summoned, in my mind's eye, I could easily conjure up the six of them: the son of the great victor of Agincourt whose wits came and went; the larger than life warrior with his commoner wife, and love of mutton stew and kissing comfits. *This* king had seen fit to knight me before his early death when the throne passed, firstly to his eldest boy who held the golden crown in his small hands for a mere seventy-seven days. After this, the dead warrior's throne was occupied (amidst a firestorm of discontent and divisiveness) by his equally accomplished, slightly crookbacked younger brother, now reviled and never mentioned. *That* king had bestowed a dukedom on my father, and an earldom on me. Then there was Madge Beaufort's boy, the miser, who'd brought peace to the kingdom and saved it from financial ruin. How could I forget *him* when he'd had me flung into the Tower after Bosworth? Yet, I didn't bear Henry Tudor a grudge, even though I knew his claim to the English throne to be as weak as a piss-poor pot of small beer. No, rather I pitied the man, secretly giving him the nickname '*Goose*' for my own amusement, and those closest to me. He reminded me of a wary gander the way he spent most of his reign nervously glancing back over his shoulder, on the look out for so-called 'pretenders', some with a far better claim to the throne.

Then there was the most recent one. The eighth Henry who'd turned out to be the most mercurial of them all (and strangely enough, as a boy, had been served by a fool called John Goose). With his ever-changing moods, he reminded me of a will-o'-the-wisp over marshland, just beyond reach, luring a man to a watery end with lights that might well prove to be false. Or a magnificent red and gold butterfly, alighting on a favoured flower for the briefest of moments, before moving on to pastures anew. Fortunately, I knew exactly why he wanted to see me today. I only hoped he'd hurry as by now, my earth-vexing knees were tormenting me, and one of the servants had forgotten to pack my meadowsweet and white willow bark cordial to ease the biting pain. I hated the discomfort because it made me remember I was a very old man.

'Nearing full four score,' I muttered aloud. 'A walking miracle in these times of ours.'

But I knew if I died tomorrow, I could go to my grave a happy man. Thanks to me, the Howards were riding high at court once more, perhaps the reason why a cushion had been provided and a fire thoughtfully lit in front of me in the brightly painted fireplace - even though a whole host of Queens of the May would be crowned a few days hence. The path from that first stinking cell in the Tower to this opulent room with its mural of long-limbed Greek heroes, and ceiling of gold and blue, studded with badges and devices, had been long and difficult.

If I closed my eyes, I could see my twelve-year-old son, Edward (a small copy of myself at the same age, all dark flashing eyes, thick mop of brown hair, and toothsome grin), hurling himself into my outstretched arms outside the walls of the Tower, upon my release. After three long years, he clung to me as if he'd never let me go.

"Father, you're like a phoenix!" he'd breathed.

"I give you my word I'll restore the family's fortunes," I replied, smiling over at Robert who'd safely delivered my three sons to me in his wherry.

Well, I'd kept my promise. Restoring the good name and wealth of a family that could trace its lineage all the way back to the first Edward, commonly known as 'Longshanks', through our connection with Joan of

Cornwall. A family having as its motto: '*Sola virtus invicta*'. Blinking away a rogue tear of emotion, I turned my gaze to a portrait of Dame Fortune on the wall next to me. I put on my spectacles in order to have a better look at this universally feared woman. Capricious by nature, she had a deceptive smile on her lovely face. Clothed in blue and gold, with a matching tall pointed hennin on her head to which a long white veil had been attached, she was standing by her formidable wheel. Her slender white hands, resting on the shoulder of some unfortunate king as she steadied him to the ground, were half-hidden beneath the folds of the blue velvet sleeves. I knew as well as any that the Dame's outer beauty belied the steeliness within as she calmly prepared to watch kings and queens, men and maids, all come tumbling down.

I felt as though someone had jabbed me with a sharp needle; it suddenly occurred to me that my chair had been placed next to the portrait with the express purpose of unsettling me. By sending me a stark reminder:

<<*Don't forget from whence you've come and to where Dame Fortune can easily return you*>>

It did not take a great deal of imagination on my part to know exactly *who* that someone was. Yet here I was to tell the tale. I allowed myself a fleeting smile of triumph at the expense of that 'someone'.

However, I was not so arrogant not to accept that on my death bed, I would be taking regrets for my (unavoidable) misdeeds, as well as my secrets, to the next life. One or two of which I'd never confess. Certainly not to one of those scurvy-valiant priests who came creeping up to the bedside. Rubbing their hands in glee at the thought of all those gold pieces about to drop into their sweaty palms as the dying unburdened their guilt, in the hope of a swift passage through purgatory. Whatever my secrets were, they were mine and mine alone to divulge or keep.

<<*Robert Warner, the wherryman, is the only person on earth*—>>

HOUSE OF HOWARD

Chapter Three

*G*ood day, Thomas. The King and I will see you now.'
As usual, Tom Wolsey had the temerity to pronounce these
words as if *he* were the most important man in the kingdom,
not the one within.

'Good day,' I replied, the gruff tone of my perfunctory greeting letting
him know I was in no mood for idle chatter. I watched him open his mouth to
utter some annoying pleasantry and then quickly snap it shut again.

I'd never cared for the man who appeared in the doorway to the outer
chamber. Nearing fifty, tall and stocky, his large blue eyes were full of
intelligence while his well-defined lips hinted at a sensual nature not supposed
to be found in a churchman. How many bastards did he have with that
woman? One? *Two.* What was her name? Joan, if my memory served
me well. Dressed in a red silk cassock buttoned down to his toes, I noted
the garment had a train so long most of the ladies at court would be hard-
pressed to match it. *<<How typical of the gorbellied footlicker>>* I thought.

On the other hand, he did have qualities I admired, however begrudgingly.
Such as his ability to work from morning to evening for twelve hours straight.
His secretary had once told me he did this *"without rising once to piss"*. I could
not deny that on many an occasion, he'd served the King well, holding the
tiller of the royal ship steady while the captain was absent. For one so lowly
born, his abilities gave him unprecedented access to a royal personage. In our
long association, as far as my feelings towards him were concerned, the pendulum had swung back and forth between tolerance and utter loathing. Once,
and only once, had we come close to anything that resembled friendship....

Today, with both of my knees gleefully aflame and determined to undo me, the pendulum was not in Wolsey's favour. I was both startled and vexed to have been caught unawares in my reverie by the accursed butcher's boy. <<*One who's had the audacity to try and equal or surpass his betters (such as we Howards) with this bat-fowling climb of his to the very pinnacle of power. Paying no heed if he knocks down a member of a noble family on his way up. Or an entire dynasty, for that matter. As he scrambles to reach rarefied air he's not fit to breathe*>> True, he was a Cardinal appointed by the Pope in Rome, but he was exactly one of those priests to whom I would never entrust my innermost secrets.

I prayed my right knee would not fail me and managed a more or less successful attempt at standing. No doubt Wolsey's sharp eyes noticed it involved my holding on for dear life to the sturdier staff the Howard carpenter had recently made for me. Giving up silent thanks to God and breathing an inaudible sigh of relief, I vowed to richly reward my servant. I could still feel the beady eyes of the Lord Chancellor upon me. <<*God's Wounds! I won't give him the satisfaction of seeing me falter*>>

'No need!' I snapped, when he attempted to take my arm.

With his love of the food and wine that was brought up from his vast kitchens, his voluminous crimson robes couldn't disguise the rolls of flesh beneath. He was certainly stout enough to support the two of us. His solicitude had the same effect on me as hearing a rat scratching on the floorboards beneath the bed, just out of reach, knowing it's going to rob you of your night's slumber. I'd known Tom Wolsey ever since he first slid into the service of this king's father (causing me from then on to rename him '*Snake*'). So I was only too aware all this show was merely his way of reminding me I was being received in *his* palace, in *his* presence chamber. And that I was *his* guest.

Again, I haughtily waved away his offer of help as he held open the heavy oak door for me. Temporarily blinded by a wall of sunlight streaming through the mullioned windows as I crossed the threshold into the large chamber beyond, for one heart-stopping moment, I nearly lost my balance. Instantly, I felt the light touch of *Snake*'s hand beneath my elbow.

'Let me help you.'

'No need,' I repeated though gritted teeth as I righted myself. Too clever to be caught out in a public insult, I was already deftly lifting my elbow beyond his reach and using it to make a grand flourish to the King....

HOUSE OF HOWARD

Chapter Four

*H*ave you heard what they're saying, Thomas?'

'Your Majesty?'

'The whole of Europe is buzzing with it.'

The young King (a couple of months shy of his twenty-ninth birthday) was a resplendent figure, clad from head to toe in May-time green. He had a most pleasing appearance: *"His skin is as clear and fair as that of a pretty maid,"* one foreign envoy, wishing to curry favour, had written home. *"His closely-cropped auburn hair is combed straight and short in the French fashion, and his red beard neatly trimmed."*

The blue-grey eyes (inherited from his Yorkist mother) beneath arched, perhaps too delicately feminine eyebrows, had a questioning look in them today. I knew they always took in every detail of the world around him.

"Hal worries his eyes are piggy, and his mouth too thin and tight," Edward had once told me in confidence. Happily, daily praise had been heaped upon Henry, sufficient to make any man's head swell. What was it his tutor, John Skelton, had once written?

> *"Adonis of fresh colour,*
> *Of youthe the godely flower—"*

'Thomas?'

I suddenly realized I hadn't yet answered Henry's question. With a little shake, I pulled myself together. 'Forgive me. Buzzing with talk of the Festival?'

Snake cleared his throat. 'Er, before we discuss that, gentlemen, may I suggest we find Thomas a comfortable seat.'

Without further to-do, I was ushered to the opposite side of the room: to a golden chair (that almost resembled a throne), with a golden cushion...beside a huge ornate fireplace. Across from me (divided by a Turkey carpet as expansive as the Narrow Sea), stood *Snake*'s walnut writing desk, near a window seat with an overhanging bird cage. The desk was littered with important looking, red-ribboned documents.

I could almost hear his wearisome proclamation: Each one is a matter of life and death.

<<*How premature of me to have thanked my stars for helping me trump the swag-bellied popinjay on my way in here*>>

In one fell swoop, he'd managed to remove me from close proximity to the King. As well as demote me in the royal eyes as if I were some witless, beslubbering greybeard, dribbling pottage down his chin, carelessly consigned to the hearth. I was to be seated while the other two stood. Deliberately hanging a huge question mark over my fitness to still serve the King. I had to hand it to the devil-monk. He was a master manipulator of situations, every inch my equal. How else could one of such meagre birth have risen so high in the royal service and remained there?

Fuming, I looked around the magnificent chamber with its walls hung with tapestries (famous throughout Europe) of cloth of gold, illustrating the triumphs of Petrarch. Hampton Court might belong to the Lord Chancellor of England (known equally as the Archbishop of York and Pope's Cardinal) but a foreigner visiting our shores could be forgiven for thinking such opulence rightfully belonged to the King. Again, the clever Skelton, knowing *Snake* had spent no less than two hundred thousand crowns on his private dwelling, penned another poem, deftly dipping his quill in poison this time:

> "*The King's court*
> *Should have excellence*
> *But Hampton Court*
> *Hath the pre-eminence* – "

Henry came to stand next to me, his face as excited as a little boy about to pick up a sword for the first time. Far be it for me to point out that responsibility for the Festival did not lie entirely with him. Although it stuck in my craw to admit it, *Snake* had done the lion's share of the work. I needed my wits about me. 'They're saying it'll be the most exciting event of the century.'

The colour was high in the King's cheeks as was always the case when he was roused to anger or any extreme emotion. <<*I've always sworn that red-headed women are more than enough for one man to handle; the same is equally true for the males*>> I went a little further. 'They're saying it's your most ambitious project yet.'

'It is.' Henry's face suddenly became serious as it did whenever the mood took him to compose verses; I knew he fancied himself the most gifted poet in the land.

'As impressive as any comet that has ever blazed its way through the night skies,' he intoned, looking at the two of us for approval. 'Leaving a fiery trail in its wake, and filling all those who observe it with awe. Already, the plans for the buildings are being compared favourably with the efforts of Leonardo, the miracles of the Egyptian pyramids, and the wonders of the Roman amphitheatres. The French....'

The King's ardour, as he continued to wax lyrical, reminded me of my Edward. That would explain their closeness - except no cloud ever appeared in Edward's skies. He was one who lived for the moment, not for the future. Hasty and often reckless, life was there to be seized. On the other hand, Henry Tudor also lived for the moment but he fully expected his deeds to be remembered with awe by future generations. So what better plan to appeal to his supreme vanity? To take six thousand of his subjects across the Narrow Sea to France...in order to meet an equal number from the rival court, in a place agreeable to both kings.

For the moment, our two countries were at peace. And every Frenchman no longer regarded by the English as the devil incarnate.

Outwardly...that is.

How could I forget it was only three years, almost to the day, since *Snake* and I knelt before Henry in Westminster Hall, pleading for the lives of Londoners who had taken to the streets to protest against the disagreeable presence of foreigners swarming around the capital. Little distinction was made amongst French, Venetian, Spanish, or Burgundian merchants: they were all seen variously as the enemy of any Englishman.

Known as 'Evil May Day', the rioting had begun when a Frenchman snatched a pair of plump doves out of the hands of a London carpenter at a market in Eastcheap.

"*Mordieu!*" he'd cried. "*You aren't fit to eat them, you scurvy knave. They're going to the table of my master, the French Ambassador.*"

Matters escalated, became ugly, lives were lost, men were punished, and I, for one, was happy to be sitting here today contemplating a brighter future. One where men would act like civilized human beings, not rabid dogs straining at the leash, intent upon doing harm to any in their way.

To celebrate this present harmony, a magnificent festival (in its final stages of preparation, as *Snake* never tired of reminding everyone) was to be held, just outside the English Pale of Calais, and the village of Ardres in Picardy, belonging to France. This friendly contest between the two nations had been lovingly orchestrated by the omnipotent *Snake*, hot on the heels of his breathtakingly bold Treaty of London, two years ago.

"*Mark my words, Thomas,*" he'd crowed at the time, "*it'll herald an entirely new vision of peace in Christendom.*"

It pained me to think the Pale was the very last remnant of English territory in France. Captured nearly two hundred years ago by the Plantagenet Edward, this pitiful one hundred and twenty square miles was all we had left from that triumphant era. Relying on a higgledy-piggledy population of about twelve thousand English, Fleming and Picard to raise the flag of Saint George—

'How apt,' *Snake* was saying, 'that everyone is calling it "The Field of Cloth of Gold" or "*Le Camp du Drap d'Or*".'

I winced at both his comment and his excellent French accent. <<*It's as if the fawning coxcomb has invented the name himself*>> Not to be outshone, I scrambled to impress with my knowledge, focusing on the outrageously expensive stiff fabric, using gold. 'Hardly surprising considering people intend to wear cloth of gold—'

'Which is all that will be seen for miles and miles,' interrupted *Snake*. 'The tents and pavilions are made from it.'

'My son, Edmund,' I parried back, using a sharp blade to remind *Snake* he was not part of a House like the Howards, 'tells me the invitations to attend are more highly sought-after than anything before.'

'As precious as gold dust,' beamed Henry. 'Which is just as it should be.'

'Exactly,' I said, ignoring *Snake* and looking straight at the King.

'And "how apt",' I continued, parroting *Snake*, 'for a royal undertaking such as yours, that by a strange quirk of fate, the old name for the Festival ground used to be "*Le Val Doré*". I am sure Your Majesty can appreciate how those remaining behind, such as myself, can't help but marvel at the idea of so great a number - as many as dwell in Norwich, our second greatest city - all joined together in splendid revelry, music, and sport. And it's all your doing.'

<<*So God mend me! I've just stripped the Lord Chancellor, Cardinal, and Archbishop of all his fair dues. In one fell swoop. Transferred all the credit to the King. Let's see how Snake follows that one*>>

'Thomas, you must forgive me but I quickly need to show the King a list of his possible departure dates from Dover. I prepared them before I broke my fast.'

I bristled as I realized he'd set off down a different path altogether… clutching a muddy-mettled list, calculated to upstage me.

'With the Emperor's imminent visit here next month,' he continued, 'it's a matter of some urgency. But we wanted to let you know we've decided to leave you in charge of the country for the duration of the Festival. Together with Fox and Warham,' he added so hastily he almost choked and his eyes began to water. Anything to downplay the importance of my role on the royal council.

"*We've decided to leave you in charge of the country*", indeed! As if I hadn't already been informed of it by my spies. How I hated the way the Lord Chancellor, when writing "*The King and I*" in his correspondence, preferred to use Latin because the grammar of "*Ego et rex meus*" meant he preceded Henry.

❧

The King turned to me. 'I apologize for making you wait but I suppose we need to get the date arranged. However, I promise we won't take long. There's something I want to ask you.'

'And I, you.'

Henry's respectful tone went a long way to mollifying me. <<*Let Snake try and have his moment in the royal sunshine at my expense. For all his bluster and bold talk, he's no more than an annoying flea that might alight on the fur of one of my hunting dogs, waiting to be picked or shaken off*>> I was but biding my time. If only he knew what I wanted to ask the King (in private) later, he'd forget about his qualling dates in an instant. It was as much as I could do not to laugh out loud, imagining an entire gamut of emotions rippling across the smug face: fury, frustration, envy, to name but three. At the very least, just thinking about it gave me as much pleasure as a man glancing down at his empty trencher to discover an unexpected last slice of succulent pork, concealed beneath a swirl of apple sauce, and a sprig of rosemary.

<<*Oh, Snake, you have no idea!*>>

Snake's lips were still puckered in an insincere smile as he looked at me; undoubtedly, he'd been peeved by the King's obvious concern for me, as well as his affection. 'I'm sure you appreciate why the matter of dates is so important.'

I fought to remain composed, knowing his clapper-clawed matter was no more than a ruse to lower my standing in the eyes of the King, as if *his* business was more pressing.

Henry glanced at me before turning to his Lord Chancellor. 'Naturally, Thomas does. He's always understood the beating heart of England.'

I was delighted to hear Henry coming to my aid in the manner of a knight thundering down the lists, his lady's favour fluttering in the breeze, atop his lance. 'I'm flattered,' I said, waiting to see how *Snake* would respond to such an unequivocal compliment that bordered on being a reproof to him.

'His Majesty's words couldn't be truer,' he simpered. 'I, too, apologize again for abandoning you.'

I wasn't surprised to see my rival easily rising to the occasion as he walked over to me and held out a goblet, as if it were an enforced peace offering.

'In the meantime, do accept some hyppocras and enjoy the view from the window. You might be able to see the new busts of two Roman emperors I commissioned from Giovanni da Maiano.'

Fixing a polite smile on my face to mirror his, and disguise the contempt beneath, I pointedly turned away from the windows with their obscenely expensive silk curtains, back to the fireplace.

<<*Why can't the hedge-born Chancellor ever have anything simple?*>>

Even the flames leaping inside the grate, with two impressive pillars on either side, seemed bigger than normal. Even so, I could feel myself gradually succumbing to the warmth and *Snake*'s irksomely delicious drink. From time to time, snatches of their hushed conversation reached me from across the carpet, breaking into my thoughts:

—'Another reason we need to decide on a date soon, Your Majesty, is to give Guînes Castle ample time to prepare a banquet—'

—'I know. I know. To outshine the one being held over at Ardres. Never fear, Tom, ours will be better. And the beauty of the Englishwomen will put their sisters across the Narrow Sea in the shade—'

As their voices floated away again, hearing this last comment drew my mind back to another time, long ago, when I'd met an exceptionally pretty young Frenchwoman. With this image in my head (the warmth of the fire easing all the pain from my bones, as well as the tantalizingly sweet taste of Ashwellthorpe Manor apple sauce sitting on my tongue), I could almost imagine myself in France again. France....

VALENTINE

Chapter Five

The same day. La Colombe.
Not far from Ardres Castle, Picardy.

J won't wed him! Not even if he waits until the end of time. He's no better than that other devil's spawn.'

'*Serpe Dieu*! If you had to take that one to husband, *mon enfant*, I would never have a moment's rest in my bed for the rest of my days.'

Valentine de Fleury placed her hand over her chest to still her thudding heart. She could feel tears pricking at her eyelids as she gazed through the window of the small chamber. '*Seigneur aie pitié de moi*,' she whispered, crossing herself.

She was standing on a stool in front of a mirror, the family's housekeeper, Béatrice, kneeling on the floor behind, the hem of the slightly threadbare blue dress in her hands. Valentine's spirits sank further when - in the distance - she caught sight of the retreating bulk of the old Baron swaying from side to side, astride his horse. He was ambling his way past the far end of the springtime garden: a riot of colour, every single inch taken up with plants, vegetables and flowers. Watching him pass between the crumbling gate posts of La Colombe's entrance, a mingled feeling of disgust and fresh despair washed over her. How could it not when she noted how his green-clothed rump was stretched almost as wide as that of his poor horse.

Valentine knew every inch of this countryside by heart. Beyond the gate, the blue-grey turrets of Ardres Castle, the newly-built home of Guy d'Ardres, the Governor of Picardy, were visible. The Castle was currently the focus of intense activity - in readiness for a magnificent banquet to be held in a few weeks time. It was to be the opening event of the Festival, mirrored by one held by the English at Guînes. Just past the Castle, in a south-westwards direction, she could make out the spire of the church of the Nativité-de-Notre-

Dame in Brêmes, adjoining the manor house owned by the Admiral of France, a close friend of the Governor.

The Festival site was set in a vast area of peat fenland, woods, and fertile farmland, with villages dotted all about. It was a pleasant place where the very blades of grass, grazed by passing butterflies, seemed to have the texture of silk. Merely looking at the slowly ripening *Rousselet de Reims* pears in the nearby trees was enough to make anyone's mouth water.

For over a century, many a little girl, including Valentine, had sat in these same fields (where bees busily hovered above the daisies), playing the game: '*Effeuiller la marguerite*'. She could picture their eager upturned little faces reciting the words, while picking off the petals one by one:

> '*He loves me,*
> *He loves me not....*'

✧

Valentine turned away from the window. Sadly, such childhood games were a thing of the past and time to find a solution was running out. As surely as the sand that ran through the hourglass above the three-legged wooden stand on the table. Feeling heavy-hearted, the heady scent of flowers in china vases in every nook and cranny threatened to overpower her. On any other day, she would have taken pleasure in the violets by the window; sea-holly by the door; the dozen pink roses on the table - or the fragrance of the bundles of dried lavender and rue attached to an iron hook on the wall, beneath the oak-panelled, broad beams in the ceiling above.

But not today.

'If only I hadn't been Queen of the May...I wouldn't have had—'

'A marriage proposal from a perfectly good man,' came the housekeeper's muffled response through a mouth full of pins. 'Ready to make you his baroness.'

'I was going to say: "suffer the attentions of a red-faced, sweaty-palmed man, old enough to be my grandpère".' Valentine turned her attention away from the lattice window and the sight of her fat-kidneyed, prospective groom, and back to her reflection in the polished steel surface of the *miroir de toilette*.

It was a long-ago wedding gift to her mother from her future husband, Valentine's father, who was then a young man of exceptional fairness who bore no resemblance whatsoever to the ageing Baron de Boulogne.

∽

Resting precariously on a makeshift stand, the *miroir* reflected a pair of anxious eyes of the palest blue staring back at her under dark brows. An admiring Ottoman cartographer visiting Ardres Castle had once exclaimed how this lightest of shades exactly matched the sun-dappled waters, lapping against the far-off shores of his homeland—

'*Par Saint Just!* Stop your fidgeting. This is the last time I'm going to alter this dress.'

Valentine rolled her eyes.

'By rights, you should have passed it on to Charlotte.'

Although Valentine was tempted to mimic Béatrice's inevitable refrain: '*And to Jacqueline—*' she managed to restrain herself. 'Then I'd have nothing to wear to the Governor's banquet. Or the Festival.'

She felt a pang of guilt. <<*It's not poor Béatrice's fault there's more than one Fleury girl to marry off, with each one needing a dowry*>>

Straightening up, Béatrice offered Valentine her hand to step down from the stool. Then she smoothed down the skirts of the dress and coiled Valentine's hair into a knot on top of her head. 'Just like a queen's crown,' she murmured, tucking in an unruly, loose strand. 'Or cloth of gold. Perfect for this "*Field of Gold*" everyone's talking about. Mind you, I've heard some folk have been forced to mortgage off their estates to pay for their clothes. They're so eager to attend they're prepared to carry their mills, forests, and meadows on their backs. Fools…every last one of them.'

'But why shouldn't they do that? I know I would.'

Béatrice reached out to stroke Valentine's cheek, keeping hold of the knot of hair with her other hand. 'Of course you would. That's because you're a young girl who's barely seen seventeen summers. And are as beautiful as an angel. You're so like your father's mother. *Que son âme repose en paix!* I shouldn't be telling you this but—'

'Telling me what?'

26

'Just after you were born, when your grandmère came to visit, one of her maids swore me to secrecy.'

'What did she say?'

'That Dame Symonne's true father was from a land in the Far North. Where they speak the language of Norsemen. Not from these parts at all.' She gave the knot a gentle tug. 'Look at this. It could be a coronet made for a baron's eldest daughter…or a sheaf of wheat carried by a Queen of the May.'

Reminded again of the source of all her present woes, Valentine twisted away, watching her hair slipping through Béatrice's fingers like a skein of yellow silk.

'No, there's no mistaking your grandmère in you,' chuckled Beatrice. 'That same maid told me she captured the heart of old King Louis. Well, he wasn't old then. He was young and very handsome. Married to a girl as ugly as sin and crook-backed. He was still only the Duc d'Orléa—'

'Enough, please!' Even though Valentine had adored her late grandmère, Symonne wasn't here to help her out of her present predicament.

<<*Or rescue me from Béatrice's marriage plans*>>

'You haven't given the man a chance, Demoiselle Valentine. I've heard not only is he extremely rich but the old King made him a baron for his bravery in Italy. And he's on excellent terms with the Governor of Picardy.'

Unfortunately, the mention of the Comte d'Ardres took Valentine back to the May revellry four days before. She thought of her white gown: the one nearly ruined when a foolish villager accidentally spilt the entire contents of a goblet of hyppocras down the front, forcing her to change into another she'd worn many times. Thereby, facing the ridicule of the Governor's son:

"*Not that old dress again, Tempête. It must have had more outings than a courtesan on le Pont Saint-Michel.*"

Noticing how easily he slipped into his old name for her, Valentine had felt humiliated but came up with the idea of dyeing both gowns for the banquet and the upcoming Festival. She kept well away from the actual process herself; after all, she couldn't afford to turn up with stained fingers. Not to mention the pungent smell of urine which the talkative dyer at the market at Ardres assured her was a necessary ingredient:

"If you want to reproduce the colours of heaven, Demoiselle, you have to make a few sacrifices. I've given you "Popingay-blue" to match your eyes. Please allow me to make a gift of it to you."

Valentine hurriedly thanked him and then ran off with the precious merchandise, with only a single backwards glance at the dyer who had a strange, almost wistful look on his face. Thank goodness he warned her about staying away from the dyeing part and the terrible ensuing stench.

The Governor's son would be sure to notice immediately.

<<*That one plays his cards very close to his chest*>> Despite her best efforts, Valentine had never been able to work out exactly what he was thinking.

She'd only seen him from afar on a handful of occasions since his return but was fearful if he breathed a single word about what happened on May Day, her reputation would instantly be in tatters. And any hopes of a future marriage to anyone - even, God forbid, the portly Baron - would be snuffed out as easily as the dozen tallow candles Béatrice lit before to help her while she did her sewing. Valentine walked over to the roses on the table and leant down as if to savour their scent. The truth was she didn't want the eagle-eyed Béatrice to see her face.

<<*No one must guess I have a secret. Especially one involving the Governor's son*>>

Valentine gave a shudder as she recalled his narrowed eyes, as green as the strands of seaweed draped across the rocks at the water's edge at Boulogne...or those of a serpent about to unleash its venom. Remembering the way he'd looked at her on May Day, there was no doubt of the wickedness in their depths.

Or that he was an opponent, both mercurial and ruthless.

<<*I wish with all my heart he'd stayed away and never come back*>>

HOUSE OF HOWARD

Chapter Six

The same day. Hampton Court Palace, Surrey.

*M*y companions were still in frivolous mood (reminding me of two small boys who couldn't decide whether to play leapfrog or piggy-back riding) as they continued to vacillate about the departure date. At present, they were more interested in the speed of the '*Henry Grâce à Dieu*' compared to the ships in the French fleet.

'It will be,' said *Snake*, raising both arms in the air and moving them from one side to the other, 'as if you've flown over the Narrow Sea to Calais.'

The King laughed. 'A flying ship? What a glorious image!' Now *that* would make the French weep with envy.'

Wearied by their inability to reach a decision, I was aware I had a far bigger picture in my head. <<*Not everyone has the time or the inclination to dally like these two. I don't*>> Being the man left running the country while King and court travelled across the Narrow Sea to play, I had far weightier thoughts to preoccupy me than the length of time it would take for the '*Henry Grâce à Dieu*' to reach Calais. As a man who'd weathered six reigns, I reflected on how far we'd progressed to even be considering a Festival such as this. And how much responsibility I'd been given.

'Not long now, Thomas,' *Snake* called over to me. 'Certainly before my new clock down below chimes four.'

Forget about the apple sauce made in the kitchens of my manor at Ashwellthorpe, *Snake*'s expression was of someone who'd managed to steal that last piece of marchpane tart. Turning my gaze back to the flames in the fireplace, I so wished I could consign the Lord Chancellor to them.

29

I knew he'd deliberately mentioned his pride and joy in the courtyard as an excuse to flaunt his wealth. Even I couldn't deny the clock was a marvel. Everyone at court had been talking about how it could tell the hour, the day, and the month, not to mention showing the signs of the zodiac, and the phases of the moon. It didn't end there. I almost suspected its French, German and Dutch creators of sorcery. How else could the bat-fowling object manage to display the high tide at London Bridge, much to the gratitude of any courtiers not wanting their barge back to be caught out by the fast-flowing rapids, present at low tide.

With a Herculean effort, I became the elder statesman once more, entrusted with the running of the country. <<*My Catholic Europe is in a state of flux. The previous century still feels like yesterday to those of us born in the mid part of the fifteenth, not in the latter - or early part of the sixteenth*>> Hardly three years had gone by since that Augustinian monk no one had ever heard of, Martin Luther, nailed his ninety-five theses to the door of the Castle church in Wittenberg, on All Hallow's Eve. Spouting some tickle-brained nonsense about reform within the Papacy and the Church.

<<*He could make a start here*>> I thought, eyeing up *Snake*, now in full flow across the room about how the English would overshadow the French for every waking moment of the Festival. He shot me a triumphant look as if to say: See, I've bested you. I've shown you who's the second most important man in the country. And it's not you!

The House of Tudor was being drawn into an enormous power struggle that had begun between the other two major Houses of Western Europe: Valois, and Habsburg - one I could envisage lasting for decades (long after I was food for worms), and be the cause of many wars and skirmishes. But war was prohibitively expensive and taxes to raise money for it always unpopular, even if the chance to fight was wholeheartedly embraced by healthy young men. The balance of power amongst the Houses was uneven, with territories shifting all the time. I'd recently glanced at a map and been startled to see the changes in the last twenty years alone.

In my long life, I'd watched allegiances among the countries of Europe (as well as the land belonging to a country), change as often as the constant flow of visitors to the Palace of Placentia. Or the customers of a bawd, touting her wares outside a tavern.

<<*Foes then friends. Friends then foes*>>

At times, my head would spin with the speed at which a situation might alter. As things stood, in the ever-shifting sands of European diplomacy, England was currently being courted by both French and Imperial representatives. Even I couldn't entirely blame the toad-spotted *Snake* for relishing every moment of the courtship with as much delight as a desirable woman who has two suitors vying for her hand. Or a man who's about to taste paradise. Almost against my will, I lifted the goblet of *Snake's* hyppocras to my lips—

Thomas Wolsey's Hyppocras

2 bottles of red or white wine

200g brown sugar

(or 3 tablespoons of runny honey)

¼ teaspoon of ground ginger

2 teaspoons of cinnamon

½ teaspoon each of cloves and galingale

A few ground grains of paradise

1) Grind all the spices together in a pestle and mortar.
2) Add to the wine and leave overnight.
3) The next day, bring the wine and the sugar (or honey) to the boil to dissolve it.
4) Strain the wine through either a cheesecloth or a paper coffee filter.

Le Menagier de Paris, France, 1393.

TRISTAN

Chapter Seven

The same day. Ardres Castle, Picardy.

ome back to bed, Monsieur Tristan!'

I gave my hose a final tug as I stood at the end of the bed. Then I turned to look at the pretty brunette whose name I couldn't quite remember. It had been a long time since I had a casual encounter such as this; I was clearly out of practice. Was it coming back to the Castle that was making me behave as though I was sixteen again?

Bonne? Bastienne? Barbe? *Barbe.* Yes, I was almost sure that was it. Past experience had taught me it was better to say nothing at all than get a woman's name wrong. Besides, I didn't want to hurt her feelings, especially as the prospect of returning to bed was tempting. How best to avoid her wrath and avert a scene? *"If in doubt,"* my best friend, Jean, advised me a very long time ago, *"use 'chérie'. You can't go wrong if you do."*

Sent by Father to the kitchens on a thankless errand to find out if more fresh turbot was needed for the forthcoming feast, I couldn't have foreseen an afternoon of lively bed sport. Stripped of her kitchen aprons and white cap, the new Ardres kitchen maid was as tasty as a sweet almond flan, with a hint of candied orange peel.

Like me, the girl was clearly no stranger to this kind of behaviour. I smiled as I watched her cunningly let the sheet slip a fraction - just enough to remind me what I would be abandoning.

<<I have absolutely no idea whether I'm the seducer or the seduced. Nor do I care>> Experience had obviously taught her that showing a little at a time to a man would have the desired effect. In the distance, I could hear the Abbey's

bells pealing for the monks to attend Nones. Glancing out of the window, I became aware of the lengthening shadows on the lawns below. On a hill in the distance, I could see the blackened ruins of the old Castle. *<<Could it be Vespers already?>>*

'*Chérie,* I have to go.'

The maid pulled a sulky face and brushed a strand of glossy auburn hair from her face. 'I suppose you're leaving to help with all the preparations. After all, your father's the Governor. And it's your family's feast.' She rolled over onto her stomach and propped herself up on her elbows, taking care to keep herself covered. 'My father's the pastry cook up here at the Castle but he couldn't even get me a job waiting on the tables. I've been praying to God every night but He hasn't helped me yet.'

I smiled at her blasphemous confession. 'You could gladly have my place. I have no wish to be there. It'll only be the same as any other feast. The real action takes place in the lists.'

The girl stared at me in amazement. 'What! You don't want to see the King and Queen, and all the lords and ladies dressed up like peacocks? I'd give my right arm to be there.'

To add weight to her argument, she thrust her arm into the air, inadvertently giving me a glimpse of what I'd be giving up if I left now. Captivated, I made up my mind not to abandon my own pleasure but to face the recriminations that would surely come my way later. '*Culpae poenae par esto*'. I was sure my long absence had already been noticed, so I might as well make the most of a bad situation.

<<Or rather, the most of a decidedly good one>>

Flinging off my hose again, I leapt onto the giggling girl, tearing the sheet away to plant a kiss upon her bared breasts. 'Perhaps I can help out where God wasn't able to. I have no use for you all dressed up. Nor for your right arm. But if you want to see those "peacocks" of yours so much, I'll make sure you do.'

The maid gave a shriek of delight. 'Oh, *merci.*'

As I moved up to kiss her on the mouth, she gave me a look of undying gratitude and then pulled me to her as if she'd never let me go....

HOUSE OF HOWARD

Chapter Eight

The same day. Hampton Court Palace.

gain, we'll be finished soon, Thomas,' said *Snake*, his excited voice breaking into my thoughts. 'Another drink, perhaps? Though we don't want you falling asleep on us.'

'No, don't fall asleep on us,' teased the King, following *Snake* across the Turkey carpet. 'How can I leave someone in charge of my country if he's a malt-worm who can't hold a couple of goblets of hyppocras without getting reeling-ripe.'

I struggled to plaster a smile across my face, hoping it was a smile rather than a grimace as I held out my goblet to be re-filled. <<*God's Gown! I'll drink the entire Palace supply dry if necessary to prove my fitness to serve the King*>> I recalled the story about the King's great-uncle. Some said the Duke of Clarence, accused of treason, had been drowned in a barrel of Malmsey wine on the orders of his royal brother, Edward. Looking at *Snake*'s self-satisfied face, I could well understand the sentiment. Little wonder my great friend, Edward Stafford, had once poured an entire basin of water over *Snake*'s shoes while holding it for the King to wash his hands. As the proud and mighty Duke of Buckingham, he'd been rightly furious that a man of his standing was expected to go cap in hand before the upstart cur of a butcher from Ipswich. Pity it hadn't been a barrel of Malmsey wine in the chamber that day instead of a basin of water.

It was high time to swat the troublesome flea. I raised my goblet to my lips. 'This is excellent hyppocras, Tom. I must congratulate you. I don't know how you manage it but you always seem to have the very best of everything.'

I peeked a look at Henry whose mouth had puckered at my comment; hopefully, John Skelton's scathing poem had left its mark. Turning a face of total innocence and spurious admiration back to *Snake*, I was gratified to see a mottled red stain on his neck that perfectly matched his robes.

<<*Play with me at your peril*>> was the message I wanted him to read in my eyes.

I sighed as they retreated back to their list of dates across the Turkey carpet. I was from a long-ago era. I knew that. From that of Henry's great-uncle, long since lowered into the grave a mere five years before his allegedly murderous brother. I had been young then. Now, I lived in times when youth ruled supreme. I knew for a fact that certain scholars were holding up their hands in despair. The faces of two men came to mind: Desiderius Erasmus, the eternally optimistic Dutch humanist, and his closest friend on earth, the English lawyer, Tom More.

"*People build cities, Thomas, only to see them fall because of the madness of princes*," Master More had once complained to me. He and his friend had lofty ideals and hopes that peace was coming to Christendom, exemplified by an increase in the glorification of virtue, piety and learning. However, the pair of them had been forced to admit that the future of Europe was resting on the relatively inexperienced shoulders of three warlike, young men—

Snake and Henry suddenly burst out laughing at some joke and I watched the King eagerly turn to share it with me. Henry came halfway across the carpet, leaving *Snake* looking as though he was sucking on a lemon. 'Tom was just saying that England is like a wealthy widow being courted by two eager suitors.' He began to act out the scene. 'As the Emperor jumps out of her bed, the King of France is waiting to push aside the bed curtains.'

I laughed politely. 'I couldn't agree more.' <<*What kind of necromancy has given the wretched Snake the ability to steal my thoughts and make them his own? What's more earth-vexing is that his thoughts mirror mine*>> Not wishing to include me in their private discussion, our esteemed Chancellor quickly drew the King back to the edge of the carpet. <<*Away from me. Youth. How fleeting it is. And how fickle*>> No wonder older folk were fretting that we had a trio of youths responsible for the fate of Europe.

The youngest - a newly-created Holy Roman Emperor no less - was barely twenty, while the oldest and longest reigning monarch of this country of ours, separated from the other two lands by the Narrow Sea - and me, by a carpet - a mere nine years his senior. I watched Henry slapping *Snake* on the back after what seemed like the Lord Chancellor's hundredth quip of the day. <<*I'd rather mount the scaffold on Tower Green than crack a smile at a single word that leaves those ever-moving, self-serving lips*>>

I knew one of the three young rulers intimately, and had met one of the other two, so I was entitled to have an opinion. I'd heard Charles of Habsburg was a heavy-jawed youth, with a face as mournful as one of my Southern Hounds. Some even jested he'd never learned to smile. On the other hand, I knew François of France, the middle member of this group in age, temperament, and geography, to be equally ready to laugh at himself as at others. And of course, standing tall and proud, across the carpet from me, was a man who would *never* dream of laughing at himself. I'd been there when a newly-crowned Henry told the Venetian Ambassador he was in charge of his own destiny:

He'd pushed his golden crown down more firmly on his head to prove his point: "*I don't choose that anyone shall have it in his power to command me—*"

∾

'So, Thomas,' said the King, covering the carpet again towards me as speedily as the '*Henry Grâce à Dieu*' over the Narrow Sea, 'we've decided that in order to keep the Habsburg faction happy, we can't be seen to favour the Valois one by arriving in Calais too early.' Always ready to play the jester, the King contorted his face. 'I told Tom it sounds like a man trying to keep both his wife and his mistress happy.' He winked at me. 'Not a task to be taken lightly, eh?'

As a man with a long and complex history with love and women, I seized my opportunity to lord it over the supposedly celibate *Snake*.

<<*Celibate? My arse! Everyone from the King to the boy who turns the spit in the kitchens knows the truth about the gleeking clack-dish*>>

'No,' I replied. 'Look how the French have tried to meddle with the date of your Festival.'

After many delaying tactics on our part, it looked as though the Festival was going to take place in June. It was originally supposed to have taken place last year but was postponed owing to the contest for the title of Holy Roman Emperor. I knew that one who was not pleased by this French and English *rapprochement* was Henry's Spanish wife…who also happened to be Charles's aunt. It irked me the way Queen Katherine remained fiercely loyal to Imperial interests. On the other hand, we English wanted to sell our wool to Spain and Flanders, and to this end, were arranging an Anglo-Imperial meeting. That was the reason we'd been trying to delay the Festival until late June or July.

Henry frowned. 'You're right, Thomas. How typical of the French to tell us their Queen would be far along with child and soon be leaving for the royal birthing chamber at Saint Germain-en-Laye.'

I watched him suck in his breath, thrust out his chest (both ominous signs), and march over to the window.

Immediately, I regretted mentioning the change of date. Like the weathercock I could see on the roof beyond, nothing was guaranteed to make Henry's mood change faster than any mention of another couple's fecundity. Even though clever little Bessie Blount had given him a boy bastard last year, he still didn't have a royal boy. And, quite honestly, looking at the Queen whose skin was beginning to wrinkle like one of my Leathercoat apples left too long to ripen, I saw almost no chance of that happening now. I glanced at *Snake* and could all but hear the cogs of his brain turning the same way as mine. To my surprise, he gave me a conspiratorial look, letting me know we were on the same side on this one. It reminded me again of other times in the past when we'd been very much on the same side, such as the day he—

<<*But I won't let myself think of that now. I can't let myself think of that now*>>

Unaware of my turbulent thoughts, *Snake* walked over to the window. 'Of course, they also complained that July is the hottest month of the year and people would be tempted to drink too much. No doubt leading to undesirable behaviour.' He gave an exaggerated shrug. 'They were clearly talking about themselves.'

Hearing a royal guffaw, I knew *Snake* had managed to avoid one of

Henry's notorious sulks, in the same way a skilled player scores a point at tennis. What else could I do but admire the man?

When Henry turned around, he was all smiles again. 'We all know the French are concerned about our earlier *rendezvous* with Charles. By the way, magnificent Roman emperors of yours out there, Tom!'

Deliberately ignoring this vexing compliment, I sought to soothe: 'You were clever to tell the French any such meeting would purely be to discuss commercial interests, and wouldn't interfere with any of their arrangements.'

I'd been there when Henry spoke to the French Ambassador. "*After all,*" he said, "*your King will always be like a brother to me now I no longer have one of my own. Nothing can alter the love I bear my dearest Francis. Nothing at all—*"

There was a knock on the door and *Snake*'s secretary appeared with an urgent message from France. To my relief, the man who'd made himself so important in Europe (that he was now indispensable) was forced to make his excuses. Despite our recent (fleeting) truce of a few moments ago, I could see the look of regret on his face as the pair of them left the King's presence (shuffling backwards...as was the custom), knowing he could no more trust me than I could him.

As soon as the door closed behind them, the King brought a hand laden with priceless jewels down on my left shoulder. 'I can't think of anyone better to leave in charge of the country than you, Thomas. My "Guardian of the Realm". I hope you don't mind not being able to set eyes on this "Field of Gold" of ours.'

'I assure you that presiding over the council is an honour and a privilege. I fear my creaking bones would find the crossing too difficult.'

'Rest assured, your task here is as important as any thrust or parry across the Narrow Sea. And with your Tom staying behind as Lord Deputy of Ireland, I'll be able to breathe easy when I take my first step on French soil.'

'It warms my heart to hear such words, Your Majesty. You know, when I escorted your sister, Margaret, up to Edinburgh to meet her future husband, an old Scottish soothsayer predicted a "Field of Gold" in my future.'

'Really? And what did you say to that?'

'I made my feelings of contempt very clear to King James.'

Henry laughed. 'That doesn't surprise me. You've always been a man who doesn't mince his words.'

For some strange reason, I could still remember almost every word the old hag had uttered in a chamber where there was neither night nor day. I was hardly about to repeat her nonsense about bloodied wedding bands involving the House of Tudor…or a match between my own House and the royal House of Stewart. Therein lay the path to madness: one that would take me straight back to the Tower. However, there was still that important matter I needed to discuss with Henry: my last piece of pork, smothered in apple sauce. One of Tom Bullen's better ideas I was about to present to the King as my own. But as head of the House of Howard, and Tom's father-in-law, that was my prerogative. Of course, if Henry liked the plan, Tom could see it through publicly, putting his head above the parapet before we knew whether or not it would be successful.

<<*Either way, I'll win. If it all ends in disaster, Tom will shoulder the blame and I'll lament him ruining my cunning scheme*>>

As usual, Henry was far too preoccupied with his own concerns to pay any attention to my mood of uncertainty. 'Now, Thomas,' he said, about to make for the door, 'I'm off to see my tailor back in Westminster about that new doublet of cloth of gold I've asked him to make. Why not come too and sup with Kate and me. I can help you down to the landing stage and you can tell me what else this ancient Scottish witch told you.'

Rising as fast as my old legs could manage, I thanked the stars again for giving me this heaven-sent private moment to put my son-in-law's proposal to the King. I was glad that Henry had the grace to wait for me, gently putting a helping hand under my elbow which I gratefully received. <<*We both know that even though my body might be failing, my mind's as sharp as it's ever been. And I'm as useful to him as I've ever been*>>

'Now Tom has gone about on his business,' he said, 'you and I can discuss lighter matters on my barge. You know how much I value your opinion. I want to know what you think of Frenchwomen. I've seen for myself they're very fair. But not as fair as our own, of course.'

I couldn't quite believe my luck. 'Your Majesty. How did you guess my thoughts? Comely Englishwomen is exactly the topic I wish to discuss with you. Or rather, one in particular. And then we may talk about comely Frenchwomen to your heart's delight. Though they do say they can be quite contrary when the mood takes them. But as we know, so can the men.'

<<*As I think of Snake, knowing how piqued he would be if he were here, I can almost taste that last mouthful of apple sauce on the end of my tongue*>>

—⁓⁓⁓—

ASHWELLTHORPE MANOR APPLE SAUCE FOR ROAST PORK

{*Pigge Sauce*}

Fat from a roasted pork joint or from pork sausages

2 large Pink Lady apples or any sweet apple

1 tablespoon of cider vinegar

1 tablespoon of brown sugar

A handful of fresh parsley sprigs/flat leaves, chopped

2 large leaves of fresh sage, chopped

Knob of butter

1 long pepper or teaspoon of black pepper

1) Slice the apples and put them in a saucepan with enough water to cover the apples. Bring to the boil. Then turn down very low and keep stirring the apples, topping up with water when necessary. About 40 minutes.

2) When the apples are completely soft, mush them up with a spoon and add the sugar, vinegar and pork fat.

3) Cook for a couple of minutes and then add all the spices and cook for a further couple of minutes.

4) Finally stir in the knob of butter.

A Proper newe Booke of Cokerye mid-sixteenth century.

—⁓⁓⁓—

HOUSE OF TREDAVOE

Chapter Nine

May 4ᵗʰ, 1520. Hever Castle, Kent, England.

secret matter. You said you had one you wished to discuss with me.'

One of the men standing at the window of the gatehouse to the inner courtyard, brushed an imaginary crumb from the embroidered sleeve of his gown. 'That's right.'

William Tredavoe waited expectantly for a moment before giving his companion an affectionate cuff on the shoulder. 'And…are you going to tell me what it is?'

'Forgive me. I was distracted by the sight of our girls coming back.'

William followed his friend's gaze to beyond the raised portcullis and the small brick bridge over the Castle's sunlit moat. He could see a laughing Cecily and Mary emerging arm-in-arm from the gardens, four of the family dogs racing in and out between them, a blur of black and brown. What a pleasing picture the two girls made: one prettily plump and full of smiles, celebrating her birthday, a respectable, newly-married woman; while the other, his Cecily - his precious only child, his pride and joy, on the brink of womanhood - slightly taller, far more willowy, with long tumbling locks that seemed to alter their shade according to her ever-changing moods or what she was doing: gleaming copper when she had her head bent over one of her books of hours, or her needlework; a leaf in autumn when she was running through a nearby forest; a burning flame when she was riding at full tilt across the fields, on her way back to Zennor Castle from Saint Ives; the gleaming pelt of a fox when she had her arm stretched back to release an arrow, tipped with grey goose feathers, from her especially carved bow of yew, her green eyes (a Tredavoe family trait, not because his wife, Alys, had looked at a snake during her pregnancy) fixed firmly on the target ahead; or a combination of all of these when she was twirling on a candlelit dance floor, with every young man in the great hall vying for a dance with her, hoping for her to bestow one of her dazzling smiles upon him, the dimple in either cheek surely enough to bring any man to his knees.

Her hair was pure Tudor gold.

Even speaking as a doting father, William knew King Hal's beautiful younger sister wouldn't be able to put his bewitching Cecily in the shade if they stood side by side.

'Look at them, Will. Can you believe it's really been seven years since your Cecily went off across the sea to the Habsburg court with my little Nan?'

'How fearful we were for their safety, especially with a war breaking out.'

William had never taken any notice of the criticism concerning his childhood friend. Tom Bullen was a good father. There were those who whispered he was so ambitious he was prepared to stand on the shoulders of any of his children (sadly, only three now after the recent loss of young Tom) in order to raise himself up in the world. William had always dismissed such accusations as the voices of envy, aimed at a man who'd clearly been favoured by the King. Look at him now. Knighted back in 1509, he'd just returned from a stint as ambassador to the court of France. In return, Tom had always been gracious about William's own success: royal recognition for his family's long-time loyalty to the Tudors, in the form of a gift of vast lands in Cornwall - to add to his already considerable ones there, and all his others around the country.

At that moment, one of the family spaniels obviously decided the gardens were far more interesting and made a dash back towards the bridge, the two girls hot on its disobedient heels, laughing and shrieking their dismay.

Seemingly losing interest, Thomas turned away from the window. 'I've had an idea for the Festival next month. It is to mirror our new close alliance with the French - which is a kind of marriage if you like - with a real life union between the two.'

44

'A real life union?' William wasn't sure he understood.

'Yes. An English bride and a French groom. To be married in the temporary royal chapel on the eve of The Feast of Saint John, and Midsummer's Day.'

'*An English bride and a French groom?*'

Thomas reached up and stroked his full, square beard tinged with russet, and lately, a few flecks of grey. 'That's right. Two strangers. Joined together in holy matrimony before the greatest of both our lands. The King has already agreed to it.'

William was impressed. 'He has? What did he say?'

'He was delighted. You know how he loves games - the more cloak and dagger the better. Of course, Tom Wolsey – or "*Snake*" as my father-in-law likes to call him – was boot-faced he hadn't thought of it first.'

'Ha! And has the couple already met?'

'Not yet. But they will soon enough.'

'Tom, this is quite extraordinary.'

'I want everyone to remember that last Saturday as both the climax of the Festival…and a symbol of our eternal friendship.'

William let out a hoot of laughter at his friend's ingenuity and the audacity of the plan. 'People will either pity or applaud the couple, depending on which view they take. England and France. A tricky match, at the best of times. Let me guess which qualities you're seeking in this English bride. Beauty,' he said, holding up his right hand and counting on his fingers. 'Wit…vast lands at her disposal…a timid disposition to allow herself to be bartered in this way.'

'All of those. However, I don't agree with your choice of words. "*Bartering*" is not at all how I see it. I think you're underestimating the honour and chance for advancement this will bring the girl's family. As for a union between England and France. Mayhap England will lead France by the nose.'

'That remains to be seen. I take it you've already found your bride.' William watched his friend quickly glance back at the open window through which they could hear the girls' laughter once more - from the cooing noises they were making, the disobedient animal safely back in their care.

'I have. And I think she'll make a splendid choice. I've also sent the French my suggestion for a groom. Actually, that part was more my father-in-law's idea than mine. And he was the one who introduced the idea to the King.'

'That doesn't surprise me in the slightest. Thomas Howard might be too old to go to France but he'll never be too old to meddle in other people's lives.'

Thomas flung his arm around William's shoulder and squeezed it in a gesture of affection. 'I couldn't agree more. Even though he hasn't been given sole charge of the country....'

'Have no fear, he'll soon be running it.'

'Well, we won't have to worry about him over in France. Now, let's go and find our good ladies and our girls and enjoy those venison pasties the King's sent me as a reward for my efforts. Elizabeth has also arranged for one of her famous gilded Marchpane Tarts to finish. An old Howard family recipe. I know it's your favourite...despite your feelings for my wife's family.'

HOUSE OF VALOIS

Chapter Ten

Two weeks later. A castle near Crépy-en-Valois, France.

A redhead, you say? Interesting. I've never bedded a redhead. Or at least not a true one…as far as I am aware. Perhaps one or two who imitated their Venetian sisters by using saffron flowers to colour their hair. Such as the ones in Tiziano Vecelli's "*Amor divino e Amor Profano*".'

The Admiral of France was not amused. Nor would he allow himself to be impressed by the other man's flawless Italian.

'We're not talking about whores here.'

'I wasn't. *I've* never had to pay for the services of a woman.'

Stung by the implication, Guillaume Gouffier, seigneur de Bonnivet, leant forward in his carved oak chair, as a not so gentle reminder of who held the power here. 'No one's asking you to "bed a redhead".'

'I thought you'd just asked me to take one to wife.'

Guillaume had never thought this request was going to be easy. Especially with Nicolas de La Barre on the receiving end. He'd known Nicolas for a long time and with each passing year, he only seemed to get trickier. *Mon Dieu!* Even his hot-headed young godson, Tristan, who was forever getting into scrapes, didn't give him this much trouble. Why the hell couldn't François have done it himself? Because he was too preoccupied with his own muddled love life, that's why. Taking a deep breath, he tried again. 'Our King is cooperating with the English to provide an unusual surprise at the end of the festivities - as well as a fitting union between our two nations.'

Sprawled in a chair opposite, the King's Master Falconer merely raised an eyebrow and distractedly fingered a golden locket, encrusted with jewels, around his neck. At his feet lay two enormous grey Irish Wolfhounds, in deceptively peaceful slumber: fitting sentries for such a master. Guillaume steeled himself, knowing Nicolas, who besides being the only man François would trust with his precious birds, was also the Lieutenant of Picardy. In addition, he was Master of the Hunt in all but name, carrying out most of the duties on behalf of the ageing occupant of the prestigious post who'd been one of old King Louis' most trusted men. Even if Guillaume hated to admit it, Nicolas's success in acquiring these posts was entirely due to his own merits.

He was known as a collector of both beautiful art and beautiful women. Guillaume could see why he'd have no problem attracting the latter, particularly in that tight-fitting doublet of scarlet and black, over a white shirt of finest Holland cloth, with billowing sleeves. Goodness knows how many ells it had taken to make the shirt. Always dressed impeccably in the latest of fashions, Nicolas certainly looked the part of the perfect courtier.

He was a man who danced to his own tune - with enviable success. With his intense dark looks, and eyes the exact shade of the Moorish dates on display upon the silver spice plate across the room, not really brown at all but black, Nicolas pleased the ladies of the court. These same eyes presently had permanent amusement in their depths - at Guillaume's own expense - he was sure of it. Heaven help the little virgin being offered up by the English as a sacrifice. The Governor of Picardy's second-in-command, although unusually cultured, was first and foremost, a man of war, as far removed as possible from their own equally courageous warrior king who had the heart of a poet. As François had recently written: "*a court without women is like a year without spring, and a spring without roses.*"

Nicolas was deliberately choosing to make matters more difficult than they need be. After a discussion with his good friend, Guy d'Ardres, Governor of Picardy, Guillaume discovered Nicolas had been without a wife for a long time. So a remarriage was well in order to sire an heir. Clearing his throat, Guillaume knew he had to tread carefully. 'Seigneur Boullan assures me the young lady in question is extremely beautiful. I met her myself long ago. And I can attest to the fact.'

This at least provoked some kind of reaction. Placing his long tapered fingers together to form a steeple, Nicolas looked pensive. Guillaume began to feel like one of the Master Falconer's prohibitively expensive birds, attached to its perch in the mews.

Nicolas's black brows knitted together. 'And quite why and when did our overweening, former English ambassador take such an interest in my affairs?'

By now, both frustrated and flustered, and uncomfortably reminded of Nicolas's legendary skill as a chess player, the Admiral had no satisfactory answer. François had received a letter from Thomas Boullan on behalf of the English King: one that caused him great mirth. *"Our Nicolas and an unsuspecting English virgin? What a delicious combination. A new-born lamb with our Wolf. Placed unsuspectingly in his lair. Excellent! See to it as soon as possible, will you, Guillaume."*

And so here he was. With the said '*Wolf*' (François's nickname for Nicolas that had always rankled with Guillaume), in the said lair - which was indeed a very comfortable one with its expensive furnishings, and lingering scent of beeswax and sweet juniper from the wood burning in the grate. The bookshelf was lined with books from ceiling to floor and on a walnut table, next to a lute, lay the most beautiful chessboard Guillaume had ever seen. It had been abandoned in mid-game, with many of the exquisitely carved, delicately painted, wooden pieces missing from one end. Guillaume took in the figures remaining on the board, each one a work of art, particularly the dazzling black knight, poised to attack, his silver lance thrust before him - his magnificent horse rearing up beneath him. Guillaume's swift perusal of the massacre that had taken place seemed to indicate very few major casualties amongst the black pieces. Why wasn't he surprised? He pitied the poor wretch who'd thought to take on the most cunning player at the court of Franc—

'I see you're admiring the chessboard I had made for me in Venice.'

'I was also admiring your play.'

'I'm afraid I can't take too much credit for that. My opponent was a novice. But a good loser, I have to say.'

'He certainly took a trouncing.'

Nicolas lips curled in a smile that had something wolfish about it. 'You could say that. Except that *he* was a *she*…and…how can I put it, the two us came to an acceptable arrangement about the conclusion of the game.'

Although Guillaume would have given a fistful of *écus au soleil* to discover the woman's identity, guessing it was someone he knew, with Nicolas, he had as much chance of finding out as the King of France becoming celibate.

'I once had an Italian tutor,' said Nicolas. 'A wonderful man from Venice, called Ippolito da Canal. He not only taught me Italian, Latin and chess, but a little of the rules of love. How the moves of chess correspond to those made in the rituals of courtship and lovemaking. Does your Cornish girl play chess?'

Such an absurd question merited a sharp retort but Guillaume managed to restrain himself. 'I really have no idea. It's hardly something Seigneur Boullan thought important enough to mention.'

'On the contrary. I've often found my most satisfying encounters have begun on the chessboard.'

Wishing to lead the subject away from the wretched game of chess, and back to that of marriage, Guillaume glanced up at the wall next to him. What he found there took his breath away. Wasn't that painting hanging there by the same Tiziano Vecelli, Nicolas had mentioned?

Priceless in value.

And the most sensuous piece of work Guillaume had ever set eyes upon. He was momentarily robbed of words, and found himself gawping like an untried boy in a stew at the portrait of a curvaceous woman standing amongst the waves. Under Nicolas's steady gaze, Guillaume's own eyes travelled down her naked body as she wrung seawater from her tumbling red locks, so long the strands dipped into the water. The scene was both intimate and wickedly carnal. In spite of himself, Guillaume found it tugging at his groin.

'Ah…my Venus,' sighed Nicolas. 'Beautiful, isn't she? Tiziano sent the painting to me from Venice as a gift. It only arrived yesterday but I had it hung at once. To think the paint is scarcely dry. And you're the first to view it. Although I have one in my bedchamber that might be more to your taste. Come. I'll show it to you.'

To refuse would seem churlish and Guillaume needed to keep Nicolas agreeable in order for him to agree to François's proposition. Besides, he was curious to see in what kind of room someone like Nicolas would entertain his women. Knowing how fiercely Nicolas guarded his privacy, he was surprised to have received such an invitation. Getting up, he followed Nicolas…through one room, up some stairs, and along a corridor until they came to the bedchamber. Pushing open the heavy oak door, Nicolas stood aside to let Guillaume enter. The room did not disappoint. If the outer rooms reflected the tastes of an owner who enjoyed being surrounded by the finest objects in several kingdoms, this one reflected the tastes of Nicolas, the lover. Guillaume suddenly felt uncomfortable being in another man's private domain; it was as if he'd made a false move at chess. And was about to lose a valuable piece as a result.

In spite of his best efforts to avert his eyes from the enormous bed with its black and gold canopy and intricately carved bed posters of solid oak, he couldn't tear them away. Matching velvet curtains, fastened by silken gold tassels, were draped around the sides. He didn't even want to think about which women had laid their heads upon the feather pillows; pulled back the sheets of Rennes linen; stretched luxuriously beneath the matching black and gold coverlet, lined with fur; or writhed in ecstasy above. There would certainly have been no need for the expensive silver warming pan hanging on the wall next to the bed: its purpose to heat the blood of the occupants.

Guillaume half-expected Nicolas's mysterious chess partner to appear from behind the bed curtains—

'That's the painting I thought you'd like,' said Nicolas, drawing Guillaume's obvious attention away from the bed and pointing at a painting hung near the window. 'It's a copy my good friend, Tiziano, did for me from one of his frescoes in Padua.'

Beginning to feel as though he was a rabbit in a field blinded by the light of a poacher's flaming torch, Guillaume managed to pull his gaze away from the bed, only to find that Tiziano Vecelli's second work was as disturbing as the first. But for a different reason. This one portrayed a nobleman, dressed in full finery, a dagger in his right hand, towering over a distressed woman on the ground, her orange satin skirts in disarray all about her. One of her arms was raised in supplication.

Guillaume glared at Nicolas. 'I can't imagine why you thought I might enjoy such a scene!'

'You don't like my "*Miracolo del marito geleso*"?'

Guillaume noticed a long thin white scar, just below Nicolas's right cheekbone. Perhaps put there by a jealous husband's rapier? Furious that he was every inch Nicolas's unsuspecting pawn from the chessboard, about to be swept away by that same dazzling black knight, Guillaume forgot about being conciliatory.

'How can murder possibly be a miracle?'

Goaded by Nicolas from the moment they'd greeted one another, he had no real idea what the Lieutenant was up to. Was he trying to remind Guillaume of all the husbands they'd both cuckolded? Or let him know how unfit he was to play the part of bridegroom to the English girl. He watched Nicolas walk up to the painting and lightly brush two fingers across the wife's cheek. Then he turned to look at Guillaume, his dark eyes gleaming in the slight gloom of the bedchamber.

'Because she's innocent and the husband only realizes his mistake when he's stabbed her. Don't worry, it all ends well. He throws himself on the mercy of a saint who revives the woman.' Nicolas gave a conspiratorial wink. 'All the ladies seem to find Tiziano's painting very pleasing.'

Hearing this last, a vexed Guillaume realized he'd allowed himself to be led by the nose by the wily Nicolas. It was time to take back control.

'I didn't come here to admire your artwork. Or discover which tricks you use to seduce your women. I came here on a mission from the King. To discuss a marriage proposition.'

Nicolas flashed a smile that wasn't one at all. 'Of course you did. Let's go back down below. And have some refreshments.'

As he sat down again, a golden goblet of malmsey wine in hand, Guillaume could tell Nicolas was impatient for him to leave. Although he'd poured them both a drink and offered Guillaume some exotic fruit and aniseed comfits from a silver platter, he was displaying a flicker of something that couldn't quite pass as interest. And Guillaume guessed his next comment wouldn't be delivered with anything that could count as respect. Nicolas ran one hand through his shoulder-length black curls as if deep in thought. Then he began to inspect a turquoise ring on his other hand, set in an ornate gold mount, holding it up to the light to better admire it. It grated on Guillaume's nerves that Nicolas was showing more interest in the qualling piece of jewellery than in the brilliant marriage being offered to him on a plate. At length, the reluctant bridegroom found his voice.

'I was wondering what my proposed *fiancée* thinks of your plan.'

Again, there was that combination of mirth and insolence in the dark eyes. The merest upturn of the wide mouth served to deepen the cleft of his chin while the hint of dark facial hair only added to the decidedly feral quality of the man. At a complete loss, and feeling as though he was sinking up to his waist in quicksand - his royal undertaking doomed to failure - Guillaume threw up his hands in a gesture of despair.

'As far as I know, her family has decided not to tell her…yet. It seems her parents needed a great deal of persuading. Particularly the father.'

'What with? A trunkful of gold coins? You make it sound as though the man wasn't easily bought. But he agreed, nonetheless, to sacrifice his daughter on the altar of his ambition. Forgive me, but quite *when* is "the bride" going to find out? When I creep into her bed at night. And inform her I'm her new husband.'

The very notion was so ridiculous it made Guillaume feel extremely foolish. 'Oh for God's sake, man! I have no idea. Before she gets here, of course. She'll have been assured of your good character.'

As he said this, it rang so hollow to the pair of them that it elicited an infuriating laugh from the Lieutenant. 'Once the bride…does find out,' he said, drawing out his words and making Guillaume wonder what was coming next, 'am I to assume such a public wedding will include a public bedding too?'

Guillaume didn't even grace this with a reply; instead he jumped up and began to pace the room. Meanwhile, Nicolas remained seated, his long legs stretched out in front of him, looking far too much at ease.

One of the dogs opened a bloodshot eye and gave a low growl, rather worryingly, its steady gaze coming to rest upon Guillaume.

No doubt, a warning of some kind.

Guillaume watched Nicolas bend down and stroke the dread-bolted beast's head. '*Calme-toi*, Mars! You'll disturb Jupiter.'

Enough. All Guillaume wanted was for this misbegotten interview to end so he could return to Paris. Although he *had* met the girl from Cornwall a long time ago, he had no idea how she turned out. From what he'd observed over the years - in sisters, cousins or daughters of others - the prettiest little girls could become the plainest of creatures, while those without a single redeeming feature in childhood, could later enthral every man they met.

Guillaume closed his eyes in order to calm himself. 'I don't understand why you're making such a fuss. She's young, beautiful, comes from a very well-connected family that's in high favour with the English King. From what I can make out, she's one of the richest heiresses in England, set to inherit half of Cornwall—'

NICOLAS

Chapter Eleven

*B*ut Nicolas was only half-listening. He'd always found the Admiral pompous - both in battle and out of it. More fop and fawner than one who deserved Nicolas's respect. With his pretty blonde looks and high status as the courtier closest to François, Guillaume Gouffier (for the last three years, granted the right to puff out his chest and be addressed as Admiral Bonnivet) enjoyed similar popularity to the King.

The two of them whored their way around the court, changing beds as often as the weathervane on Ardres Castle changed direction. Nicolas had thoroughly enjoyed making his old rival squirm. Bonnivet deserved it. <<*Sent by the King to do his dirty work when François is no doubt doing his own dirty work with the luscious Françoise de Foix*>>

The look on Bonnivet's face when he'd first clapped his eyes on Tiziano's paintings, particularly the one of Venus, had been most gratifying. The greedy expression in the Admiral's pale blue eyes had reminded Nicolas of a starving prisoner, fettered and manacled, then led into a great hall to be confronted with a banquet table, laden with food and drink. Only to realize that every last crumb and drop belongs to his captor, not him. Bonnivet had certainly been riveted by the sight of Nicolas's bed, his face a study of absorption, as if he was trying to guess the name of every single woman who'd lain in it.

<<*How ill-mannered*>>

As for the purpose of Bonnivet's visit, the idea of a new bride was not such a bad one. Nicolas had been alone for several years. After the first disturbing experience of marriage, he'd been in no hurry to repeat it. Fortunately, he didn't want for female company. Although he'd done very little to deserve it, there seemed to be no shortage of women clamouring to be part of his life...mostly to no effect.

⸙

He knew the English girl would probably have a face like a horse; in his experience, wealthy heiresses with a shortage of suitors invariably did. Why otherwise would any father agree to let his daughter be married off in such a strange fashion? Especially, to one with the reputation Nicolas knew he enjoyed. <<*The father must be a fool. Or callous for not telling his daughter what he's done. Does he really care so little for her?*>>

As for being "*in high favour with the King*", anyone could say that. The royal butcher, baker or candlestick maker. A man who'd met the King once. Or not at all. Who could tell? Perhaps King Henry had agreed to help the father offload his burden onto an unsuspecting Frenchman in return for past services. The girl was probably not only horse-faced but possessed hair, not burnished Titian at all, but mottled copper.

He imagined her to be heavy-boned and clumsy, unable to move across a dance floor with grace or hold a tune when accompanied by a lute, and so meek and mild she never uttered a word, certainly not to object to such a terrible fate as this proposed marriage. She would be unlettered and unable to speak any other language but her own. She would definitely be dull in the extreme. Even if she *was* a redhead. In France, such a woman was thought to have an excess of passion and haughtiness, but their English sisters were clearly different.

Bonnivet seemed too eager to rush him into a decision, giving him no time to discover the truth about his ill-favoured bride. No matter. Having a new wife would make little difference to his life - apart from the sons she would hopefully provide; unfortunately, they would not be the most attractive of creatures. But once her duty was done, he would have a choice of countries in which to abandon her while he attended to his own—

⸙

'Demoiselle Cécile's related to the Governor of Picardy by marriage. Through his Cornish wife.'

Related to Guy d'Ardres? <<*Related to Tristan d'Ardres*>> who just happened to be the Admiral's godson. Nicolas knew he would be hard pushed to decide which of the two deserved his contempt more. However, as usual, the honour would have to go to Tristan. Even with all this Cécile's other failings (apart from having a name, Cecily, so close to the French, he was able to pronounce it with ease), Nicolas couldn't think of anything less appealing than an affiliation with Tristan. It was already bad enough she was from Cornwall, a place that was almost like a separate country from England. He was still smarting from the loss of one of his best ships, '*Le Nicolas*', off the Cornish coast, this past Christmas Day. Even though the cargo had been worth half a king's ransom, and to his great regret, his crew had probably all met their end in a watery grave, most of all he mourned the loss of the gold and ruby necklace, priceless in worth and sentiment, presumably now adorning the seabed far beneath the Celtic Sea.

"*Sunk without trace,*" he'd been informed, when first told of the fate of '*Le Nicolas*'.

<<*Damned Cornish thieves!*>> Notorious for their skills as pirates, they either captured their prey on the high seas, or weaved in and out of secret inlets in their vessels along the perilous, seventy-mile Cornish coastland. They worked in tandem with local smugglers, waiting to catch out an innocent ship with a false beacon shining its light onto the treacherous black rocks - instead of leading the vessel to the safety of harbour. Then they would pounce, stripping the ships of their entire cargo with the efficiency of a dog picking a bone clean. Nicolas had no idea what had happened to his ship but guessed that pirates and smugglers had far more to do with it than the ferocious December storm, mentioned in a cursory note that had arrived for him a couple of months later. At the time, he'd found it a little strange that Bonnivet, as Admiral of France, in charge of all things maritime, was never informed of such a major incident, or taken any interest in the loss of a French vessel in English waters.

"*You win some games, you lose some,*" was the only comment he'd made, while giving a shrug. "*With your skill at chess, you should know that by now.*" His amusement had been palpable. "*It seems not even the patron saint of seafarers with whom you share your name was able to intercede on your behalf.*" The Admiral had finished off with a remark so irksome Nicolas felt tempted to punch him: "*I've heard there's a prayer used on the southern coast of England that goes something like this: 'Oh Lord, protect ships at sea from the storm...but if they have to run aground, please let it be on our shore.*'"

∽

Sitting up straighter in his chair, Nicolas started mulling things over in his mind. He'd been about to refuse point-blank to take on the Cornish girl when a different possibility presented itself. What sweet revenge on Tristan to have power over this cousin of his. His mind made up, he picked up a bright red cherry from the small Venetian glass bowl next to him and popped it into his mouth, thinking how apt this luscious fruit was associated with virginity, ripe to be plucked. He turned towards the Admiral in the manner of one who meant business. 'I would expect to become a baron for my pains. And receive a sum of one hundred and fifty thousand *livres tournoi*, to be paid on the day of the wedding.'

The look on Bonnivet's face was a picture of outrage, his pale cheeks flushing, and his eyes watering with emotion - as if in pain. 'A baron! Wasn't a seigneury enough? Or being chosen as a Chevalier of Saint-Michel. Or your most recent appointment as Master Falconer.'

<<So he still hasn't forgiven me for the past>>

Nicolas knew for a fact that Bonnivet had stood in his way of receiving anything higher than a seigneury, convincing the King he'd already been more than generous. What pleasure then to keep the other man dangling for a little while longer, before tugging on the rope. 'Unfortunately, honoured as I am to have received these titles, I fear my future bride will be less than impressed with a husband who is merely entitled to wear a crimson hood and a gold chain around his neck. After all, if I'm to be married to an Englishwoman who, according to you, will own most of Cornwall one day, for the sake of appearances - and French pride - I have to at least appear her equal. A lieutenancy and a seigneury won't be enough.'

<<Checkmate!>>

∽

To his disgust, the Admiral's face reflected his defeat. They both knew Nicolas had won again. But didn't he always? This time would be no different. Although he felt tempted to ape Bonnivet's taunting words about "*losing some games*" back to him, he resisted the urge.

Now the matter had been settled to his satisfaction, he reached out for his lute and began idly strumming - after he'd wearily sworn to keep the plan secret from the rest of the world until the day itself. He let the remainder of the Admiral's drearily fulsome, obviously false description of his future bride, and details of the magnificent wedding feast, float over his head. Why would he give a fig that the chapel at the forthcoming 'Field of Gold' would be lit with candlesticks brought over from Westminster Abbey in London. Or that he and his bride would sip wine from gold chalices, also transported from the Abbey.

Nicolas laid his lute to one side, hardly bothering to stifle a yawn of boredom at Bonnivet's nonsense. Nevertheless, he couldn't escape the fact he'd agreed to take on a new wife. As he considered this, he suppressed a sigh at a distant memory, his mind drifting back to that other time he'd stood at the altar....

HOUSE OF HOWARD

Chapter Twelve

The same day. London.

I don't know why but even the thought of Tower Hill turns my blood to ice,' I told Robert and John, as their wherry passed it on our left.

'A guilty conscience, perhaps?' joked John. 'You're not climbing up there any time soon, I hope, Uncle Thomas.'

'No, I plan to take my head to the grave with me.'

Robert made a slicing motion with his oar. 'Alack! Plenty haven't managed it.'

<<*So true*>> Pretenders, as well as nobles with more than just a drop of blue blood running through their veins, had prowled around the precious throne for decades, ready to pounce at any sign of weakness. Great families such as my own, or the Staffords, watched their fortunes rise or fall, depending on the favour of the King. One week a high-born noble (such as myself) might be supping on swan and quails at the King's table, the next, gazing morosely through the bars of a cell in the Tower, weevil infested horse bread, made from ground-up beans, at their feet, wondering whether they'd ever see the light of day again. Not everyone was lucky enough to have forty shillings a week spent on them, as I'd been. Or be under the watchful eye of Sir James Radcliff, the obliging Lieutenant of the Tower.

It was not even twenty-five years since thousands of Cornishmen had marched towards London in fury at the first Tudor King's taxes, only to see the tarred heads of their leaders displayed on the south end of London Bridge. Although *Goose* was naturally inclined towards peace and clemency, in this instance, he'd known a show of strength was essential if he wished to keep his throne. And he did wish to keep it. Very badly—

'I was just thinking about *Goose*,' I said.

Robert's oar paused in mid-air. 'Old King Henry.' He hurriedly crossed himself. 'God rest his soul. He's on your mind because of the Tower?'

'I suppose so. I was imagining his horrified expression if he could witness how many coins have spilled out of the coffers to pay for his son's whimsical "*Field of Gold*".'

'I thought you two told me *Goose* wasn't averse to spending money in the early days to promote his family,' said John.

I pulled a blanket over my knees. 'You mean, while I was festering in the Tower? You're right, though. Sir James Radcliff told me that not one week after poor Richard met his end on Bosworth Field, *Goose* happily spent over three hundred pounds on gowns of cloth of gold and velvet, and a doublet of crimson and black satin. And not long after I was released, I discovered he'd spent five and a half thousand pounds on clothes for himself and his burgeoning family.'

Robert rested his oar on the side of the wherry. 'From that time onwards, whenever pretenders such as Perkin Warbeck—'

'The Flemish boy pretending to be Richard's nephew and namesake?' asked John.

'Aye. Whenever any of that ilk crept nearer to the throne, your Uncle Thomas said *Goose* would respond by flinging money at the problem. Out upon it! If that wasn't the sign of a man terrified for his safety and his crown, I don't know what was.'

'Uncle Thomas, as Lord High Treasurer these past two decades, you know more about money than anyone in the kingdom.'

'I do know one thing,' I said. 'Unlike *Goose*, who raided England's Treasury to impress, his son raids it to excess. As he's done from the very first day he threw himself down on *Goose's* vacant throne and immediately requested a new cushion of cloth of gold to replace the slightly faded, red velvet one.'

Robert shook his head. 'Marry! That's what comes from having three young lads running Europe.'

'Or a Stewart on the throne of Scotland,' said John. 'By the Might of Mars! Uncle Thomas can vouch for the Scottish thistle using every opportunity to give its neighbour a nasty scratch. Shamelessly exploiting its "Auld Alliance" with France while making life as difficult as possible for us in the south.'

I shrugged. 'I've always told any monarch seated on the throne of England to keep one eye on the Narrow Sea beyond and the other firmly on the volatile northern border above.'

'Don't forget Wales and the Dublin Pale,' said Robert. 'We might control that troublesome pair but in my opinion, they make uneasy, if not downright unwilling bedfellows. Only a tavern tosspot would ignore them.'

Robert lay down his oar and sat on the wooden bench across from me. 'Let the son row his father and uncle for a while. Old bones need a little rest. Besides, you and I need to sort out Europe. What about this Valois King, Thomas? He's had his throne for five years now. What kind of stuff's he made of?'

'François? No different from those before him. He wants to keep the crown of Milan and capture that of Naples.'

Robert grimaced. 'Tush! Italy's become both a great prize and the bloody battlefield of Europe.'

'What about King Hal?' asked John. 'Our very own "Tudor rose". Isn't he still lusting after what he considers his rightful crown of France? He makes no bones about coveting his neighbour's country. Not just the tiny strip around Calais where the Festival's to be held.'

'That's why he styles himself "*King of France*",' said his father, stretching his arms above his head, undoubtedly to alleviate the soreness caused by the frantic rowing under London Bridge. 'They're all as bad as each other, that's what I think.'

I nodded, recalling a recent occasion when Henry had paced ceaselessly up and down the chamber like a caged lion. 'The French certainly make much of the fact we English have been prone in the past to rid ourselves of troublesome monarchs - by fair means or foul.' I pretended to be the Valois François, adopting a sneering French accent:

'*Fi! Let my English brother try to steal my crown again. He'll soon discover the Tudor rose is no match for the French fleur-de-lys.'*

My two wherrymen friends laughed; they loved it when I did impressions. Being with them was akin to inhaling camphor to clear a pesky head cold. Often, I'd return to Parliament with my thoughts in order after a ride on the river.

'What about the new Emperor, Uncle Thomas? Doesn't Charles of Habsburg have similar status to the Pope in Rome now?'

'I fear he does. I've given up trying to list the staggering amount of territory over which a boy, still wet behind the ears, rules. Unless I'm mistaken, it includes Germany, the Austrian Archduchies, the Low Countries, eastern Burgundy, Savoy, Spain, and most of northern Italy, as well as Naples.'

'I've heard his secret desire is to reclaim the lands of his Burgundian forebears in eastern France,' said Robert. 'They say the very thought is enough to make his famous Habsburg jaw jut out more than usual. Is that true?'

I pretended to stroke an enormous chin. 'The English Ambassador overheard him saying he'd get the lands back if it was the last thing he did on God's green earth. According to our man, Charles said this with such passion it caused the courtiers around him to tremble and grow pale, lest his ambition could not be fulfilled.'

∽

'All our passengers are talking about the Festival,' said John. 'For weeks, all I've heard is who'll be the best jouster, which archer will have the surest aim, who'll have the stronger wrestlers, us or them.'

'*Snake* says he's taking the best horses in the land with him,' I said, not bothering to hide my contempt. 'He intends to present the heavenly music of royal choirs, and bring out the most talented actors to perform elaborate masques.'

Robert snorted. 'Go to! It sounds as if God in heaven couldn't achieve more if He came down to earth.'

I smiled at the comparison. 'According to the loose-lipped braggart,' I said, easily slipping into *Snake*'s voice and mannerisms: '"*all this and much more is to take place against a backdrop produced by extraordinary wizardry. The finest painters, sculptors and craftsmen in both lands have been commissioned to build a festival ground beyond men's wildest dreams.*"'

'I can almost hear the sound of thousands of nails being hammered into wood by the carpenters,' said John.

Snake was an easy target to mimic and poke fun at:

'"*In this magnificent setting,*"' I said, flinging out my arms, '"*twelve thousand members of the French and English Courts will gather. Each lord or lady will be a peacock, vying to outshine all others in clothes and finery. And so transform this colourful food and wine spectacle into an equally glorious feasting of the eye.*"'

I wagged my finger. 'If I was even ten years younger, I'd be fighting tooth and nail to be there—'

'God's Truth, yes!' exclaimed Robert. 'If only to prove to men and women alike there's still life in the old dog yet.'

I reached out to clap him on the shoulder. 'Sometimes, I think you know me better than myself!'

That made John laugh. 'It sounds as if all those nobles will be feasting their eyes on more than their food. Give us some more *Snake* bragging, Uncle Thomas.'

Smiling, I obliged. 'The other evening, he addressed everyone in the manner of a schoolmaster about to reward his favourite pupils.' I pretended to straighten an imaginary cloak: '"*For once, the more serious pursuits of politics and war are to be abandoned in favour of this unique opportunity to bask in the June sunshine, and play with kings and queens.*"'

Robert was shaking with laughter. 'He could be sitting here next to me.'

'Best not. I might be tempted to tip him in,' said his son. 'I wager all the guests cheered.'

I rolled my eyes. 'Yes. And he got a beaming smile from Henry.'

Robert reached over to tuck my blanket back over my knees. 'There are those that say that when prickly France meets blustering England, instead of instant antagonism, true love sometimes springs up and begins to flourish. In such instances, the delicate fleur-de-lys may deftly entwine itself around the fragrant English rose, with no fear of being pricked by sharp thorns—'

I thought again how much the King had liked Robert that far-off time. 'Then let's pray there aren't any thorns over in Calais.'

As I gazed at the Thames ahead, I considered how talk of the Festival was taking place not only on water but also on land; I recalled all the comments I'd heard:

"By Saint George! How can you possibly need a gown of cloth of gold, as well as all the others?"

"Will we find Frenchmen more charming than our own?"

"Who'll break more lances…us or them?"

"Can their court really be that dissolute?"

Across the Narrow Sea, I knew there was equal anticipation and excitement. Being very familiar with the French court, it didn't take a huge leap of imagination to imagine what was being said there:

"Dieu merci, they speak our tongue, not just their own heathen one!"

"I've heard Englishwomen kiss on the mouth when greeting guests."

"Will their King be taller than ours?"

"Perhaps I'll find a wife amongst the English—"

'So, Uncle Thomas,' said John, 'you're supping at the Palace and then stargazing again with the King and Master More. You've got a good clear night for it.'

'How did you manage to stop *Snake* butting in?' asked Robert. 'I know you two are going through one of your bad patches.'

'You always remind me of an old married couple,' guffawed John. 'You can't live with each other. But you can scarce live without each other either.'

I shrugged. '*Snake*'s got far more important things on his mind than me right now, John. Besides, he's risen so far above all of us, he's nearly touching the stars.'

'Then let's hope he fares better than Icarus,' Robert said, rolling his eyes (and showing off the knowledge that had come from spending decades in the company of learned men crossing the Thames), 'flying too close to the sun. And he remembers that the higher you climb, the further you fall.'

HOUSE OF HOWARD

Chapter Thirteen

*Later that evening. On the roof
of the Palace of Placentia, Greenwich.*

I never feel so at peace as I do up here,' said the King, looking up at the velvety night sky: a dark canopy, liberally sprinkled with stars.

I always found it a strange, womb-like experience when the earth below turned almost completely black - apart from the faint glow of candlelight dotted here and there. This was when the sky above, with its moon and stars, came into its own. Allowing us to see in all their glory the stars and planets that played such an important part in our daily lives: influencing our wellbeing, our actions, our temperaments and our fortunes. I'd always told my children to reach for the stars and never had it seemed more possible than this evening.

Our sole means of lighting at this very moment were the blazing torches propped up against the wall, or the occasional flash of light from the world beyond the Palace walls. Perhaps a lantern attached aloft to a pole by a wherryman such as John Warner, grateful for half a groat for rowing a nobleman to a secret assignation with his mistress further up the Thames, taking advantage of an absent husband. That splash I'd just heard might well be his oar gleefully dipping into the water on a promise of extra money for speed.

Next to me, the royal under-secretary, Tom More, was examining an astrolabe belonging to the King, an impressive looking circular instrument of gilded brass, cupped in his hands.

'The Norman who made it for me inscribed the winds in Latin around the edge,' said Henry.

Even though I was sorry to hear a Frenchman had produced such an exceptional specimen and not an Englishman, I was still impressed by its beauty, as well as the ability of something so tiny to give others valuable information about the position of the sun, moon, planets and stars. I was pleased that for once I had no need of my silver spectacles. 'It makes me feel very small and humble, standing here in the starlight,' I said.

Tom looked up from the King's astrolabe. '"*Non est ad astra mollis e terris via.*" According to Seneca the Younger, there is no easy way from the Earth to the stars. I have to admit, it's at times like this I feel closest to God.'

'It's interesting that we all feel so differently,' said Henry. 'Yet the same.'

I could see Tom smiling. His features had a luminous glow to them in the torchlight on this roof of the world. I always felt his face reflected his flair for perspicacious insight and rapidity of mind. Around forty, he was a man of middling height, with a large nose and somewhat thin lips. He had a fair complexion and his large, clear blue eyes gazed out calmly about him. To my mind, it was a face that men would trust. His wide forehead and rather short neck only added to the impression of one prepared to devotedly serve his master.

<<*After nearly eighty years on this earth, I've learnt to read a man or a woman's face*>> Perhaps the only hint of the existence of a 'secret place' within Tom's soul which he kept well-hidden from the prying eyes of kings was the tell-tale dimple on his chin and the long nose, with the tip pointing down a little towards his mouth. As someone who happened to possess similar features, albeit in a far thinner face, I recalled how a recent guest of mine had told me that, according to a current study of Aristotle's physiognomical teachings, they indicated an individual who was honest, reserved, and self-effacing. I would be the first to admit that such a description was far more suited to the clever lawyer than me.

I continued from where the King had left off: 'I draw comfort from men and women feeling the same wherever they are in the world. I like the way the Governor of Picardy is equally likely to cross himself in fear at the sound of thunder in the heavens above as a merchant in York, a painter in Milan, or a princess in Spain.'

'It's true a cosmos exists that is a miracle of God's handiwork,' said Tom.

I gave a little shiver. 'But it's also a fearful thing.'

The King put his hand on my shoulder. 'There isn't one of us in Christendom who hasn't trembled at the sight of hailstones the size of eggs, knowing they're the work of Satan.'

I pointed up to the maze of stars above our heads. 'Don't you both find it unnerving how each comet and eclipse seen in the skies has the potential to bring forth disaster and disease?'

We lived in an uncertain world. All three of us had heard tales, or knew from personal tragedy, how a man, woman or child could be in perfect health one moment, and then die from the dreaded sweating sickness in a matter of hours. Doctors (knowing that every human being was governed by the four humours), when faced with either a megrim or a bout of melancholy, or any other ailment, would dispense their somewhat experimental cordials accordingly.

Tom walked over to the edge of the battlements and gazed down at the river. 'Everything under the sun - be it animal, mineral or vegetable - has its place in this world of ours.'

'You mean, as in a game of chess?' asked Henry.

'Exactly,' replied Tom. 'Wasn't it the so-called "Spider King of France" who said that the conditions of this world are akin to a game of chess. Each person is in the place and degree suitable to his or her estate while the game lasts, but when it is finished, all the pieces go back into the bag without any distinction made.'

Henry began to laugh. 'So I am to be placed back in a bag with a common thief and a bawd, am I?'

Tom looked serious. 'Your Majesty, everything is as it should be in our world. Thus, the lion and the king mirror one another as rulers of their kingdoms. Equally, it is accepted that the proud eagle soars uppermost in the skies; the diamond is the most desirable of gems; and the mighty oak, the first amongst trees.'

I fingered my black velvet cloak. 'Even the clothes on a man or woman's back are dictated by their place in society. Cloth of gold, velvet, and silks being strictly reserved for royalty and the upper echelons of the nobility.'

'Quite right, too,' said Henry.

❧

I'd often marvelled at Tom's ability to avoid offending this most easily-offended of monarchs, certainly more so than any of the other five kings I'd known in my time. Tom once told me he'd learned the lessons of his youth well; as an apprentice lawyer at New Inn, he was required to debate a legal point of a court case every evening after dinner. The documents were placed next to a large ornate saltcellar until the meal was finished, and then two junior barristers were selected to debate on either side of the argument.

'Speaking of cloth of gold,' said Tom, 'we must all give thanks to God that He has finally seen fit to put the two greatest kings in Christendom together on the same soil. Gold is the natural colour of kings and the "Field of Cloth of Gold" is the perfect setting.'

'Are you suggesting the French king and I are equal, Tom?' asked Henry, unable to resist teasing our solemn companion. I so wished I could see the smile on Henry's face reach his eyes.

Unlike the odious *Snake*, Tom More was no idle flatterer. I waited to see how he would extricate himself.

'Sire, if you will permit me to be so bold, I believe the waters which have separated our two countries until this moment have been to the detriment of France.'

'Go on,' said Henry, his voice curious, remarkably, his demeanour not showing any signs of ruffled feathers.

Tom made a graceful gesture with his hands. 'I am sure Thomas here will agree with me that King François has much to learn from you. I've heard he has long been desirous to do so. I am also convinced that the two of you are overly modest about your own achievements and that the amount that you can teach one another is as equal as the hours between dawn and dusk.'

Bravo! Pure poetry to the King's ears to be told he was a shining example to his brother monarch. I felt like applauding. Instead, I took the conversation to a lighter place, certainly a safer one:

'I do know one thing. On either side of the Narrow Sea, young noblewomen are in a state of feverish excitement hoping for a glimpse of the pair of you.'

✍

For a few long moments, the three of us stood on the Palace roof in companionable silence, enjoying being inside the dark cocoon, free to contemplate the mysteries of the universe outlined above our heads. I was the first to speak: 'France and England as foes. England and France as friends. Why does history always have a habit of repeating itself?'

'*Thucydides!*' exclaimed Henry and Tom together, before dissolving into laughter.

'Thucydides?' I repeated, at a loss.

'The Greek historian,' said Tom, 'who believed that in accordance with human nature, historical events are likely to repeat themselves at some future time - if not in exactly the same way, then in one very similar.'

I knew of old how much Henry enjoyed such discussions as these, grabbing them with his hands, kneading them into shape as if he were a baker producing the best manchet loaf, and they the dough. 'Throughout the ages,' he said now, 'a philosopher or politician might well have regarded this as proof of human weakness or stupidity, an inability to learn from past lessons. An astrologer might have looked to a shift in the planets above, their movements reflected in events below. Whatever the reason, no one can deny patterns exist that are endlessly repeated.'

'I'm nought but an old soldier,' I said, 'yet, that makes sense to me.'

<<*If I'm able to solve problems in a wherry on the Thames, then why not on this starlit rooftop? If only we lived in a world where Robert and John Warner: men of water, could join in this lively debate with Henry Tudor and Tom More: men of land. On a regular basis, not in an extraordinary encounter between king and subject*>>

≪

Tom turned to me. 'Standing here makes me more aware of the two worlds into which we are born.'

'*Two?*'

'Yes, whenever a baby breathes its first breath on earth, he or she is entering two worlds. The first is the narrow one where they will soon enough start to go about their daily life: perhaps learning their letters, toiling at a job, taking their leisure when possible, celebrating the seasons of the year, feasting or fasting, making love, raising a family. All in all, mostly unaffected by what is taking place in the other world.'

I thought of the wherrymen at Number Ten, Turnpin Lane. 'And the second one?'

I could tell by the expression on Henry's face that his quicksilver mind was racing ahead. Even as my own was puzzling over Tom's words. 'That's the wide one far beyond their hearth and home,' the King declared, 'of which they may come to know very little, depending on their position in society, and their opportunity to travel. Am I right, Tom?'

'You are,' said Tom. 'Consider it, gentlemen. We live in an era when it takes an entire day to travel twenty or thirty miles on horseback, depending on the state of the roads. And even if you are able to afford a horse - a king, such as Your Majesty here; your queen, Her Majesty, within the Palace; or the Emperor across the Narrow Sea, must seem as remote as God Himself. With very little means of communication, for most people, almost everything of any importance takes place in the first world.'

'But what happens when the two worlds collide?' I asked. 'When people are forced to look up from the supper on their table and look beyond the front door of their dwelling. To watch patterns endlessly repeat themselves.'

'Ah,' said Tom. 'This has happened in Europe, on numerous occasions. Here, territory has always shifted on a regular basis, as have the relations between the countries. If we look more closely at England, Scotland, and France, for instance, we see that Scotland has long desired independence from England. As for England and France, the area around Calais (besides others) has been a bone of contention between the two of us for many a long year. In one month from now, it will be a place of celebration. But how about in ten years…in twenty…in fifty…even in five hundred. Will it remain the same?'

'Nothing really changes,' mused Henry, 'or as our French friends say: *"Plus ça change, plus c'est la même chose."'*

For a while, I listened to the two men continuing their debate but eventually my mind took off in a totally different direction. It was obvious to me that even in the narrow world of the family, history was prone to repeat itself. If I chose to look down the long tunnel of generations of Howards and their forebears, and into their various closets of closely guarded secrets, no doubt I would soon discover that many things such as looks, behaviour, and riches were passed down. In addition, circumstances would often be repeated in a very similar manner, to such an extent that two members, separated by hundreds of years, could easily feel two parts of a whole. It was hardly a surprise then that delving into a family's background and its secrets could be both rewarding and perilous.

At my advanced age, I lived for the present, not what was left of the future. As for the past, I viewed it as a series of skirmishes: some well-fought, bringing a sense of heady satisfaction…others not so rewarding, bringing only frustration. <<*Then there were the one or two occasions that left me so bloodied I feared I'd never rise to my feet again. But, of course I did*>> I could quite neatly divide my soon-to-be four score years into equal parts: the final one beginning in 1497, the year when the Cornish and Scots seemed intent upon creating chaos and devastation throughout the land….

PART TWO

FIRST LOVE

'And when Love speaks,
the voice of all the gods
Make heaven drowsy with the harmony.'

'Love's Labour's Lost'
William Shakespeare (1564-1616).

HOUSE OF TREDAVOE

Chapter Fourteen

Twenty-three years earlier. Saint Valentine's Day, 1497.
Zennor Castle, Cornwall.

*Y*ou have no choice. You have to wed the Frenchman. It's all been arranged.'

'I don't give a fig! I've never even met him.'

'You know what he looks like. You've exchanged portraits.'

'I don't want a roynish portrait! Or to be forced into wedlock because the monks at Saint Buryan asked Father to send their mead over to Sir Edward Poynings at Calais. How earth-vexing that the Comte d'Ardres tasted it, asked for more, and found out about our family. And me.'

'But he did. And now I fear you must wed his son. King Henry favours both our trade with the French, and the match.'

Grace shook out her hair in a cloud of burnished gold. 'I don't want Guy d'Ardres. I want Ned. I love him.'

William was trying hard to remain patient. Inwardly sighing at the gargantuan task that had landed on his boyish, twenty-one-year old shoulders, he gazed past his younger sister, seeking inspiration in the slate-coloured February skies, beyond the lattice windows of the chamber. When he spoke, his voice was unnaturally quiet considering the dangerous subject matter…for fear of being overheard. Heaven forbid what would happen if news of this secret liaison got out. He'd only found out by chance yesterday when he saw Grace and Edward Howard in a foolhardy embrace in the courtyard below. He'd been aghast. How he wished their beloved mother hadn't perished from the sickness two years before; she would have known exactly what to say and how to act. All he could do was try his best.

'I have no idea what's possessed you. Edward is a Howard through and through. You know how ambitious that family is and how far they've fallen. They still haven't recovered from being on the wrong side of King Henry at Bosworth—'

'It's not Ned's fault his grandsire was one of King Richard's closest allies.'

'Much good it did either of them. Both slaughtered on a battlefield.'

'So why are you so against the Howards now?'

'Everyone's heard the rumours about Edward's grandsire having a hand in the disappearance of the little princes for financial gain. Helped by Edward's father. There are still whispers about how the Howard titles of duke and earl, given by Richard a few days into his new reign, were bought with blood—'

'That's scurrilous gossip!' interrupted Grace, letting out something akin to a hiss. 'Tavern talk by those too far gone in their cups. Alys Pendeen's mother thinks Margaret Beaufort had a hand in it. Mistress Matilda says Margaret's always been like a wildcat who'd claw anyone's eyes out if they crossed her in her ambition to put her son on the thron—'

'Hush, sister! That's the King's mother of whom you're speaking. Men have been hanged for less.'

Yet, he knew he was powerless to Grace's indignation.

'You know our own mother used to say Cecily Neville, King Richard's mother, never stopped loving him. Moreover, Mother said that the princes' mother still favoured the King after their disappearance. And that no grieving mother would have treated the murderer of her sons so.' Grace gave a little toss of her head. 'I don't know why we're even talking about this, Will. None of it has anything to do with Ned.'

'Perhaps not, but some facts about the family can't be disputed. After Bosworth, they lost those titles and Edward's father was thrown into the Tower. Before Henry Tudor exiled him to look after the North.'

Grace swept aside a strand of blonde hair that had fallen across stormy green eyes. 'Ned says the Earl has done a magnificent job there. And is quite restored to the King's good graces. Or "*Goose*" as Ned's father calls him.'

'You and I both know the Howards are at the mercy of the Tudors. And need all the help they can get to crawl their way back to the top again. '

'I don't care about any of that. I love Ned and he loves me. He's asked me to marry him. His mother is very ill and he wants us to be wed as soon as possible.'

As she said this, she turned away, reaching down into her pocket. Then she thrust out her left hand in a defiant manner. On it was a gold ring, its slim band adorned with stars all the way around.

William was appalled. Matters had clearly gone even further than he suspected. He knew his hot-headed sister only too well and dreaded to think how far that was. If only he'd noticed something before now. Edward Howard had been staying with Roger Trewellis and his family at Mount's Bay for several months, supposedly working in the trading business of his father's old friend. William now knew the reality to be quite different; it explained why Edward hadn't returned home to the Howard home in Norfolk for the twelve days of Christmas. Instead, he'd accompanied the Trewellis family to Zennor for Twelfth Night. William was almost certain Lord Trewellis and his family knew nothing of the clandestine relationship either, and that the two lovebirds had successfully managed to keep it away from prying eyes…until now. It explained Grace's recent frequent absences from the Castle, ostensibly to pay visits to friends, or satisfy a sudden fancy to visit a dressmaker's in Penzance to discover the latest fashions in London. William frowned. As a Howard, Edward had enough gold coins in his purse to find a suitable love nest for the pair of them, as well as bribe any over-inquisitive servants.

He tried to stay calm. 'It's impossible. You're betrothed to another. Besides, Edward hasn't asked his father's permission, I take it. Be reasonable. Even if Edward is only the younger son and not the Howard heir, his father's probably got some eye-wateringly rich heiress earmarked for him. Why would he ever agree to a marriage with a Cornish family such as the Tredavoes when a rebellion here looks more likely by the day. No one wants to pay taxes to fund a war with Scotlan—'

'But we're loyal to this King. Father fought for him at Bosworth. Look at how much land we were given as a rewar—'

'Grace, everyone knows how suspicious the King is. And Thomas Howard knows it better than anyone. With pretenders like Perkin Warbeck making false claims to the English throne while up in Scotland, and men like King James supporting him, besides stirring up trouble on the border, he's right to be worried. The Howards have to keep their noses out of trouble. It's only a matter of years since your Ned's father managed to claw back the earldom of Surrey from Henry Tudor's good graces. He's not about to risk everything again for a match that would displease him.'

Grace put her hands on her hips, her expression defiant. 'It's not fair. I know you're sweet on Alys—'

'Alys Pendeen isn't a Howard!'

'What about Tom Bullen? Your best friend's wooing Lizzie Howard and you haven't mentioned that.'

'Nothing is certain. The fact Thomas Howard is even considering a union with a Bullen shows you how precarious the family's position is. Before Bosworth, he and his father would have looked down their long noses at any family inferior to their own.'

To William's consternation, Grace suddenly looked as if all the fight had gone out of her. Her eyes welled up and William noticed a piece of parchment she'd picked up and was clutching in her right hand. Fearful it might contain the whereabouts of a forthcoming assignation between his sister and her lover, William reached out and snatched it from her. Caught by surprise, Grace let out a cry of protest but she was too late. William was already reading the words written in an elegant but bold hand, with many flourishes and an ornate signature beneath:

" *To my beloved Grace, my future wife.*

May I let Master Geoffrey Chaucer speak for me:

"*Ther sat a queen*
That, as of light the somer-sonne shene
Passeth the sterre, right so over mesure
She fairer was than any creature....

* * *

78

{'There sat a queen
As in brightness the summer sun's sheen
Outshines the star, right so beyond measure
Was she fairer than any creature.'}

* * *

*"This was on Seynt Valentynes Day
Whan euery foul cometh ther to chese his make."*

{'This was on Saint Valentine's Day
When every fowl comes there his mate to take.'}

*Ever yours,
Ned* "

A pair of lovebirds indeed! Seeing Edward Howard's handwriting seemed to bring to life the youth himself. If Grace was an exceptionally pretty young girl, then her intended groom possessed equal charm and presence. A year or so younger than William, dark-haired and bright-eyed, he had the wiry build of his father, Thomas, but in that slender frame lurked an ebullience that was evident everywhere he appeared: in the tiltyard, at the butts, trapping a deer, in his big infectious laugh as he'd swept William's fifteen-year-old sister off her feet on the dance floor of the great hall in Zennor Castle this past September - the place their paths had first crossed. He was certainly larger than life—

'Will, I said, give it back this instant!'

Looking at Grace's anguished white face, William came to a difficult decision. He had no wish to worry his father, still mourning their mother, but glad of the advantageous match next month between Grace and the highborn young French nobleman (a widower) - tipped to follow in the family footsteps and become a future governor of Picardy. William knew he must be the one to put a halt to this madness. And swiftly. God have mercy! If Grace and Edward

Howard were already lovers, every chime of the clock in the courtyard below counted. There was no other option; he would have to go and see Thomas Howard.

Having glimpsed the Earl once over at Mount's Bay, his heart sank at the daunting prospect; knowing his beloved only sister might never forgive him made him unduly harsh.

'I think this has gone far beyond Valentine Day love missives, Grace.' He looked pointedly at the stomacher of his sister's green gown. 'For your sake and that of the Tredavoe family honour, I can only hope that if a child results from this folly, it will favour *you* in looks and not its father....'

HOUSE OF HOWARD

Chapter Fifteen

Six years later. 11th August, 1503.
Holyrood Palace, Edinburgh.

I frowned at the black chess piece I was holding in my hand: the Queen. My chance to seize back control in a game I was losing. It should have filled me with a feeling of triumph but instead it reminded me of the delicate task that lay ahead. By God's Nails! How to break it to the proud, fashionably-dressed, young Scotsman seated opposite me in a chair of state in the impressive oak-panelled chamber, with his personal coat-of-arms: the red lion of Scotland, guarded by two unicorns, above his head - as skilful at playing chess as he was at ruling his country - that his wilful child bride (now safely abed, worn out by her tantrum) was demanding the removal of all seven Stewart bastards from the royal nursery before she would agree to set foot in Stirling Castle: one of her husband's wedding gifts to her.

<<*Damn the Tudors!*>> As a Howard, I was fiercely loyal to whichever king was on the throne of England: Lancaster, York, or Tudor. But this afternoon, I'd found myself cursing *Goose* for the unseemly outburst by his thirteen-year-old daughter, Margaret. It had taken all my self-control not to give her a well-deserved slap on the cheek; indeed, my wife had need of her entire arsenal of soothing and kind words to calm the girl down and prevent me doing something that could cost me a lifetime's career. After all the money that had been spent on a royal progress for her along the Great North Road... through England and southern Scotland, she was acting like an insufferable ingrate.

Not for nothing had I offered up a silent prayer in York Minster for the girl's dead Yorkist great-uncle, Richard, my former master: a king who'd shown me only respect and gratitude. I certainly hadn't had to crawl on my hands and knees to him, as I often felt I was doing with *Goose*. Thanks to him, I was, at times, reduced to a condition no better than a dog snuffling in the rushes on the floor of a great hall, hoping to find a few scraps beneath the high table.

∽

I cleared my throat. 'Your Majesty, there's something pressing we need to discuss.'

In reply, James of Scotland arched a dark eyebrow, the corners of his wide mouth turning down. He shifted his lean body against a couple of blue and red velvet cushions behind him. 'I trust 'tis nothing we canna overcome, Thomas. After all, here ye and I are playing chess after fighting on opposite sides six years ago outside Berwick. Where, I might add, ye turned down my challenge to single combat—'

'Wisely, I believe. I had the disadvantage of an additional thirty summers to your twenty-four. And you the advantage of being a king compared to a mere lieutenant.'

'Pity! 'Twould have been interesting to see how the red lion fared against the white one,' said James, tugging at the embroidered neck-band of his shirt and letting me know he was familiar with the lion on the Howard coat-of-arms, inherited from my ancestors, the Mowbray dukes of Norfolk.

'I can see you like to play games, Your Majesty.'

James laughed. 'I've calculated I am but two moves away from winning this one. So let's raise a glass and drink a wee dram of *aqua vitae* while ye tell me what it is that's gnawing at your innards.'

'Better luck with a game of backgammon next time,' he called over his shoulder as he walked across the sumptuously furnished chamber (undoubtedly containing newly acquired tapestries, silver plate and chairs from Bruges). He seized two goblets and filled them with the fiery brown liquid so beloved of the Scots. I noticed an impressive turquoise ring on one of his fingers catching the last rays of evening sunshine. Impressed by the King's perspicacity, I was a little nervous, an emotion alien to me: a seasoned warrior used to plain speech and thrusting myself into any breech that came my way. But I hadn't been dealing with the King of Scotland: a man with an enormous passion for life, probably the best educated monarch in the whole of Europe, fluent in several languages, including Flemish, Italian and Spanish; highly intelligent and possessing an admirable curiosity in the world about him. I'd heard his interest in medicine extended to being able to set a broken limb, pull a tooth, or apply a leech to a wound. He was also a man with a vision for the future; I knew he'd given orders for the eldest sons of his barons and major freeholders to be educated to increase the number of judges.

This was a ruler of a land of wild moorlands and spectacular lochs, marshes and reed-gilded pools: home to crane, bittern and heron. In contrast to the land below Scotland, trees and hedges were scarce except for the enormous forests of pine in the Highlands. Here, caterans, with their thirst for blood, were as dangerous as the wolves that still roamed. Scotland was a land of water; its capital city was surrounded by lochs; its winter seas so perilous that no ship was permitted to sail between the Feast of Saint Simon and Saint Jude, at the end of October, and the Feast of Candlemas, on the second of February. James was a worthy successor to Robert the Bruce, hero of the Battle of Bannockburn, against we English. A victory as impressive as Henry of Lancaster's Agincourt. The Spanish Ambassador, De Ayla, described how the King actively sought out danger in battle, and at times flew into the fray before he'd even given the order to fight, not the mark of a good captain. Hard to believe the rumours that the man before me had in some way been involved in the assassination of his own father when a callow youth. I'd heard tell that in the weeks before his birth, a startling portent, in the shape of a bright comet, visible to the naked eye (even in the noonday skies), had left a fiery trail in the heavens above from mid-January to mid-February. James was renowned as a soldier, a formidable jouster, for his impeccable manners and charm - one equally comfortable in his colourful court pursuing gentler pastimes.

And *women*.

His success with women was legendary (even though his last mistress had, to his enormous sorrow, been poisoned); no wonder looking at him now. Handsome, brimming over with good will, yet possessing a certain earthiness I could see would send the females giddy, it seemed that none could resist an invitation to the royal bed...which was exactly why I found myself in this unenviable position today. The solemn oath the Earl of Bothwell made in Richmond Palace last year, in his role of proxy for the King of Scotland: to forsake all other women for the remainder of his life, was about as likely to be realised as the Pope in Rome to take a wife. Or the hogsheads of finest Gascon wine (transported throughout London on carts) to quench the thirst of those celebrating the ceremony around multiple enormous bonfires that same evening, being found the next morning with a single drop left inside.

Seventeen years older than his new bride, as far as I was concerned, James had genuinely wooed Margaret Tudor and shown her nothing but kindness up until this point. He'd certainly been generous: providing her with red and purple velvet curtains for the hangings in her chamber, and cloth of gold for the curtains of her bed of state. He'd even taken it upon himself to commission an Edinburgh goldsmith to produce a crown for his queen out of dozens of coins from his Treasury. Before the wedding, he'd unexpectedly arrived in Dalkeith, supposedly on a hunting trip, but in reality, to meet Margaret in relaxed surroundings, take supper, play music, and put her at her ease. No expense was spared, and the gold coins with their emblem of the thistle, came pouring out of the royal coffers as readily as the ones in the kingdom below.

A born crowd pleaser, in Edinburgh, James leapt onto a palfrey (a gift from him to his future bride), impressively not touching either stirrup, and then asking for her to be lifted up behind him. Of course, his subjects went wild at the sight of her in cloth of gold, trimmed with black velvet, with her arms wound around their King, in cloth of gold, bordered with black fur. William Dunbar's poem, '*The thistle and the rose*', incorporating the badges from both countries, was greeted with equal enthusiasm. However, I wouldn't blame him if all this fuss ceased now; in fact, I half-hoped it would. No woman had any place challenging a man who was her lord and master, especially not a strong-willed young girl, not long out of the nursery.

I only hoped he wasn't already thinking the thirty thousand golden nobles Margaret Tudor was to bring with her as a dowry (of which I'd handed over ten as a first instalment yesterday) was an unfair exchange. It was but three days since I'd worn cloth of gold and the Order of the Garter around my neck to lead Margaret down the aisle, accompanied by the Archbishop of York. We'd returned to Holyrood Palace after her coronation to sup our fill of the magnificent feast provided for our pleasure. The royal high table, a few inches higher than all the rest, groaned with an abundance of delicacies: Boar's Head with its own jelly decorated with the arms of the two countries, roast swan, crane. Watching the King and new Queen (their feet resting on a beautifully embroidered lyare) nibbling their way through the dozen courses served to them on golden plates, with the freshly-painted coat-of-arms above their heads, depicting an entwined thistle and rose, topped by a crown, I'd had a sense of a job well done. I was able to enjoy the festivities: music, dancing and skilful conjuring within the Palace, illuminated by all the bonfires in the streets. We all admired the acrobat who danced with the agility of a sprite, plucked from thin air, on ropes in the courtyard the following day. My Agnes and Muriel joined in the fun, cutting James's long beard and being well-rewarded for their pains with fifteen ells of cloth of gold each. All had been well. Until now….

When I'd finished explaining the problem, James of Scotland leant back in his chair and made a steepling gesture with his long fingers while a slumbering hunting dog at his feet let out a contented snore. I half-expected one of his beloved hawks to appear from nowhere and come to rest on his wrist. Once, when younger, I knew he'd paid almost two hundred pounds for a single hawk.

He did not speak for a few moments and I prepared myself for the onslaught of rage about to follow. To my surprise, he brushed the material of his doublet of cloth of gold, then gave a little chuckle, his expressive face alight with mirth.

'So…my wee Tudor bride has stamped her foot, has she? I'm sure that didna please ye at all, Thomas.'

Lulled by the pleasant sound of the King's lilting accent and not at all offended at finding myself the butt of gentle teasing, I could afford to be gracious. 'Well, I must say, she caught me by surprise.'

James was still smiling. 'Och, in a bairn's head, even the word "mistress" must seem a verra big one indeed. I've heard her father didna indulge himself outside the marital bed.'

'No. King Henry and your Queen's late mother were devoted to one another.'

'So my sources have informed me. A rather pleasant state of affairs for a royal couple to find love at the altar.'

Admiring the roll of the Scottish King's 'r' s which seemed to turn every sentence into something that resembled poetry, as well as the way he said the word 'my' as if it were the French '*ma*', I couldn't help comparing James's speech to the dry tones of the far older *Goose* in the land below. Not wishing James to think he was being given a lesson on how to conduct himself by the English, my reply was deliberately half-hearted:

'But rare for a royal couple to do so. And in my book, a man should not be told by anyone how to act in these matters.'

'I couldna agree more. Tell me. Is it true you're a happily married man?' This caught me unawares. 'It is.'

Again, there was mockery in the King's warm brown eyes. 'And why would ye no' be with the lovely young Countess for a wife. Ye were fortunate to find love so quickly after your first lady wife died. Dame Fortune didna even grant ye a full summer to mourn her if I remember rightly.'

If I'd been a woman, I know I would have blushed. Glancing over at the abandoned chessboard, I had the feeling I was about to lose another game. 'It was not a question of marrying for love. But rather a way of honouring my dead wife's family by marrying her cousin and keeping them close to the Howards.'

As I spoke the words, I knew exactly what James Stewart must be thinking. My late wife, Bess Tilney, a wealthy widow, much sought after by other suitors, *had* served me well and given me three living sons and two daughters. Four more sons and a daughter hadn't survived childhood but such was the way of the world. She and I had both lived past the turn of a full half-century, loyal companions until the end but with any passion (if it had ever existed) long since extinguished. How good it had been to feel power surging through my body anew; oh, how eagerly I'd sunk into the trembling arms of my second wife, twenty-year-old Agnes, on our wedding night: a virgin bride for the taking with her soft yielding flesh and wide frightened eyes. Not only had she hardened my cock but she'd gone some way to restoring my youthful vigour in the bedchamber.

James was nodding his head. 'I understand. And who am I to comment on the ages between bride and groom when I've just wed a wee maid myself.' He lifted his goblet to his mouth but suddenly paused and set it down again. 'One thing puzzles me though. Your eldest son and heir managed to bag the daughter of King Edward after his death, thanks to your family's closeness to his brother, Richard. But your second son is bound to a rich widow two or three years older than yourself. Are ye no' concerned about the future of the Howard line? After all, the life of an heir can be snuffed out in an instant and then ye have to look to the spare for the future.' He crossed himself. 'Forgive my bluntness, Thomas. But take my bride's brother. One moment young Arthur was "*the rosebush of England*". The verra next…nourishment for worms.' He hastily crossed himself again, as did I. 'And the poor Queen risked her life to give her husband and England another son.'

'She did indeed.'

'Died on her thirty-seventh birthday, if I'm no' mistaken? With the wee lassie she'd just birthed no' tarrying long on this earth. 'Tis a great sorrow that of the eight Tudor children, born hale and hearty, just three remain. Such is the will of God, and the capriciousness of Dame Fortune.'

I was taken aback by such accurate information. No, he wasn't mistaken. Then he knew just how much the King mourned her.

'May the stars look down favourably on the House of Stewart, Your Majesty. And give you many healthy heirs.'

'I thank ye for your kind words. Och, let's hope King Henry lives long enough to let his new heir at least sprout some hairs on his wee chin and grow a pair of proper ballocks. How old is the lad now?'

I was certain he already knew the answer to that question. Even so, I couldn't be seen to show any disrespect. 'Prince Henry is twelve years old.'

James took my goblet and walked away to refill it. He didn't seem to be able to sit still for anything longer than a few minutes and, even then, he was drumming his fingers on the armrests of his chair of state, or tapping his feet. Little wonder he and his household of about a hundred rarely spent more than a few weeks in any of his palaces. Apart from the fact that the King and his court were fleeing bad odours (and would only return when fresh rushes had been laid, and the garderobe flues cleaned), the man was as restless as my favourite black stallion, presently snorting and stamping in the stables outside. He was also very well-informed. By God's Wounds! He seemed to have the ages of the entire world engraved upon his brain. And every vital fact at his fingertips. <<*I shouldn't be surprised*>> I told myself, recalling James's easy patronage of the Pretender, Perkin Warbeck. It was another example of his often ingenious statesmanship. What better way to get yourself recognition in Europe as the monarch of an independent country from England than harbouring such a person at your court. At the same time, forcing his English rival to open up a huge number of coffers to counter his border raids and the threat to English security. Ingenious, indeed. It also brought him one step further to his goal of bringing peace to the rest of Europe, and leading the armies of Christendom against the Turk.

What was it a Spanish ambassador once wrote about James? That he had as high an opinion of himself as if he were *"Lord of the World"*. How could any of us forget the story of the same ambassador and his companion? Sent by Queen Isabella and King Ferdinand on an embassy to the court of Scotland, they were instructed to pave the way for a marriage between their daughter, Katherine, and young Arthur Tudor, by persuading the Scottish King to give up Warbeck. Unfortunately, a further letter, advising them to flatter and deceive James Stewart, arrived before the unfortunate diplomats. Breaking the seal of the royal correspondence without a shred of conscience, what sport James had at their expense in the gardens of Stirling Castle. He reminded me of a sleepy, seemingly tame lion, inveterately charming with his winning smile, but quite capable of raising a menacing paw if pushed beyond the limit.

I wondered if James of Scotland had a spy in my household. His dark brown eyes seemed to have the ability to stare into a man's very soul. And what he said was true. Elizabeth Stapleton (or *"Old Bess"* as my son and heir,

Thomas, called her in private, a sneer on his thin face) had brought Edward enrichment but no cradle in their house would ever be filled. Drinking rather too deeply of the burning liquid in my goblet, the Devil's own drink, I almost had a coughing fit. 'Sometimes,' I rasped, 'a young man needs the steady influence of an older woman.'

How true that was in the case of my favourite son, a boy too easily given to rashness and foolish actions; even so, I far preferred Edward to his older brother, Thomas, a cold fish - or Edmund, his useless younger brother, a wastrel in the making if ever I saw one. After the avoidance of that disastrous match involving Edward six years ago (thanks to the resourcefulness of a Cornish girl's brother), I'd whisked my two older boys away up here to Scotland, knighting the pair of them after a treaty had been signed with the man now settled into his seat again.

James downed the contents of his goblet in a single gulp as if it were milk from the dairy. 'So, the father marries a woman the same age as his son, and the son does the same in reverse. Ye Howards certainly have a curious way of behaving.' He winked at me. 'But I think we both ken who got the better end of the bargain.' He slammed the empty goblet down on the table in front of him. 'Now, to business. Ye needna worry. I have no wish to offend my little Queen who is still grieving the loss of her mother. I will make sure her demands are met. Heaven knows, I've spent enough on the castle in Stirling, refurbishing the chapel and building myself a great hall as grand as anything your King has at Eltham. So I want her to like it. I've made arrangements for my mistress to take up residence in Darnaway Castle up north. My bastards will also be removed forthwith but there's a favour I'd like to ask of ye in return....'

HOUSE OF STEWART

Chapter Sixteen

*J*ames Stewart was enjoying this parry of words. He had the greatest of respect for the formidable Earl of Surrey; the man had very few grey strands in his head of thick glossy hair, was surprisingly slight in stature, and almost graceful in his movements for one of the most respected and feared warriors of the age. His looks were quite remarkable for someone in their sixtieth year; heaven only knows what those dark intelligent eyes had witnessed in his long, spectacular career at court and on the battlefield. The Earl had a slender face, not one belonging to a man who allowed his appetite to get the better of him in the great hall. James smiled to himself as he took note of the wide sensual mouth beneath a long nose, leading him to believe that matters were verra different in the bedchamber. Of course his company was more interesting than that of the young Tudor girl, although she'd be a satisfactory enough wife, especially once she was old enough to start breeding. She'd brought him what he desired more than anything else: recognition in Europe of Scotland as a separate country to England. No' a mithering northern bairn tied to its English mother's apron strings. The wee Margaret was also pretty enough, musical, adequately intelligent, agreeable if a little stubborn and spoilt. He'd already heard about her earlier screaming fit from his mistress.

"I told ye she wouldna be as easy to control as ye thought," Janet Kennedy had teased as she sat astride him before in his bedchamber, twisting and turning her glorious body until he began to moan aloud. She'd bent down to stroke his face, her full breasts with their soft nipples tantalisingly close to his lips. *"We redheads never are. Just because she still has the body of a wee lass doesna mean she isna already thinking with the mind of a grown woman."*

After his mention of a favour, James could see from Thomas Howard's clever face he was dreading what was coming next. Instead of asking for it though, James decided to delay his question. As in chess, war - or life itself - surprise was a better tactic. 'Have ye ever been in love, Thomas?'

A startled look appeared on the Earl's face but then his dark brown eyes softened and his voice became gentle, undoubtedly mellowed by the excellent *usquebaugh* - its flavour conjuring up for James the peat fires over which the barley had been dried on the Isle of Islay.

'Once. Long ago. She was my first love. Ten years younger than me. A redhead—'

'In my own experience, they're the most capricious but also the verra best of women. Their hair gives them fire inside and out.' James reached up and ruefully touched his shoulder where Janet had bitten him before in the throes of passion. 'Pray continue.'

'Dame Fortune played me for a fool. The girl was everything I could have wanted: beautiful, quick-witted, nobly born—'

'Why didna ye wed her?'

'I met her the very day of my wedding. On the eve of May Day. I could almost hear the Dame's spiteful laughter.'

'So ye could only admire her from afar.'

The Earl's laughter rang around the small chamber. 'Don't tell me you believe that for a second, Your Majesty. Let's just say that by the end of May Day, she was a maid no longer.'

James was intrigued; for a nobleman to seduce two women on consecutive days, with one of them his new bride, was no mean feat.

'Of course, it didn't take long before I got the two of them with child.'

James let out a long whistle of admiration; whereas it was perfectly acceptable for a king to sire bastards, he could see the problem here. 'So your first love was quickly married off?'

'Not long after the Harvest Moon in September. To a man as far away from Ashwellthorpe Manor in Norfolk as possible…in Cornwall. Who knew nothing of our liaison. But Dame Fortune hadn't finished with me yet. What malicious glee she must have taken in the birth of a daughter to my love on the very next May Day.'

'Do ye think the bairn could be yours?'

The nostrils of the Earl's long nose flared. 'I would have walked barefoot every mile, or ridden like the wind across the whole length of the land to that young woman's bed, if need be. Luckily, I had connections near their family home in Cornwall. Her new husband had trade dealings with the Trewellis family, near Mount's Bay. And as one of Lord Trewellis's oldest childhood friends (who owed me for one or two royal favours I'd done for him over the years), I had little difficulty persuading him to arrange for John Pendeen to be absent each summer for six weeks, on trips over to France.'

James gave a snort of amusement. 'So the wee lassie was yours.'

'Yes. And I planted a son and heir in her husband's cradle the year after that. But when the babe died a few months later, she decided it was punishment for her sins and refused to see me again.' He let out a sigh and waved his hands with their long slender fingers (more those of an artist than a soldier, James noted) in a dismissive gesture. 'But enough of my maudlin story, what of your first love?'

'A French lass. With hair as dark as the Scottish corbie that flies above our crags and ravines. And eyes as black as the sea coal brought down to the Palace from the Firth of Forth. She was visiting her relatives here in Edinburgh. I was seventeen. She a year younger. For a short time, I was able to pretend I was no longer King of Scotland but just a lad in love.' James shook his head. 'I fear like yourself, the stars didna favour me any more than they did ye. Consequently, my own tale is equally star-crossed, with no happier ending. Mirroring yours, my sweetheart was soon with child. Having no husband to cover her tracks, and being no scullery maid or tavern wench, but born of the French blood royal, albeit distant, it was a disaster. To avoid a possible scandal and breach with France, she was spirited away to a nunnery on the island of Iona where she gave birth to a wee boy.'

'One of the children in the nursery?'

James could still feel the grief welling up inside him in some dark place which he rarely visited. 'No. Neither of them are there. He was sent back to France to live with a childless couple…distant relatives of Madeleine.'

'And the mother?'

James could hear the sorrow in his own voice. 'She never left Iona. But died shortly after the birth.' Unable to relive the painful memory further, James tried to lighten the mood. 'Have ye ever loved a Frenchwoman, Thomas?'

'Sadly not. Though not for want of trying. I did meet one once in Calais who had eyes so light and hair so fair you'd think she was an angel come down from Paradise. One of my men discovered there'd been a secret dalliance between her mother and a visiting ambassador from one of the lands in the Far North.'

'So ye failed? That does surprise me. Ye strike me as a man used to getting your own way.'

The Earl gave a wry smile. ''Tis true. But I had a rival so powerful, so charming, so handsome, twenty years my junior to boot - there was nothing I could do.'

'Och, ye must mean a king.'

'He wasn't then. But he *was* a future one. Why would a girl want me when she could have Louis of Orléans?'

'It seems we kings can cause many problems when we so desire—'

As if on cue, there was a loud knocking on the door....

HOUSE OF HOWARD

Chapter Seventeen

*S*lightly apprehensive at the unexpected intrusion, I jumped to my feet as a woman dressed in a gaudy scarlet gown stalked into the chamber with cat-like grace, the earthy scent of heather trailing in her wake. With her flaming red hair reaching down past her slender waist, I immediately guessed this must be Janet Kennedy, mother of at least two of the offending bastards in the nursery in Stirling. She was a magnificent specimen, in her early twenties, graceful, glowing with health, and unlike the querulous little Tudor brat, very sure of herself. She had the air of a woman who knew exactly how to please a man. Returning my bow with a deep curtsey, she raised her pretty face up to mine, displaying her thickly-lashed brown eyes and full wanton mouth that instantly made me think of all kinds of acts strictly forbidden by the Church. I was almost certain she'd deliberately loosened her bodice to display her rounded breasts in all their glory. My tongue inadvertently moved to wet my lips but I snapped my mouth shut. I had no wish to be shown up as an ageing lecher, a laughing stock, a sot. *<<Besides, why do I have need of a mistress when I have all the opportunity in the world to fasten my lips around a youthful pair of breasts every time I enter the marital chamber>>*

I looked across at the King who began introducing his mistress and another far older woman with snow-white hair who'd just entered the room.

'This is the favour I mentioned earlier. Lady Gordon is soon to leave for Darnaway but was verra curious to meet a man of whom she's heard so much. And this is her auld nurse, Mairghread, a woman famed at our court for her gift of second sigh—'

'*Aie!*'

With all my focus up until now concentrated on the considerable attributes of Lady Gordon, I'd hardly acknowledged the new addition. That is, until the old crone began pointing at me and shrieking at the top of her voice in what I supposed must be that heathen tongue, Gaelic:

'*An ruadh diùc! An ruadh diùc!*'

Unnerved by the creature and having no idea what she was screeching, I glanced at Janet Kennedy, trying to keep my expression pleasant.

Having the air of one who was thoroughly enjoying the little spectacle, mischief bubbling up inside her until it reached that pair of gleaming brown eyes, the King's mistress went through the motions of an apology. 'Ye must excuse my nurse, Sire, but she's from Stornaway, up in the Far Isles, and is verra excitable.'

James smothered a chuckle. 'Although our good poet, William Dunbar, describes the way the people there talk as "*the roup of raven and rook*", no one can deny the beauty of their poetry, the melodies of the clareschaw, or the pretty pictures they carve on their standing stones.'

<<A pox upon such stuff and nonsense. I'm being cursed by a shard-borne sorceress!>>

'What's the woman saying?' I asked the King, who was wearing an equally amused expression as his saucy mistress. *<<Damn them both!>>* I suddenly felt mightily uncomfortable in this unfamiliar chilly northern land where the only decent commodities to leave its shores were wool, hides, salted salmon and coarse woollen cloth. No wonder they had to travel to the Low Countries to purchase coloured cloths, cushions, books, silverware and wine, and a hundred more such luxury items, to bring back to a country bogged down in mud and misery. The sun never seemed to set during the summer (for that matter, hardly bothering to rise during the winter months) and strange lights could be seen in the night skies; for instance, if I stepped outside at this late hour, the daylight had failed so little I might fancy myself back in the chamber with the Tudor girl. It was as if I was being pursued down one of Edinburgh's narrow cobbled streets, heading from West Bow towards the Mercat Cross with no way ou—

'"The Red Duke". She's calling ye "the Red Duke".'

James said something to the old woman and then looked at me. 'I told her she must be mistaken for ye are an earl not a duke.' He motioned for the four of us to be seated at the small walnut table where the chess set lay permanently abandoned. This new game (with its two additional players) seemed to be proving far more appealing to my host than the last.

'Why don't ye calm yourself, Mairghread,' said Janet. 'And tell this man his fortune.' She repeated it in Gaelic while putting her hand on the witch's arm. Putting one hand up to protest, I slowly lowered it again. I fought to keep my temper in check - or at least, not let it show. I couldn't believe I was being forced to make a foray into accursed necromancy but knew I had no choice but to accept. My own master, *Goose*, definitely less colourful but far older and wiser, would never have subjected a foreign visitor to such rough treatment.

The old woman was looking at me with a mixture of hatred and terror in her bright blue eyes while grasping hold of a talisman around her neck and whispering what sounded like curses under her breath. But at least she'd stopped cackling about some confounded red duke. King James handed me another *aqua vitae* and watched as I downed it in one quick motion. He laughed and pointed a finger at the witch.

'Best wait to hear what old Mairghread has to say, Thomas, before ye decide to drown your sorrows.'

As he said this, the witch was speaking very fast to Janet Kennedy who proceeded to translate:

'…She says ye were born when the sun was setting on the Ram. And the goat rising in the East. That ye will have a verra long life, with many offspring from your loins…but your greatest joy will also be your greatest sorrow….' The King's mistress hesitated for a moment or two. 'She says it will be nothing less than ye deserve—'

At this, the witch rose to her feet and began pointing a bony finger at me again, spittle spraying out of her thin lips. I glanced at Janet Kennedy who was no longer looking as though she was enjoying this game to the same degree as before. She raised an eyebrow at the King who nodded his head, giving her permission to translate for me.

'She says your House began its existence at a time when great evil was afoot. And even if ye didna commit wicked deeds yourself, your House is still tainted. And will be forever more. Your titles will continue to ebb…and flow… on a river of—'

'*Aie!*' The old hag began clutching at her scraggy neck and making gasping sounds as if someone was strangling her.

<<*Would it might be me*>>

Janet Kennedy had a look of fear in her eyes. 'She's saying: "I see Death stalking your House! Making it awash with blood". And repeating: "The Red Duke".'

In a frenzy now, pushing her white hair back beneath her dark bonnet, the witch drew out a very old pack of cards from beneath her grey kirtle and began shuffling them. Seizing one, she held it up with a look of triumph on her wrinkled old face. 'It's the Wheel of Fortune!' cried Janet, showing that she, too, knew rather too much about necromancy for my liking.

'She's saying, "Beware the House of roses!"' Janet continued, '"for the thorns will draw blood from your own. I see a tall tower and men of your House imprisoned within."'

I was hardly impressed by that; she'd probably heard her mistress discussing my past with the King.

Janet gave a shudder as she looked at me. 'She says, "some will never walk out alive."'

I watched the old woman hold up two cards, showing a dark-haired woman and a fair-haired one, both seated on a throne. Janet cleared her throat. 'She's picked the Queen of Swords and the Queen of Wands and is saying, "Your children will bear queens, not kings. That will bring your family to its knees." Mairghread sees two wedding bands. "Red. Red. Both of them steeped in the blood of your House."'

"*Your children will bear queens, not kings.*" Was that a strange Scottish expression I hadn't heard before? I couldn't believe my present misfortune: to be trapped in a room with two Scottish witches when all I longed to do was crawl into my own bed and take Agnes in my arms. But I could see I was not about to be spared anytime soon. Janet was clearly excited by something she'd just heard. 'She says your destiny is inextricably tied with my lord and master.' She gave James Stewart a loving look before turning back to me again. 'There will be at least one marriage between your two Houses. One day, far in the future, one of your House will inherit a country. But to no avail. Just as is right and fair, in the end it will come back to my master's kin.'

Perhaps it was overindulgence in the demonic *aqua vitae* but I could no longer make head nor tail of a single word the witch was saying. I was tiring of her ridiculous antics; she deserved no better than to be left in the stocks near the Mercat Cross until the flesh rotted from her brittle bones.

'She says she can see two castles,' said Janet. 'With your kin in both. One in the land of lilies, the other on our own shores. And a Field of Red. She's talking about a Field of Red. And blood, so much bloo—'

I flung both arms into the air. 'Oh, can't she see anything more original than that!'

When Janet Kennedy translated it for the witch, she turned a pair of unnerving opaque blue eyes on me. This time the King stepped in as interpreter when she began to babble afresh. '"Dinna be so hasty. There is, too, a Field of Gold. In a land across the seas. But ye won't be there. You'll be in charge of your own land."' James ran a hand through his dark curls. 'It seems Dame Fortune has great things planned for ye, Thomas. I canna help but wonder what she has in store for me.'

I fear I could no longer help myself. I began to laugh and once I'd started, I found it impossible to stop. <<*A Red Duke...a Field of Red. A future generation of Howards on the throne of England. Me in charge of a country. And now a Field of Gold*>> If - as the old witch predicted - I was going to live to a grand old age, I would stake any gold I held in my fist between now and then, that never in my lifetime would there be a Field of Gold....

PART THREE

THE POLITICS OF MARRIAGE

'Omnis ardentior amatur propriae
uxoris adulter est.'

{'Excessive affection in marriage is a
sin worse than adultery.'}

Peter Lombard 1100-1160
'De excusiatione coitus.'

Nicolas

Chapter Eighteen

July 16th, 1504. Château de Chantilly, Oise, France.

No wonder you can't hold a sword properly. Not even a wooden one. "*Anne*." What a knotty-pated name for a boy.' Nicolas was in a bad mood. Brought here against his will on his thirteenth birthday (which, as usual, had largely been ignored, apart from another unwanted prayer book to "*atone for his sins*", as his mother said with a disapproving sniff when she handed it over), he saw no reason to be friendly to the heir of one of the wealthiest families in France. The Montmorency family, neighbours of the La Barres, lived in a huge château, set in a marshy valley near the Nonette River, with acres of rolling land around it. Forbidden to use proper swords without adult supervision, Nicolas and the Montmorency boy had been shooed into the enormous gardens of the château by their parents, like a couple of errant goslings.

The boy in front of him, who was one or two years younger, had a defiant look in his blue eyes. 'It's not just any old girl's name. I'm named for my godmother, Anne of Brittany. Queen of France. Which is more than you can say about your fly-bitten name.'

Although Nicolas admired his spirit, he couldn't resist lunging forward with his sword, striking Anne far harder than he intended on the left arm. 'I speak with my sword, not my lips.'

Rubbing his arm and attempting to ward off further blows by holding up his shield, strengthened with layers of deer horn, Anne stared at Nicolas. There were tears in his eyes from shock and pain, as well as a look of disgust on his face. 'Then you're a milk-livered miscreant. Striking a man before he's ready. You wouldn't last a day in François's band.'

Stung into shame, knowing Anne was right about his behaviour being unchivalrous, sent Nicolas into even more of a sulk. 'Who's François?'

It was Anne's turn to have the upper hand. 'Now, who's *"knotty-pated"*? François. He's the young Count of Angoulême, heir presumptive to the throne of France. His mother, Louise of Savoy, invited me to join his band of comrades at Amboise.'

With that, Anne stalked off, dropping his sword and leaving Nicolas alone in the gardens. As usual, he'd ending up feeling left out. On the outside of this little band of boys he'd never heard of until today. Spurned. A figure of scorn. Sometimes, it was as if he was all alone in the world…and nothing was about to change on this birthday.

Nicolas couldn't help being impressed by Anne's mention of François d'Angoulême. One of his tutors had explained that if King Louis died without heirs, François would one day take his place on the throne. Becoming king seemed to be a perilous affair. As a child, Louis had merely been a cousin of the reigning king at the time, poor misshapen Charles who'd had so many good intentions. He remembered what his tutor had said about Charles six years ago:

"Who could complain about anyone who loved the sunshine and beauty of Italy as much as he did? What a terrible way to die, hitting your head on a low doorway after a game of tennis."

King Charles had fallen down dead on the spot, leaving the throne and the road to glory to his heir, Louis, Duc d'Orléans. However, with only one daughter in the royal nursery with his new wife, Anne of Brittany (widow of the unfortunate Charles), and no female allowed to take the throne, it seemed as if the royal office might be open to contenders again. Nicolas had often overheard his parents discussing the fiercely ambitious Louise of Savoy and her hopes for her son. Widowed at nineteen, the Countess had been left to raise two small children, one of whom was François. Nicolas only hoped François's childhood was happier than his own….

On the way to the Montmorency estate from their home this morning, they'd stopped at the cathedral in Senlis so his devout mother could pray.

"You should do so as well, Nicolas," she'd said, tight-lipped. *"I've never*

known a boy more in need of prayer. Perhaps Anne de Montmorency will be able to show you how to behave better. He will be a great lord one day. And make his father proud of him." The words "*unlike you*" hung in the air like the stench of rotting meat.

His mother's cruel words were akin to water being shaken from the back of one of the ducks on the river that flowed through their estate. Nicolas had heard them so many times before: how his one mission in life was to be a dutiful son to his father, to carry on the La Barre dynasty in a way agreeable to his parents. Trying to understand why they both treated him as they did, Nicolas often wondered whether it was because they'd both been so old when they had him.

Bored, he'd wandered into a small alcove and sat staring up at a marble statue of the Virgin Mary, standing on a stone bench, holding her infant son on her hip. Wound around her and her baby was a pink shawl that matched the fringed carpet beneath her feet. In front, two large winged angels leant in protectively, while behind, a magnificent arched stained glass window cast a soft light into the immediate area. Nicolas would never admit it to anyone but whenever he saw an image of the porcelain-featured Virgin, it troubled his soul and made him wish his own mother could show him even a *soupçon* of tenderness.

He couldn't remember a single gesture of affection from either his rather austere mother, with her sour face, or his unsmiling father. Perhaps it was for the best they were absent for long periods of time, following the court around the country. The only problem was they left him in the care of a harsh nurse: one who spent a great deal of her day clutching a pitcher of good red wine, pilfered from his father's cellar. She also meted out regular beatings to him from a very young age.

The La Barre family stronghold was situated halfway between Senlis and Crépy-en-Valois, and was a sombre place indeed. Even with candles lit everywhere in the winter months, it was very dark inside and oppressive; this wasn't helped by the thick walls or the narrow doorways. Servants who might as well have been covered in cobwebs, scuttled to and fro in the gloom to serve their unhappy young master. With no brothers or sisters, he'd spent an extremely lonely childhood in his parent's castle, with only his pet falcons for company. The army of tutors his parents enlisted to ensure he had an education fit for a prince didn't count. They were being paid to teach him, not to show him any particular kindness. Sometimes, he felt as though he had a tutor for every topic under the sun - not to mention, a riding master, a sword master, a jousting master…the list went on and on, with each one of them giving him advice for the future.

Nicolas remembered how the royal Master of the Hunt, an acquaintance of his father's, had personally supervised his training:

"*Hunting will toughen you up, boy,*" he said. "*And give you an idea what to expect in war. You'll learn what it is to feel your body burn up with heat, or become so cold, you'll fear for your limbs. Then there's the hunger—*"

The riding master had expected no less of Nicolas: "*You'll never shine at the King's court if you can't acquit yourself in the saddle,*" he once scolded a ten-year-old Nicolas when he was lying in the dust for the fourth time that day, trying not to cry.

Even his jovial Venetian tutor, Ippolito da Canal, an expert chess player, brought in to teach Nicolas Italian, had been unforgiving when Nicolas made a mistake in his choice of moves during their first few games:

"*You have the making of an excellent chess player, Nico, but you have to remember the rules. I'm teaching you 'The chess of the mad queen'. Unlike in the olden days, she has astonishing new powers on the board. And the bishop can move horizontally. Even the humble pawn, so adored by the common folk, is permitted to jump two squares on its first move.*"

His mind and body tested to the hilt by all these subjects, Nicolas never had any real friends. He was forbidden to mix with the local boys (who mocked him, anyway, for his wealth and privilege) and had no young cousins of whom to speak. Once, when he was about nine, a Castle carpenter took a liking to him and carved out and painted exquisite wooden tournament figures, so lifelike that Nicolas shouted out in joy when he first saw them. Sadly, this pleasure had been short-lived.

The very next day when he jumped out of bed early, excitement waking him from his slumber, his head filled with all the mock battles he was going to stage, he raced to the small chamber next to the stables, only to find his precious new toys hacked into dozens of pieces. The carpenter was shocked at the pitiful sight, and furious at the decimation of his painstaking work.

"Tell me who did this and I'll give them the thrashing they deserve!" he cried.

However, Nicolas had kept his counsel, even though he knew exactly which sly-eyed village boys were responsible for the cruel act of vandalism. When he finally tracked down the culprits, he was fit to burst with rage and indignation. It was an unfair fight of two against one, leaving him with a long scar down the side of his face. The injustice of it all made him determined to become the strongest and fittest amongst all the youths of his acquaintance: a goal he was resolved to achieve—

To Nicolas's surprise, in the middle of these woeful childhood memories, Anne de Montmorency suddenly reappeared with two goblets. Holding out one to Nicolas, it was clear he didn't bear a grudge for the incident with the wooden sword.

'Come on, let's go to the stables and I'll show you my new horse,' he said.

Once they'd left the scene of Nicolas's crime behind, their two swords abandoned on the ground in the shape of a cross, as if in a gesture of peace, relations seemed to improve between them. Nicolas was full of praise for the horse Anne's father had purchased for him at the market at Senlis.

'I can teach you a new kind of running jump, if you like,' he told Anne. 'It's one I learned from my riding master who's from Naples.'

Unfortunately, after his first successful leap, there were no more to follow by either of them and soon the pair found themselves on the floor of the stables, bruised and battered but in fits of laughter. Nicolas didn't think he'd ever laughed as hard in his entire life. Time passed so quickly that he was genuinely sorry when a servant came to usher them back inside to their parents.

As usual, his own were waiting for him in the great hall with faces of stone as he walked towards them, probably because his clothes were now filthy and there was straw in his hair. In contrast, Anne's smiling mother (confusingly, bearing the same name as her son) walked forward and put her hands on Nicolas's shoulders. 'From what the servants tell me, and from what I can see, you two have been having a good time. Your red faces are telling me you're both in urgent need of a drink to quench your thirst.' She turned to Nicolas's parents. 'Why doesn't your son stay behind and return to Amboise with Anne for a while. It will be company for Anne on the way back and Nicolas would enjoy playing with boys of his own age.'

From the look of horror on the face of his own mother, Nicolas immediately guessed his case was hopeless. He would never get the chance to find out what it meant to be in François d'Angoulême's precious band. But to his great surprise, his father suddenly spoke up:

'I agree. Thank you for the kind offer.' He looked at Nicolas's mother. 'I think it might do our son some good.' It was as if he was referring to a knave beyond redemption, and a trip to Amboise, some kind of punishment for a misdemeanour, not something to be relished.

She pulled a face. 'B-but Jean—'

'Think who he might meet at Amboise,' Nicolas's father said.

'Exactly,' said Guillaume de Montmorency, with a broad smile. 'Let us not forget, Denise, those boys playing with François d'Angoulême today are our leaders of tomorrow. Especially if he becomes king.'

'Louise seems to think that might happen,' said Anne's mother. 'She told me soon after her marriage, she visited an Italian hermit who had a reputation as a miracle worker. He predicted not only would she have a son but he'd become king of France.'

Nicolas didn't care what this François d'Angoulême would become; all he cared about was that he wouldn't be accompanying his parents back to his life of isolation but would, according to the Montmorency family, amongst other sports and pastimes, be riding, playing tennis in an enclosed court, built especially for the purpose, and shooting at the butts.

'Thank you, Mère. Thank you, Père,' he said, taking care to keep his eyes lowered in case they saw the delight there and changed their minds.

NICOLAS

Chapter Nineteen

*A*fter his parents bade him a frosty farewell, a joyful Nicolas flew back inside to join Anne. The next day they set off bright and early and after several long days of riding, Nicolas found himself on a horse next to Anne and his father, crossing a bridge and staring up at the blue-turreted Château of Amboise, perched high above the River Loire. The sun was shining in a cloudless blue sky and his spirits were soaring as high as the skylarks above, singing their glorious song.

'You'll like all the boys,' said Anne. 'Especially François. He's not even ten yet but he's great fun.'

After his experiences with the village boys, Nicolas couldn't help feeling apprehensive. 'Tell me who's in the band again.'

'Me. François. Philippe Chabot. Robert de La Marck. The Duke of Sedan's son. François calls him "*The Young Adventurer*". He gives us all nicknames.'

'What's yours?'

Anne laughed. '"*Know-all*". Because he's always asking me questions to which I know the answer.'

'Why "*The Young Adventurer*"?'

'Because once, when he was only ten, Robert went running up to King Louis, offering to go off to battle for him.'

'What did the King say?'

'He said he was grateful but Robert was still too short and would help him more by going to live in Amboise to train with the Dauphin.'

'Who else will be there?'

'Well, there's Guillaume. From the Gouffier family. He's seventeen. Older than the rest of us. And, I suppose, the real leader of the band.'

'What's his nickname?'

'"*Gascon*". Because François says his nature is as sunny as his place of birth.'

'I wonder what mine will be.'

'We'll have to wait and see. François is so clever he never makes a mistake when choosing a name.'

If there was such a place as paradise on earth, Nicolas decided Amboise was it. Although he knew he was only there for ten days, he was determined to make the most of every moment. Anne had been correct about the other boys; they all greeted him with friendly grins, apart from Guillaume Gouffier who held back, mistrust in his blue eyes. He was obviously waiting to see if this visitor would be any kind of threat to his own position.

Suddenly, all the years of hard work - in both his studies and his pastimes - seemed worth it. François's mother, Countess Louise of Savoy, was a tall elegant woman who spoke excellent Spanish and Italian, besides her native French, and doted on her son and daughter, Marguerite, a pretty girl of twelve. Nicolas decided she was the perfect mother: present all the time and choosing accomplished tutors for her children.

'Some say they're like "*un seul coeur en trois corps,*"' Anne told Nicolas.

When it became clear the Countess approved of him, for the first time, Nicolas felt grateful to his parents for giving him such a good education.

'I'm glad Anne's father brought you here, Nicolas,' she said on the second day. 'You'd be a worthy companion for my son.'

'Thank you, Madame la Comtesse.' Filled with happiness and pride, he looked over at the impish François who was smiling at him; however he also took note of Guillaume who was not.

Two days later, Louise came into the gardens, looking for her son. With an imperious wave of the hand, she gathered all the boys around her. 'I have something very special to show you,' she said, holding up a gold medal while pulling François to her side. '*Mon amour,*' she said to him with a tender smile, 'I ordered a medal to be struck with your head in profile on one side, and a spectacular lizard on the other. A Salamander is a mythical reptilian creature supposed to thrive in fire and, according to legend, is immortal. François's grandsire used it to represent himself. From now on, François, your motto will be: "*No trisco al buono, stingo al reo.*" Can any of you boys translate that for me?'

"'I feed the good fire and put out the evil,'" said Nicolas without hesitation. Years of study with a short-tempered Latin tutor who had a tendency to throw a primer at Nicolas's head if he made a mistake, had honed his skills.

He was rewarded by a smile of approval from Louise, a smirk from François, *The Adventurer*, and Anne, and a glare from *Gascon*.

To Nicolas's delight, being tall and strong meant it didn't take him long to excel at everything he attempted. After one particularly vigorous game of tennis in the enclosed court, built especially for the purpose, followed by firing darts from a small gun at a target on the wall, and shooting at the butts, when he emerged the victor of all, François begged him to join them permanently. If he noticed the thunderous expression on *Gascon's* face, he chose to ignore it.

'You've got the surest aim of all of us, Nicolas,' he said, his eyes shining as he pulled an arrow out of the wooden cask. 'I'd love to have you in my band. I'm sure Maman will agree.'

Once he learned that Nicolas knew how to cast goshawks (famed for their ill temper and deadly accurate slaying of birds flying low) from his gloved fist, the matter was decided. Basking in his new near godlike status, at the end of the visit, Nicolas waved happily to his friends, confident he would be back within a fortnight. So it came as an even greater blow when the La Barres refused Louise of Savoy's offer point blank, afraid that being in the constant company of a boisterous band of boys would distract their son - as sole heir to the La Barre fortune, and keeper of the family's good name - from the exceptional education they had planned for him. No matter how hard Anne's parents pleaded with them, nothing would deter them from their insistence on Nicolas continuing his education…by himself…in the La Barre family home. In the end, only to appease the Montmorency family, and avoid giving offence to the persistent Louise of Savoy, did they begrudgingly agree to three visits a year, lasting no more than three weeks each. Knowing he must be content with this paltry amount of time made Nicolas determined not to let it deter from his enjoyment. Nothing his parents did could touch his happy memories, such as galloping through the trees in pursuit of deer, or feasting in the great hall with his new friends. If he kept these images in his head, he hoped they'd be enough to tide him over until he could return to Amboise....

∽

April 24th, 1505.
The Château of Amboise, Loire Valley.

'I wish you didn't have to leave tomorrow, *Wolf*,' said Anne. 'It's always more fun when you're here.'

'I don't think *Gascon* would agree with you.'

'That's only because you beat him at everything. Hawking, hunting, tennis, shooting at the butts. You name it. You should have seen the look on his face when your falcon came back before his.'

The two of them were lying on a grassy bank, above the tennis court, their racquets by their side. Hearing the admiration in his best friend's voice gave Nicolas as much pleasure as a bee collecting nectar. He never tired of being addressed by the epithet François had bestowed on him after his second visit to the château.

"*Wolf!*' *You must be called 'Wolf'. You remind me of one because you are fearless, intelligent, fair, a lively member of the pack, and you only show your temper if you are wronged.*"

So, from that day forward, Nicolas was known as '*Wolf*'. Of course, he never mentioned it to his parents; he could well imagine their reaction. His father had been in a very ill humour of late; from the few snippets Nicolas had picked up, it seemed Jean de La Barre had angered King Louis who was seriously ill for the second time back in April. By siding with Queen Anne (a distant relation of Nicolas's father) who wanted little Charles of Habsburg as

110

a son-in-law, not François, Jean de La Barre managed to incur the wrath of both the King…and Louise of Savoy.

Nicolas knew Louis and Louise wanted François to marry the royal princess, a girl called Claude who, according to Anne, could not be improved by the brush strokes of even the most talented artist in the world, using the most colourful pigment, dye, oil and gum.

"My mother says she's plain enough to crack a mirror, has two eyes that meet in the middle, and two hips that are askew and make her limp," he'd said, his eyes wide with horror.

Nicolas couldn't imagine someone as lively as François d'Angoulême being saddled with such a pitiful creature. However, that seemed to be the way of marriages: adults arranged them for their children to suit their own purposes. Without a care for the feelings of those concerned. He dreaded to think what kind of girl his parents would produce for him to marry in order to enhance the La Barre line.

In the distance, he could hear his name being called by one of the others.

'That's *The Adventurer*,' said Anne. 'He probably wants to play "*La Grosse Boule*" again. He's desperate to replace you as champion.'

Nicolas loved this Italian game, probably because he'd managed to beat Guillaume hollow the very first time. It was a game played in pairs, requiring the players to knock an enormous air-filled ball back and forth, using a piece of tin strapped to their forearms.

Nicolas jumped to his feet, always stirred by a challenge. 'Come on then, let's find him so he can try.'

However, when they reached *The Adventurer*, Nicolas was surprised to see his father's cousin, Berthault, Vicomte de Bridiers, with him. He'd always shown great kindness to Nicolas, unlike Jean de La Barre, but unfortunately his visits to Senlis were infrequent.

Most unusually today, his gentle face was creased in a deep frown. 'Nicolas, I am afraid I haven't come to see you for pleasure. Instead, I come bearing some very sorrowful news.'

Immediately, Nicolas's heart was in his mouth. Had something happened to his horse? Or to his beloved falcons. He couldn't imagine anything worse than that.

Berthault de Bridiers cleared his throat several times as if he also wished to clear away what he had to say: 'My boy, I regret to have to tell you that both your parents caught the sweating sickness while you've been here. And that they're...dead.'

TRISTAN

Chapter Twenty

21ˢᵗ May, 1506. Ardres Castle.

y mother had tears in her eyes as she spoke: 'You're far too young to be fretting about your future, Tristan. Your brother had no right to mention the Church to you. And what you said simply isn't true. Your father is not a cruel man. He is bound by centuries of family tradition. In the eyes of the world, depriving the world of an Ardres bishop would be a mortal sin. From the day he is born, it is the duty of the younger son of the House of Ardres to enter the Church. Nevertheless, as a loving mother, my heart is breaking to think of—'

'Gilles won't have to go and live in a monastery one day. Nor will Nicolas. It's not fair!'

My mother wiped a tear from my cheek and cupped my face in her hands. 'Gilles is your father's elder son and will become Governor of Picardy. Nicolas has no father. That's why he came to live with us.'

'Why couldn't he have gone to live in a monastery instead? I hate him being here.'

There was reproach in my mother's green eyes. 'That's not very kind of you. This is Nicolas's home now. You must try harder to get on with him. It was wrong of you to overturn the chess board the other day in a fit of *pique*. He was only trying to teach you chess because your father asked him to.'

'I don't care. I'm glad I hid all the pieces. And I'll never tell anyone where I've put them. Not for so long as I live. Not even when I am making my confession to the priest on my death bed.'

To my surprise, this seemed to amuse my mother. 'So like your father. Always so happy and full of joy and laughter.' She stroked my forehead. 'But also full of spirit and bold words.'

'I'm not like him at all. I hate him! I hate Gilles! I hate Nicolas! He's as fen-sucked as that pendant he wears around his neck all the time.' My throat suddenly began to throb as if it might close completely and I could feel my lip quivering. 'I hate everyone...except you.'

'Oh, come here, my poor love,' soothed my mother, pulling me onto her knees. 'You might be eight years old and growing up fast, but you're still my little lord...with Tredavoe blood flowing through your veins.'

Knowing we were alone in my mother's bower, without any maids present, and I couldn't be ridiculed by Nicolas for being a weedy minnow, clinging to my mother's skirts, I buried my face in her soft chest, inhaling the familiar sweet smell of violets.

♨

The moment Nicolas de La Barre entered the Castle on New Year's Day, I decided I hated him. He hated me, too. Once, when he teased me, I charged at him and the servants had to drag us apart. How unfair that my father was furious with me...not Nicolas.

"You're my son and should know better!" he shouted at me when I complained.

Nicolas never missed an opportunity to torment me so it was a relief he'd been invited to the betrothal of the new Duc de Valois and little Claude of France, far away from Ardres Castle.

'I'm glad Nicolas has gone away,' I said. 'I hope he never comes back.'

I'd forgotten my mother had very strong opinions about the betrothal: 'Those poor children!' she cried. 'I can imagine how they're feeling, standing in a draughty chapel in the Château of Plessis-lèz-Tours, being forced to say their vows. At six, Claude is little more than a baby. And François d'Angoulême is but eleven.'

But I wasn't interested in two strangers I'd only vaguely heard of and never met. I was only interested in the fact that Nicolas was not here.

'Why can't Nicolas stay there?' I mumbled into my mother's chest.

She tenderly smoothed my hair. 'Because he belongs here now, *chéri*. When Berthault de Bridiers asked your father if we'd be willing to take him because he and his wife felt they were too old, your father and I discussed the matter at great length. It was not a decision we came to lightly, knowing we had to think of you and Gilles as well.'

'So why didn't you say no?'

'We decided we had enough love to give all of you. And, according to the Vicomte de Bridiers, Nicolas has had very little of that in his life up until now.' My mother lifted up my hand and placed it on her stomach which felt rounder than usual. 'I only hope you're going to be kinder to your little brother or sister when they come.'

Horrified by her words, I leapt off her knees. 'No, I don't believe it! I don't want you to have another baby. You nearly died last time. Just like Gilles's mother did.'

My mother laughed and grabbed me by the shoulders, planting a kiss on either cheek. 'By the will of God, this time will be different to the others. Believe me, child, I have no intention of leaving this earth. Who else would scold Gilles when he makes mischief, or separate you and Nicolas when you're intent on killing one another.'

NICOLAS

Chapter Twenty-One

28th June, 1506. Ardres Castle.

*R*obine de Croisic.'

The name, when he repeated it out loud, rolled around the roof of Nicolas's mouth, making it feel as dry as sawdust. Watching François d'Angoulême make his vows last month, his voice echoing around the chapel (as he stood next to odd looking little Claude of Brittany in the Château of Plessis-lèz-Tours), had stirred up feelings of intense pity in Nicolas for the newly-created duke. Little did he know then that, within weeks, he would be joining the ranks of young men forced to wed for the sake of land and money.

He could feel Monsieur Guy's eyes on him as the two of them stood at the window of the Count's study, the waters of the lake sparkling in the distance.

'Robine was unwell and couldn't attend her cousin's betrothal last month. So, of course, the two of you weren't introduced. Indeed, Berthault de Bridiers only discussed the possibility of your marriage with her parents after you left.'

Nicolas began to feel distinctly unwell as he looked down at the silver buckles on the straps of the Count's black leather shoes. <<*What would Monsieur Guy do if I vomited all over them?*>> Knowing Robine de Croisic was Claude of Brittany's cousin, his mind was now crammed with memories of King Louis's lame daughter, none of them flattering. Perhaps Robine was even uglier; what if she was so crookbacked she couldn't even stand up straight to say her vows? Immediately, images of François's future bride were replaced with ones of his own: an unsightly girl with eyes that crossed in the middle, a nose so long (possibly with a wart on its tip) she couldn't eat proper—

∾

'You're very quiet, Nicolas. I thought the match might have given you pleasure. And, at the very least you'd be giving a whoop of joy. After all, the Vicomte has managed to arrange an extremely advantageous marriage that will instantly link you to royalty. You should be grateful to him.'

<<*I don't want to be linked to royalty!*>> Nicolas wanted to yell the words out loud, but, of course, he remained silent. Thankfully, the feeling of nausea had passed but its place was taken by one of crushing defeat: acceptance that he was a condemned man, with nowhere else to go but to the altar where a noose would be placed around his neck, one he could never remove...until death. 'I *am* pleased,' he managed, the words sounding far off and so lacking in conviction Monsieur Guy couldn't fail to notice. Or be offended.

'I've seen men look happier when they've been told they need to have several teeth pulled.'

Nicolas knew he was behaving churlishly and struggled to at least sound interested. 'When will the marriage take place, Monsieur Guy?'

'Not for many years yet. But the betrothal is planned for September.'

Monsieur Guy's words didn't make sense. 'I don't understand.'

'Surely you didn't think you were going to marry an eleven-year-old girl. And a sickly one at that. Her parents would never allow it.'

All of a sudden, great waves of relief began surging through Nicolas's entire being. He found himself gasping out the words: 'So I don't have to leave Ardr—'

A smiling Monsieur Guy reached forward and clapped him on the back. 'No, no, if that's what was bothering you. You don't have to leave any of us for many years yet. Not until Robine reaches maturity.'

<<*And maybe she won't ever reach it*>> Nicolas imagined Robine already laid out on a slab, as cold as marble, her eyelids closed on her pitiful squint, above her long nose, for all eternity.

<<*Dieu ait pitié de son âme!*>>

Nicolas badly wanted to cross himself. He was a little shocked at his swift arrival at such an abrupt end for a girl he'd never met. He'd taken great comfort in Monsieur Guy's innocent words: "*and a sickly one at that*", even though he knew imagining the death of another was wicked in the extreme, not to mention grounds for so many Hail Marys he might as well never rise up from his knees again. He reasoned that if Robine de Croisic was so lame she couldn't even walk up the aisle without help, perhaps a shortened life would be a blessed relief for everyone. Particularly himself. And he shouldn't be feeling too guilty for his callousness; after all, if Monsieur Guy wasn't staring straight at him, he would fall to his knees this very minute and give thanks to God for his reprieve. Surely that was recompense enough.

'Come, my boy, and take a seat. You look very pale. I realize it's a great deal for you to grasp all at once.'

<<*Can he read my thoughts? Or at least the part about me falling to my knees*>>

'I hope you're not too disappointed you can't marry the girl right away. But you're only just coming up to your fifteenth birthday so you have plenty of time to wed. Just be thankful the age difference isn't the other way round. Gilbert Talbot, over at Calais, was telling me recently about one of his oldest friends, an English earl who has married off one of his sons to a woman even older than himself. What kind of man would do that, I found myself thinking. At least, you know that at the end of your wait, you'll have a girl who can bear you sons.'

The feeling of nausea making an unwelcome reappearance at the very idea, Nicolas was glad when this particular conversation was cut short by the entrance of Bernard Guillart, the Ardres family steward, looking for his master.

Guy d'Ardres stood up. 'Stay here, please. There's something I need to discuss with you. Oh, and take this. It's a gift for you from Dame Grace.'

Left alone in the study, Nicolas looked down at the small walnut box the Count had handed him, wondering what it contained. Presents that he liked (now plentiful), and not dusty old prayer books that he didn't, were new to him. Eagerly, he fingered the tiny metal key, wondering what kindness Grace d'Ardres was showing him this time. He'd never met anyone quite like her -

someone who belonged to a land across the Narrow Sea - as beautiful inside as she was out. From his own experience, she didn't even begin to correspond to his idea of a mother; besides, at twenty-five, she was too young. He thought of her more as a beloved fairy, always smiling, always good, making him feel this was his home now. As did Monsieur Guy, six years older than his wife, as darkly handsome as Dame Grace was fair, extremely cultured...yet a fine warrior, both caring and just. He'd had no difficulty in replacing Jean de La Barre with Monsieur Guy in the role of a father. Giving a twist of the key, Nicolas flipped open the lid and laughed out loud when he saw what was inside. Thirty-two exquisitely carved chess pieces...to replace the ones the fen-sucked Tristan had hidden.

Tristan.

The bane of Nicolas's life. His mind went back to how they'd met after the death of Nicolas's parents last April. The Vicomte de Bridiers, *in loco parentis*, had arranged for Nicolas to join the Ardres family, saying:

"We have three grown-up sons and two daughters of our own and, although we'd love to keep you, it wouldn't be right."

Again, Amboise was suggested as a possibility but after a chance visit to Bridiers by Guy d'Ardres, both Berthault and his wife thought that joining the refined household of the Governor of Picardy - equally a champion of learning and physical accomplishments - was the perfect solution for their orphaned ward. They knew Nicolas's parents had twice before turned down the opportunity for their son to permanently join François d'Angoulême and the other young lords at Amboise. So, at least, it seemed as though the final wishes of the La Barres were being fulfilled.

Unfortunately, upon their death, what little that was left of the La Barre fortune was needed for the upkeep of the family home until Nicolas came of age. The rest was already forfeit as a consequence of Jean de La Barre's arrogance and folly for daring to plot against the King when he lay gravely ill. This had resulted in a subsequent fall from the all-important royal grace, and the family being cast into oblivion. All that remained to Nicolas from his childhood days of great wealth (and loneliness) was a turquoise ring and a golden locket Berthault had found amongst his father's few surviving possessions, the rest having already been sold off. They were pieces of jewellery Nicolas had never set eyes on before; he vowed to always wear the ring on his right hand, as some kind of filial duty to a man and woman who'd never loved him but were nevertheless his parents.

The first time he'd picked up the locket, he was curious to find out what lay inside. With a sense of excitement, he'd gently prised it open to find a miniature portrait of a dark-haired girl hardly older than himself. He had no idea who she was other than she looked rather familiar, so she must belong to the La Barre family (although his mother had never mentioned a younger sister, nor had his father). Besides, she was far too beautiful to resemble either of them. Nicolas drew great comfort from gazing at her face; once, when he was being fanciful, he decided that she was trying to warn him about something.

<<*Something about money*>>

"*The fact you're penniless,*" Berthault had explained as gently as he could, not long after this, "*means that one day in the future you'll have to wed an heiress in order to start rebuilding your family fortunes. In the meantime, Guy has offered to bring you up with his own two sons. Helped by a small contribution from me.*"

As far as Nicolas was concerned, the situation was ideal; becoming part of the noble Ardres family, and finally having two *quasi* brothers, seemed even more enticing than Amboise. Except that it hadn't worked out like that at all....

NICOLAS

Chapter Twenty-Two

*A*fter that first meeting with Tristan d'Ardres on New Year's Day, Nicolas had pitied the poor monks at the monastery where Tristan would one day live:

<<*God have mercy on them, having to deal the vexing dewberry*>> he'd thought.

Even though Monsieur Guy had asked Nicolas to teach Tristan chess, it was an unmitigated disaster, leading to an upturned board on more than one occasion. Nicolas had never found the chess pieces the qualling little hugger-mugger hid the other week, forcing Dame Grace to replace his precious chess set. It was obvious the younger boy never ceased to regard Nicolas as a rival for his father's attentions and affection, particularly when the Governor gave Nicolas expensive presents, or Dame Grace praised him. What was even more clay-brained was how he seemed to apportion some kind of blame to Nicolas for the fact he was destined for the Church and Nicolas was not. Unfortunately, Tristan's bat-fowling behaviour often drove Nicolas to distraction, making him act almost as badly in return.

Thankfully, the Count's other son, Gilles, a couple of years older than Tristan, was affable enough. He was the product of Monsieur Guy's first marriage to an Italian countess who'd died giving birth. As a tribute to her memory, the Count always employed a few Italians, including a tutor for his children. Nicolas already spoke good Italian because of his former tutor (who'd taught him chess) but it had improved leaps and bounds since his arrival at Ardres. What a pity his relationship with Tristan showed no signs of heading in the same direction—

'I think it's time you and I had a conversation about women,' said Guy d'Ardres, re-entering the chamber and seating himself in a chair opposite.

Nicolas swallowed hard, certain that the Count and Countess must have seen him looking at one or two of the Castle maids.

It was as if Monsieur Guy guessed his thoughts. 'Have no fear. It's nothing you've done. It's only that you're reaching an age when young women will start to become, how shall I put it, interesting.'

<<*He's certainly right about that*>> Half a dozen pretty maids immediately sprang to mind, all giggles and coy looks. Now he knew he'd been sentenced to a life with the ugliest girl in Christendom, he might as well make the most of the time left to him. 'Yes, Monsieur Guy, I do find them interesting. Though I've never touched any of them,' he hastily added.

The Count's brown eyes were warm and reassuring. 'You will. That's why you and I need to talk. It's a very complicated business, I can assure you. Do you know anything about how to prevent a girl getting with child?'

In the absence of lively company around the Castle, apart from the odd occasion when the naturally idle Gilles would agree to accompany him on a walk or go riding, Nicolas had spent many hours in Monsieur Guy's study, making use of the unusually large collection of books. 'Yes, I've been reading about it.'

'Ah, preparing yourself, I see.'

Nicolas blushed, not wishing to be seen to live up to his nickname, '*Wolf*', intent upon praying upon innocent lambs in Ardres Castle.

<<*Whatever would the Countess say about that?*>> 'No, I like reading books about medicine.'

'What did you discover in your research?'

'That most women employ several methods to avoid getting with child.'

'Such as?'

'Trying to guess their fertile days; making use of a small knot of wool soaked in vinegar; or a tiny bundle of herbs. Or in some cases, merely saying a hasty Hail Mary. Others use amulets of herbs or flowe—'

'I think some of those quacks would be trembling in their boots if they heard you,' laughed Monsieur Guy. 'Tell me about the amulets. I don't know much myself.'

Encouraged by Monsieur Guy's praise, and his delight at finding that adults such as the Bridiers and Ardres were genuinely interested in what he had to say, Nicolas got up and walked over to one of the shelves where he picked out a small book. 'Here's one I was reading a few days ago: "*A treatise on ailments and good health*".' Quickly finding the page he was looking for, he read aloud, effortlessly translating the Latin into French: "'*Many a time has my surprised tongue suddenly happened upon an amulet hidden between a pair of particularly ample breasts. Once I sat bolt upright, my desire instantly evaporating when the woman beneath me, although exquisitely formed and very alluring, informed me that the amulet around her neck contained the anus of a hare.*"'

Monsieur Guy's lips twitched. 'I can see why this book made such an impression on you. But as you know, things can be very difficult for women, both before and after childbirth.'

'Yes.' Nicolas had read that women might turn to rue, mint, or juniper to either prevent an unwanted pregnancy - or rid themselves of it, even though this last was strictly against the law. It seemed that many a charge of witchcraft had been laid at the door of any women assisting in such an activity. He watched Monsieur Guy get to his feet.

'Well, I think our conversation is at an end sooner than I thought. You've taught me a few things I didn't know. I'm certainly well-prepared for the talk I'll need to have with Gilles sometime in the future. Of course, it's not one I'll ever need to have with Tristan.'

'Thank you, Monsieur Guy, for taking the time to help me.'

'Don't fret about your future. You'll make little Robine a splendid husband.'

Thankful the Count couldn't see his face as he opened the door, Nicolas made a vow right then and there. <<*If anything happens to the Croisic girl, the next time the possibility of marriage arises, it will be to a woman of my own choice*>>

CECILY

Chapter Twenty-Three

July 7th, 1508. Pendeen Manor, Cornwall.

 could feel my mother's eyes upon me, fretting I was all right. I dearly loved my grandam, Matilda, and had begged my parents to let me come and say goodbye. I'd overheard them saying that at seven, I was too young to understand such things...but I knew better. Although it was nearly high summer, the heavy velvet curtains were drawn and candles lit all around the bed. Grandam's bedchamber was filled to the brim because so many people wanted to see her off on her final journey, including my two uncles, Richard and Stephen. Next to her, Father Roger was muttering some kind of prayer.

My grandam was an old lady, I knew that.

"*I can't grumble, Cecy,*" she'd said to me recently. "*I've seen fifty-five summers. More than most women.*"

Looking at her now, lying there so small and fragile in her long white nightgown, her once glorious red hair (that had always seemed to have a personality of its own), tied neatly in plaits, I understood she would never see another summer.

The door opened and one of the servants came in bearing a wooden basket filled with pink roses, their exquisite perfume replacing the heavy scent of incense. My grandam gave a faint smile when they were laid on the table next to her.

'Yet more,' she croaked, her voice as thin as her frail body. 'But then he's always had a garden full of them.'

I looked up at my parents to find out who '*he*' was. I knew it couldn't be my grandsire because he'd died a few years ago.

'I told you her mind was wandering,' my mother whispered to Father.

To my surprise, Grandam Matilda turned to look at me, her blue eyes as bright as ever. I could have sworn she gave me what looked like a wink as she shooed away Father Roger's right hand. It was hovering over her face with a crucifix as he prepared to sprinkle holy water on her with his other one.

'Come,' she beckoned to a nearby servant girl, holding a ewer of scented water, 'arrange my pillows so I can sit up. And all of you,' she carried on, her voice a little stronger now, 'can leave. If you've come to watch an old lady die, I'm afraid you'll be disappointed. It won't be today.'

My mother took Grandam Matilda's small hand in hers. 'Please don't distress yourself.'

Helped by the maid, my grandam used all her strength to push herself up onto the pillows. 'I want to spend some time alone with you and my granddaughter.' She gave a feeble clap of her hands. 'The rest of you, go. Go now!'

❧

'Open the curtains. And a window,' my grandam instructed the maid. 'It's so hot in here! I'm not ready to be stitched into my shroud yet.'

'Aye. Right away, Mistress Pendeen.'

My mother filled a goblet and held it to Grandam Matilda's parched lips. 'Here, drink this.'

Lifting her head a little to take a few sips, my grandam fell back against the pillows. I could see the effort was almost too much for her. 'Alys, give Cecy one of my roses.' she gasped.

I took the rose and held it to my nose. 'I think this is how heaven must smell.'

Grandam Matilda tried to laugh but it turned into a coughing fit that made her eyes water. 'It's a Damask rose, child,' she managed eventually. 'They're very special.'

'Why, Grandam?'

'Because the first ones were brought over from Syria by the crusaders. They bloom twice a year, in spring and summer. For me it is the flower of love. It was the first gift he ever gave me. He told me he was going to plant a rose garden for me down here.'

'She's talking about Grandsire John,' said my mother to me in a low voice. 'My father always sent your grandam a single Damask rose every year on May Day, my birthday. And he always pretended not to know who'd sent it. Looking at all the ones that keep arriving, we think he must have left instructions with someone for the tradition to continue even after his death.'

Grandam Matilda made a small tutting sound and pointed a finger at my mother. 'Don't be tickle-brained, girl! He wasn't pretending because he didn't send them. But he was a good man and I loved him for it. He used to tease me it was a pirate chief, wealthy and wicked, who sent my rare roses. Or a fat old neighbour of ours who always made a point of kissing my hand for too long with his wet duck lips whenever we met. Of course, I knew all along it was your father who was responsible. I loved John for his kindness but I loved your father more. Far…more. With all my hear—'

My mother interrupted my grandam's ramblings and patted her hand. 'Hush, Mother, you're tiring yourself. You need to sleep.'

Grandam Matilda shook her hand free. 'Tush! What on earth do I need to sleep for when I have to teach the little one about love while I still can? She's always been more like me than you ever were. You've got too much of your father's common sense about you. But thankfully none of his devilry. Or mine. Sometimes, he's too clever for his own good. That's why your William has been the perfect husband for you. Gentle and kind. Just like you.' She held out her bony hand to me. 'Come and sit on the bed, child.'

Taking care not to hurt her, I clambered onto the bed that seemed enormous now my grandam had become so small. She pinched my right cheek but her grip was so feeble I hardly felt it. 'A little witch, Cecy. That's what you are. Not like your mother but a true De Lacey, like me. So many of us have the second sight, it's fitting your mother married into a family with a mermaid and a dolphin on its coat-of-arms.' She picked up a strand of my hair. 'Red. Like the Welsh dragon. But also gold like the sun. Men will fall over themselves one day to bask in your sun.' She turned her face away towards the open window. 'Like they did with me.' Closing her eyes, her voice was becoming weaker again as if she'd almost used up all the words left to her on earth. 'Like *he* did with me.' She smiled at me. 'I promise you, even though I won't be there to see you wed, I'll be watching over you. And the man you wed. Keep that rose I gave you. Forever.'

My mother pressed her hand to Grandam Matilda's forehead. 'Cecy, go and fetch the doctor. Too much talk has made her feverish.'

Jumping down, I raced to the door but not before I heard my grandam murmur: 'I only wish he could meet you one day. He'd be so proud to have a granddaughter like you—'

VALENTINE

Chapter Twenty-Four

26ᵗʰ March, 1509. La Colombe.

*G*randmère Symonne's garden, behind the little cottage at the bottom of the estate, was her pride and joy. Valentine knew its contents off by heart: one side was taken up with beds of roses, lilies, columbines, and yellow gillyflowers; and the other with such useful herbs as rosemary, mugwort, wild marjoram and parsley. Besides this, there were periwinkles in plenty, wild poppies and golden kingcups, as well as a thriving vegetable garden that supplied the kitchens in the main house with delicious produce such as spinach, onions, gourds and pumpkins.

'I like your garden so much, Grandmère,' said Valentine, who'd come to visit with her younger sisters, Charlotte and Jacqueline, and their nursemaid, Bonne.

After the death of old Grandpère Pierre, Valentine's father had brought the widowed Symonne from the Fleury family seat near Rouen and built a big house for her and her servants. It was shut off from their own property by a thick hedge. *"Which will give you a little peace away from your lively granddaughters,"* Valentine's papa had said when she first arrived.

'Valentine loves to help me, Anthoine,' said Grandmère Symonne to her guest, a tall man dressed in a long brown robe, wearing a crucifix around his neck. Valentine knew he was the abbot of the nearby Anderne Abbey.

He smiled at Valentine. 'You can learn much from your grandmère. As can I. May I congratulate you, Symonne, for making your garden a veritable paradise all year round. It seems to change every time I come.'

'I do my best. I've tried to arrange it so that it yields green vegetables to feed us during every season.'

'How exactly?'

'I discovered by chance that old cabbage stumps left in place all through winter yield small sprouts in the spring. Charles always teases me that the trees in *my* garden yield better plums, peaches and mulberries than the ones in his own.'

'And better ones than in our kitchen garden back at the Abbey, I have to say.'

Outside the front door were two fruit trees, and an exquisite rosebush Grandmère Symonne had grown from a cutting she brought back from her own garden, as well as a group of elms. 'Those trees over there are almost as old as God, Father Abbot,' said Valentine, trying to prove how well her grandmère had taught her.

The Abbot laughed. 'I'm sure they are, my child.'

'They're certainly as old as when the earliest crusaders took their leave for Jerusalem,' said Grandmère Symonne. 'I might know about growing plants and trees, and the benefits of many plants for our health, but the Reverend Father knows more about some rare plants I'm growing.'

Abbot Anthoine beckoned Valentine over to a corner in the garden. 'If you ever fall prey to illness, child, don't listen to those miserable quacks who want to bleed you dry with their leeches. Not when you have the remedy right in front of your eyes.' He bent down and plucked a few leaves from a green plant, pressing them to his nose. 'Basil. Good enough to eat, but also excellent for the digestion. Before too many weeks, your grandmère will be able to help those with breathing difficulties by giving them a newly flowered sprig of mint. And see here, a few leaves of rue have been known to cure those suffering from the sweating sickness....'

As the two grown-ups continued to chatter about herbs above her head, Valentine leant into her beloved grandmère's waist, knowing she was her favourite. Her grandmère had exclaimed over her beauty before, kissing her, telling her she was like a little princess with her long fair hair.

"*Just as I was at six.*" Opening a pretty little box, she held it out to Valentine. "*Here. Take a confiture de noiz. I know how much you like them.*"

✥

'I was so sorry to hear Grace lost another babe last week,' Grandmère Symonne was saying. 'I've sent over some angelica root and yarrow leaves to the Castle to make a tisane. Thank goodness all went well at Tristan's birth. Though I do recall he came too early. I was visiting Charles and Athénaïs at the time and remember how poor Guy was beside himself with worry. He'd already lost one wife to childbed and was desperate not to lose a second.'

Abbot Anthoine shook his head. 'News has just come from court that the Queen's lost another one too,' he said.

'Where did the Countess and the Queen lose their babies? Have they found them yet?' asked Charlotte, as she wandered up to stand on the other side of their grandmère, taking her thumb out of her mouth to ask the questions. Her brown eyes were wide with curiosity about the disappearance of the two babies.

Valentine knew from their mother's experience what had really happened. 'Of course they haven't!' she chided her sister.

Grandmère Symonne stroked Charlotte's long dark hair and bent down to give her a kiss. 'Go back to Bonne now, there's a good girl.'

Happy that she was considered old enough not to be sent away, Valentine vowed not to say anything foolish. Creeping away, she sat down unnoticed on a little stone bench at the end of the herb patch.

'Guy told me when I visited the Castle that he's going to take Grace to England over the summer to raise her spirits,' said Abbot Antoine.

'Poor lamb. Sometimes I think she only wants another son so Tristan won't be the younger one and have to go into the Church. After all, with Gilles and Nicolas, she's already got three boys.'

'I fear you're right. Between you and me, never was there a boy less suited to holy life than Tristan d'Ardres. I am a very patient man, but at times I've felt like tearing out what little hair I've got left at the antics of the rascal.' He reached up and touched the top of his head. 'It's already turned as white as your snowdrops.'

Fortunately, Valentine managed to suppress a giggle; she didn't want to be sent to play with her sisters as this conversation was far too good to miss. She wanted to hear what else Abbot Anthoine had to say about their neighbours' son.

<<Grandmère Symonne's friend might work for God. But he gossips just like the maids in the kitchen>>

'Tristan has no more interest in learning about the ways of the Church than I have learning the latest dance steps from the court,' said Abbot Anthoine.

Valentine opened her mouth to say how much she liked dancing but then closed it again. It was obvious the two adults had no idea she was there.

'It can't be easy for Guy. Having two sons as stubborn as a pair of mules, from what I can make out. According to Gilbert Talbot whom I visited last week in Calais, as you say, Tristan is refusing to learn the ways of the Church, and Gilles is refusing to learn the proper ways of a nobleman. Of course, it's a tragedy they weren't born the other way round. Tristan would have made an outstanding knight and Gilles would have made a—'

'Very lazy priest,' laughed Abbot Anthoine. 'That leaves Nicolas. But unfortunately, he isn't Guy's blood son.'

'More's the pity. I've watched him grow into an exceptional young man. But with no money, he'll have to wed the Croisy girl when she's old enough. Now that's a tragedy, as you and I both know. Pairing such a handsome young boy with a girl so plain she'd wilt a flower just by looking at it. I know it took all Grace's powers of persuasion to get him to go ahead with the betrothal once he'd set eyes on her. I felt so sorry for him that day, looking so pale and forlorn, standing next to her in the church.'

'Such strange pairings are the way of the world and the will of God, I'm afraid. I hear Robine de Croisy is related to our good Queen so it's an excellent match for the boy.'

Grandmère Symonne gave a sniff. 'Well, let's hope she can give him sons, and has more success at breeding than the Queen. After all, the blame for any absence of children lies with the woman.'

'Not in your case. You had no problem producing healthy sons.'

'That's true. Even though God saw fit to take three of them before they reached manhood. But thankfully not my Charles.'

'That was part of God's plan for them. You fulfilled your duty to your husband by giving him sons. Of course, Charles was stronger than the others. That's because he—'

Valentine watched her grandmère put her finger to his lips. '*Chut!* Don't even say the words aloud. You're the only person in the world who knows my secret. Apart from *him*, of course. Queen Anne must never find out. Trust me, an angry jealous woman like that would be a bitter foe indeed. Even though it happened long ago, and we've only seen each other in private a handful of times since, our behaviour has been as chaste as yours and mine. "*You know how to give a man a healthy boy and raise him to manhood,*" is what Louis said to me after she lost a boy. I know he despairs. Counting the number of times Anne was with child when she was married to King Charles before Louis, including the little boy who only lived a few years, her attempts must have reached nigh on a score by now.'

'All of which pleases the Countess of Angoulême no end.'

'Louise of Savoy? Yes. Who knows what lengths she would go to get the throne for her son. I know it's not true but there's even been talk of hemlock being added to the Queen's soup.'

'While I don't believe that either, I've heard Louise keeps a journal and gleefully records each lost child as the removal of an obstacle for François.'

'That sounds just like her.'

Grandmère Symonne was looking thoughtful. 'I wonder why God allowed me to bear children when other women such as Grace and the Queen find it so difficult.'

'Perhaps that was His way of rewarding you for the sacrifice you had to make.'

'Giving up Louis, you mean.' Valentine watched her grandmère rest her head on Abbot Anthoine's shoulder. 'How well you know me, my dear friend. How long it seems since you left the Abbey at Jumièges and came to our house in Rouen. I was so grateful to Pierre for choosing you as the family confessor.'

'As I was to you for telling Guy d'Ardres I'd make an excellent abbot.'

'It was my way of ensuring I could see my good friend whenever I came to visit my son.'

'How young you were when we first met.'

'Sixteen.'

'I was twenty-six. When I was sixteen, I still thought I might be Pope.'

'When I was sixteen, I'd already been wed a year.'

'To a man old enough to be your *père*. With grown children of his own.'

'But daughters. Not the sons he needed. How those girls hated me. And made my life a misery. So when Louis walked up the steps to the manor one day as part of that hunting party, it was as if someone had lit a thousand candles, never to be extinguished again. I know he felt the same.'

'I remember that time very well. You reminded me of a flower turning its face to the sun, dear Symonne. Even though I knew it was a sin for you and Louis to be together while Pierre was in Paris, how could I judge you? After all, a possible future king doesn't marry a woman. He marries a country.'

'I thought I would die of love. He thought he would too. He told me I was the only thing that prevented him from flinging himself off the castle battlements at Blois. Anything to avoid returning to a woman he found so repulsive.'

Abbot Anthoine shook his head. 'Crookbacked Jeanne with her unfortunate face. Another fine young man forced to marry a girl who was…to put it kindly…deformed. No wonder he wanted you so badly.'

Valentine's grandmère gave him a playful punch on the arm. 'Are you trying to flatter me? I don't think Louis ever forgave "The Spider King" for forcing his daughter on him, taking malicious glee in the fact that Jeanne would never be able to bear him children.'

'It was a clever way to end the bloodline of a rival for the throne, you have to admit. King Louis certainly deserved his nickname. Like a spider, he lured his enemies into his web and entangled them, with no chance of escape.'

'Fortunately, he didn't succeed in destroying *my* Louis.'

'Nor did his son manage it either.'

'I always thought Charles and his sister, Jeanne, resembled a pair of frogs. Don't you remember how Louis and I used to call Charles "The Frog King"?' She tutted. 'My poor Louis. He went to great lengths to divorce Jeanne in order to marry Anne but has had no more success in getting a boy on her than Charles did.'

'We are fortunate to understand the workings of childbearing so much better than we did before. Now we understand that the delivery of a healthy boy, as you might expect, is the product of faith and reason.'

Grandmère Symonne laughed. 'Whereas the delivery of a girl comes from a defect in the workings of nature.'

'Or the result of inclement conditions at the time of conception such as a moist south wind. The Queen must pray for a healthy boy next time.'

'In the meantime, let you and I pray that God sees fit to keep both Louis and my Charles safe in Italy.'

'Amen.'

∽

Valentine watched them both cross themselves several times as they said this. Why did grown-ups make the sign of the cross so many times a day? Didn't their hands ever grow tired? She had no idea who most of these people were, or what they were talking about.

<<*Grown-ups always seem to have so many secrets*>>

As she grew older, she was beginning to understand that only a priest knew all your secrets. Abbot Anthoine and her grandmère had talked about some strange things. There was an angry jealous queen; someone called Louis who wanted to throw himself from the battlements of a castle (which must surely hurt); a king who was really a spider; another one who was a frog; and a third who was forced to marry a country. She had no idea how a king could marry a country. <<*How folly-fallen!*>> Giving a little shrug and being careful not to make a noise, she got up and tiptoed down the path, leaving the pair deep in conversation....

∽

'I don't understand why Maman is being so quarrelsome, Grandmère,' said Valentine, when Abbot Anthoine had left. 'She made Charlotte cry this morning.'

'One day,' her grandmère smiled, 'you'll understand that when a woman is with child, sometimes strange moods come upon her. It is not for us to question why but to try and help her through it. Here, Jacqueline,' she said, handing Valentine's sister a small basket. 'You can help me pick some

134

hollyhocks and cherry blossom for your mother.'

Valentine followed them down the garden, her mind still firmly on babies. The arrival of a new baby in the household had taken place what seemed like every year, for as long as Valentine could recall. The one before last - a boy - had sadly breathed his final breath just before Valentine crept into her mother's chamber. He'd already been washed in wine and rubbed with butter to prevent harmful air from getting into his pores.

"But to no avail. Death was waiting for the poor mite just around the corner," the Fleury housekeeper, Béatrice, had pronounced in solemn tones.

This image was so terrifying it haunted Valentine for many a sleepless night, long after her tiny brother had been buried in the churchyard of Notre Dame de Grâce. Fortunately, not every birth ended this way and this was a time when everything would be in uproar. The younger girls would run wild, knowing that after delivering a new babe, their mother would not leave her chamber for a full fourteen days. It was just as well their father was equally preoccupied with welcoming visitors, making arrangements for the christening, and fetching the wet nurse. Last year, no one noticed when Valentine disappeared for hours with a little band of village children to pastures far afield. As far as she was concerned, putting up with her mother's ill humour was worth it if a new baby brought her such freedom.

27ᵗʰ March, 1509. The kitchens at La Colombe.

alentine liked Danielle, the wet nurse, who would soon be moving in to help with the new baby. A plump young woman from the village, she'd recently given birth to her second baby. Valentine loved to sneak into the warm kitchens and watch her with her tiny son. Today, she wandered aimlessly into the kitchens and, seeing Danielle and Béatrice, quickly hid herself in an alcove.

'Thank goodness I've got too much milk for my own baby - scrawny little devil he is,' Danielle was saying. 'I swear, Béa, little Symonne guzzled so much last year and got my *tétons* so big, my Emile said I reminded him of one of his cows down in the field coming in for milking. *Par la Mère de Dieu!* He was just sulking because I wouldn't let him touch me while I was suckling. I don't know how many times I've told him it turns the milk sour. I couldn't afford to waste a precious drop fooling with him - not with the little princess up here at the manor waiting for me!'

Danielle gave a loud laugh and Béatrice joined in most heartily. 'Sometimes men don't know what's good for them,' the housekeeper said. 'When my Didier took me to wife, he couldn't get the ring on. He always jokes he knew right then I wouldn't be docile—'

Wondering why Danielle's husband wanted to touch her all the time and what '*docile*' meant, Valentine decided to go and find her mother. It wouldn't be long before Maman had to go into a chamber upstairs that had been especially prepared for her. Unlike the friendly atmosphere and idle gossip of the kitchen, this room would be like a tomb, sealed up to prevent harmful fresh air from entering. Her mother always insisted upon having at least one window uncovered so she could gaze outside to stave off what (in Valentine's opinion) must surely be long hours of boredom. She wasn't exactly sure what '*giving birth*' meant but it sounded dangerous.

Although the Fleury family never actually lacked for anything, they still borrowed hangings for the walls of the special room (portraying pleasant scenes of love and romance, rather than hunting or fighting), as well as carpets and other pretty objects from their friends. Before baby Symonne's birth, Valentine knew that Tristan d'Ardres' parents had sent over an especially fine set of Venetian glasses.

She started to climb the stairs to her mother's bower but then suddenly remembered how angry Maman had been two days before on the Feast of the Annunciation. She blamed everyone for making too much noise outside her window after taking part in the annual sport known as '*clattering*'. The entire village, including the Fleury family, gathered with anything in their homes that made a noise: a kettle, a mortar, a drum, a frying pan, a basin. The object of the exercise was to go - armed with these objects and torches - deep into the forest and make such a din that the nesting ring doves would be paralyzed with fright and keep completely still. Then each man would load his harquebus and...*Bang!* A shower of bullets would bring down a torrent of ring doves on their heads.

Valentine's mother - who usually took part in the sport - was in a sheep-biting mood. "*As if this racket wasn't bad enough,*" she complained, "*afterwards I had to endure the sound of the villagers making merry below my window. Not to mention being sickened by the smell of suckling pig roasting over a fire.*"

For once, Justin Leblanc, the village drunk (who was also the best rebeck player in the village) was sober. There were calls for him to play some music so that the dancing could begin. The sweet notes of his rebeck charmed everyone - except Valentine's mother. Maître Jacques, the family cook, jumped up to accompany Justin on the hautboy whilst Phélix, the pastry cook, picked up his lute. Even Abbot Anthoine was persuaded to take part in the dancing, something he didn't dare mention to her mother later when she scolded him for allowing his flock to run amok.

"*Of course I'll admonish the villagers, Athénaïs,*" he said, wiping the sweat from his brow with a large white handkerchief.

Valentine also remembered the smile on the face of her nursemaid, Bonne, as she danced around the bonfire, hoping all her wishes would come true. Valentine had previously watched her toss some pins into the foaming waters of a nearby fountain.

"*If they reappear near the surface,*" Bonne said, "*it'll be a sign I'll wed the swain of my heart.*"

Skipping down the stairs again, Valentine set off in search of her father. She adored him and couldn't bear the thought of him leaving tomorrow to join King Louis' army.

She found him downstairs in his study and tucked her hand in his. 'Come for a walk with me in the gardens, Papa.'

He smiled at her. 'How can I refuse such an invitation?'

As they walked away from the main house, Valentine asked him something that had been bothering her. 'Do you like the King?'

'Yes. He's a good man.'

'So why is he making you go to Italy? I don't want you to. I don't like the sound of war. It's too dangerous.'

'*Dangerous*' was Valentine's favourite new word which was just as well as it seemed to describe perfectly what adults wanted to do a great deal of the time.

'Sadly, it is, *ma puce*. But King Louis needs my help. He's not getting any younger and has been very ill twice. Pope Julius thinks Venice is growing too powerful in northern Italy and has formed something called "The League of Cambrai" to curb its power. Not only that, but Louis has a claim to Milan through his Visconti grandmère.'

Valentine didn't want to hear about 'war' when she didn't understand what it was except that it was what little boys did when they grew up. She especially didn't want to talk about it on their last day together. The two of them soon reached the vegetable garden and orchard behind the house; Valentine loved to wander down to the paddock just beyond where she would spend an hour or two petting and feeding apples to Cassandre, her little mare. If Bonne was with her, she was allowed to run over to the brook, fighting her way through the overhanging willows to fetch Cassandre some water. Her father had once shown her a secret door at the far end of the field, for his use only, through which he entered and left when he didn't want to be seen. It was also a way of avoiding the unpleasant smell of the stables and the courtyard. On the grey stone archway above the door, some words in Latin had been engraved: '*Inveni portum: spes et fortuna, valete.*' Valentine's father had translated them for her that day: '"*I have reached harbour: hope and fortune, farewell.*"'

"*But don't you go getting any ideas, young lady, about hopping off somewhere,*" he'd teased, replacing the key to the door in its hiding place.

'Child, I believe you've inherited your love of the outdoors from my side of the family,' he was saying now. 'As you know, your grandmère is passionately interested in her herbs.' He took a deep breath, thrusting out his chest as they paused at the top of a hill. 'I love to watch the changing seasons and all they bring. Sometimes I come here very early in the morning when only the ploughman and the oxen are up, making their way up and down the field over there, attached to the yoke. I'm never truly alone for there's always the tuneful chorus of a hundred birds - making me glad to be alive. You can be sure a few of them will be greedily feasting on some nice fat worms which have come out of the furrows of the newly tilled soil.'

'Ugh! I hate worms.'

Her father patted her head. 'They're part of nature, *ma petite.*'

'Like the birds?'

'Yes.' He pointed to a couple of Black Redstarts flitting above the hedge.

'If you pay attention, you might be able to see a fox. Birds are our friends and we should give them due respect. Any farmer worth his salt will understand their language. For example, a lone heron standing on the shore of the lake over at Ardres marks the beginning of winter. If you want to know if fine weather is on the way, look out for a swallow flying high in the sky. And to tell if rain is coming, look out for that same swallow skimming low over the water, or listen for the voice of a green woodpecker. I've lost count of the times I've seen those two birds right before I've felt the first drop of rain on my hand. But take comfort if you hear a little owl hooting its heart out in the middle of a rainstorm. For it knows better than you that sunshine is on its way.'

'And if the hens don't take cover from the rain, it means it won't stop,' chipped in Valentine, who'd heard some of this before.

'Clever girl. Even the geese and ducks in that pond down there know rain is almost here by the way they start diving into the water without a break. If you suddenly become aware of the croaking of frogs, don't be surprised. Like the rest of our four-legged or feathered friends, they too can feel the weather changes. Even our old house can tell when we're in for a storm - if you put your hand on the walls, you can actually feel the moisture there.'

'Don't we know anything for ourselves?'

Her father laughed. 'Of course we do, *mon enfant*. A calm autumn usually means strong winter winds; thunder heard in the morning is a sure sign of wind, and at midday - rain. Wait until the autumn, and when you see the sheep running wildly across the fields, it means winter's coming fast.'

'Was a south wind blowing when I was born, Papa?'

'What a strange question. Why do you ask?'

'Abbot Anthoine said girl babies are blown in by the south wind.'

Valentine looked up at her father. 'Why do Maman's friends always come when she has a baby?' She hated seeing the sharp-nosed Dame Brinon who had yellow teeth and usually said something unpleasant to her. 'Do they say something to make the baby come down the chimney?' She knew that some babies came into the world that way and could get hurt. Others, she'd just learned, were blown in by the north or south wind.

Even the thought of that horrible woman was enough to give Valentine nightmares. Her father stroked her cheek. 'No, they come to make a caundle for your mother and be with her when the baby comes.'

'What's a "*caundle*"?'

'It's wine with spices added to it. All new mothers drink it.'

Unfortunately, Valentine knew she'd have to endure Dame Brinon a second time; after the baby arrived, her mother had to lie down in a darkened room for the first three days because this thing called '*childbirth*' was bad for the eyesight. Then her friends would come back to be served a special meal prepared by Maître Jacques.

It was with a slightly heavy heart when Valentine heard it was time for her mother to be 'churched' since this meant the end of her freedom. Last year, they all trooped off to the church of Notre Dame de Grâce (with a bag full of coins for the priest) for a special thanksgiving service. Bonne had recently explained to Valentine that it was regarded as a cleansing process for the new mother after being tainted by childbirth. Valentine had no idea what '*tainted*' or being '*churched*' meant. She only knew that when the priest read Psalm 121 while her veiled mother knelt in one of the pews reserved for new mothers, she would have to start behaving herself again.

Valentine's father let out a sigh. 'You learn everything so quickly I've lost count of the number of times I wished you could have been a boy.'

Knowing how excited her father was about the approaching birth of her little brother: a prince waiting to inherit his kingdom, Valentine's eyes filled with tears. She thought of the life-size hobby horse, and a small jousting toy on wheels he'd purchased from a travelling fair.

Her father wiped away a tear from her cheek. 'Forgive me, my pet. Not a word of it is true.'

Valentine understood it was important for her mother to produce an '*heir*'. Her father had explained this was someone who took over the family home when they grew up. In some parts of France, such as Picardy where they lived, it couldn't be a girl, only a boy.

"But what will happen if Maman only has girls?" she'd asked him recently.

"La Colombe will pass to a male cousin of mine I've never met."

As Valentine didn't want a stranger to come and live in their house with them in case she didn't like him, she hoped the baby stretching her mother's belly to bursting point was a boy. And wouldn't come down the chimney and end up next to her other baby brother in the churchyard of Notre Dame de Grâce.

As they walked towards the brook back in the direction of the orchard, her father began telling her about the tasks this 'heir' would be expected to complete when he took over the Fleury estate. 'I'll expect you to help me teach him as soon as he is old enough,' he said.

'I'd like that.'

Her father crouched down and gently turned her head in the direction of the orchard beneath. 'Look down there, daughter. You'll find all kinds of sweet fruits.' He ruffled Valentine's hair. 'Such as a delicious apple for your sweetheart.'

'But I don't want a sweetheart. I only want you.'

Her father chuckled. 'Trust me, that will change someday. And when you are grown and visit La Colombe with your own family, you'll be able to enjoy juicy pears and apricots from your brother's orchard, or carrots and cabbage from his kitchen garden. And beyond, stretching out like a blaze of summer sunshine on a July morning, will be his fields of wheat and barley.'

In the distance, they could hear the sound of horses' hooves clattering into the courtyard. Her father looked at her. 'All this will belong to your brother someday. He'll ride through that same archway, seated on a fine horse, servants rushing up to do homage to the lord of the manor.'

'He'll be so handsome. Just like you.'

'Thank you, my Valentine. But it won't be easy for him. You and I will have to teach him how to manage his estate well. It will take up most of his time and if he has to go off to Court or serve in the King's army, as I do sometimes, he'll have to leave a good man in charge.'

❦

Valentine knew that as a girl, she was supposed to be at home spending her time in preparation for marriage, learning her letters, working on her stitches and practising her dance steps, amongst other things - unlike a boy whose education took up more time. Her parents often called her *'fidget'* because she could never sit still. She found learning tiresome, far preferring the freedom she felt running in the fields, learning to ride her little pony, or twirling around in the great hall, pretending she was grown and dancing with a swain. Valentine was secretly glad she wasn't a boy. She did 'boy tasks' anyway such as accompanying her father, his steward and several servants, around the estate, watching them carry out various tasks and begging to help where she could. This involved checking on the traps they'd set for the foxes who were stealing the hens or geese; pruning the young bushes in the orchard which she learnt, had to be tended in keeping with the phases of the moon; sowing the new seeds her father had brought back from his travels; deepening the ditches in the woods, and fishing in the stream down by the paddock. Sometimes, her mother would join them, especially if one of their tenants needed medical aid.

Her father had even taken her with him once or twice when he went hunting with his greyhounds and running dogs, placing her on the saddle in front of him. As they pursued foxes or roebuck, he took care not to trample down the wheat in the fields. With the wind tangling her hair as they galloped across the fields, it was one of the few times Valentine's father seemed to be truly carefree. Her mother worried about him spending so much time with the family steward poring over the accounts in his study. *"Come, Charles, that's enough now,"* she'd often say.

Valentine tugged on her father's sleeve. 'I promise to be your "son and heir" until the north wind brings my baby brother here.'

'I'm glad. Now, I think it's time for us to go back and see your mother. Have no fear. I'll be back from Italy before you know it.'

CECILY

Chapter Twenty-Six

1ˢᵗ June, 1509. The battlements of Zennor Castle.

'Where would you end up, Cecy, if you sailed in a straight line from Zennor across the Celtic Sea?'

I thought for a moment, admiring Nan for always asking more interesting questions than my other friends.

'You'd probably end up in Cork. In Ireland. Where Perkin Warbeck first became known. Before he came to Cornwall.'

'My father says the Pretender deserved to be hung as a traitor at Tyburn. And that old King Henry did the right thing.'

Both of us hastily crossed ourselves in case the soul of the dead King was lurking somewhere in purgatory. After all, he'd only been dead these past six weeks.

'My Grandam Matilda believed Perkin *was* one of the Yorkist princes in the Tower. Richard of Shrewsbury. Duke of York. She wanted to shelter him here in our Castle. But Father refused. He told her not to meddle in affairs that could cost us our lives.'

Whenever I mentioned my dead grandam, I could feel tears pricking my eyes and found it hard to swallow. Even though it was almost a year since her death, time had done very little to ease my pain. I sometimes thought about the strange thing that had happened at her funeral: how a beautiful pink rose (from the two score laid upon her oak coffin) seemed to fall...or rather fly straight into my lap as my uncles and my father bore the coffin up the aisle. I'd placed a couple of petals from it next to the others that were already in my favourite Book of Hours: a copy of one owned by Cecily of York, the new King's aunt, after whom I'd been named. Whenever I opened it, I'd take great pleasure in knowing the rose petals would be pressed together for all time...in honour of Grandam Matilda.

144

Next to me, Nan was staring straight ahead of her, her brown eyes in her pale face, intently fixed on the distant horizon, as if trying to see the cobbled streets of Cork where the young Warbeck, dressed in clothes of the finest silk, had first caught the attention of the residents. After a while, she got bored and turned her back to the Castle battlements. 'My family's got relatives in Ireland,' she said. 'The Butlers. They live in Ormonde Castle.' She tossed back her long black hair (of which she was so proud), with its sheen of red. 'Perhaps I'll marry one of them one day. If it pleases me.' All of a sudden, her dark piercing eyes were searching my face for an answer. 'Whom will you wed, Cecy Tredavoe? A soldier or a sailor. A tinker or a tailor.'

∽

'None of those. I'm going to be like Hildegard von Bingen.'

'Who's that?'

I was pleased I knew someone Nan didn't. 'She was a Benedictine abbess. Hundreds of years ago. A mystic. She managed to have all the men, even the Pope himself, hanging onto her every word.'

'She sounds very clever.'

'She was. Not only did she write plays and poems but she composed music.' I sang a couple of lines from one of my favourite songs:

'"*Columba aspexit*
Per cancellos fenestre."'
{'The dove peered in
Through the lattices of the window.'}

'What's that? It's very beautiful.'

'It's called "*Columba aspexit*". One of my tutors told me Hildegard once begged the Pope in Rome to instruct the then kings of France and England to make peace. Two men she described as "*dangerous beasts*".'

'She was brave to do that.'

'Very. But she also knew a woman's place. In order to avoid offending so great a man as the Pope, she excused the mere woman's voice she used to protest as: "*the small sound of the trumpet*"—'

'It's just as well Lizzie Stafford and Mary are down below with our mothers. They hate any talk of books and learning. You know my sister always says the same thing: that she only needs to learn to read and write her name so she can write a love letter. She says it's far more important to look pretty, dance, play an instrument or two, sing, ride a horse, and, as lady of the manor, tend to simple wounds. Everything else makes her feel motley-minded.'

'I'd be motley-minded if I talked about boys all day long like those two.'

'So would I. But it doesn't mean I don't think about whom I'm going to wed.'

'We can find out if you like.'

'What do you mean?'

'Grandam Matilda taught me how to tell fortunes.'

Nan's dark eyes grew wide. 'Was your Grandam Matilda a witch? I sometimes think you are, Cecy Tredavoe. When you know when things are going to happen before they do.'

I gave a shrug. 'I can't help that. I've always been able to do it. Since I was very little. Yes, some said my grandam was a witch. But mostly she was known for her ability to bewitch men.'

Nan's mouth curled into a pout. 'I'd like to do that one day. Wouldn't you?'

'No, a lady abbess rises above such things. And, besides, she's already a bride of Christ.'

'Oh, don't be so prim! You won't be able to make merry if you become an abbess. Why do you want to become one anyway? I know you find the priest's sermons at Hever as boring as I do.'

'That's true. But you're wrong about not being able to make merry. My cousin's going to be a bishop. And he likes to make merry.'

'I haven't met him. What's his name?'

'Tristan.'

'Where does he live?'

'France.'

France.

A country across the Narrow Sea that meant very little to me, apart from the fact that my Aunt Grace had married a French count and lived with him near the English town of Calais. They had a son together, as well as another one by her husband's first marriage. Giving me a cousin who was half-Cornish and half-French.

'I'd like to sail across the Narrow Sea one day,' said Nan, taking a deep breath of Cornish sea air. 'Father's always full of praise for the courts of France and Burgundy.'

I looked around the battlements. 'I never want to leave here. I have everything I could possibly want right in front of my nose.'

Nan gave me a nudge. 'Come on, my Lady Abbess, I want to find out whom I'll wed. And whom you'll wed…when your nunnery becomes too dismal for you.'

'Oh, very well. Wait here.'

⁊

Returning a short while later from a secret raid on the kitchens, out of breath and hot…but victorious, I emptied a little knapsack onto a linen napkin on the ground next to Nan. Out tumbled several red Pendragon apples, handfuls of cherries that had ripened very early this year, and a tankard of small beer I'd managed to fill without being seen.

'First of all, we have to eat all the cherries,' I said, taking a swig of the beer to quench my thirst, before handing it to Nan. 'We need the stones, you see.'

'I like this game,' she mumbled, accepting the tankard while devouring cherry after cherry in her eagerness to find out what the future held for her.

Eventually, when the pair of us had a small mountain of cherry stones piled up next to us, I picked up two apples. 'We can't eat these yet.'

'So what are they for?'

My future as an abbess entirely forgotten, I was suddenly as excited as Nan. 'To reveal the names of the men we'll both marry,' I replied.

⁊

I handed Nan an apple. 'Turn the stem slowly and as you do, say the letters of the alphabet. When the stem breaks, that will be the initial of your future husband's first name.'

With a look of intense concentration, Nan began to twist the stem. 'A...
B...C...D...E...F...G...H,' she chanted as if she were in a schoolroom. 'Oh,
look it's snapped. H.'

I rubbed my hands together. 'That means your husband's first name will
begin with H.'

Nan looked disappointed; I knew she'd been hoping for a J because she
liked one of her older brother, Tom's, friends called John.

'Now it's your turn, Cecy.'

I grabbed hold of the stem of an apple that was sturdier than Nan's. In not
time at all, I'd managed to get to the letter M.

'No, it was an N,' protested Nan. 'It didn't quite break off at M. So, now
we have the first names of our husbands. How do we find out their second
names?'

'Patience. Pick up the broken stem and poke the apple until the skin
breaks.'

Nan began to prod the apple as she recited the alphabet again, easily
reaching P without piercing the skin. I put my hand over hers.

'You're not doing it hard enough. At this rate, you'll reach the letter Z.'

We both laughed as we said in unison: 'And no one has a surname
beginning with Z.'

Nan took up the stem again with renewed vigour but we couldn't decide
whether it finally pierced the skin at S or T. I picked up my own apple and, to
our great amusement, stabbed it with so much force it almost went through on
A. By D, it had certainly gone all the way in.

'I think it went through on B,' said Nan.

'That's only because the apple was a little rotten where I was trying.'

Not sure if she was to marry a man whose first name began with H and
second with S or T, and I, to marry one whose first name began with M or N,
and last name with B or D, we were a little disappointed. 'Let's play a different
game,' I suggested. 'Using the cherry stones.'

❦

Nan looked at me expectantly. 'So what do we do?'

'We're going to ask some questions. First, the profession of our husbands.'

'How do we do that?'

'Pick up a handful of the stones and lay them next to each other in a long row.'

Nan seized some stones and quickly did as I said. 'And now?'

'We're going to count together, using a little rhyme Grandam taught me. When we run out of stones, that will be your husband's profession. Listen to me and then repeat the rhyme yourself.

'"*Tinker, tailor, soldier, sailor,*"' I began, '"*gentleman, apothecary, ploughboy, thief.*"'

'I'm certainly not tying myself to a rascal who'll end up on the gallows,' Nan giggled, as we counted together.

'Gentleman,' I said. 'You're going to wed a gentleman.'

After we discovered I was to wed a soldier, I explained the next question to her. 'We do exactly the same thing but this time, we want to know what kind of garments we'll wear when we're wed. "*Silk, satin, muslin, rags.*"'

It was a relief to discover that neither of us would find ourselves in rags, rather Nan would be in silk and I in satin. 'I think your husband's going to be richer than mine,' I teased her. 'Now, let's find out how we'll travel to the church: in "*a coach, a carriage, a wheelbarrow* or *a cart.*"'

Again, Nan was to travel in a slightly grander fashion than me. 'Let's see if I can finally beat you. We're going to find out where we're going to live,' I said, repeating the options of: '"*palace, castle, cottage* or *barn.*"'

Of course I didn't beat her. 'I don't mind living in a castle,' I said. 'Only kings and queens live in a palace.'

'Or a lady's maid. Perhaps, I'm going to wed one of the King's servants and live in the royal palace with him. What's next?'

'Finding out when we'll wed. But as today is your birthday and you're only eight like me, I'm going to have to alter the numbers a little: '"*ten years, twenty, twenty-five, never.*"' We can't find out the exact number of years but it'll be the nearest to the one we choose.'

'So, I *will* be wed,' said Nan, pointing to the final cherry stone in dismay, 'but not for twenty-five years. Forsooth! By the first of June in twenty-five years I'll be creeping to my grave. Not to a church door. You, on the other hand, will be wed in ten. At least, I'll be living in a palace.'

~

As she said these words, one of those strange feelings came over me that I'd had before (Grandam Matilda used to say I had the gift of second sight from the De Laceys, her side of the family); it was as if I was aboard a galleon, rocking to and fro on the high seas, dipping and diving over huge waves, the sails of the vessel billowing like a giant's handkerchief. I was glad we were seated on the ground otherwise I was certain I would have fallen, unable to keep my balance. Even my vision was shifting as I looked at Nan for I could have sworn I saw a golden crown upon her head. And then, as swiftly as it had come, the sensation vanished and my sight returned to normal.

'Maybe I'm going to be queen of a foreign land,' Nan said, putting on a silly voice. 'Where the king likes old women.' She bent over, pretending to be a crone and pulling a hideous face.

I was slightly taken aback that Nan (who'd noticed nothing) seemed to have acquired the ability to read my mind.

'I can't be Queen of England,' she went on, 'because our new King is about to wed the Spanish princess at the Palace of Placentia. They say he bought over three hundred pounds worth of jewels from a Parisian jeweller.'

'Father told me he bought a thousand pearls and wears a gold collar around his neck to which a diamond as big as a walnut is attached.'

'I've heard he's quickly becoming known as the "the best dressed king in Christendom."'

I reached over and dug her in the ribs. 'Let's hope your old king is equally fashionable.'

~

'It's a shame we're not older,' I said. 'Then we could go to court. And to the wedding.'

'Father says if old King Henry ruled over a "*Winter Court*", then this one will rule over a "*Springtime Court*". That's because the new King and Queen are so young and neither of them have any parents by their sides. Three are dead and the Queen's father lives far from England. My grandsire came to Hever last week and was as angry as a wasp. He kept hopping from foot to foot.' Nan let out a little laugh. 'I'm sure he'd like to take a rod to the new King. "*A Tudor rose with thorns*", he called him.'

I shuddered. 'Your Grandsire Howard? The thought of meeting him scares me.'

'Grandsire Thomas scares everyone. Except perhaps King Henry. That's what Father told us. He can't wait to see what will happen. He says it'll be like watching an old stag locking horns with a young buck. Fighting until one of them draws blood. Father's got no complaint with the King because he's promised to knight him at his coronation.'

I was thinking about the royal wedding in ten days. 'Imagine if we went to the wedding. We could wear our silk and satin.'

'You'd fit in perfectly with your red hair. You know all the Tudors have red hair. Mother says you look just like the King's younger sister, Mary. And everyone says Henry is as handsome as that knight who ran off with King Arthur's wife.'

'Sir Lancelot?'

'That's right.'

'One of my tutors told me Camelot was really Tintagel Castle. Here in Cornwall.'

'One of Tom's tutors told us it was either Winchester or Cadbury Castle.' Nan turned to face me. 'I wonder whom we'd find more handsome. Sir Lancelot or King Henry.'

PART FOUR

THE TUDOR ROSE

*' If you could see how nobly
how wisely the prince behaves,
I am sure you will hasten to England.
All England is in ecstasies. '*

William Blount, Lord Mountjoy to
Desiderius Erasmus. 27th May, 1509.

HOUSE OF TUDOR

Chapter Twenty-Seven

June 28ᵗʰ, 1509. The Palace of Westminster.

lone in his bedchamber, Henry Tudor was counting on his fingers. Eighteen years exactly since he'd first entered this world. Sixty-nine days since he'd become King of England. Seventeen days since he'd wedded and bedded his new queen. Four days since Midsummer's Day when they'd both been crowned in Westminster Abbey....

Yet, still he felt the frustrating yoke of boyhood around his neck. Older but no wiser heads than his own, were preventing him from setting foot on the path to glory. Men such as Thomas Howard, and Richard Fox, his Lord Privy Seal (the Bishop of Winchester's name reflecting his wily character), amongst others, all advising him to keep the peace in Europe and adhere to the craven, fawning League of Cambrai (supposedly against the Ottoman Turk, but, in reality, a means of attacking the Republic of Venice and dividing up the spoils), signed shortly before his father's death by all the major rulers, including the Pope himself. Louis of France had certainly benefitted from the alliance with his magnificent victory against the Venetians in Agnadello, last month.

Suddenly overcome by a fit of pique at the thought of this, the young King snatched up his small mirror of Venetian glass (a gift from the Republic's ambassador), framed by a rich border of silver. He stared into its smoky depths, speaking to his reflection as if to a trusted friend: 'I'm not a callow youth, all fingers and thumbs, unable to perform on a battlefield (given half the chance)... or in a lady's bedchamber. That's why I married Kate in such haste, to have her father, Ferdinand's, support against France. My grandsire, Ned, fought for his throne at the battle of Towton when he was the same age as me. And the fifth Henry nearly met his death at the Battle of Shrewsbury, two years younger.

I'm no fool! But here am I…hero of nothing but running at the ring. I might as well be a stable lad for all the chances I've had so far to prove myself.'

The reflection frowned back at him and then declared: 'All I want is to be King of England and France! And the rest of Europe to be dazzled by the deeds of England's eighth Henry.'

There was a long established belief (which Henry knew delighted his people) that the French feared the English. The same Venetian ambassador who'd given him the mirror had added fuel to this theory by referring to the Earl of Shrewsbury as a member of the "*terrifying Talbots*". According to Andrea Badoer, a mewling French child could be instantly subdued by an adult with the threat of an approaching Talbot:

"'*If you don't behave yourself, the Talbots will get you in your bed!*' is what they say,*" he'd told Henry, his cronies, Kate, and a few of her ladies, after a banquet last week. They'd all moved to a more intimate chamber to sample the spice plates and copious amounts of wine being served at the void. Henry took great delight in telling everyone the room was lit by a great number of his dead father's most expensive wax candles; they'd been discovered by Henry's groom of the stool, hidden away in a store room.

"*More often than not,*" Andrea told them, "*such an utterance, made in a moment's anger, results in months of nightmares in the nursery, robbing many a nursemaid of her sleep, and causing her to rue her hasty words.*"

How everyone laughed. Will Compton, his loyal groom of the stool, and Ned Howard, proceeded to make snarling noises and hideous grimaces, stamping their feet and chanting: "*We're the 'terrifying Talbots'. And we're coming to get…you!*" as they grabbed a giggling Anne Hastings and Lizzie Bullen around their tiny waists.

Henry knew it wasn't just him who felt this way about the French; this hostile attitude permeated every level of society, right down to the lowliest stable boy or tavern wench. No French merchant living in London was allowed to attend an English cloth fair, and any unfortunate to be caught out at night without a candle, were more likely than not to be thrown into the nearest prison, accused of spying. Indeed, England was a country that had been waiting for the right monarch to come along and reconquer France....

❧

Taking part in war was a dream Henry had cherished for as long as he could remember, the desire for it coursing through his veins as forcefully as the desire for peace had coursed through those of his father before him. As far back as the days in the royal nursery when he'd drifted off to sleep, his little head filled with knights of old slaying fiery dragons.

Up until the age of ten, he'd grown up in the shadow of his older brother, Arthur, universally adored and known as the 'Rosebush of England'. But when the healthy, fifteen-year-old heir to the throne suddenly succumbed to illness, Henry was thrust into the limelight. It was a role he relished and the moment his ageing father breathed his last, Henry had seized the crown with both hands and swept his dead brother's wife to the altar, intent upon flinging opening his father's bulging coffers. His father had been a notoriously miserly king; when he chose to be extravagant, it was for the purposes of show alone - not out of sheer enjoyment. One Spanish ambassador had quipped: "*Once a gold coin goes into one of the King's strong boxes, it never sees the light of day again.*"

There was many a one who grumbled Henry was wont to pay the equivalent in depreciated coin. The ambassador wasn't alone in having the image of the King in his counting house, counting out his money; some wag even put pen to paper and wrote a poem about it....

'Well, the people need not fear,' said Henry out loud to the empty bedchamber, 'a new king sits upon the throne now.' He picked at a diamond stud on his doublet. 'Who is as likely to be called a miser as the Pope in Rome to take a wife.'

❧

Henry knew he was already extremely popular with his people, having easily won their hearts with his youth, vigour, and warm-heartedness. One of his best friends in the world, Ned Howard, teased him that he reminded everyone of a heroic six-foot-two giant: their very own English version of a Greek god. Around him, many of his courtiers (especially the women) waxed lyrical about the awe-inspiring proportions of his body.

"*Do you realize you're fast becoming a legend, Hal,*" Ned had said the previous evening. "*I've heard that Andrea Badoer wrote home to Venice how the ground shakes beneath you when you move.*"

It's certainly not because I'm fat, thought Henry now, patting his slender thirty-one inch waist. 'Nor am I ugly', he whispered, smiling at his reflection as he picked up the mirror once more. The image that stared back at him had prompted John Skelton to write some most gratifying lines of verse:

> "*Our prince of high honour...*
> *Our king, our emperour...*
> *Our welth, our wordly joy.*"

The fact his former tutor had been employed by his father to teach him the niceties of English grammar and Latin: necessary tools for diplomacy, was of no consequence. Henry knew he could trust the words of his newly appointed poet laureate; John was no idle flatterer intent upon catching himself a court appointment.

Henry set the mirror down on the walnut table next to him. He had no need of it to tell him he looked every inch a handsome warrior king: one capable of leading his country into worthy battle. A whimsical thought entered his head: <<*Who knows, one day far in the future, the victory of Agincourt might seem a mere skirmish. A glorious interlude that came to nought, begrudgingly given a few lines in the history books. Or perhaps none at all. The fifth Henry remembered as a pale shadow, a leader for a day, no longer the warlike hero who brought the kingdom of France to its knees*>>

The King started to walk towards the door where he knew members of his council were waiting patiently on the other side. Ned Howard had warned him his father was on the warpath again about keeping the peace with France.

"*Humour the old man, Hal, I beg you,*" he'd pleaded yesterday. "*Otherwise it'll be me getting it in the neck again for not acting my age. It won't be my sisters, Lizzie and Muriel. As two of your Queen's ladies, they will remain blameless. After all, my fourteen years of seniority to you are supposed to have given me some kind of superior wisdom.*"

Grinning, Henry remembered how Ned's jovial comment had led to a fierce swordfight in the presence of all their friends. Eventually, a lightly blooded Ned had been forced to concede defeat with hands held in the air and a point of the sword at his throat. Examining the scratch on his hand, he'd laughingly renounced his claim to possession of a superior wit.

Stretching with all the grace of one of the Palace tomcats as he remembered his victory, Henry gave voice to the thoughts that were gathering momentum with every step he took, turning him into the greatest conqueror that had ever walked the earth. 'Yes. Hundreds of years from now, poor Henry of Lancaster will be recalled as a firework that gave a few moments pleasure. While I...I will be the blazing comet that lit up the night sky - a wonder, a miracle.'

Henry reached out for the ornate wooden ringed door handle, altered last week to bear his personal crest. He began to turn it. 'The only name still on people's lips...will be mine!'

All of a sudden, he paused and turned swiftly on his heels. No. Let his councillors wait; they'd forced him into this hateful position of peace. He felt like punishing them, knowing some of them had been waiting for upwards of two hours. As for the ancient ones like Thomas Howard, his Lord Treasurer; Richard Fox; William Warham, his Archbishop of Canterbury and chancellor; and Thomas Ruthall, his secretary and Bishop of Durham: the so-called 'voices of reason' and to a man, originally his father's closest advisors, he hoped their disapproving old bones were giving them suitable hell.

Throwing himself down gracefully into his oak chair, he reached out for a quill, blowing on the swan's feathers before dipping it into the iron gall ink in the small pot next to him.

'Now is the time to let all those curmudgeonly greybeards know what kind of life I intend to lead,' he announced to the mullioned windows across from him. He began to hum the first bars of a new song. As he finished, the perfect title came into his head, one he knew would please Kate...and all his friends, especially Ned, Charles, and Will Compton. Smiling broadly at his own wit, he began to write:

'*Pastime With Good Company*

Henry Rex, King of England

Pastime with good company
I love and shall unto I die;
Grudge who list, but none deny,
So God be pleased thus live will I.
For my pastance
Hunt, song, and dance.
My heart is set:
All goodly sport
For my comfort,
Who shall me let?

* * *

Youth must have some dalliance,
Of good or ille some pastance....'

HOUSE OF HOWARD

Chapter Twenty-Eight

August 11ᵗʰ, 1509. The lists at the Palace of Westminster.

I raised my arm in greeting to my second son as he bounded up the steps of the royal box which was magnificently decorated in blue velvet, damask and cloth-of-gold. Clad in his tournament clothes, *en route* for the nearby arming pavilion, Edward was a striking figure of a man. I knew his expressive dark eyes, wide curved mouth, and strong Howard nose had gained him many female admirers. Not as tall as the new King, of course, happily, he possessed the exact build of the recently deceased Henry, my '*Goose*', of whom I'd grown quite fond by the end. How pleased I'd been when Edward was selected to wear the dead King's armour and take part in the funeral procession. He might be smaller in stature than the present King but he nevertheless had the strength and skill to be a first rate jouster <<*which has proved to be very useful for the entire Howard clan*>>....

As usual, it took him a while to reach my side, laughing and joking with all he passed as hands reached out on all sides to grasp his or pat him on the back, head, or shoulders. My popular boy. Everyone knew how high he was riding in the royal favour and perhaps hoped that touching him would increase their own standing. Where Edward was concerned (the son who most resembled me in appearance), I felt that mixture of fierce paternal pride and unfettered love, coupled with a keen desire to throttle him for not keeping the Tudor pup in order. My '*Tudor rose with thorns*'. How many times had we discussed how he could do it? This morning had been a perfect example; all of us in the royal council had told young Henry that it was his duty as reigning monarch to keep the French happy and honour the Treaty of Cambrai and its goal of peace in Europe. <<*But what did the over-excitable snipper-snapper*

do? Cause a scene with the new French Ambassador, the abbot of Fécamp>>
I was still cringing from what I'd witnessed: the look of outrage on the fleshy features of Antoine Bohier as the King of England proceeded to insult the King of France.

A few weeks before, Richard Fox, William Warham, and I had sent a letter to Louis of France on behalf of young Henry, urging for peace to continue between our two countries. Louis of France was still basking in glory after his astounding victory over the Venetians back in May. Someone had rightly said that in one day, the Republic of Venice was stripped of everything it had taken eight hundred years to conquer. With this in mind, I was still smarting from our King's words as he'd turned to look at all of us this morning:

"Who wrote this letter? I ask peace of the King of France! Who would not dare not look me in the face, still less make war on me."

Of course, the three of us kept our mouths firmly closed (*<<safety in numbers>>*) but I knew the other two would be inwardly seething too. The Tudor stripling had only been on the throne a mere five months yet already he was threatening to bring chaos thundering down on our heads. Didn't the artless blockhead realize he had no heir to succeed him? The precious Tudor dynasty *Goose* had worked so hard to build up could be snuffed out as quickly as it had sprung to life. It was the same as young Hal's absurd desire to take part in the jousts: as near to the act of warfare he could manage. That lawyer, Tom More, the same age as Edward, had written about the dangers, saying how we'd all seen the tournament ground *"drenched with the life blood of stricken knights—"*

'Good day, Pater. I see you're alone today.'

I warmed to Edward's special name for me: one he'd used since the schoolroom when he tried to come to grips with Latin, with little more success than me. On other occasions, when we were engaged in playful banter, he'd call me '*Phoenix*', and tell me that, thanks to me, the Howard star was shining very brightly in the Tudor firmament. Never boasting that it was equally because of him (which was the truth; the King wanted lively young men to play with, and old men, like me, only when it was time to work). But that was my son, always knowing when to push himself forward and when to take a step backwards. Apart from one or two rare exceptions.

'I have left your stepmother behind at Framlingham. She's with child again.'

Being the same age as my Agnes, I noticed a shadow cross my son's face as he looked over to where his red-faced second wife, an even wealthier widow than his first (though not as old), was fanning herself. She might be paying to keep my son in a life of luxury, but at nearly fifteen full years his senior, her days of childbearing duty were well and truly over. At least Edward had two bastard sons to his name, I thought, to quell my slightly uneasy conscience for urging him into the match.

Not one long to brood long, Edward quickly offered me his congratulations. 'Though I'm surprised you have such good news to impart. Judging from your face, you are carrying the worries of the world upon your shoulders.'

My son sprawled across two of the chairs, seemingly oblivious to the present diplomatic crisis at court, smiling and waving at two of his friends strolling towards the arming pavilion. He was so like one of my lovable hunting pups I felt all my annoyance of a few moments past evaporate. I should not forget Edward's friendship with the King was worth a thousand gold crowns to the Howards. 'Forgive me. I was thinking about this morning's meeting with the French Ambassador.'

'Ah, that.' Edward pulled an apologetic face. 'Believe me, I had no idea what Hal was going to say. Besides, he does exactly what he wants.'

Sucking in my breath a little at my son's easy sobriquet when referring to the King of England, I glanced around to see if we could be overheard. I had been one of the first to arrive and the box was relatively empty. I immediately relaxed. <<*I have nothing to fear; only a favourite of the King would be allowed to shorten his name thus. Instead of fretting, I should be proud and pleased*>>

◈

I watched my son stifle a yawn, probably after too much carousing with his irrepressible eighteen-year-old master the night before. Seeing my frown, Edward sat up and straightened his lawn shirt. 'Pardon me, Pater. I thought you were going to complain about Hal's latest poem.'

'The one poking fun at his decrepit old advisors? Like me. Who think he's ruled by his young head. You don't need to tell me one of the verses was aimed at me. The one beginning:

> *"I pray you all that aged be*
> *How well did you your youth carry?*
> *I think some worse of each agree."'*

Edward grinned at my recital. 'Hal meant no harm. He speaks so highly of you. He's just flexing his muscles against those older than him. It's only normal.'

'I know you're right, son. 'Tis a tragedy he has no older relatives left to help him. With his grandam's death the day after his birthday, that was the last of the elders he might have listened to. Trust Madge Beaufort to go out so dramatically....'

'Choking on a piece of swan, you mean. There must be better ways to go.'

'Yes. The old fool has left her precious grandson all alone now.'

'And his queen is far from home.'

'With only a scheming father to guide her. I wouldn't trust Ferdinand of Spain further than I could throw him. So I know I shouldn't judge young Hal too harshly for the letter business.'

I deliberately used my son's pet name for the King to show my sympathy for the tricky situation in which the orphaned royal youngster found himself. But as a mark of respect and, in keeping with my advancing years, I would only refer to him as 'the King' in public.

Edward nodded in agreement. 'I assure you that inside he acknowledges all the help you give him.'

That was going too far. 'Do you really expect me to believe he says that to William Compton as he's wiping the royal arse.'

'Hal would laugh if he heard you say that.'

I beckoned Edward closer. 'Tom More said to me only last week the young King is like a lion. And if he knew his own strength, hard were it for any man to rule him.'

Edward's grin widened. 'Master More has a clever way with words. And knows how to play to the King's vanity. He'll go far.'

'What else would you expect from a lawyer,' I grumbled, 'claiming humility with their silver tongues while all the time lining their pockets with gold.'

'I don't blame Hal on this occasion. That French Ambassador's like a puffed up windbag and deserves to be taken down a peg or two. He has a face like a bulldog chewing a wasp; or a giant toad, with those bulging eyes of his.'

Amused by my son's all too accurate description, I didn't scold him too much. 'Nevertheless, he is the ambassador representing a country we want to keep close.' I let out a sigh. 'I was hoping bedding the Queen every night was going to rid our King of some of his choler. Putting those fiery ballocks of his to good use, begetting England an heir. Still, I suppose I should see it as a small mercy that's he's joining me here in the viewing chamber, and not you in the arming chamber.'

Around us, the royal box was filling up (although Henry and Katherine had not yet arrived) and Edward stood up to leave. Just then, there was a commotion at the far end and I spotted the French Ambassador with a face indeed remindful of a bulldog chewing a wasp. He was having some kind of altercation with a steward. His hat was slightly askew and inside his long abbot's gown, he was flapping his arms around in the manner more of a large angry bird than a bulldog. I could almost hear the screeching from where I was sitting. I could certainly see what was wrong. No place had been reserved for him.

'Grace!' gasped Edward and I was gratified to see his face had turned as white as his shirt. At least, my son realized the importance of court etiquette.

'Yes, it is a disgrace,' I muttered, all the while knowing exactly who had given orders for this public insult: the royal latecomer. He was deliberately biding his time before making an appearance, probably hidden behind some curtain watching events unfold, knowing him. 'Go and sort it out will you as you leave, Edward.'

I watched my son making his way over to the far side of the box where the furious ambassador was standing with a man and a woman, still gesticulating wildly. Thank God for Edward. He would remedy matters. Unfortunately, I hadn't bargained with the extent of the worthy prelate's ire or him having the sensibilities of a woman with an attack of the vapours; just as Edward reached the small party, the French Ambassador let out a roar and turned on his heels.

Disaster!

I looked around. Still no sign of Henry or Katherine. She was probably in on the joke; what else would you expect from the daughter of the King of Spain? Edward was speaking to the couple and pointing in my direction. I stood up, understanding they must be of some importance and connected to the ambassador - perhaps his relatives. I knew I must do everything necessary to appease them. Edward gave me a final brief wave and disappeared down the steps as the pair reached me. Luckily, he'd sent a page ahead to make the introductions:

'My lord, may I present the Governor of Picardy, Guy d'Ardres, and his wife, the Countess d'Ardres.'

'And this is my son, Tristan,' said Guy d'Ardres as a young boy came to stand next to them.

By the Rood! Now I would have to speak French. They were certainly a very handsome family, the boy favouring his mother entirely in his looks. I'd noticed a definite flutter of female interest as the Count strode across the box, his entire demeanour suggesting frustration, not a hint of a smile in either his dark eyes or in the firm set of his mouth. On any other day, I would have been more than happy to entertain the Countess, a beautiful young creature with blonde hair and green eyes, fine-boned, almost otherworldly, like a dweller of a fairy marsh. However, the prospect of using my rusty French on her was most displeasing. I'd never had much truck with languages, even though I'd once spent time at the Burgundian court of the great Charles the Bold. The sword was the only implement in life for which I had any respect. And the pesky

French saw no need to learn our tongue when so many lands used their own clapper-clawed one.

Fortunately, there was only a minute or two to exchange greetings before there was a rustling around us, a swishing of dresses and clang of swords, signalling the arrival of the royal couple as people stood up in deference. On the other side of the box, I caught sight of my eldest son, Thomas, and his wife, Anne of York. The marriage might have made my son, brother-in-law to old *Goose*, and uncle to this present one, but what was the good of that with no issue to show for it. A poor breeder Anne had turned out to be, with puny infants who'd hardly survived the childbed, unlike her older sister, young Hal's mother. Now heading towards her mid-thirties, there wasn't much hope of another heir in that cradle to replace the one that had died last year. <<*No wonder Thomas looks as though he spends his days sipping verjuice*>> Next to him, my feckless third son was wearing his usual expression: that of a man who awoke in the morning expecting the day to deliver its usual round of disappointments and imagined wrongs. With my own enormous brood about to grow again (hopefully with another boy, not a girl to join the gaggle Agnes had already produced), I had no time at all for this male runt of my previous litter, though I supposed I'd have to find him a wealthy widow sooner rather than later. God help any woman who found herself a-bed with Edmund, a man ill fortune seemed to follow as surely as Dame Fortune smiled on his older brother.

<<*My Edward*>>

Normally, the moment the King and Queen had taken their seats, a trumpet would be blown and a herald step forward to announce the day's events. There were murmurings around me as people began to wonder at the delay. However, the reason for it soon became abundantly obvious as the portly French Ambassador made a somewhat startling re-appearance in the royal box, ostentatiously bowing to his royal hosts as he lowered his large backside onto a chair that had hastily been provided for him. I was relieved young Hal hadn't asked for one that was sure to break beneath the substantial bulk demanding shelter of it; it would be quite typical of his slightly cruel sense of humour. *<<Those of us with older heads upon our shoulders know that such a trivial (but humiliating) incident can rapidly lead to a broken treaty between two countries>>*

'I wish his chair had broken,' whispered the young French boy next to me, obviously having similar thoughts to my own, or rather of those of the King. He wasn't addressing me but his mother who immediately put her finger to her lips. The fact he didn't like the ridiculous shrill-gorged abbot didn't surprise me; what did surprise me was that he was speaking English.

'Hush, Tristan!' his mother whispered. 'Don't let your father hear you, for pity's sake.'

Out of the corner of my eye, I could see a sulky expression on the boy's fine features and when he spoke, his voice was fierce: 'What! Don't tell me you care what happens to that droning old boar-pig. I wish he'd crawl under a stone and die. Then he and Papa wouldn't be able to pack me off to his hell-hated monastery in Fécamp. I thought you were on my side, Maman.'

'Tristan! Not here. Not now.'

Listening to the young rascal's outburst (which I found most entertaining; nobody could accuse him of not having spirit), I could imagine how relieved his mother must be to hear the piercing tone of a trumpet below us. Interrupting what was obviously a very raw subject between the two of them. I couldn't quite work out her accent; however, there was the slightest trace of something. As for the boy, he was clearly one of those gifted souls who (unlike me) had room in his head for not only two whole languages but probably a whole host of them.

I knew Edward was first up to fight against his brother-in-law, Tom Knyvett. The two of them, together with Charles Brandon, were easily the three best jousters in the kingdom. As they rode into the lists, wearing the respective colours of their Houses, to the sound of their names being called, there were cheers on all sides of the arena. Again, I had a warm feeling inside. I had done my Muriel proud in my choice of a second husband for her after John Grey left her a widow. Young Tom was as dashing as her second brother, and she'd been kind enough to name her eldest son after her third, who hopefully would take after him in nothing else but name. She was still the same lively girl who'd once cut the beard of James of Scotland before his marriage to Princess Margaret, never forgetting the fifteen ells of cloth of gold she received. How long ago that seemed now but every time I thought of those weeks spent up in Edinburgh, it was with great affection. Muriel was my favourite daughter, much like Edward in character, more outgoing than her sister, Lizzie, who had married Tom Bullen, against my better judgement. The problem with that one was that he was always trying too hard. Unlike Edward who never had to try at all. Still, I suppose that was preferable to Edmund who wouldn't know what 'trying' meant if it hit him in the face with the force of a dozen gauntlets.

Tom and Edward had jousted against each other so often they could probably have done so in their sleep. As they thundered dramatically down the lists towards each other, milking their performances to the very last drop, I watched them splinter an equal number of lances. However, when they passed me on the final course, something odd happened. For a split second, Edward seemed to lose concentration as he glanced up in the direction of where I was seated. I was disconcerted; one of the main rules of jousting was to keep your eyes squarely ahead of you at all times. As he did this, there was a gasp from the young woman next to me and I distinctly heard her murmur my son's name. Or rather: "*Ned!*"

Luckily, Edward managed to regain his composure and went on to take the round from Tom. However, I was left puzzling about what I'd just heard. There was not a shred of a doubt in my mind I was mistaken. The small cry had come from her very heart. <<*Strange. Almost as if she knows Edward*>>

Chapter Twenty-Nine

*B*efore the next competitors arrived, I decided to strike up a conversation with the young Englishwoman. Fortunately, the Governor of Picardy was being avidly quizzed by an admiring female, simultaneously using both her French and her wiles.

'Madam, I am pleased to hear you are from these parts,' I began. 'Although I do speak some French, it's no time for an old man to attempt to perfect it.'

A pair of the greenest eyes I'd ever encountered stared straight into my own. They reminded me of the luminous waves lapping against the hull of a ship in the Narrow Sea.

'I'm sure you manage very well, Your Excellency.'

I was startled. Was she being charming or giving offence? Hard to tell. 'I can't quite place your accent.'

'I grew up in Cornwall.'

'And your family name?'

'Tredavoe.'

Nothing else. No smile. No attempt to make any conversation. Her son was watching us, a curious expression on his face. Was his mother always this unforthcoming?

<<*Tredavoe*>> An unusual name. But one I knew I'd heard somewhere before. 'Would I know your father?'

'He's dead.'

Now I was certain she was being ill-mannered but could not think for the life of me why. 'Do you have brothers or sisters?'

'One brother. William.'

<<*William Tredavoe*>> A pair of anxious green eyes under a thatch of blonde hair suddenly came to mind. I had an excellent memory for both names

and faces, and despite supposedly being a greybeard of sixty-five, I could easily remember events of forty years ago. Except, in this case I didn't have to. Suddenly, I understood exactly who this woman was and what she and Edward meant to each other. It had been the same year I'd done battle with James of Scotland. How many years ago was that now? I sucked in my breath as I counted back in time, half-wishing I hadn't set out on this particular path.

'How old are you, boy?' I asked her son, trying to keep my tone light.

'He's nearly twelve, Your Excellency.' This time I was sure there was a challenge in the woman's lovely eyes, as if daring me to ask the question.

But I didn't need to. Although on the outside, he was her son through and through, I didn't need to be a Scottish soothsayer to be certain that on the inside, he was a Howard through and through. On closer inspection, I could see he had Edward's slight build, slim face, and most telling of all, the distinctive Howard nose.

<<So, she did give birth to a child with my son>>

Fortunately for the boy, he'd inherited his mother's startling green eyes behind which his bastardy could be well hidden. I even remembered her name. Grace. *<<Of course>>* That's what Edward had said when he spotted her at the entrance to the royal box. Not "*disgrace*". No wonder he nearly took a tumble. I was pricked by a twinge of shame. Although she'd clearly married very well, I succeeded in halting '*First Love*' in its tracks, snuffing out the future before it even had chance to begin. Edward only had two bastard sons to show for his efforts at fatherhood. Nothing from between the marital sheets. *<<Well...he has three of them now>>* I wondered if the French father knew he was bringing up a Howard by-blow. Preparing him for the Church by the sound of things. *<<God's Teeth! I can no more see a Howard male in the Church than I can the Pope entering the lists>>*

The memory of what had happened between Edward and Grace was as fresh and crisp in my mind as if it were yesterday. The girl's brother had ridden up to Ashwellthorpe Manor one bitterly cold February morning in 1497, asking for an urgent audience with me. Luckily, Edward and his brothers were out hunting and their ailing mother in her chamber. There was no need for me to bother her with something she couldn't mend. I remembered congratulating the boy for his good sense in realizing a union between our two families was impossible. I could even conjure up our likely conversation:

"*As you probably know, William, these past dozen years have not been kind to the Howards. The last thing we need is an alliance with a family in a corner of the world upon which the King frowns.*"

The boy's face was ashen and his manner anguished. "*I understand. But Grace must never find out I've been here. She's my only sister. And if I were to lose her—*"

Although I recalled hearing a humming in my head so loud I could hardly concentrate, I reassured him that neither of us was going to 'lose' anyone. I told him I needed to take a walk in the gardens to clear my head; standing by the moat, watching the carp in the waters beneath, weaving their merry dance, it came to me what we must do. Hurrying back up to my study, I explained to William it was imperative he follow my instructions. He was to return to Zennor Castle and persuade his sister to go ahead with the French wedding. Hearing this, he became further distressed.

"*She'll never agree to that. I've already tried. And besides, what if there's a babe to worry about?*"

I remained extremely calm, as calm as the millpond on the other side of our village. "*William, all you have to do is listen to me. If you'd been at the English court even for a sixth of the time I have, you'd realize that in order to succeed in life, you sometimes have to do things differently. Of course your sister won't agree to wed another man unless—*"

"*Unless?*"

"*Unless you explain to her that she must proceed. If there's a chance she's with child, she must go ahead for the sake of your family honour. Tell her time is against her. She must wait for Edward to speak to me. And then wait for me to obtain permission from the King. Assure her marriages can quickly be dissolved if an impediment is discovered. And the person trying to dissolve it important enough.*"

"*I don't understand.*"

I remembered feeling sorry for the lad; his anguish at betraying his sister was making him beef-witted. *"Let her think Edward will come and get her wherever she is. Bringing with him the assurance of an annulment."*

"Even in France?"

"Especially in France. Remind her the child she might be carrying is a Howard. And reassure her I'll speak to the King on their behalf."

"What about Edward? He'll never agree to give up my sister."

"Leave him to me."

William Tredavoe galloped away to help his sister compose a letter to my son (to be sent when she reached France, not before; this was vital to ensure that Edward couldn't carry out some foolish last-minute dash). In the letter, they would explain she might be with child and was only marrying the Frenchman for the sake of appearances, knowing the marriage would soon be dissolved.

Dealing with Edward proved more difficult than I'd first imagined. In order to give myself time to prepare everything, I made a trip to London, thus preventing him from having that all-important conversation with me. When I returned about a week later, I could see he was itching to speak to me but still I delayed. Finally, when I could put him off no longer, I led him into my study and sat listening while he discussed his desire to wed the Cornish girl. It soon became obvious he had genuine feelings for her. I would bet a golden crown he had his horse outside, ready and waiting to cover the countless miles to join her. What was it about the furthermost tip of Cornwall that seemed to cast such a spell over the males in my family? I put this latest disaster down to my enduring friendship with Roger Trewellis from Mount's Bay. He'd helped me out once long ago when love drew me southwards, and it seemed he'd also been instrumental in the introduction between Edward and this Grace Tredavoe. A star-crossed meeting of which I'd known nothing…until it was too late.

Poor Edward. He stood no more chance with the trap I'd prepared for him than a fly getting entangled in a spider's web. By now, I was able to act my part with perfection.

"Edward, this is so strange. 'Grace Tredavoe' did you say?"

I could still recall his expression of surprise; he'd obviously been preparing himself for a completely different reaction from me: at the very least, an explosion of rage, certainly not this muted acceptance. When I spoke, my tone was mild.

"I received a letter this morning from my old friend, Giles Daubeney—"

"The Lord Deputy of Calais?" Edward looked perplexed, no doubt wondering in which direction our conversation was headed.

"That's right. You won't believe it but he mentioned your Grace in his letter."

A deep frown creased my son's brow and I could see him swallowing hard. *"What did he say?"*

Making a small movement (that unbeknownst to my son, masked my inner triumph), I turned to the table next to me and casually picked up the letter and handed it to him. As he read the words (which I already knew by heart because I'd dictated them to a scribe myself), his expression changed and his face became as chalky as the parchment. *"W-wed,"* he stammered, *"Grace wed him?"*

"I don't know who 'he' is, my boy, but yes, it seems she has wed him."

Edward flung the letter back on the table with great force. *"I don't believe a word. I must go to her at once."*

I hadn't been expecting this. Reaching out, I put my hand on his arm. *"Edward, please see sense. For whatever reason, your Grace has wed another man and is now in France. You'll soon learn that young girls in the throes of first love can transfer their love as swiftly as they change hands or point their toes in a Gavotte. Quickly bestowing their kisses elsewher—"*

"Grace isn't like that, Father! She loves me."

I pretended to look sympathetic. *"Then prove it to me. Write her a letter this very day. And when I see evidence of her love for you by return of messenger, I'll do everything in my power to free her from the marriage. I'll even ask Giles Daubeney to help me."*

❧

Looking back, I thought about what happened next. As I brushed that first letter he wrote to her against the flame of a candle in my study, I wondered how many more would follow. Shortly afterwards, Grace's first letter from France arrived, no doubt sent via the trusted Cornish maidservant I'd been told she was taking with her. I'd told William the best way to succeed was to keep as close to the truth as possible: to make his sister believe the letters she sent were reaching Edward. Well, they reached Ashwelthorpe Manor…just not my son. In the end, there were so many I lost count. With every burnt (unopened) intercepted letter I flung into the grate, I fervently hoped their passion would gradually be extinguished. To my relief, after several long months, the correspondence ceased. Strangely enough, at exactly the same time on either side of the Narrow Sea. It was as if Grace and Edward both awoke one morning and decided to give up the ghost on their doomed love affair.

I waited a further nine months and then showed Edward another letter supposedly from Giles (also dictated by me), telling of the future count and countess's joy at the (fictitious) birth of their first son. After that, Grace Tredavoe's name was never mentioned between us again. When it came to marriage, I had no problem persuading Edward to eschew younger women and embrace all the financial possibilities a rich widow, ten or fifteen years his senior, could offer him, even if it meant no child could come from the marital bed.

❧

Perhaps it was for the best there was no further opportunity to converse with the Countess d'Ardres during the interval. After our brief conversation, she pointedly kept her back to me and spoke to her husband and son in French, obviously wishing to block any further intrusion into her life. I didn't altogether blame her. In her head (even if she couldn't prove it), I'd stolen her chance for happiness with my son. I was somewhat gratified to note she seemed perfectly relaxed in her good-looking husband's company and had clearly captivated him. I looked over at Tristan and for a fleeting moment, wished I could get to know my grandson better. Fortunately, such a crook-pated thought was quickly dispelled by the start of the action. As a man with my exceptional vigour, I had no need of a grandson when I was awaiting the birth of a son from my second marriage. I was grateful to Charles Brandon for having the crowds in fits of laughter by his display of horsemanship. My newly-found grandson let out loud whoops of encouragement as Charles made his black stallion pirouette around the stands. <<*So like his real father*>>

Towards the end of the day, the herald stepped forward and announced there was to be a slight change to the schedule:

'For your pleasure, two "Stranger Knights" are going to fight.'

<<*'Stranger Knights'*?>> I wasn't sure I liked the sound of this. Edward certainly hadn't mentioned anything. Of course, the crowd loved it when two knights rode out with visors down and with no identifiable coats-of-arms. I didn't need to look behind me to know the King would be enjoying this. My grandson certainly was.

The two 'Stranger Knights' ran four courses and broke as many staves. For some reason, I wasn't able to enjoy the display as much as the crowd around me. I was wondering why this was when disaster struck. There was a deafening sound as one of the knights knocked the other to the ground. I'd seen men lose their lives at a tournament for less. Several men ran up to the felled knight, one of them, Edward. I was alarmed when I recognized terror in his demeanour as he started pulling at the man's visor. <<*What in God's name is going on*>>

By this time, the felled knight's opponent had dismounted and reached the little group. Edward sprang to his feet and threw his cap into the air. 'God save the King!' he cried, as the second 'Stranger Knight' pulled up his visor.

Immediately, there was a buzzing akin to that of a thousand bees: word had quickly spread that the two 'Stranger Knights' were none other than the King and his groom of the stool. The watching crowd was immediately shocked into realization it could have been their beloved King lying there stricken. Instead, it was poor Will Compton who should damned well have kept to his task of wiping his master's arse instead of joining him in the lists.

I felt a mixture of fear and fury. And frustration with my son for being part of this and keeping it from me. But then I glanced over at the shining face of Edward's bastard son and began to calm down. <<*I was young once, fought and risked my neck on countless occasions. Like Edward, I had a first love, and lost her too*>> I should be pleased that sharing the King's secret meant Edward was riding higher in his favour than almost anyone else in the kingdom, apart from the hapless Will Compton, Charles Brandon, and two or three others. I watched as the groom of the stool was carefully carried out of the arena, thinking: <<*this is a day of not only surprising discovery but one when I should be counting my blessings*>>

TRISTAN

Chapter Thirty

*W*hy can't we stay longer? I want to meet the King and Queen.'

I could feel all my joy and high spirits draining away like the contents of an upturned tankard, left unattended at a banquet. In the distance, I could still hear music and laughter coming from the lists and could well imagine King Henry congratulating all the knights who'd fought so hard.

<<*Would that I could be amongst them*>>

My father was clearly in no mood to listen to any protests. 'Because, Tristan, I promised Antoine Bohier we would dine with him at Fulham Palace. I've accepted William Warham's invitation now.'

I didn't care how angry I made him. 'Why can't he go by himself?'

My mother laid a warning hand on my arm. 'It's been a very trying day for the Abbot. I think he was expecting something quite different when he was appointed French Ambassador. Not the public insult he received today. He doesn't want to dine with the Archbishop of Canterbury and be the sole Frenchman there.'

At least her remark made my father smile. As she always did. Turning to her, he lifted her hand to his lips and kissed it. 'Louis should have appointed you as ambassador instead, *chérie*. Though I couldn't bear to be parted from you for long.'

My mother smiled sweetly at him before giving me a sidelong glance as if to say: *I've saved you this time, I'm not sure if I can again.*

I felt so angry about being made to leave just when everything was getting more exciting. I wanted to know what happened to one of the Stranger Knights, whether he'd survived his fall. I kicked several stones on the path in front of me. 'Who was that old man you were talking to?' I asked my mother. 'The one you were rude to?'

My father whipped round on me in a fury, making me think of a male lion protecting his territory. Yet, in doing so, attacking his own cub.

'Tristan! Watch that tongue of yours. I can never imagine your mother being rude to anyone.'

I felt like switching to English to exclude him but knew I would lose my mother's support if I did that. *"It's not fair to your father to speak English in front of him,"* she'd always say. *"He can't help it if English is such a difficult language to learn."*

Then he should try harder, I wanted to retort but never did. I loved my mother more than anything or anyone on earth and could never imagine saying one word to wound her. Besides, not being able to speak English worked to my advantage as it meant my father never had any desire to accompany us down to Cornwall.

"You go, Grace," he'd said this time. *"They're your people and you deserve some time alone with them. To speak your own tongue. It would be selfish of me to keep you to myself all the time. William and Alys know they're welcome to come to Ardres Castle whenever they want. With little Cecily, of course."*

'Who was the old man sitting next to us?' I asked again, changing the wording of my question to keep the peace.

'That was the Earl of Surrey,' answered my father. 'From what Antoine Bohier tells me, he's a very colourful character.'

'Had you met him before, Maman?' I asked.

'No, I'm unfamiliar with any of the Howards.'

My father gave a shrug. 'I realized he must be the same earl Gilbert Talbot was telling me about: the one that wed a young girl on the death of his first wife. But keeps marrying off one of his sons to rich old widows. I wonder if it was the one we met today. You English certainly have a funny way of doing things,' he said, smiling at my mother.

Whenever I was irked with my father…which was often, I thought of myself as English. Whenever something in England irked me, I thought of myself as French.

<< Today, I am definitely English>>

'Couldn't you and I stay a little longer here, Maman? I want to explore London more.'

My mother understood me so well; she'd known how much I admired the "Stranger Knights". How I wanted to be like that one day. Not a fusty old priest, dried up inside and out.

She reached out to stroke my hair. 'I'm afraid it's not possible this time. We have to get back to relieve Nicolas of his duties. It's not fair to leave him alone for too long. I know Bernard Guillart is with him but even so. He's still so young. And your father has already done it once this year when he accompanied King Louis to Italy.'

Apart from my joy at travelling alone with my mother down to Zennor Castle, the other positive thing about this trip was that Nicolas had stayed behind. As usual, whenever we travelled to England, Gilles went off to visit his relatives in Venice.

"Unfortunately, I need a member of the family to remain in Ardres Castle to represent us," my father had said to Nicolas. *"But I promise I'll take you with me on my next trip."*

"To the next war?" Nicolas asked, his face alight with hope while looking pointedly at me, knowing I'd never be asked to go.

"Let's not wish for war," my mother said. *"It's bad enough when it happens."*

Even though I'd been pleased to hear Nicolas getting a reprimand, it wasn't enough to make up for being asked to be a priest, not a soldier.

I continued to tramp bad-temperedly along next to my parents, leaving behind all the merrymaking as we made our way down to the river's edge. How clay-brained that we had to catch a barge to the Bishop's palace at Fulham to attend some sleep-inducing supper. I rued my ill luck: to have the full-gorged Abbot of Fécamp looming large in my life, a man who, according to my fly-bitten father, regarded me as *'already one of his flock'*, was bad enough. To make matters worse, I also had to deal with the venomed Nicolas, his spiteful remarks, taunts and general ability to make my life hardly worth living. If only I could be given the chance to prepare a large pot of soup for the Abbot and my worst enemy, not forgetting to season it with a few seeds of white henbane for good measure.

When we arrived at the small landing stage, I caught sight of the Abbot already seated upon William Warham's impressive barge, his massive red bulk looking worryingly capable of capsizing any river vessel.

'*Viens ici*, Tristan,' he called out, a beslubbering smile painted across his face, his scarlet cheeks wobbling as he spoke. He patted the wooden bench. 'I've saved you a place next to me.'

PART FIVE

YOUTH MUST HAVE SOME DALLIANCE

'Dulce bellum inexpertio.'

{'War is sweet to those who have not tried it.'}

Desiderius Erasmus
(1466-1536).

HOUSE OF HOWARD

Chapter Thirty-One

Two years later. September 30ᵗʰ, 1511. Calais harbour.

oes the King know you're here, Tom?'

'I neither know nor care.'

Gilbert Talbot reached out and patted me on the back as we walked along the quay. The wind was buffeting the pair of us with as little mercy as it was showing the ships moored there, many of them proudly flying the flag of Saint George. Their huge white sails were flapping wildly, with all the vigour of a row of voluminous bed sheets, hung out to dry in the gardens of the Palace of Westminster by the chapped hands of the royal laundresses.

Several times we passed a merchant or two trying to strike a hard bargain with a fearsome looking captain or his boatswain, their voices rising above the shrieking wind as they tirelessly haggled. Glancing at the crestfallen face of one merchant we passed, tugging his cloak about him, I guessed not a single keg of wine, sack of wool, or ell of cloth, was going to make its way to the nearby warehouses anytime soon from the hold of the boat he'd just left.

It was an effort for anyone to make themselves heard above this racket but next to me, Gilbert was making an admirable attempt. <<*Fortunately, my ears and eyes (and all parts of my anatomy) are still in excellent working order despite my mature years*>>

'How long have you and I known each other?' he yelled. 'Nigh on sixty years, I'd say. Since before I was breeched and you had your first hornbook. Easily from when the Yorkists and Lancastrians started ripping each other's throats out.'

I waited until there was a slight lull in the wind before replying. 'You mean, just after we lost Normandy for good?'

'That's right.'

'It should have been the end of you and me at Bosworth Field.'

'Because you begged me to finish off the job Henry of Richmond's men had begun?'

'Yes.'

'Ask me to kill my boyhood friend? Because you wanted to fall on the sword of one gentle born.'

'You refused to humour me, you dog-hearted whoreson.'

'A fine way to talk to the man who saved your life, Tom Howard. I think it's earned me the right to ask you what's happened between you and the King.'

'What! How he dismissed me from court like a pox-riddled doxy from a stew. I'm still smarting from the indignity.'

'Ha! You always did have a way with words.'

The wind suddenly dropped completely so we could hear each other again. Right on cue, the sun came out, bathing us in pleasing warmth. Immediately, I felt my mood lift and was even able to smile back at my friend. We'd both aged, of course, and I could see that (unlike me, who prided myself on still having the wiry frame of one of my prize whippets) a love of his second wife, Audrey's, cooking had added flesh to Gilbert's bones. The approach of old age hadn't completely passed me by either. My knees were beginning to ache and I had more silver threaded through my hair than before. But to me the streaks were a badge of honour.

<<*Evidence of a long life, lived well and to the full*>>

Gilbert still had the same ready smile he'd always had, and his slightly faded blue eyes reflected the same wisdom and humour I'd long set store by.

'It's true,' I said. 'That toad-spotted, bum-bailey of a royal almoner, *Snake*, couldn't wait to write to Richard Fox reporting my disgrace. There was such a red mist in my mind, I could think of nothing else to do but come to you. I rode like the clappers to Dover and jumped on the first vessel crossing the Narrow Sea.'

'And I'm very glad you did. I take it you tried again to dissuade the King from declaring war on France.'

'I did. But the Tudor boy is as stubborn as a mule. He's determined to risk his royal neck in the lists and has got his sights set on the spoils of war. The treaty Fox, Ruthal, and I negotiated last March is as good as dead. All Henry thinks and talks about is invading France.'

Gilbert laughed. 'He certainly lives up to your description of him: "*A Tudor rose with thorns*". I wish to God he and Katherine hadn't lost the prince in January. Maybe it would have calmed him down.'

'But they *did* lose little Henry. And nothing and no one can turn his head away from the idea of leading an army over the Narrow Sea.'

'It doesn't help that Henry's father-in-law—'

'That wily old fox, Ferdinand.'

'Yes. It doesn't help he's joined forces with the Pope, declaring the French got more out of the Cambrai agreement than either of them—'

'Or that Rome has invited Henry to join a Holy League against France. He's acting like a moonstruck maid, meeting a swain in a meadow.'

'Speaking of lovesick swains, Tom, doesn't Henry realize the Pope is panting after Venice? And Ferdinand after Naples. Not France.'

'That flap-mouthed Andrea Badoer—'

'The Venetian Ambassador?'

'Yes. He's stoking the fires of war, telling the King that old Louis of France wants to be "*monarch of the whole world*".'

Gilbert rolled his eyes. 'We can only pray the good ambassador falls into the Grand Canal on his next trip back to Venice.'

By this time, we'd almost reached the end of the quay. It felt good to be able to talk like this to an old friend who understood my predicament, even if he couldn't help me out of it. Just offer me food, board and good counsel for a few days. I knew I was exaggerating a little out of frustration. Young Hal hadn't actually dismissed me, merely suggested I might like to spend some time with Agnes who was expecting another child. A second boy, I was certain of it. There was nothing wrong with Howard seed: perhaps another thing about me that didn't sit well with the royal pup. <<*A man of nearly seventy able to produce what a youth of twenty cannot*>>

'What about your boys, Tom. Can't they help out? Try to change the King's mind.'

I let out a dismissive laugh. 'The King doesn't like Thomas. Not that I blame him for that. You know my eldest is a chilly devil at the best of times; even his dogs don't care for him. And Henry has no time at all for Edmund. Nor do I blame him for that either. Sometimes I think 'tis both a miracle and a tragedy that one survived the childbed. Animals seem to know much better than humans how to deal with those too puny to survive.'

'He's a fine jouster.'

'A loggerhead, for sure. Instead of showing cunning like Charles Brandon - and all the others - did back in the lists in February, either tying with the King or letting him win, what does my idiot of a third son do? Knock the proud young Tudor pup to the ground so many times he must have been choking on the dust in his mouth.'

'God's Teeth! Henry will never forgive him.'

'He hasn't. Edmund hasn't been invited to a single joust since that day.'

'You've got new boys to follow.'

'Yes. William in the cradle and another in the belly.'

'What about Edward. He's still in favour.'

'Yes, but for some boil-brained reason, he spends his time dripping poison about James of Scotland into the royal ear. When the Venetian Ambassador has finished dripping poison about France into the other one.'

'Ah, I see your problem. It must be hard for you. Especially as you struck up such a good rapport with the Scotsman when you went up for the wedding.'

'I did. I can honestly say James deserved every word of any praise I heaped upon him back then. Truly a king amongst kings. Whereas I swear our own sometimes shows less sense than my Lizzie's little George.'

Gilbert pointed straight ahead. 'How about a visit to "*The Sign of the Ship*" to drown our sorrows? I know for a fact a cargo of the best Malmsey arrived from Madeira this morning, by way of La Coruna.'

As we headed in the general direction of the church of Saint Nicholas, I glanced up at the wooden houses with their crowstepped gables, all huddled together as if for safety, some of them with sizeable gardens. I'd always had a soft spot for Calais (a town rising starkly from the sea, encircled by high walls, showing off its turrets and battlements with pride), ever since my own father brought me here on a trading trip when I was twenty. It was a few years before he became Deputy Governor, my friend, Gilbert's, current post. If it was true that affection for a place can be in someone's blood, then it was in mine. Coming back to see Gilbert, I felt that connection again, perhaps the same sort of bond a woman has for her unborn child: a pull as strong as one of the tidal currents in the water beyond the harbour. Little wonder the town was known as 'the brightest jewel in England's crown'. It was a place teeming with traders and seamen, rubbing shoulders with the local folk. With a grand flourish, Lantern Gate Street wound its way through the middle, the hustle and bustle of its shops, including my favourite goldsmith's, a constant reminder that the laudatory epithet given to Calais was entirely deserved.

We paused in front of a very large house, obviously belonging to someone of rank, set back in a plot of land, more meadow than garden. Two youths and a younger boy were taking full advantage of the space to engage in a game of what looked like '*Pallone*' as it was called in Italy, or '*La grosse boule*', over the border here in France. The three of them looked to be having the time of their lives, using both hands and feet to navigate a large ball made of leather and pig's bladder around the field.

'Those are Guy d'Ardres' boys,' Gilbert said.

'Guy d'Ardres?'

'The Governor of Picardy. I've known him since he was a young boy. I was delighted when his father chose an English wife for him. He and Grace must be inside visiting the Baynhams.'

Of course, hearing Guy d'Ardres' name again, my interest was immediately piqued; if I was not mistaken, the third member of the group, as blonde as his brothers were dark, was my very own grandson, *Tristan* (grown taller since I'd last seen him). I was not about to confide in Gilbert, not when I hadn't even mentioned it to the boy's own father. Only my wherryman friend, Robert Warner, knew my secret and the only one he'd tell was the Thames. Fortunately, the Count and his wife had taken their son and left the tournament early the day I met them, rather than waiting to mingle. I'd felt a mixture of relief and disappointment at not getting to know the boy better. But had decided it was for the best; Edward didn't need anything to distract him from his brilliant destiny: certainly not a thwarted love affair that belonged to the past not the future. As a way of making reparation, I'd given my first-born son with Agnes the same name as the boy's Cornish uncle. It had somehow seemed the right thing to do.

One of the group in front of me seemed particularly talented, the darker of Tristan's older two brothers (obviously from an earlier marriage); I watched as he hit the ball repeatedly, never missing once. I'd gladly welcome that kind of skill into the English army any day.

'The Governor should be proud of his sons,' I said.

'Well, they're not all his sons. One of them is his ward. Guy took him in when he was orphaned. He's the one playing as though his life depended upon it.'

At that moment, the youth he was referring to gave the ball a resounding kick, causing it to land right at our feet. I watched him come running over, his gait so graceful it was if he was gliding across the grass, his feet barely making contact with the ground. He'd make an excellent horseman. In fact, with that kind of instinctive use of his eyes and entire body, he'd excel at any sport. And in any war.

Beside me, Gilbert reached out to pat the boy on the back. '*Bien joué*, Nicolas!'

This name brought back a memory of a brother of mine who'd died young. The youth in front of me who was about nineteen or twenty, looked pleased but there was also a guarded expression in his eyes. Up close, he was every inch a nobleman; with his dark intense looks, I could see he'd be a draw for all the women. There was obviously a touch of vanity there too, I thought, as my eyes were drawn to a turquoise ring on his right hand. <<*I have a strange feeling I've met this Nicolas before but as he's French and lives in France, I know it can't be possible*>>

❦

The sound of a child's voice calling out my grandson's name interrupted my thoughts. Looking down, I saw an exquisite little girl of about eight or nine, holding the hand of an older woman.

'Tristan!' she called again, but was studiously ignored.

With their unusual eyes and fair skin and hair, there was no mistaking the family bond between woman and child. Gilbert introduced them as Symonne de Fleury and her granddaughter, Valentine. He and this Symonne began an animated conversation in French but after a few perfunctory sentences in the bat-fowling tongue, I turned my attention back to the ball game. For some reason, I found my mind wandering to another time: my second visit to France....

It was nearly twenty years after my first, a month before King Edward's death. I could almost feel the chill March winds biting into my skin as I recalled how he'd sent me to Calais on a mission. Happily, I'd been introduced to a young Frenchwoman at a banquet thrown by the Deputy Governor at his home, the old Staple Inn, just off Lantern Gate Street. I'd long forgotten her name but not how she captivated me, distracting me from the cold that seemed to seep into my very bones. I hadn't thought about her since that far-off day when I confided in the King of Scotland. Admitting to him that to my disappointment, she'd only had eyes for the young Duc d'Orléans (as King Louis was then known). Not for me. But what eyes they'd been. Even though more than a quarter of a century had elapsed, I could still remember them: a perfect copy of the palest blue summer sky. If my memory served me correctly, I hadn't bothered pressing my suit; instead, I took a different Frenchwoman to my bed that night who'd served me perfectly well.

I turned back to the other three, away from the game where a squabble had broken out between Tristan and the Governor's ward. I wasn't surprised; once or twice I'd noticed my grandson deliberately kicking the ball away from the older boy. I chuckled to myself; whoever this Nicolas was, he hadn't bargained on having to deal with a Howard bastard in the family nest.

❦

'*Non! Ce n'est pas vrai.*' Symonne de Fleury had a smile on her lovely face. For a woman of over forty, she was still a great beauty.

'I think I'd best retire from the conversation,' Gilbert murmured to me. 'The little one's telling her grandam to beware because I'm one of the warlike Talbots sent to create havoc in France.'

I burst out laughing. 'I've never seen anyone less likely to frighten small children. Now, if it were me she was talking about....'

'I don't know what I did to make her say it. Before that, I was telling her grandam she has a following of grey-haired suitors beating a path up to her house so long it would stretch the entire length of Calais and back again.'

'The good lady is a widow?'

'The most eligible the length and breadth of the Pale of Calais and Picardy.' He lowered his voice. 'Not for her lands or jointure, it must be said. But for her beauty. That once captured the heart of the present King of France, so I've heard.'

I was startled. <<*Surely, it can't be...can it?*>> However, I was given no further time for thought as my grandson's quarrel with Guy d'Ardres' ward was becoming more boisterous. The two boys were facing each other at close quarters, their features contorted with rage. I could hear my grandson pushing the older boy to the limit with his taunts. Did Tristan have no sense at all? His foe obviously had every advantage if any punches were thrown. Tristan's older brother was doing his best to calm the situation but to no avail. By now, goaded beyond endurance, Nicolas had raised his arm, prepared to strike.

'*Smettila, Nico!*' I heard Tristan's brother saying as he stepped between them.

'Italian...Spanish?' I asked Gilbert, curious.

'Gilles's mother was an Italian countess so Guy employed an Italian tutor for the boys to honour her memory.'

My friend moved forward to intervene, but there was no need. Guy d'Ardres' ward took a step backwards from a red-faced Tristan and held up his hands. He was pale and his mouth was set with anger but he remained in control of himself. The mettle of a good soldier.

If only the lad were English born, not French, I'd take him straight back to Norfolk with me. <<*If this foolish war goes ahead (which seems more and more likely), we'll need every good man we can lay our hands on*>>

NICOLAS

Chapter Thirty-Two

Hallowtide, 1511. Ardres Castle.

ith her long eyelashes and creamy skin, the young woman sleeping so peacefully next to him, resembled more an angel from above than the alluring wanton of the night before. Even her very name suggested purity: one whiter than the driven snow. Four years older, Blanche Dufresny seemed to have lived four lifetimes when it came to the art of love. At twenty-four, the Countess's maid had already seen one husband to the grave, without regret, Nicolas guessed, having met the wheezing greybeard once. He was certain she hadn't learnt her tricks of the trade in the old man's bedchamber. Blanche was soon to be wed again to another ageing widower who'd flung a sack of gold at her father the moment he set eyes on her.

Fortunately for Nicolas's youthful masculine pride, not all the ideas last night had been hers. Reaching out, he gently touched the corner of her full mouth which was still slightly stained with dewberry juice. She stirred but not enough to waken. He gave a satisfied smile, knowing himself to be the reason for her exhaustion.

When she'd arrived at his bedchamber last night at the arranged time, after a passionate kiss or two, he quickly helped her unlace. Discarding her clothes with kittenish grace, she stretched out on his bed, anticipation in her shining eyes. Nicolas walked over to a table and picked up a silver platter (pilfered from the Castle kitchens) upon which were scattered some late ripening dewberries he'd picked in the woods earlier in the day. He cared nothing for the warning that at this time of year they were to be avoided because the Devil had spat on them. Blanche reached out to take one but he pulled the platter away.

"They're not for eating," he teased. *"At least not for you to eat."*

Slowly peeling off his scarlet and white satin doublet and hose as if he were in no particular hurry for what was coming next (which wasn't true at all), he noted Blanche's sharp little teeth gnawing at her bottom lip. Reaching out for a few of the sweet berries, he surprised her by sprinkling them over her luscious body, finding it deeply arousing to watch her squirm her way through the anointment. However, her giggles soon turned to gasps when he took two berries and pushed them hard against either nipple, waiting until the red tips hardened before swooping down with his mouth, licking away every last drop of the juice. He did the same with a few more he'd dropped on her belly, devouring them in the same fashion until she could bear it no longer. Grabbing him around the neck, she pulled him down on top of her and languidly slid her legs apart, murmuring: *"You've won me, mon seigneur, now take your prize."*

Blanche. He pushed a strand of her long black hair from her cheek.

<<*What would Dame Grace say if she knew how her demure lady's maid behaved past the witching hour, and with her own ward, no less?*>> Nicolas was sure she wouldn't approve at all. It seemed a fine irony Blanche had been selected to play the harp with four other young women in the candlelit chapel this evening to aid the souls of the dead in their passage through purgatory. He'd take great satisfaction watching her as she plucked the strings of her harp with those wicked fingers of hers, an imaginary cloak of dewberries adorning her narrow shoulders.

Dame Grace always liked to celebrate Hallowtide; he knew it made her feel less homesick if she performed the time honoured rituals of her Cornish childhood: under her tutelage, the villagers of Ardres now lit bonfires and went around from door to door, masks upon their faces, perhaps reciting a poem or two in exchange for a spiced soul cake. Dame Grace had explained that each cake symbolized a soul in purgatory. She also mentioned a custom peculiar to Scotland:

"There, it is usual to go around the village with painted and even blackened faces. If the welcome the mummers receive isn't considered warm enough, all kinds of mischief will be unleashed on the house dwellers."

"I like the sound of that," Tristan had laughed. *"I can think of some unwelcoming house dwellers in our very own village. Or even here in the Castle."*

As he listened to Blanche's even breathing and felt her warm flesh pressed next to his own, Nicolas thought how fitting it was that today should be the qualling miscreant's fourteenth birthday. Hallowtide was known as the day when the veil dividing this world and the next was at its thinnest, allowing the souls of the deceased and evil spirits to walk the earth unchallenged.

∽

Thankfully, Nicolas got on well with Gilles, finding him happy-go-lucky - bone idle, of course, preferring to spend his time dicing, or playing cards than charging around the countryside like his younger brother and Nicolas. Right from the start, the two of them had always competed in everything and, until recently, Nicolas, being bigger and stronger, had no problem winning. But things were beginning to change. At the Feast of the Assumption running at the ring this past August, the conniving, earth-vexing Tristan had almost but not quite managed to best him.

"Same time, next year, Nicolas," he'd said, clearly intending it to be a challenge, not a compliment.

"Same time, next year. And the result will still be the same."

<<*Ventre Saint Quenet!*>> Thus far, Nicolas had no equal at the joust in the whole of Picardy.

∽

At least, there was one area in which Tristan would never be able to take part. <<*Love…and women*>>

As a future churchman, they weren't supposed to play any part in his life and once he left to join the monastery his father had selected for him, there would be very little chance for him to discover what he was missing. Which left the field wide open for Nicolas. After that long-ago talk with Monsieur Guy, he discovered his company was not displeasing to the females in the Castle - even though his heart had never truly been touched by any of them. He'd stumbled for the first couple of times in the game of love and could still be as nervous as a boy about to take part in his first joust when faced with a woman like Blanche. Over the past five or six years, he'd invented his own set of rules, now finely honed. Monsieur Guy had a vast library, including many romances such as '*Tristan and Iseult*'. The ladies of the Ardres household had a particular fondness for these tales and Nicolas would often be called to the Countess's boudoir to read aloud. His audience, including Blanche, smiled and sighed as they bent over their needlework, their needles flying in and out of the tapestries on their laps. There seemed to be an intimate connection between the threads of the love stories to which they were listening and the ones they were stitching.

Dame Grace (in the role of a cherished mother) made Nicolas want to behave like a knight in a courtly tale, not an ill-mannered boor, more suited for the stables than a lady's boudoir. '*Le Roman de la Rose*' was her favourite book and some lines could have been written about him:

> '*Ou vintième an de mon âage*
> *Ou point qu'Amors prent le paage*
> *Des jones gens.*'
> {'When I the age of twenty had attained -
> The age when love controls a young man's heart.'}

Courtly behaviour was complicated and Nicolas didn't want to make any mistakes. He preferred to draw matters out as he had with Blanche - taking time to make his intentions perfectly clear...then wait. Where was the satisfaction if there was no hunt at all - or the quarry too easily won? Most of his attempts at seduction had been little more than a stolen kiss or two. Perhaps a few more daring caresses, but further intimacy, he mostly chose to forgo.

After all, he owed due respect to Monsieur Guy and Dame Grace for taking him into their home. He was different from many of the young men of his acquaintance, relentless in their whoring, hardly able to remember a face - let alone a name, a few months hence. Although he was known to like female company, he guessed he'd bedded a tiny fraction of the number of most other youths of a similar age. If a month…or even three…or four passed without finding solace in a kiss, it was preferable to taking what he didn't want just for the sake of it.

There were several possibilities of how he might begin the game of love, depending on whether the woman was high-born like Blanche - or one of the Ardres Castle servants. If from the nobility…or married: a single burning glance - very fleeting - across the great hall might suffice; a shared laugh over some jest, perhaps even made by the husband or betrothed (this always added a delicious frisson to proceedings); the most casual of brushes against the woman's forearm (never anywhere more intimate) in passing, that could be construed by others as accidental - but never was; the merest extra pressure of the hand towards the end of a rendition of the sedate bass dance (*that* was guaranteed to set both pulses racing); catching the woman's eye just as he was about to place a goblet of wine to his lips, devour a piece of meat - or bite into a fig (this made it easy to get his message across, although it rather spoilt the fun; the chase had to be at least interesting); the same went for holding a woman's gaze a fraction of a second too long - or using the opportunity of having her full attention to place his forefinger innocently upon his lower lip and rub it several times in a rueful manner: in a mirror image of what he wanted to do to her; many an enjoyable encounter had occurred after stroking his chin thoughtfully, always immediately looking away afterwards - making the woman wonder what it would be like to feel those fingers doing the same to her body; only once, when he couldn't wait to take a young woman to his bed, had a whispered invitation in her ear resulted in capitulation that very night.

The methods for a member of the servant class were different - but equally effective. Nicolas never treated these females with anything other than respect, but he was able to make his actions far bigger and bolder: a pretty serving maid's hand would be laughingly grabbed and pressed to his lips; he would bow graciously to another as thanks for some service performed, such as returning a freshly laundered shirt to his bedchamber; he would compliment a kitchen maid on the excellence of the food that day; a stray hair helped back into its place beneath a cap was perfectly capable of winning an already partially willing heart.

His male rivals might resent him but what they failed to comprehend was that not one of Nicolas's actions was ever feigned. That would have made him shallow...or even devious. And never once had he been called to the Governor's presence to defend his behaviour.

Blanche snuggled up to him and put her head on his chest but still did not awaken. She was young and beautiful but age had been of no account to a crusty old Spanish soldier who'd visited the Castle long ago with his voluptuous, but no longer youthful mistress. Someone asked him why he hadn't chosen a pretty young thing instead.

In response, the soldier let out a roar of laughter and slapped his thigh. "*Because....* '*A las visperas se conoce la fiest.*' *And I happen to have a penchant for hot-loaf delicacies. Experienced bakers always say it's much easier to heat an old oven than a new one. So, if you want to eat better bread, or a tasty quinny, you need to find an old oven.*"

As the weak October sun began to light up the bedchamber, Blanche finally stirred, arching away from him while she stretched her arms above her head. She gave a little yawn and kicked herself free of the sheets. Nicolas found it amusing how her nakedness didn't seem to bother her in the slightest.

She reached up and stroked his face. 'Your reputation did not disappoint. For one so young, it seems you have learnt a great many things.'

'I think I learnt a few more last night. What do you mean, "*my reputation*"?'

Blanche gave a pretty fluting laugh. 'Let's just say I know I'm not the only harpist who's attracted your attentions.'

Nicolas ignored this. Another of his rules was never to discuss one female with another, especially as, on this occasion, only a kiss had been exchanged, nothing more. 'Your future husband's a lucky man,' he said.

Her answer came out on a pout. 'Oh, *him!* Let's not talk about him. I will soon be a wealthy woman with a fine house and, in return, he will have my body. All I can do is pray that God is as lenient as He was last time, and quickly summons him up to heaven. And hope he doesn't have an heir who secretly changes the will.' She stroked Nicolas's chest. 'Shame you have to make a loveless match with a rich young girl who makes your skin crawl.'

'Who said that?' he asked, shocked into brusqueness.

Blanche smiled at him. 'Oh, you know how people gossip, *chéri*. Besides, you would make a woman a fine husband, not only in the bedchamber, but out of it."

Nicolas bristled at both her cruel but deserved comment about Robine de Croisic, and the reminder of his own future marriage. As far as he was concerned, the less he thought about his unfortunate *fiancée* the better. The memory of the white-faced young girl holding his hand in the chapel haunted him. It had been no place for the sickly-looking Robine with her stick-thin body and troubled eyes. Still, it didn't feel right to let a woman like Blanche talk about her in insulting terms.

'I have no time to dwell on such matters,' he said.

Blanche planted a kiss on his cheek. 'Oh, you sweet boy. So young and untried still. One day a woman will come along to capture your heart. Until then,' she continued, running her hand down from his chest to his navel, tugging at the golden locket he always wore, 'the time is ripe to play.'

Not sure he wanted to be treated like a plaything, Nicolas put out a hand to stop her. In return, she caught hold of his hand in hers and held it up to the light.

'What a beautiful ring. I noticed it last night but I was…how shall I put it…a little distracted.'

Nicolas stared down at the turquoise ring and said in a flat voice. 'It was the only thing of any value my parents left me. That and the locket. '

'I can assure you the gold band, in addition to the turquoise, makes it worth a king's ransom. So if ever you find yourself without a crust of bread, you won't starve. The locket looks very valuable too. What's inside it?'

'A drawing of our old house in Crépy-en-Valois.' He had no intention of sharing his secret with Blanche and was glad she seemed satisfied with his answer.

'Do you miss your parents?'

Nicolas hesitated. 'No. My old nursemaid once told me I was the devil's spawn.'

'What a cruel thing to say to a child!'

'I probably deserved it. I think it was during one of her beatings.'

'Your nursemaid *beat* you?'

'Only after she'd been drinking. She also said she'd swear on the bible my mother had never given birth to me. Which meant the Devil must have fathered me.'

'Did you tell anyone what she'd said?'

'My mother. When she returned a couple of months later.'

'What did she say?'

'She rushed up the stairs and dismissed the old harridan on the spot. So I suppose it wasn't such a bad thing, after all.'

'And your father. What was he like?'

'No better than my mother. Neither of them showed me any tenderness. But then I showed none back.'

Blanche reached out and stroked his face. '*Mon pauvre*. No wonder so many females flock to you. All of them wanting to rescue the little lost boy trapped within.'

Nicolas gave a short laugh. 'I think they want to do more with me than that.'

Her fingers began tiptoeing their way down his chest but again, he held her hand fast. 'Aren't you fearful I'll get you with child?'

Blanche sat up and leant on her elbow, looking at him, her eyes narrowed. 'Why do you think I agree to marry such rump-fed old moldwarps? Certainly not for the pleasure of it. If I should fall with child, they'll be delighted and brag about it to all and sundry. So,' she finished, brushing her hands over her breasts, 'there's nothing to fear. I'll be a married woman by Yuletide and can continue to take my pleasure where I choose, both now and in the future.'

Even though Nicolas was slightly nonplussed by her brazen approach to marriage, he had to admire her. In her eyes (perhaps to justify her faithlessness), she wasn't so much treating her husbands badly as giving them the chance to recapture their youth. For his part, Nicolas liked to think he treated women well. This included never making his intentions either public - or obvious. He didn't aspire to the role of the traditional courtly lover to be found in all the romances he'd read, playing out his moves in a great hall for all to see: first worshipping a woman from afar, then reciting poetry at her feet - or performing knightly tasks to gain her favour.

With this in mind, he seized Blanche's wandering hands and pinned them above her head. There wasn't a moment to lose as the Castle was beginning to stir around them and their absence below might soon be noticed. This time, he took her swiftly and without preliminaries, her ensuing cries of ecstasy and his own gratification, a fitting conclusion to their long night of passion.

VALENTINE

Chapter Thirty-Three

January 5th,1512. The Eve of Epiphany
(La Fête des Rois). La Colombe.

he King and Queen are coming to La Colombe for the Feast of
Epiphany! Together with their girls and the Angoulêmes."
How many times had Valentine heard that in the past few
weeks? Royal fever had seized the manor house, affecting every member of
the household from her parents, now the Baron and Baroness de Fleury (since
the King rewarded her father for his bravery during the Battle of Agnadello)...
to little Louis, the newest kitchen *galopin*. Valentine only wished it could be
over and everything return to normal.

Today, it was the turn of Phélix, the pastry cook, to behave like a cornered
bull in the nearby field when a tiny corner fell off his confectionary
masterpiece. 'A subtlety is made entirely of sugar and used to amuse,' he told
Valentine and her younger sister, Charlotte, as he impatiently pushed the piece
back into place. He pointed at some large, conical sugar loaves in the corner
of the room. 'One pound of sugar costs more than I make in an entire month.
But you know how it is with those who have money - they like to show it off
to others.'

Valentine knew the longing on her face must be obvious; Phélix often
teased her about her love of confectionery. 'You can either eat a subtlety,' he
said, 'except in March when we may eat nothing sweet - or, if I use wax, they
make a wonderful table decoration. But judging from your face, Demoiselle
Valentine, like my own daughter, Barbe, I've no doubt which one you'd
choose.'

'Oh, eat it please!'

Now his masterpiece was fully restored, the pastry cook's mood was lighter. 'Come, *mes demoiselles*, and look at these colouring materials. You shouldn't always have white as your colour. If you want to have violet, you heat the flowers in a mortar with a little hard sugar and then soak them in rose water and gum tragacanth. Blue lichen magically turns a dish red or blue depending on what I mix it with. You can use cinnamon to give you the colour of walnuts but if you want a lighter brown, you have to blend the cinnamon with ginger. Or use sandalwood. I use saffron to make yellow and young barley blades. And parsley to make green. Carrots or leaves from the Dragon's Blood plant make a sanguine colour which, as you know, is the colour of blood.....

Leaving Phélix to his sugary duties, the two little girls advanced deeper into the heart of the kitchens. They were always a haven of comfort and warmth - from where, thanks to Maître Jacques, the head cook, Valentine would leave with her belly satisfyingly full. Even from the other end of the house, the commotion from within could be heard, and the appetizing aroma of a multitude of different dishes would waft in all directions. On Christmas Day, following a day of fast, and before the feast, her mouth had positively watered from inhaling the rich aroma of roasting meat, spices and newly-baked bread. The kitchens had been a hive of activity, with a variety of servants bearing silver salvers, scurrying to their destination, much too preoccupied to cast so much as a glance in the direction of Valentine or her younger sisters. It was the same today; neither her mother nor her father had any time for them, not with all the preparations for the Feast of Epiphany banquet making the adults behave as if they'd sat on a nest of wasps.

With time on her hands, Valentine had brought Charlotte to the kitchens, knowing they'd find a warm welcome there. On their left, hung Maître Jacques' armour: countless rows of frying pans, colanders, cauldrons, hanging kettles, copper and brass boiling pans, wooden stirring spoons and holed spoons, as well as saucepans and skillets, meticulously arranged in order of size. Nearby, stood a battalion of perfectly sharpened knives: each one a trusty soldier waiting to go into battle. From the shine on the pewter spoons, horn spoons, and silver ladles, anyone could see how much pride the cook took in his collection of cooking utensils.

Valentine had heard chilling tales of how the terrifying English might one day come and kill them in their beds. It was bad enough that one of the fearsome Talbots was Deputy Governor of Calais. Sometimes, when she remembered, she sank to her knees and offered up a prayer: *"Please God, may the only army in Picardy be the one in our kitchens, hanging on Maître Jacques' wall."*

Arranged neatly around the kitchens were vital pieces of equipment: hampers, baskets for carrying foodstuff, pot-hooks, oven shovels, roasting spits and skewers. A large sack of unshelled almonds stood in one of the corners, just below a little statue of Saint Gertrude.

'Why's she there?' asked Charlotte.

'She's supposed to be protecting the kitchen from rats and mice.'

Valentine was pleased she knew the answer; after all, she'd be nine in a few months and Charlotte still only eight. Walking past several shelves of plates of wood, silver, pewter and gold, and some cupboards containing fine linen and white cloth, Valentine suddenly came to a standstill in front of another one. She loved this shelf.

'Look at those books, Charlotte.'

There, in pride of place (as if they were members of the nobility) sat two heavy tomes on cookery: presented to the cook the previous two years by Tristan d'Ardres' father. It was a running joke between Valentine's father and the Count that the Fleury cook was the Baron's most valuable possession, much coveted by Guy d'Ardres. Charles de Fleury had jested that the Governor of Picardy's extravagant New Year's gifts to Maître Jacques were intended as a bribe to leave his present employer and move across to the Castle.

Only three or four people were ever allowed to touch the books: Maître Jacques, the young boy in charge of polishing them on a weekly basis, and whomever Maître Jacques (who could barely write his own name) could persuade to read out some recipes to him. This included the Fleury family steward - and Valentine, who sometimes ducked behind the nearest door when she saw the cook striding in her direction. Luckily, he had an excellent memory, and all his recipes, together with all the quantities, methods of preparation, ideal flavours and appearance, resided quite happily on imaginary shelves in his head. However, he still liked to hear the details of the lives of those cooks who had gone before him.

Valentine had never bothered to learn the long titles of the two cookery volumes but knew that one had been written more than a hundred years ago.

'Who wrote that one?' asked Charlotte, pointing to the book on the left, her brown eyes big with curiosity.

Valentine wasn't about to let her sister know she had no idea.

'It was a rich Parisian,' said a male voice from behind them.

The girls whirled around to come face to face with a youth of about sixteen or seventeen, not far off six feet tall, powerfully built, and dressed entirely in green satin. Although he wasn't conventionally handsome, his pale oval face with lively hazel eyes - almost the same hue as his shoulder-length hair - his over-long nose, and shapely mouth, together with his fine clothes, made it obvious he'd stepped out of the French court.

'He was an extremely old man,' said the boy. 'He knew a great deal about many topics and decided he was the best person to educate his fifteen-year-old bride. His book is at least three hundred pages long, and besides recipes, has advice for his poor young victim on everything from hawking, and looking after horses...to how to pray.'

'Are you the King?' asked Charlotte, to Valentine's disgust.

She gave her sister a hard nudge. 'Of course, he isn't, you jolthead! The King's very old. So old I don't even know how old he is.'

The boy in front of them started to laugh. 'I'm not sure the King would be pleased to hear that.'

'You've got a very long nose,' said Charlotte in a matter-of-fact voice, as if it was the most natural thing in the world to say to a complete stranger.

Valentine was mortified. <<*What's wrong with Charlotte today? It's as if some evil sprite has taken control of her tongue*>>

Luckily, the boy didn't seem to mind. 'Some call me "Foxnose". Behind my back of course.'

Valentine decided she liked this newcomer with his clever face that reminded her of a satyr - but one always on the brink of laughter. Even so, he was an interloper in the Fleury family kitchens, and as the most important member of the family present, it was up to her to straighten matters out. She put her hands on her hips. 'Who are you then?'

The boy gave a deep bow, whether to mock or flatter, she couldn't be certain.

'May I present myself. François d'Angoulême. Duc de Valois.'

∽

Valentine thought his name sounded familiar but couldn't remember where she'd heard it. 'Last week, I helped Maître Jacques make a *confiture* with walnuts, pears, carrots, turnips and gourds,' she said, to prove she had equal importance to a duke in the kitchens. 'But my favourite is *confiture de noiz.*'

François smiled at her. 'What about the other book on the shelf?'

Fortunately, Valentine knew the answer. 'It was written a few years later by the Duke of Savoy's cook. His talents were extraordinary,' she said, getting into her stride. 'He could produce a feast out of thin air. That's why his master begged him to put quill to paper.'

'For his own personal glory, no doubt. What a shame I can't wait to hear more. But I'm off to Ardres Castle. To meet a friend of mine.'

'Who?' asked Charlotte, forgetting her manners again.

The boy smirked. 'I call him "Wolf".'

Seeing that Charlotte was about to open her mouth again, Valentine prodded her in the back. Although she, too, was intrigued to find out the identity of the Duke's friend, she merely bobbed a little curtsey as he left.

∽

From across the room, Maître Jacques called out to them. 'I need your help today, Demoiselles Valentine and Charlotte.'

He lifted a linen cloth to his face to mop the sweat from his brow. The Fleury family cook was a large man in his mid-thirties, with a broad chest and round stomach, suggesting he was fond of sampling his own creations. His bright blue eyes usually sparkled merrily beneath his auburn curls. But they weren't sparkling now. They were troubled and his forehead creased with lines of concentration. 'Demoiselle Valentine, can you find the part in the book where the Savoy cook writes about the feast with sixty dishes. I'm fretting I haven't ordered enough food. I want to know how much Master Amiczo needed for one that lasted a mere two days, but yet had so many dishes.'

Walking past her sister with her nose held high in the air, Valentine reached up and carefully lifted the heavy book down from the shelf. In no time at all, she'd found the passage: '*A hundred cattle,*' she obediently read, '*one hundred and thirty sheep, one hundred and twenty pigs, two hundred piglets, two hundred lambs, one hundred calves, two thousand hens and twelve thousand eggs.*'

'*Mordieu!*' Maître Jacques exclaimed. 'That's not including all the fish, wild game, fruit, herbs, spices, sugar, wine, candles and firewood. Think how many butchers he must have needed, how many scullions to scrub so many plates and cooking utensils. Think how many recipes he'd have to juggle in his head, depending on whether it was a meat day or a fast day....'

Valentine knew that on a fast day, when only fish was permitted, and domestic and wild meat were not even allowed over the kitchen threshold, a cook had to be inventive to make up for the lack of dairy products.

"*This is when almonds become a cook's saviour,*" Maître Jacques had told her more than once, "*giving us butter, cheese and milk.*"

Pulling down a large white apron from a hook above his head, the cook was smiling again. 'You can help me make a *torte.*'

Returning with the cheese, eggs, and herbs he needed, Valentine watched him crack several eggs into a bowl before handing Charlotte a wooden spoon.

'Beat those for me, please.'

Valentine knew cooking was a complicated business because of the four humours the Greeks had discovered: warmth, cold, moisture, and dryness. 'I always forget which dish belongs to which humour,' she said. 'And I'm sure Charlotte doesn't know at all.'

'Yes, I do,' came back her sister's indignant response but, of course, when pressed, she wasn't able to provide a single example.

Maître Jacques reached up to his spices pouch for some pepper. 'Human beings are naturally warm and moist, *mes demoiselles*, so a cook should ensure that any foodstuff not corresponding to this description should be corrected by using either dry or moist heat. Or by adding appropriate condiments. Onions can be fatal if not fried to remove their moisture,' he told them as he diced one so rapidly that had Valentine blinked, she would have missed it. 'Beef, being a dry meat should always be boiled...never roasted. Eels should first be killed by burying them in salt to remove their moisture.' He grinned when he saw them shuddering at this last image.

'Then there is the order of foods that are served,' he said, as if telling himself as much as them what he needed to do for the comfort of the Fleury family guests. And especially the royal ones he was about to serve.

'In order to open the stomach, a cook needs to provide such vegetables as cabbage and lettuce, fruit such as peaches, and fowl such as chicken. At the end of the meal, he must ensure his guests eat some cheese, but not one that is too old or too dry....'

VALENTINE

Chapter Thirty-Four

January 6th. The Feast of Epiphany
(La Fête des Rois). La Colombe.

alentine glanced up at Monsieur Jacques' precious books as she made her way through the kitchens. It was well-lit in here with candles blazing all around the room, making up for the weak rays of the midday sun.

Although Maître Jacques would often grumble that by the time spices arrived in his hands from the Levant, they'd lost their pungency, there was still a delicious aroma of ginger and cinnamon. Valentine loved the exotic aromas wafting out of the cook's large leather spice pouches: cloves, nutmeg, the peppery smell of grains of paradise, cardamom, galingale, mace, anise, and last but not least, that reddish-yellow powder called saffron.

"The king of all the spices!" Maître Jacques would say as he tipped a little into one of his concoctions to turn it a bright yellow, in the same way he used parsley, sorrel and Saint Benedict's herb to turn his food green.

<<*Finally, it's the day to be dazzled by Kings and Queens*>> The entire house had turned into a place Valentine no longer recognized as home: her mother had shouted herself hoarse; her father looked worn out; the servants were rushing around from the top of the house to the bottom. Valentine half-expected to see one or two sitting on the chimneys, giving them a last-minute polish. The guest list and where everyone would sit, according to their rank, had been repeated so often she knew it by heart:

"King Louis and Queen Anne at the high table, above the salt, together with the two princesses, Claude…and little Renée (who would only put in a

brief appearance at the beginning of the feast). *The Angoulêmes, the Comte d'Ardres and his family....*"

Valentine knew there were strict rules concerning the seating arrangements; the most important diners absolutely had to be placed at the high table, upon a raised dais. It was the thankless task of the Fleury family steward to decide which families would take precedence over others. Needless to say, those placed at the bottom of the great hall, to the far left of the top table - the lowliest of all the positions - would be offended.

As she walked into the main part of the kitchens, Valentine could hear the cook's voice barking out orders to the beleaguered kitchen boys, their bodies running with sweat - in spite of the tall window which took up one side of the room, allowing cool air in through its shutters. They all had blackened faces and red eyes as they built up a huge fire with a combination of firewood and coal.

'Swing the pot over a big fire,' Maître Jacques was saying to one of them. 'Not a little fire that will merely warm the pot. And take care not to taint the meat with the smell of burning wood.'

Almost without turning his head, the cook instructed another boy on the other side of the kitchens: 'Cook and stir that Cameline sauce for the length of three Paternosters. Not one word more, not one word less.'

And to another, he called: 'You, over there, bake the bread for as long as it takes to walk around an acre field....'

On either side of the fire in the grate, logs were piled in readiness. The wall above was blackened from the flames and a cauldron was suspended over the fire, its dark contents bubbling enticingly. The smell of the strips of bacon draped over some chickens was making Valentine's stomach rumble. Nearby, sat half a dozen *galopins*, including Louis, the new *galopin*, a boy of around seven or eight who'd been given the vital task of turning some pigeons on the spit.

Valentine looked at the cook. 'Louis has got a very important job, preparing pigeons for the King and Queen.'

'That's true. A *galopin* has to decide which is the best heat for the meat.

Swan, turkey and bustard need a slow fire but if I'm cooking pig, quail or pheasant, he has to do it far quicker.'

Although Louis was puffing out his chest in pride at the cook's praise, it was hot thirsty work and Valentine guessed he'd much rather be in the larder, sitting on a sack of flour, drinking a small beer to quench his thirst. Even though she felt guilty leaving the poor boy to his hard task, it was to the larder she was heading herself. She didn't want to be late as she had an important meeting there....

As she made her way past work tables, chopping blocks, extra fireplaces and sinks, to the end of the kitchens, Valentine felt a twinge of excitement. It was pleasantly cool in the larder, in contrast to the heat of the main kitchen. Perhaps that was why so many servants seemed to be coming and going all the time, fetching and carrying various items of food. Sitting on a sack of flour, she looked around to see if there was anything tasty to sample. She glanced down at the huge tubs of salt near her feet and then up at the shelves above her head, straining to see if there was anything interesting in the earthenware preserving jars.

On the other side of the room, barrels containing salt fish, olives and dried fruit were intermingled with wooden boxes containing marmalade, and wicker baskets which were used to transport anything from coal to fruit. A pot of verjuice made from crab apples sat next to its matching neighbour to which sorrel *purée* had been added, turning it green and into *verjus vert*. Further along the shelf was a jar of orange rind preserved in honey. Large sides of bacon and salted meat hung behind bottles of olive oil and neat rows of assorted candles.

Valentine wrinkled her nose at the slightly musty smell from the cellar below where barrels of wine, ale and beer were stored. In October, there'd been an unusually severe frost and she watched the servants bring in the logs, piled high in the corner, as well as the fruit on the shelf above.

Her gaze fell on a spiral staircase which led up to the garret above; how many times had she felt glad not to be one of the poor servants who had to live with the unpleasant smell. Although there was a granary above the room she shared with her sister, Charlotte, and their nursemaid, Bonne, where rye, wheat and fruit were stored as well as the clean linen, she didn't mind the sweet smell of the apples. Quite often, she would creep up there when she was supposed to be in bed, sink her teeth into a nice juicy apple, open a little window, and stare up at the stars, with the refreshing feel of the north wind on her face.

∽

A mouth-watering apple pie with figs, raisins and spices, and a crust gilded with eggs, placed on a long oak table, next to a gooseberry tart, suddenly reminded Valentine of why she was here. She looked around the larder trying to find it….

<<Ah, there it is!>> At the far end of the room, next to the window to keep it cool, was Phélix's magnificent sugar subtlety, depicting the Fleury family manor - decorated with the family crest of lions, swans, and a golden sun. Beside it, two young boys, seemingly placed there by Phélix as sentries, looked as though they were applying the finishing touches to a couple of little sugar figures. Now all she needed to do was wait.

A short time later, the far door slowly opened and she looked up expectantly. Except it wasn't who she'd been waiting for. It was an old man she'd never seen before, dressed in expensive clothes. He had grey hair, a long nose, kindly eyes of greyish blue, and a mouth that didn't look as though it had ever shaped itself into a complaint. On his head, he was wearing a black felt cap with what looked like a large gold coin attached to the front. Valentine felt sorry for him; he was obviously someone's ancient grandpère who'd lost his way. Or perhaps a family retainer who'd been kept on out of pity. For some reason, he seemed to be staring at her in a most peculiar manner.

'I feel as though we've met before,' he said, sitting down on a neighbouring sack of flour.

Was this what happened when you lost your wits? If you managed to live for half a century or more. He seemed such a gentle soul, she felt no fear. She decided to try and put him at his ease.

'I don't think so. Though I met someone yesterday who my nursemaid told me is going to be the next king.'

This seemed to capture his interest. 'Really, what was his name?'

'François. He's got a big nose. But that doesn't matter if you're king, I suppose.'

'You mean, he has a nose bigger than mine?'

'Yes, but you're not the King so it doesn't matter, does it?'

From the twinkle that appeared in his blue eyes, the old man seemed to find this amusing. So he still had enough wits to appreciate humour. She was glad of it.

'And what's your name, pretty little maid?'

'Valentine de Fleury, Sire. And yours?'

'You can just call me Louis.'

So the man was a servant of some kind. She smiled at him. '*Louis*. I like that name. It's the same as the new *galopin* who started in the kitchens after Christmas.'

'Perhaps he was named for our King?'

'No! The King's far too old. He's even older than you. Who would want to be named for him? He thinks of nothing else but going to war in Italy. And making others risk their lives by going with him.'

The old man laughed. 'I see you have a very poor opinion of your monarch, young demoiselle.'

'I do. We're not allowed to have a King and Queen of the Bean today because the real ones are coming to dine. Papa said it would be disrespectful.'

'Ah, I see your point. Well, as we already have a "Young Louis", why don't you call me "Old Louis"? I've just been talking to your grandmère and parents. Your grandmère and I are old friends.'

Valentine stared at him open-mouthed; perhaps his wits weren't so addled after all. Could he have been one of her grandmère's servants in her house in Rouen…although 'friend' was a strange way to speak of his former mistress. 'You worked for Grandmère Symonne?'

He thought for a moment. 'Yes, I suppose I did. A long time ago. You favour her so much in looks that's why I thought I knew you.'

Although Valentine wondered whether a servant should be talking about her grandmère…or indeed to the daughter of the house in this manner, she was enjoying their conversation. Unfortunately, she had no choice but to bring it to an end. 'I'm very sorry Old Louis but you'll have to go now. I'm waiting for someone important to arrive. And they won't want anyone else to see them in here.'

Slipping easily into his role of respectful servant, the old man got up to leave and kissed her hand. 'That sounds intriguing, but I quite understand your predicament. I hope to have the pleasure of your company again, *ma petite demoiselle.*'

Valentine jumped down and gave him a dainty curtsey before almost pushing him over the threshold in her haste to see him to go. Then she closed the door behind him with a resounding bang.

A few moments later, the door opened again. Standing there, towering above her was a glowering Tristan d'Ardres, wearing what looked like a new black doublet and hose. There was an almost demonic expression in his slanting green eyes, the same one that had been there an hour or so earlier when she informed him he would be acting as her lookout in the larder. She'd witnessed so many of his misdeeds she no longer knew for which of them this particular foray into blackmail was responsible. Threatening to tell Tristan's father seemed to work like the words of a magic spell. <<*Every time I utter them he's forced to do my bidding*>>

Going back to sit on the sack of flour, next to the one so recently occupied by Old Louis, she looked up at the Comte d'Ardres' son. 'You don't have to look so horn-mad, or behave so churlishly. François and Old Louis are far better-mannered than you.'

Tristan gave her a strange look but said nothing.

'All you have to do is guard the entrance to the larder,' she went on, 'while I do something inside.'

He ran one hand through his unruly dark blonde hair. '*Do something*, you little harpy. What exactly?'

'It's none of your affair. Just stand there until I come back. And don't turn around.'

Leaving a scowling Tristan to go and guard the door, Valentine told the

214

two boys that their master needed them right away. The moment they'd gone, she tiptoed over to the subtlety as stealthily as a thief in the night, thrusting out a greedy hand—

'*Serpe Dieu, Tempête!*' Tristan cried out. 'What on earth do you think you're doing?'

But it was too late. Valentine was stuffing an entire castle turret into her mouth. 'Just tasting to see if it's as good as it should be. In caysh all the adultsh eat it before I can try it.'

'Valentine!' he yelled again, making a desperate lunge for her and grabbing one of her wrists in his—

But there was no time to do anything further as footsteps interrupted them and a glowering Maître Jacques suddenly appeared above them. The cook's face was puce - either from rage or the heat of the kitchens, it was hard to say. However, when he realized who the interlopers were and what Valentine had done, fortunately he saw the funny side of things.

'Monsieur Tristan, I don't think we should tell either your father or Phélix what has happened to his beautiful creation. We'd better place the blame on one of the cats. And call back Phélix's helpers to repair the damage. Come with me, you two.'

Startled at being discovered, and ignoring Tristan's furious glances, Valentine gulped down the rest of the evidence. Glancing up at Maître Jacques as he ushered them out of the forbidden area, she felt a wave of shame wash over her. She could imagine the cook comparing her and Tristan with little Louis. Although they deserved a scolding, they'd been born into the nobility and must always be treated with the greatest of respect by the kitchen staff - even when they were misbehaving.

Maître Jacques must have seen how hot and tired little Louis looked. 'Go and fetch a small beer, *mon galopin*,' he said. Then he walked over to a nearby wooden dresser and pointed at a platter. 'This peacock has been cooked in the classical fashion. There's nothing that can beat a good "Peacock Royal". That's why it's known as "food for the brave". And has given rise to a proverb: *"Thieves have as much taste for falsehood as a hungry man for a cooked peacock."'*

'It looks as though it's still alive,' said Valentine.

'Ah, *ma petite,* that's exactly how it's supposed to look at the end. However, the first thing I did was break its neck and slit its throat open. Then I took off its skin, feathers and head in one go.'

Valentine knew the cook was in his element, discussing his favourite topic, oblivious to any squeamishness from his listeners. For him, slicing up animals and birds was a means to an end and she knew he never gave it a second thought. Whether it was removing the tongue of a lamprey to bake it with cinnamon, grains of paradise, and serve it with a hot sauce...or skinning an eel to serve it with onions and parsley in a *Soringue.*

From long experience, she could tell he was warming to his subject. Next to her, a stony-faced Tristan was starting to grow restless, moving from one foot to the other. Bound to this place by her threats, and now those of the cook who was in full flow, she could imagine he was boiling with rage inside.

'One of my helpers dusted the peacock with cumin before roasting it and leaving it to cool,' said Maître Jacques. 'As you can see, we have positioned it on this large platter as if it were still alive, and re-covered it with its own skin and plumage, its tail fanned all around.' All of a sudden, he paused. 'Are you quite well, Monsieur Tristan? I've never seen you without a smile on your face. Is it the demands of our little demoiselle here that have snatched it away?'

Valentine gave Tristan no chance to reply. 'I haven't snatched anyone's smile away. I thought you were my friend, Maître Jacques.'

'I am. But I'm not sure I could say the same for Phélix if he were to find out about his subtlety.'

Valentine was willing the cook not to remember about Phélix's famous *Fête des Rois* cake: the one containing a bean, enabling whoever found it to become king for the day, creating mayhem. If Maître Jacques remembered they weren't allowed one this year, there was a good chance they'd never get out of the kitchens. And Tristan would never forgive her.

To her relief, the cook patted her on the head. 'Now,' he said, 'you must excuse me. I need to make my stuffing of parsley, sage, eggs, and pork for my chicken. We're serving *Poulaille farcie* later. I also need to check we have enough packets of woad to baste the bird and the meatballs once they're cooked. Then I must attend to my sauces. I have to prepare a cheese sauce to accompany the roasted kid which - I'm told - is served in all the best households in Milan. I hear it's a particular favourite of your father's, Monsieur Tristan. As for you, Demoiselle Valentine, *ma petite poupette*, although I'm not sure you deserve it, I've prepared your favourite rose-sugar dragées and honey-coated ginger, not to mention *filberts* dipped in sugar and dates. I might even make you a *crêpe* with honey batter if you're lucky....'

When they finally managed to escape the cook's clutches and were standing outside the kitchens, Tristan immediately rounded on her. 'That's the last time I'm ever going to do your bidding, Valentine de Fleury. No matter what you threaten to tell my father.'

As he marched off into the courtyard, angrily brushing flour from his clean doublet, a not at all daunted Valentine stood with her hands on her hips and called after him: 'Well, you'd better make sure you're good then!'

LA COLOMBE CAMELINE SAUCE

70g white bread, toasted
180 ml red wine
4 tablespoons of cider vinegar
1 tablespoon of brown sugar
¼ teaspoon of the following:
Cinnamon
Ginger
Cloves
Mace
Grains of Paradise
Salt
½ long pepper or ½ teaspoon of black pepper
3 saffron threads

1) Break up the slices of toast and soak them in red wine and vinegar. Break them up more as they get softer.
2) Grind all the spices together, using a mortar and pestle.
3) Place the bread, wine and vinegar mixture in a blender for one or two minutes.
4) Place mixture in a saucepan and add spices.
5) Leave it for an hour or two in order to let the spices infuse it.
6) Add sugar. Taste. Adjust spices/sugar according to preference.
7) Gently heat in a pan until thickened.
8) Pour into a sauce bowl and serve.

Le Viandier de Taillevent (1350).

—◦◦◦—

CECILY

Chapter Thirty-Five

1ˢᵗ May, 1512. Saint Michael's Mount, Cornwall.

glanced at Tristan next to me, tapping his feet on the dark velvet hassock, and drumming his fingers on the back of the pew. For some reason, the usually jocund Archpriest, John Arscott, our host for the next few days at Saint Michael's Mount, had decided to make his morning sermon in the Lady Chapel the most droning one of all time. I'd promised Tristan a stay to remember in this magical castle, shrouded in mystery, cut off from the mainland for many hours each day. It was only accessible on foot, or by boat, as a means of delivering goods, or *in extremis*, rescuing those unsuspecting souls caught out by the incoming tide.

<<*And what have I managed to produce for my favourite cousin?*>> Utter tedium. I pitied my mother at the far end of our pew, seated next to Father and Tristan's mother. What a dismal-dreaming way for her to celebrate her birthday. To keep myself awake, I gazed around the richly adorned chapel, past the high altar and the swathe of silk suspended from the ceiling (with a small gold box attached to it, containing the Host), over to the magnificent rose window. Behind me, by the door, hung a painting of the Archangel Michael slaying the dragon, his two feet atop the beast, his enormous wings fanning out behind him. Everyone knew the tale of how some fishermen had long ago seen him standing on a rocky ledge on the western side of the Mount. To my left, by the wall, I could see my favourite relic: the jawbone of Saint Appolonia, the patron saint of toothache. I knew her grisly story by heart. As punishment for her refusal to worship a false god in Alexandria, she'd had every single tooth in her mouth painfully pulled out before she was flung unceremoniously onto a pile of blazing faggots.

❧

I loved to visit the Mount with all its thrilling legends and events that had taken place there. I'd told Tristan about Perkin Warbeck, the Pretender to the throne of England, whose life had ended so unhappily. It was only a mere fifteen years (the same year Tristan was born) since Perkin landed at Whitesand Bay near Land's End, and made his way to the Mount with his Scottish wife, Lady Catherine Gordon. Theirs was a marriage arranged by the mischievous James of Scotland to annoy his Tudor neighbour. I remembered how much the Pretender used to fascinate Nan and me before we were old enough to truly understand his tragic story. I'd known Perkin claimed to be Richard, Duke of York, one of the two little brothers who mysteriously disappeared in the Tower of London. Just thinking about them always sent a shiver down my spine. Sadly for Perkin and his beautiful wife, having the support of many who still sympathized with the House of York was not enough. Although he was proclaimed King Richard IV in Bodmin, Perkin was captured in Beaulieu Abbey, near Southampton. I loved the part of the tale where his wife remained faithful to him until his execution two years later, even when she found out the so-called truth about him, uncovered during torture: that he was nothing more than the son of an impoverished boatman from Tournai.

"*It was the man I loved, not the king,*" she was reputed to have said. Her charm, beauty, and bravery at the court of the first Henry Tudor won her the title of 'The White Rose of Scotland'. Whenever we came across to the Mount for a service and stayed behind to dine, I would find a particular window and stare out through the narrow slit to the Narrow Sea beyond, pretending to be Lady Catherine, pining for her lost love.

I was extremely proud to be Cornish, relishing how we always stood up for ourselves. No wonder our present King's father once described our county as "*the back door of rebellion*" when we rose up to support Perkin. Today, I felt I had a little of that rebellious spirit in me. I usually enjoyed the services in the Lady Chapel but all I wanted to do now was escape. How I wished I was outside, up on the church tower, next to the stone lantern used by the monks to help fishermen find their way back home in the darkness.

<<Free...with my face held up to the morning breeze>>
With a feeling of despair, I glanced back at Saint Appolonia, as if seeking a miracle. All of a sudden, an idea came to me: one so bold and striking in its simplicity I felt quite light-headed. Digging Tristan in the ribs, I whispered I had terrible toothache and thought I might faint if I didn't go outside. Although he looked surprised, he mimed my affliction to his questioning mother and followed me to the door.

<<Freedom. At last>> It was as well that Tristan burst out laughing when he realized there was nothing wrong with me. 'Cecy Tredavoe, I swear you're the Devil's own servant!'

But I noticed the admiration in his eyes. It made me wonder how young girls behaved in France; perhaps they were more demure, not so unruly. 'Wouldn't a French girl do that?' I asked.

'I know one as madcap as you. She might only be eight or nine but if you're the Devil's servant, then Valentine de Fleury is the black imp that sits upon his shoulder.'

I was prevented from asking him more about this little fiend by the appearance of Gabrielle, my young French nursemaid, obviously sent by my worried mother to see what was wrong. Unfortunately, Gabrielle knew me far too well for anything else but suspicion to register in her brown eyes. Quick thinking was called for to avoid the pair of us being marched back into the Archpriest's never-ending service.

'I can't help it if I've got toothache,' I said, clutching my jaw. 'If you don't want to ruin Mother's birthday, *ma chère* Gabrielle, you must go back and reassure her that Tristan is taking care of me.'

'*Mais, bien sûr, Demoiselle Cecily.*'

However, I could see her demeanour belied her outward show of concern. No matter. I'd won. Although she gave a few disbelieving tuts and some expressive Gallic shrugs, we both knew my argument about spoiling my mother's birthday was too strong.

'*Merci*, Gabrielle,' I managed to get out to her retreating back, even with a tooth that might not last the day. Her response was to mumble something unintelligible in French.

Tristan smirked. 'It seems your visits to some cove or other are about to be stopped forthwith.'

I didn't care. <<*A few tears and caresses always do the trick with the kind-hearted Gabrielle*>> The moment the door closed behind her, I grabbed Tristan's hand and began to pull him down the path towards the final resting place of relieved pilgrims, Saint Michael's chair, a carved-out place in the rock, hanging perilously a few hundred feet above the sea.

'Where are we going?' he demanded.

'To Marazion. There's a small fair there today. For May Day. It'll be fun. Though, of course, not as good as the ones over at Penzance, especially the Saint Bartholomew fair in August.'

'But what about the May Day celebrations to take place here today?'

'We'll be back long before those begin.'

'And what about the tides? We don't want to find ourselves cut off.'

'Stop fussing like a mother goose, pecking at her chicks! You're talking to someone who knows every tide off by heart. You seem to forget I live in a castle surrounded by the sea on three sides. We've got ages before the causeway closes today. At least until noon.'

<<*Or is it eleven? No matter. An hour is neither here nor there*>>

That seemed to pacify him; I could tell he was as eager as me to go to the fair from the way we almost flew down the side of the Mount, along the well-trod Pilgrim's Way, past the ancient well, once home to a giant named Cormoran, tricked into falling into its murky depths by little Jack, a local boy. Cormoran had been wreaking havoc in the villages across from the Mount, stealing livestock, and even babies and young children to appease his appetite. Jack came up with the idea of digging a pit during the hours of darkness. As the dawn broke and the sun appeared in the sky, the little boy called out to the giant who stumbled out of his cave into the blinding sunshine and fell headlong into the trap Jack had laid for him.

With all my efforts centred on reaching the causeway below, I didn't stop to show Tristan the heart of the giant, embedded in the cobbles of the winding path. In no time at all, we reached the causeway. What exhilaration I felt both to have escaped, and to be running barefoot with Tristan towards the mainland, my own and his laughter lost on the wind. In one hand, I held my red leather shoes, and in the other, the skirts of my matching kirtle of the best Flemish cloth, held up high in a most scandalous fashion. The mingled tang of salt and seaweed was as heady as any jasmine scent from the Far East, worn by a lady in her boudoir to seduce her sweetheart.

'You can be Perkin Warbeck, and I'll be Catherine Gordon!' I yelled back as I sprinted ahead of my cousin, as sure-footed as a goat that has committed every stone to memory. 'You can't catch me!' I panted into the wind, wondering whether his little Valentine would enjoy this adventure as much as me.

⚘

The fair was even better than I'd hoped for and every stall we came across as we pushed our way through the throng of May Day revellers, offered fresh delights.

I spent ages trying to decide whether I wanted the rag doll with red hair or yellow hair.

'You must have the red one to match your own,' said Tristan.

Luckily, I'd unearthed two silver groats in a pocket of my kirtle, enough, as I jested, to make us Lord Perkin and Lady Catherine Bountiful for the day, free to buy our heart's desire and bestow gifts upon any we saw fit. I was delighted when I spotted some coloured bangles on the tray of a passing peddler. They would make a perfect birthday gift for Mother, in addition to the nightgown I'd painstakingly embroidered for her. A short while later, Tristan took a fancy to a small gleaming dagger which I instantly bought for him.

'After all, I might need you to protect me,' I said, feeling very grown-up (far older than my eleven years) as I placed it in his hands. Tristan took his cue from me.

Dipping into the practised bow of a courtier, he pretended to doff an invisible cap. 'At your service, my Lady Catherine.'

'My Lord Perkin.' I dropped him a laughing curtsey back. However, I was soon distracted by a stall selling all kinds of sweet goods, including my favourite, gingerbread.

The sun was beginning to rise higher in the sky but we were too engrossed to pay much attention. Wiping away the sticky gingerbread from the side of my mouth, I wandered over to a peddler and bought two juicy green apples for us.

Tristan bit into one of them. 'I'll be sick if I eat much more. Especially as there's going to be an enormous feast for your mother's birthday. Shouldn't we be getting back soon? The clock just chimed twelve.'

I gave him a haughty stare. 'No, that was eleven. I counted it especially.'

I could see Tristan was having too much fun to protest. To be honest, I wasn't entirely sure I had only counted eleven chimes but knew we had ages yet. As I'd told him, the tide didn't start to come until after noon.

I made him laugh when I presented him with a small knight astride his charger.

'You should be buying me a crucifix,' he said, his mouth curling in a wry expression. 'My father would approve of that.'

'Never! You were born to be a knight not a monk.'

Although I'd met Tristan's French father, Guy, once, I didn't like what my cousin told me about him. The boy who'd raced down the hillside before in search of adventure was never going to be suited to life in a monastery. From the beaming smile on my cousin's face, my words seemed to please him a great deal. <<*I want him to forget about the future and live for the present…just for one day*>>

Marazion May Day Fair Gingerbread

250g clear honey

200g fresh white breadcrumbs

1 teaspoon ground cinnamon

1 teaspoon ground ginger

1 long pepper or 1 teaspoon ground black pepper

3 strands of saffron

To decorate: Fresh box leaves, such as marjoram or bay leaves or basil. Whole cloves to keep the leaves in place

1) Slowly bring the honey to the boil in a saucepan.
2) Turn the heat down very low and add the spices. Cook for a couple of minutes and then gradually add the breadcrumbs, stirring all the time.
3) The mixture should be very stiff, if not, add a few more breadcrumbs.
4) Turn out onto a board and roll it flat until about an inch thick.
5) Line a shallow rectangular tin with greased paper and lay the mixture flat inside. Press it down with your fingers.
6) Place it in the fridge for two hours.
7) Turn the pan upside down and place the gingerbread on a plate.
8) Cut it up to your own taste. Squares, hearts, diamonds. Roll some into balls if you so wish.
9) Decorate the top by taking a whole clove and pressing it into two leaves of your choice.
10) It stores well in a tin.

Two fifteenth century cookbooks 1425-1450.

CECILY

Chapter Thirty-Six

aught up in Tristan's good mood, I was happy for him to take part in an archery competition. About twenty archers, of all ages and sizes, were lined up ready to take part, cheered on by a sizeable crowd.

'But only if I can join in, too,' I said.

Tristan looked surprised. 'I didn't know you'd ever used a bow and arrow. Or a crossbow.'

'Father gave me one of each as a New Year's gift last year. I'm not very good yet but you'd be surprised how resourceful Lady Catherine can be when she sets her mind to something.'

Tristan shrugged as he watched the man in front of the equipment tent hand me a smaller lighter crossbow, giving me a broad wink as he did so.

'Good for you, little maid. Even if you have no hope of beating your friend here. Most wenches I know are too busy with talk of fripperies and their sweethearts to pay a mind to men's sports.'

Taking the man's words as a challenge, I awaited my turn with a mixture of mounting excitement and trepidation. There would be several excellent archers amongst the group, one of whom I guessed might be Tristan himself. In front of us, an artificial popinjay, especially built in sections, had been placed on a wooden mount. It was our task to take aim at individual pieces of the bird, winning points for each one. The main prize, and the part each of us, of course, yearned to hit, was the heart section of the popinjay. Whoever managed this, also known as the 'king shot', would be crowned champion.

Walking up to the line chalked along the grass, I passed Tristan looking very pleased with himself, carrying a pair of leather gloves, his prize for hitting one of the legs. 'Good luck, Lady Catherine. Make sure you don't hit anyone by mistake, won't you!'

Frowning at this loud remark which made everyone around me draw back several feet, I took a deep breath. Then I lifted the crossbow up to my shoulder, aimed it at the bird, pulled the trigger and fired….

'*The heart!* The wench has hit the heart!'

I allowed myself a small smile of triumph. <<*What Tristan and the man running the competition (a pair of naysayers) don't know is that I've got one of the best archery tutors in Cornwall*>> He was always full of praise for my coordination, telling me he'd never seen anything like it in either lad or maid. Of course, as an only child with indulgent parents, it helped I was able to spend as many hours practising as I wished.

As we walked away from the makeshift butts, I glanced down at the posy ring now adorning a finger on my right hand. After a fair amount of scrabbling around amongst the stallholders, a more suitable prize had been found for a female winner than a brace of pheasants (almost certainly) poached from the land of a local lord, perhaps even our own. I twisted the gold band (still a little big for me) with the fingers of my other hand, admiring the stars engraved around the circumference. On the inside, written in black were the words: '*My brightest star, my one true love. N.*' Even though I knew the ring (like the pheasants) was probably stolen, I vowed never to take it off but wear it in memory of this happy day.

Not long after this, the clock chimed again. However, instead of the reassuringly long twelve chimes, there was the unmistakably ominous sound of not one…but *three* single chimes.

Aghast, we stared at one another.

'Three o clock!' gasped Tristan.

'Quick,' I said. 'Follow me. There's not a moment to lose.'

Racing down the cobbled streets of Marazion, we soon found ourselves standing on the shore again, looking back towards the Mount. We were also looking at the waves beginning to swirl against the shore at our feet, and the much higher ones at the end, near the entrance to the Mount.

'We'll never make it in time,' Tristan said.

'Of course we will.'

'We won't. When does the causeway reopen?'

'Not until late evening. Come on. I promise you we'll be fine. Stop acting like a whey-face. Surely you don't mind getting your clothes a bit wet. Think how sad it would make our two families if we missed my mother's birthday celebrations.'

'Very well. But I'm not happy about it. Not at all.'

Deep down, nor was I. As a Cornish girl born and bred, I knew it was sheer folly to attempt a crossing in these conditions. As we began the journey back across the partially covered causeway, I could hear my father's voice in my head, warning me as he'd done so many times before:

"Never cross the causeway if you see large waves at the far end. The high tide is fickle and has a mind of its own. It can come in much faster than you think. Before you know it, it'll take away both your breath and your life."

With all our wits needed to reach the other end as fast as possible, we stopped talking. The wind had risen slightly so all I could hear was a whistling in my ears. I was beginning to think perhaps we should have stayed to watch the May Day celebrations in Marazion, and danced around the maypole after the crowning of the Queen of the May. <<*We would have been in disgrace, but at least we would have been safe*>>

Even though I knew this part of Cornwall like the back of my hand, all my former feelings of joyous rebellion quickly turned to terror as the first large waves reached us, about halfway across, nudging at my waist and the top of Tristan's legs. An icy reminder of what was to come. My right hand tightened around the precious rag doll that had given me such pleasure a short while ago. I didn't dare glance at my ring as I needed all my concentration. As we progressed, slipping and sliding on the seaweed tangled around the cobblestones, and with the waves rapidly inching their way up my body, I realized the trinkets were nothing compared to the loss of our lives. Although

I was a strong swimmer (certainly better than Tristan, I was sure of that, even though in my folly, I hadn't even asked him if he could swim), I knew my heavy skirts would soon drag me down into the unforgiving depths. Praying to Saint Nicholas to save us from drowning would not be enough. <<*Is this divine punishment for running away from a sacred church service? Or accepting stolen property*>>

'Stay calm,' I instructed Tristan, but even to me my voice sounded hollow.

To stop the panic that was threatening to take over, I tried to concentrate on something else. All I could do was pray my Father's pet name for me would come in useful now. Since I'd been quite small, Father had called me '*Morvoren*' in jest. Pronounced Mor*VOR*en, as Mother always painstakingly told any visitors from up country who overheard him using it - came from the two Cornish words: '*mor*' meaning 'sea' and '*voren*' meaning 'maiden'. Taught to swim by one of the Mount boatmen (with me decently clad, of course), I took to swimming as if I'd been '*born with fins instead of legs*', Father once teased me. Learning to swim, although not a pastime that most people felt the necessity to try, for me, my father's little '*maid of the waves*', it was an absolute necessity. After all, we lived in a castle perched high above a sea with gentle swirling currents that could give pleasure, but also - with no warning at all - turn into something far more ferocious, and snatch away a precious life.

How shocked my parents would be if they knew how often I coerced Gabrielle into taking me to Pendour Cove, otherwise known as Mermaid Cove, on account of the frequent sightings of a mermaid. Gabrielle would stand with a mortified expression on her face while I dove in and out of the waves, wearing only my cotton shift, with all the ability expected of *Morvoren*, that other part of my self.

"*Zut alors! Demoiselle Cecily, you take care!*" Gabrielle would call out in high-pitched, distressed French.

"*Oh, don't bother your head about me,*" I cheerfully shouted back, waving my arms wildly, "*mermaids can't drown!*"

"*Mermaids can't drown.*" My foolish words were coming back to haunt me. By now, the icy water was just above my chest and I was being held aloft by Tristan who was struggling to keep afloat himself. I heard him murmur something in French, perhaps some kind of prayer. I remembered the Mount boatman telling me people who are drowning see their whole lives appear in front of them, very slowly, every good deed and bad deed appearing until in the end—

'*Cecily! Tristan!*'

Was I dreaming? Was I already dead?

No, neither. Coming towards us at what seemed supernatural speed was a small rowing boat, scudding across the choppy waves as if its (and our) lives depended on it. What untold relief it was to see Father's anxious face, waving and shouting as he drew up next to us, accompanied by two of the Mount's boatmen. Tristan and I were too shocked to speak as we were dragged over the edge in our sodden clothes, frozen to the bone, not quite able to believe our lucky escape.

As my terror subsided, guilt at the worry I'd caused everyone began to take hold. This only increased when we reached the shore and I caught sight of the anxious little group awaiting our return with drawn faces and clasped hands, supposedly at the Mount to celebrate a birthday but now to give thanks to God for two young lives that had been spared. Our poor mothers. There was certainly no punishment...only a huge bear hug from Father who wrapped me in a grey woollen blanket while throwing one to Tristan, and a half-whispered admonition from my poor white-faced mother who grabbed my hand and kept hold of it as though she'd never let it go again. I felt utterly wretched. Particularly when my Aunt Grace showed no such reserve as she rained kisses and tears galore down on us.

'You foolish, foolish children!' she sobbed. 'How could I ever lose you, Tristan? My precious son. My only child.'

'I'm fine, Maman,' Tristan soothed. But I couldn't help noticing how he returned her warm embrace with equal passion.

TRISTAN

Chapter Thirty-Seven

May 4ᵗʰ, 1512. Zennor Castle.

*S*o your Valentine didn't recognize the King of France and dismissed him from the kitchens of her house as if he were a mere servant.' Cecy clapped her hands together. 'How beguiling.'

My cousin was stretched out on the battlements of the Castle next to me, her long red hair fanning out around her. I decided she could equally belong in one of those Italian paintings we had in our own castle, as in the depths of the green sea far beneath us, darts of light dancing upon the scales on her mermaid's tail as she swished it back and forth.

'Don't forget,' I said, recalling my horrified amusement when Valentine told me what she'd done, 'she also met the Dauphin of France. I shudder to think what the little hoyden said to him. I call her "*Tempest*" because she turns my life upside down whenever she's around me.'

'I hope I'll meet your funny friend one day. I'm sure I'd like her.'

'I am sure you would, too. Fiendish demons, the pair of you. Both sent to earth with one aim alone—'

'To torment you, my dear coz.'

The next moment, Cecy flung herself upon me, a look of triumph on her elfin face as she began tickling me.

'Stop! I beg you, Cecy. Isn't it enough I'm a prisoner in your Castle, forbidden to leave unless accompanied by a French girl not much older than myself?' I looked over to the edge of the battlements where Cecy's nursemaid was talking to one of the servants. 'Which, I have to admit, would not be such a bad thing. Gabrielle's grown very pretty of late—'

The tickles turned into playful slaps. 'Don't you dare! I've already heard you trying to flatter her.'

'It's irksome you speak such good French.'

Unfortunately, that was true. My clever cousin spoke far too many languages for my liking: she'd had Gabrielle with her since babyhood and - besides English and Cornish - spoke fluent French, as well as excellent Latin, and even a smattering of Italian she'd learnt from various tutors, thanks to my Uncle William's insistence on an education equal to that of the new Queen of England.

'Father always felt it was important that I learn French so I wouldn't feel out of place if ever I visited our family across the Narrow Sea.'

'You mean, my father and Gilles?'

'Yes. I'm a little fearful about meeting your father again. After the other evening.'

I knew exactly to what she was referring: a conversation we'd overheard by chance between her father and my mother, following our near drowning. After a quick recovery, consisting of changing into fresh dry clothes and a goblet of warming mead each, spiced with cloves, rosemary and ginger, we'd danced around the maypole until we were fit to drop, eaten our fill at the feast, and lived every moment as if it were to be our last. Yawning our way back up the winding staircase to our bedchambers at the top of the Mount, exhausted but happy, we suddenly heard angry voices coming from a chamber on the first floor. Realizing that the door was half-open and that it was my mother and Cecy's father within, we paused to listen, standing with our backs to the wall, trying not to make a noise. It soon became obvious they were quarrelling about us:

"He should have known better. He's nearly fifteen. Cecy's only just turned eleven."

"She's hardly an angel."

"Thanks to your son, she nearly became one this afternoon."

"This is no time to jest, Will."

"I'm not. I'm deadly serious. It's hardly surprising Tristan's so wild, with a father like his."

"That's not fair! Tristan is not to blame for his father's words or deeds."

There was a long moment of silence. *"Of course, he isn't."* Cecy's father sounded as contrite as a sinner in the confessional. *"Forgive me, my dear sister. I don't need to tell you how much I cherish Tristan. I fear the events of this afternoon have sent me boil-brained."*

From the sound of weeping that followed, I could tell my Uncle William's loving words had touched my mother. I guessed that by now he was holding her in his arms, trying to soothe her. Feeling guilty Cecy and I had caused such pain to our loved ones, I decided we should leave them in peace. Holding a finger to my lips, I pulled my cousin back up the stairs. Fortunately, the next morning when we all broke our fast, laughing and chatting away, it was clear everything was back to normal, and brother and sister as close as ever.

⊷

'You mustn't be afraid of my father,' I told Cecy now. 'His bark is worse than his bite.'

'But my father said it's his fault you're so wild.'

'Only because he wants to send me to a monastery and I don't want to go. Now, let's talk again of more pleasant matters. Namely, the fair Gabrielle. I could teach her some Cornish.'

'Cornish? You don't know any.'

"'Whegyn ow holon.'"

Cecy burst out laughing. 'Trust you to know *"Darling of my heart"*! I can't imagine which of our maids taught you that one.'

'My lips are sealed. You're lucky to live in such a beautiful place.'

'I know. But I do get lonely. Even though I've got my Pendeen cousins living so near.'

'What about those friends of yours you've told me about? The two sisters.'

'Nan and Mary?'

'That's right.'

'They live in Kent. A full ten-day's ride from here. So I don't get to see them as often as I'd like. I wish I had a brother like Gilles. It must be such fun.'

'It is but he and I are very different. And besides, he's not my full brother.

Sadly, my mother didn't have any more living children after me.'

'Nor mine after me. Though, like yours, she had no problem getting with child.'

I shook my head. 'However hard they tried, it always ended up in disappointment, didn't it.'

'It doesn't matter Gilles is only your half-brother. I have to make do with Gabrielle. Sometimes, I make her play with me on the green below the Castle.'

'What do you play?'

'My favourite game. Where I pretend to be famous women from history.'

I couldn't help laughing as she jumped up and began marching around, arms akimbo, to show me what she meant.

'One day,' she said, her straight nose in the air, 'I'll be the haughty Eleanor of Aquitaine who married Henry Plantagenet and gave birth to her last son—' She suddenly bent over double, pretending to clutch an enormous belly, 'When she was an old lady of forty-five.'

'What else do you do?'

'I fling out orders to my imaginary minions.'

'What kind of orders?'

'Oh, I don't know. *"Bring me a goblet of wine! Write me a poem this instant! Compose a song for me!"*'

'Poor Gabrielle. Having such a tyrant for a mistress. I pity the poor man who has to take you for a wife.'

Cecy stuck out her tongue at me. 'Don't pity Gabrielle. She's usually asleep on the grass long before then.'

'Do you still want to be like Hildegard von Bingen when you grow up?'

'I'm not sure. Maybe I'll live in a castle instead. Nan's going to live in a palace.'

'What as? A queen,' I joked, until I saw Cecy's hurt expression.

'Oh, I'm sure you're right,' I hastily corrected myself. 'You'll live in a castle and your friend in a palace.'

I meant what I said about pitying the husband who wed my cousin; unless he was as clever as her, she'd run rings around him.

⤙

Cecy broke off as if she'd suddenly remembered something more important. 'What about that other boy who came to live with you. The surly one you detest.'

Her question took me aback. 'You mean, Nicolas?' I stared down at the grey sea. 'Now, there's someone who makes me wish I was an only child.'

'He can't be that bad.'

'Oh, he is, I assure you. Every bit as bad. And worse, besides.'

Cecy gave my arm a gentle punch. 'Then I'd like to meet him to make up my own mind. And you can stop brooding. I've got a treat planned for you.'

'Does it involve water?'

'No. I've persuaded my parents to let me take you to Saint Senara tomorrow to show you the church.'

'Accompanied by the lovely Gabrielle?'

My cousin let out an exaggerated sigh. '*Mais naturellement.*'

I closed my eyes, enjoying the warmth of the sun on my face. 'Why would I, of all people, want to visit a church?'

'Because it's not any old church. According to local folklore, the Mermaid of Zennor once lured a young man to a watery grave, so besotted with her was he.'

I opened one eye. 'Don't you think we've had enough of watery graves for one week?'

Ignoring me, Cecy continued with her story: 'At this time, the population of Zennor was well-known for their healing powers and their beautiful voices. I remember loving the story of the Mermaid the first time I heard it.'

Lying here so close to the sea, with the seagulls circling overhead before swooping down to the waves to retrieve their fin-flapping prey, my interest was piqued. 'Go on,' I said.

'One day, a young woman of almost unearthly beauty appeared in the chapel in the village of Saint Senara, joining in the singing with the sweetest voice any of the congregation had ever heard. As she left, one of the young men called Matthew Trewhella, a parishioner with the best singing voice in the village, leapt up from his pew and dashed after her.'

I made a snorting noise. 'Then, he's a fool. Never pursue a maid who shows no interest in you.'

'Ssh! Don't interrupt. Neither of them was ever seen again. In their honour, the church ordered a local carpenter to build what we today call "The Mermaid Chair" because of its carving of a mermaid on one side.'

'And I suppose you go and sit in that very chair, pulling your pretty bone and ivory comb, with its double row of different sized teeth and decorations of flowers and ribbons, through your long red hair, pretending to be a mermaid.'

My cousin was staring at me in astonishment. 'How did you know?'

'Because, my dear Cecy, you are like an open book. Very easy to read.'

'Easier than your Valentine?'

I'd told my cousin about the subtlety crime which made her laugh.

'She's certainly not *my* Valentine. But in answer to your question, yes. Far easier. For one so young, that one has a staggering amount of mischief stored up in her brain. She has no interest whatsoever in books or learning, just a natural cunning, worthy of the wiliest vixen.'

It was true. As if having Nicolas living under the same roof wasn't bad enough, I had to endure the constant mischief-making of Charles and Athénaïs de Fleury's eldest daughter. Unlike my cousin (whose life was one long happy adventure, living in one of the most spectacular castles in England, loving all those around her, and being loved back), Valentine feared nothing and no one. <<*Cecy doesn't know how fortunate she is to have so much solitude in her life*>>

Down below, we suddenly heard a gong summoning us to supper. Getting up, I stretched my arms above my head. 'Enough of all this talk of mermaids. I'm as hungry as a wolf howling at the gates of the Castle.'

'Thankfully, you won't find one in these parts. You'll have to go much further north. Or up to Scotland. I've heard they're such a problem for travellers there they've had to build special houses for people's protection. I never want to go to Scotland.'

'Nor I. Now let's go down.'

'Yes. Two of my uncles are coming to dine. They've just returned from London and always have plenty of gossip.'

TRISTAN

Chapter Thirty-Eight

A short while later, I sat down in the great hall with my mother, my cousin, her parents, and her uncles, Richard and Stephen Pendeen. It was a magnificent room with the Tredavoe coat-of-arms displayed above the fireplace, a dolphin and a mermaid on either side. Below, etched in gold, was the family motto: '*Dum spiro spero.*' Although I had a talent for Latin, I had scant liking for it after being subjected to long dismal-dreaming hours of study. However, I knew it meant: '*As long as I breathe, I hope.*' Portraits of Tredavoe family ancestors hung on the wall. Vaguely, I tried to find my own features in the various ones looking back down at me, some with stern expressions, others far less so. That was certainly true of my late grandsire, Hugh Tredavoe. I could hardly remember him but his spirit, imbued with humour and grace, lived on between the gilt frame in the painting that hung above the frieze running the length of the wall, depicting birds and animals. The same was true of my pretty, fair-haired grandam, Margaret. Although I'd never known her except in the portrait next to her husband, I felt drawn to this gentle soul with her kind smile. <<*As for resembling any of the other motley crew on the wall, just as with the portraits of my other ancestors back in Ardres, the only person in the world I seem to favour in looks is my mother*>>

Richard looked around the table and shook his head. 'I always feel as though I'm surrounded by a family of cats with green gleaming eyes when I come to sup here. Alys, Stephen, and I stand out in present company.'

'Mother's got Grandam Matilda's blue eyes,' said Cecy, next to me.

'And you her red hair,' he replied.

'And her mischief too, from what I hear,' said Stephen, laughter in his voice. 'It's just as well you're a Cornish mermaid.'

Cecy and I looked at one another a tad sheepishly at this reminder of our escapade at the Mount.

✍

What a treat it was to be served a steaming bowl of warming pea pottage, with its extra ingredients of ginger and saffron, brought back from London by Richard on his previous visit. I had a sudden feeling of well-being, surrounded by those I loved the best in the world. These last twenty miles before Land's End were as wild as the inhabitants themselves, but they were like paradise to me. <<*Somewhere I can be myself and forget about the dread-bolted future my father has mapped out for me*>> Once again, relief washed over me that he never came down to my mother's childhood home, instead, stopping short in London whenever we travelled to England. He'd been once and said that the days spent in travel were far too long when he could be enjoying himself in London, visiting several French friends who'd made their home there.

Cornwall was a beautiful place, with its ancient stones as old as time itself and where magic would weave its spell on all those who took a single step on its soil. One of my favourite places was Zennor Quoit, about a mile from the Castle, an ancient burial chamber with supposed magical powers. Cecy had taken me there on countless occasions, the two of us standing upon the huge stone slab, our arms outstretched, sometimes beneath the light of a full moon, and a velvety night sky of twinkling stars.

When the November winds blew icy blasts throughout Zennor Castle, and the huge waves of the Celtic Sea below broke against the rocks with great force - the fun-loving, silver-finned dolphins that came to frolic in the warm blue summer waters, long since departed - at night, there would be whispered ghost stories around the fire. Strange shadows would sway on the stone walls in the light of the dancing flames and the guttering, strong-smelling tallow candles would hiss and splutter until - with a sound like a quick sigh - they'd go out, leaving fear and eeriness in their wake. At this point, Cecy's mother would come bustling into the kitchen bearing fresh, far more fragrant, beeswax candles, scolding the servants for filling her child's head with nonsense, even though she'd know very well it was Cecy who'd wheedled the stories out of them.

"*Cecily Tredavoe, how many times have I told you not to torment our poor servants!*" she once said in an exasperated voice when I was staying with them.

"*That's what comes from allowing your daughter so much freedom,*" my

Uncle William complained. *"Sometimes I think we've bred a little savage between us…even if she does speak five tongues. With that flaming red hair of hers, just like her grandam's, and those sea-green eyes (perhaps the only part of me she's inherited), I half expect a sixth to come out of her mouth at any moment. Mermaid!"*

Her father was correct about Cecy being like her grandam. There was a portrait of Matilda de Lacey (as she'd once been) hanging in my cousin's bedchamber. With the neckline of her dark velvet gown plunging to indecent depths, and her famous russet hair loose about her shoulders, rippling down her back, her expression was both bold and mocking. It unnerved me how her deep blue eyes would follow you around the room, seeking you out wherever you were standing. Not surprisingly, she'd been popular with the men, evident from what Cecy told me last week:

"Some used to say my grandam was a witch. Seducing any man who came near her. She certainly had the gift of second sight, like so many de Laceys. She told me I have it too."

"I can believe that."

"When Mother and I went to see her when she was dying she was very confused. She kept talking about another man who sent her pink roses."

"'Pink roses'?'

"Yes, Grandsire John loved her so much that on each May Day he used to send her one to mark the birth of their first child. My mother. He always made us laugh by joking it wasn't him who sent the roses. Even though everyone knew it was. When she died, we discovered he'd arranged for two score to be placed on top of her coffin."

"So instead of leaving money to pay for masses to be held for his soul, he left money for her roses?"

"He left money for those, too." My cousin gave a little twirl. *"Who can blame her for wishing she had a mysterious admirer? It sounds more exciting. To have someone who loves you so much they'll follow you to the grave and beyond. I hope someone loves me that much one day…."*

∽

The talk at the table had turned to politics, especially so today; everyone was waiting for Cecy's uncles to report back on the latest events in London.

'The big news is that Sir Edward Howard was appointed Vice-Admiral while we were there,' Richard said, raising a spoonful of pea pottage to his lips. 'It's up to him to control what happens in the Narrow Sea. He was probably given the position because he did away with James of Scotland's man, Andrew Barton.'

'Not to mention the fact he's one of our King's best friends,' added his younger brother. 'People still talk about the joust at Greenwich nearly two years ago when Howard took on a German giant called Gyot and felled him.'

Richard blew on his soup. 'He started off in Henry's household as a standard bearer. Earning around forty pounds a year for the privilege.'

Uncle William leant forward in his chair. 'Unlike a labourer in the fields beyond Zennor who earns a paltry two, or a skilled shipwright over at Mount's Bay, who earns twelve.'

'Edward Howard is Nan and Mary's uncle,' Cecy told me.

'Who was Andrew Barton?' I asked.

Richard smiled as he dabbed his mouth with his napkin. 'Well, Tristan, what you have to say about Barton rather depends on whether you're Scots or English. For them, he was an honest sailor, acting as a privateer in their King's employ, but for the English, he was an unscrupulous pirate, wreaking havoc in the Narrow Sea, attacking and pillaging boats belonging to their merchants.'

'So the Scots aren't happy he's dead,' I said.

'Not at all,' said Stephen. 'They're particularly vexed with Edward Howard who boarded Barton's ship, "*The Jenett of Purwyn*", after his death, killing some and capturing others. Our King was gleeful when Howard arrived back in Blackwall, on the Thames, with both of Barton's ships, complete with the remaining crew as captives.'

For some reason, the name 'Howard' rang a bell, but I couldn't remember where I'd heard it before. 'I like the sound of Edward Howard,' I said, imagining myself on the deck next to him, fighting the warlike Scots. There was probably a wolf or two aboard to make it even more dangerous.

'He's Nan and Mary's favourite uncle,' said Cecy. 'They like him far more than their other two.'

'His brother, Thomas, lost his wife back in November, so I've heard,' said Stephen. 'So he'll be sniffing around for a new one.'

'The wife who was old King's Edward daughter?' asked my aunt.

Stephen nodded. 'That's right. Princess Anne of York. Trust the Howards to manage a wedding in Westminster Abbey. However, nothing lasting came out of the match, I'm afraid—'

'You mean, all their children died?' asked Cecy. She glanced at me and I could tell she was thinking of our earlier conversation.

Stephen picked up his goblet of wine. 'Yes. And there won't be any Howard boys from Edward. Though he's a handsome fellow, popular with not only the King but the ladies. So I'm sure there's more than one Howard bastard around the place. But he makes it his business to only wed old women who can put money in his purse, not warmth in his bed, or heirs in his nursery.'

My aunt glared at him to remind him Cecy and I were listening. I liked Stephen Pendeen. His stories were always more colourful than those of his brother.

'Was the old Earl in London when you were there?' Aunt Alys asked her brothers.

'Yes, I think he was,' said Stephen. 'But we didn't see him.'

Cecy gave a little shiver. 'There's an enormous portrait of him in the entrance hall at Hever. I'd rather welcome the Devil into my home than him.'

'Cecy!' admonished her mother. 'Despite what you might think of Thomas Howard, that's no way to speak of your elders and betters.' She turned to the other adults. 'Having said that, I've never envied Tom Bullen, having that one as a father-in-law.'

'I met him a couple of times when Father took us to Trewellis Hall when we were young,' said Stephen. 'His son, Edward, was there once. He was a few years older than me but I remember him captivating the great hall with his stories.'

'There's no denying the Howards are a good-looking bunch,' said Richard. 'With those big dark eyes of theirs that seem to stare right through you—'

'And their long noses that make them seem haughtier than any noble alive,' said Stephen. 'I have an appetite for their women. Both of Thomas Howard's daughters are as tasty as a Mousehole Starrey Gazey Pie. William, your friend, Tom Bullen, must have given a whoop of joy when he got Lizzie Howard.'

'He did.'

'Have you met Edward Howard, Uncle William?' I asked.

My uncle gave a shrug. 'Once, if I remember rightly. A long time ago. I'm never in London for long enough to meet anyone important. Besides, why should I go there when I have everything I could possibly want here?' He reached out to pat my mother's arm. 'And never more than when my dearest sister and nephew visit.'

My mother, who'd been quiet during the conversation and didn't seem particularly interested in this Howard family, grasped his hand and gave a little smile that wasn't really one at all. Perhaps she was missing my father and it was making her sad listening to the tales of the thrilling Vice-Admiral. We knew Father was safe because the French Ambassador, old Abbot Fécamp, sent word he'd returned home from the recent battle in Ravenna, Italy. France, together with her ally, the Duchy of Ferrara, had been victorious against Spain and the Papal States. Although I felt a cold-hearted varlet for thinking it (considering my father risked his life every time he went to war), the fact he always insisted my mother and I come back to Cornwall whenever he was away fighting for the King, or accompanying him on his travels around France, only worked to my advantage. It was also no bad thing that Nicolas was left behind to watch over Ardres Castle in the absence of its lord and lady.

All of a sudden, I noticed the colour drain from my mother's cheeks.

'Wherever did you get that ring, Cecy?' she asked, clutching her throat and staring at my cousin in horror.

Startled, I looked over at Cecy who'd flushed bright red. I immediately knew it must be the ring from the archery competition.

'I won it, Aunt Grace,' Cecy answered in a small voice, guilt written all over her face. Both of us had known such a valuable ring belonged in a lady's boudoir, not on a stall in a Marazion market.

'For being the best archer…better than all the men,' I put in, trying to make light of the situation.

'"*Better than all the men*"!' Stephen let out a roar of appreciation. 'That doesn't surprise me, Mistress Minx.'

My mother held out her hand. 'May I see it?'

Cecy slipped it off her finger and held it out to my mother. 'Here.'

Not a trace of colour had returned to my mother's cheeks and I noticed tears in her eyes.

'Is it yours, Grace dear?' asked Aunt Alys in a gentle voice.

My mother didn't reply but sat staring at the ring.

'It's got something written on the inside,' said Cecy. '"*My brightest star, my one true love*". And there's the letter "N".'

Stephen laughed. '"N"? It must be an initial. Perhaps a woman's name. Nan, for example? Or a man's. Nicholas. A secret admirer from your past?'

Cecy's father glared at his brother-in-law. 'Don't be foolish! Grace was wed to Guy far too young for anything like that.'

Stephen held up his hands. 'Forgive me. I meant no offence.'

I was surprised Cecy's posy ring was causing such a stir, or that my normally affable uncle seemed as shaken as my mother by its appearance. After what seemed the longest time, Maman finally spoke. 'Here, Cecy, have it back. I used to have one quite similar but it was stolen soon after I got it. It's so long ago now I can't even remember much about it. Only that it probably belonged to my mother, and I was sad to lose it.'

The mystery of the ring solved, Richard begged my mother to sing a song in French. 'You have the sweetest voice, Grace.'

My still white-faced mother took a few moments to compose herself and then she smiled at us. 'This is a poem by Christine de Pisan,' she said, closing her eyes. 'It's called *"Deuil angoisseux"*, and was set to music by Gilles Binchois:

> *"Fierté, durté de joye separée,*
> *Triste penser, parfont gemissement,*
> *Angoisse grant en las cuer enserrée,*
> *Courroux amer porté couvertement*
> *Morne maintien sanz resjoïssement,*
> *Espoir dolent qui tous biens fait tarir,*
> *Si sont en moy, sanz partir nullement;*
> *Et si ne puis ne garir ne morir."*

> {'Disdain, harshness without joy,
> sad thoughts, deep sighs,
> Great anguish locked in the weary heart.
> Fierce bitterness borne secretly,
> mournful expression or without joy,
> dread which silences all hope,
> are in me and never leave me;
> and so I can neither be healed nor die.'}

It was a song I'd never heard before, one whose words and tune were as melancholic as its title. As I listened, it was as if a part of me had stepped out of the Maytime Castle and our family celebration, and was wandering the road to London in search of the enigmatic Vice-Admiral.... My mind drifted back to all that had been said about Edward Howard. Although we'd been discussing his family, we hadn't mentioned the mooted war between England and France.

<<*How I long to be part of it, fighting the—*>>

I stopped short. *Whom* was I fighting? The English or the French. Should

I be happy the French had won a resounding victory at Ravenna, even though they lost their handsome young commander, Gaston de Foix (beloved by all the women). Or should I be siding with England who staunchly supported the Pope in Rome? Two castles were home to me: Ardres and Zennor. I belonged equally to both. And whichever one I happened to be in when war broke out, I'd be on the wrong side in the other.

Confused, I glanced up at the portrait of my great-grandfather on the wall. A Cornishman, born and bred, Thomas Tredavoe's family line stretched back through the generations, right here in Zennor, to the beginning of time. The venerable old man seemed to be staring straight at me, his green eyes as bright as they'd probably been in life.

I could almost hear him reprimanding me. *'You'll find out, my boy, that war is a fool's game. With no winners. Only losers.'*

I only hoped he wasn't right or that I wouldn't feel like a traitor, not knowing whether to support Louis of France…or Henry of England.

ZENNOR CASTLE THICK PEA POTTAGE

2 slices of white bread, blended into breadcrumbs

1 egg yolk

1 teaspoon (5 ml) chopped parsley

½ teaspoon (2.5 ml) fresh ground ginger

3 threads of saffron

½ pint (275 ml) milk

350g can of peas, drained

1) Blend the breadcrumbs, egg yolk, parsley, ginger and saffron.
2) Bring the milk almost to the boil. Pour in the peas and the breadcrumb mixture.
3) Bring to a boil slowly over a low heat, stirring with a wooden spoon. It should be a very thick consistency by the time it's boiled.
4) Put it into a blender for a couple of minutes.
5) The pea pottage may be served as a soup or as a vegetable side dish.

A Book of Cookrye, A W 1591.

HOUSE OF TUDOR

Chapter Thirty-Nine

November 1ˢᵗ, 1512. The Feast of All Saints.
The Palace of Placentia, Greenwich, Kent.

he King was in a good mood. He had lately come from the Queen's bedchamber where thoughts of black-haired Maud Brereton with the saucy expression and welcoming arms, had spurred him on to perform with much greater ability than usual.

Yes, he had every reason to be pleased with himself. Afterwards, while sharing a cup of spiced wine, Kate had assured him his magnificent efforts would bring forth another boy-child. Her next words still rang most pleasantly in his ears: *"It's true what they say about you, my lord…that already you're a great king…and one day you'll be the most powerful ruler in Christendom."*

Henry could almost hear her husky voice with its marked Spanish lilt, reassuring and praising him as she always did when they were alone. He stretched luxuriously, flexing every muscle of his body. Smiling to himself, he slipped a ring onto one of his fingers and adjusted the frill on his wrist. His wife's words echoed almost exactly those of his trusted adviser, Thomas Wolsey. Henry silently gave thanks to Dame Fortune for surrounding him with such competent people. Wolsey was a man who'd so impressed the King, his father, by managing to travel to the Emperor's court in Flanders and back again in three days (accomplishing the near impossible, by taking a barge from Richmond to Gravesend, travelling by post horse to Dover, sailing to Calais within three hours, and arriving in Flanders the next day; all done again in reverse) on a diplomatic mission, that he'd made him Dean of Lincoln on the spot. Positions and royal favour soon started to flow into Wolsey's hands. From a humble background, within a remarkably short time, he'd become Royal Almoner and general confidante to the royal family. From the moment Henry inherited the throne at the tender age of seventeen, Wolsey was invariably by his side with soothing words:

"Leave this tedious matter to me, Your Grace. Go...go and enjoy yourself with your friends. After all, as the whole world knows, youth must have some dalliance. Take your time. And when you return, it will all be done."

The excellent Wolsey had been extremely useful recently; his expert knowledge of the area of France around Calais (acquired during time spent there as secretary to an English lord), enabled them to work closely together on future plans.

To invade France and seize the glittering prize: the throne.

How King Louis's victory over the Pope and Spain six months ago still rankled. However, it also provided Henry with the perfect excuse to take up arms against France under the guise of a 'holy war', in defence of Pope Julius. Hoping for Henry's support in his bid to expel Louis from Italy, the Pope had sent the new King of England gifts: a Tudor rose of solid gold, one hundred hard Parmesan cheeses, and copious amounts of Italian wine.

Henry was looking for any excuse for war and a chance to prove his worth in the eyes of the world. Finally, he had the backing of (most of) his government. If he could take France, what was to prevent him from organizing a crusade against the Ottoman Turk? Or becoming Holy Roman Emperor. Everything was possible. At least in his own head...if not in the head of his disapproving Lord Treasurer, Thomas Howard.

It would certainly go some way to make up for his recent humiliation. Back in June, Kate's father had played him for a fool in Spain, promising to help him take Bayonne in south-west France, but instead abandoning him and taking the Kingdom of Navarre for himself. He'd made England a laughing stock in the courts of Europe. What ignominy for Henry to know - through no fault of his own - that two hundred thousand ducats had been spent and two thousand English lives sacrificed.

He walked over to the window and was pleased to see his best friend, Charles Brandon, heading in his direction. He was glad. Charles played a central part in his life and always made him feel much better about everything. They had been close for many years, ever since Charles's father was slain at Bosworth Field, allegedly by Henry's great-uncle, the Yorkist villain, King Richard. Following the death of Charles's mother in childbed, Henry's father had taken the young orphan in and brought him up with his two sons, supposedly as a companion for the older. But it was Henry not Arthur who had more in common with Charles, even if he was a good six or seven years younger than the orphaned boy. True, many regarded Charles as more brawn than brains, as big as Henry, bluff and hearty, but with none of the sophistication or charm of his master. Henry didn't care. He likened his circle of friends (many of them also his tournament companions, collectively known as 'the King's Spears') to the ingredients of his favourite green apple tart: each one played a part towards the finished product, whether it was the apples, the egg, sugar, ground ginger, butter, saffron, cinnamon or flour. <<*What does it matter if Charles is the plain old 'egg' and not the more exotic 'saffron' or 'ginger'?*>>

'It makes my blood boil,' Henry said, a little while later as they strolled through the gardens, 'to have to listen to my scoundrel of a father-in-law. Do you know what he dared write to me? That although we English show promise in the arena of war, we are yet "novices".'

'He had to say that to excuse his own behaviour in Navarre.'

'I still blame Tom Howard for bringing the men home. A bunch of cowardly curs you know I wanted to string up from the nearest tree.'

'Tom and Edmund aren't a patch on their father, the Earl. Or their brother. Our Ned.'

'Don't even mention Edmund Howard's name to me. Every time I see his face I want to punch it.'

'I don't blame you. Any man who doesn't wait until his opponent is ready at the lists doesn't deserve another day at court. All of us agreed you were a hero continuing to joust in such bitter weather, especially when your horse started having problems. I know I would have given up long before. It was probably Edmund's idea to leave Fuenterrabia. Playing into the hands of the old naysayers at court.'

'By the Mass! You know how sick I am of being told by my Archbishop of Canterbury and my Lord Chancellor that I should *"consolidate"* my father's *"successful domestic policies"*.'

'Hal, William Warham was your father's man before yours. Richard Fox, too.'

'Fox might be Lord Privy Seal but he's my man now. So is Thomas Howard who sometimes seems to forget it. If that meddling Earl dares treat me like an insolent pup one more time—'

'You mean, not treating you as if you're taking your father's hard-earned money and squandering it abroad.' Charles gave his huge booming laugh.

'That's right. The flap-mouthed moldwarp had no choice but to come back with his tail between his legs last summer after I sent him packing from court.'

'But he also came back and together with George Talbot, negotiated a treaty with Spain.'

'To save the honour of his sons.'

'To be fair, Hal, it wasn't the Earl's fault Ferdinand is as slippery as an eel and as two-faced as Janus. As for his tail, it's not such a bad one. It's managed to produce two sons in as many years!'

Henry didn't care if he sounded bitter; it was a blessed relief to be able to express his true feelings to a trusted friend. 'Unlike me. Who's had to endure a girl child born dead and then have my precious boy live for but two months. Sometimes, I swear I can see Thomas Howard's beady eyes on Kate's flat belly. Just as I can imagine my fiendish Scottish brother-in-law gloating whenever he picks up his boy prince in the nursery. Why should Margaret have more luck than Kate? Dame Fortune can be a vixen at times.'

Charles sighed. 'Unfortunately, that's true. But no one could ever accuse the Howard men of having poor seed.'

'Or their women lacking beauty. Even though she's past thirty, Lizzie Howard has eyes that beckon a man to the bedchamber.'

'I've always thought Tom Bullen has the air of a man who's walked off with the best hen in the coop.'

'If Kate didn't please me so much, or I wasn't anxious not to unsettle her humour, or the workings of her womb, I'd take Lizzie to bed in an instant.'

'That really would put old man Howard's nose out of joint.'

'Then he'd be a fool to take on the King of England. I've even thought of sending the old meddler back to the Tower but haven't because of my affection for Ned.'

'Thomas Howard is too useful to you. Better to have the Howards working for you then plotting against you.'

'Maybe. But I still can't abide the way he treats me. Even though I've got my way over France, Thomas Howard and all the other greybeards he consorts with would prefer me to stand by like some beetle-headed pumpion. Rightly despised by every other ruling monarch of Europe...but becoming richer by the day—

'God's Fury! What a lot of twaddle. The Earl should never have told you to honour the treaty with France you signed a year after your father's death. Who gives a tinker's farthing it's tradition to keep the peace.'

Soothed by Charles's words, Henry paused to pluck a climbing red rose (normally associated with summer love - but not today) from a nearby bush, inhaling its rich scent before attaching it to his doublet. He turned and took a white rose from the other side of the path and handed it to his friend. 'Who, indeed. Look! The red rose of my father's house of Lancaster and the white rose of my mother's house of York. Together making the red and white rose of the House of Tudor. I want to show everyone exactly what we're made of. If they think I'm about to take a single step down a road pointing towards peace, they're wrong. Thank God I have Tom Wolsey to do my bidding. He understands me as well as you do.'

He was rewarded with an enthusiastic slap on the back from Charles. 'How can they expect you to champion peace when the road towards war is beckoning with all the allure of a siren of the waves, eh?'

'Or the allure of Will Brereton's pretty cousin.'

That stopped Charles in his tracks. 'I can tell from the smirk on your face you've made progress in that area since we last spoke. Lizzie Bullen's honour may be safe but that of Will Brereton's cousin surely is not.'

Henry assumed an expression of mock innocence and put a finger to his mouth. 'My lips are sealed.'

Charles's dark brown eyes were dancing with mirth. 'Suit yourself. But you and I both know I will find out. I always do. Now, I've heard that Paulo da Lodi—'

'The Milanese Ambassador?'

'Yes. I've heard he wrote home to his master, the Duke of Milan, that you're *"as hungry for war as a lion"* and have *"a burning desire to fight the French".*' Charles pretended to give a silent roar and made a clawing gesture with his hands.

This drew a laugh from Henry. 'Signor da Lodi is a clever man. Tell Wolsey to invite him to supper tomorrow. But first, I want you to go and find as many of our friends as you can and bring them to me....'

As far as Henry was concerned - and many in his court - going to war was in his blood. After all, hadn't Mars, the mighty God of War, declared himself in favour of his own father, Henry of Richmond, not far from the town of Market Bosworth, on a hot August day twenty-eight years before. So why shouldn't God and Dame Fortune be smiling down upon him as he prepared to realize his greatest ambition?

Back in his private rooms, as he looked around at the eager faces of his friends, Henry was reflecting how this particular Feast of All Saints held a promise all of its own. Loudly humming his most successful composition to date, *'Pastime with good company'*, he broke off suddenly to address his attendants:

'Charles, send word to Will Compton to bring me my surcoat of hawthorns - and my best baldric and my sword. And I need you to shave me.'

He wanted them all to know the King of England was feeling as pleased as an archer whose arrow has just hit the 'heart'.

'Youth must have some dalliance,
Of good or ill some pastance,' he sang in clear, high tones.

'Ned - you can fetch the fool to amuse us while we work. You Howards deserve to be amongst the first to hear the news.' He started to chuckle. 'Even if it will send your good father into a fit of apoplexy.'

'*Company methinks them best,*' he continued, thoroughly enjoying the sound of his own voice.

'*All thoughts and fancies to digest* - Oh, and so does that brother-in-law of yours. What an excellent ambassador to the Low Countries, Tom Bullen's turned out to be. He clearly has the ear of Margaret of Austria.'

❧

The men were used to their monarch's boisterous behaviour but this was different; the last time he'd been in quite such high spirits was at little Henry's birth: now a bitter-sweet memory. Henry's boon companions smiled at one another, already guessing the reason for his exuberance this morning. It was only six months since Ned Howard had come racing down the corridor to tell them he'd been made Vice-Admiral of the King's Fleet. "*I can't wait to see my father's face when I tell him!*" he'd cried.

All eyes were on the King as he began to pace up and down the room. It was clear he had plans for all of them. He turned to face them and winked at Charles Brandon.

'Gentlemen, prepare yourselves. We're going to war! And no one is going to stop us. Certainly not my arrogant Scottish brother-in-law who should be going down on one knee to do homage to me instead of siding with our enemy, France. I've heard he knows no fear on horseback and can easily ride from Stirling to Aberdeen, and then on to Elgin, in one day. He might have been on the throne for two decades, and I only three years, but it doesn't give him the right to challenge my authority.'

Charles put his hands together as if in mock prayer. 'They say he forgoes meat on Wednesdays and Fridays, will not mount a horse on Sunday, even to attend mass, and before he attends to any state affairs, has to hear at least two masses.'

Henry made a scoffing sound. 'Does he have to ask God's permission before he swives my sister…or any of his other whores? You forgot to mention how he feigns piety during Holy Week by entering a friary in Stirling and fasting with the brothers inside.'

'No doubt smuggling in a "sister" from outside,' said Charles. 'To keep him company in between the vigils.'

Ned made a graceful lunging movement, holding an imaginary sword. 'James Stewart might be skilled at the longbow, crossbow and hand-culverin, as well as able to play a vigorous game of tennis and win at long bowls. But let him disobey the Subsidy Act at his peril. It's his duty to be "*the very homager and obediencer of right*" to you.'

Henry grinned. 'If he disobeys, you might have to take another of his ships. He seems to forget my Grandsire Edward sent his own brother, Great-Uncle Richard, to invade Scotland and make the Scottish King's brother regent. Brother paired with brother. Of course those were the days before Richard showed his true colours—'

'You mean, that he was a serpent capable of killing two little brothers!' exclaimed Charles, his lip curling in disgust. Around the room, Henry's friends gave a collective shudder.

Wishing to shake off this horrible image and return to the matter in hand, Henry held up his hand. 'Forget the Treaty of Perpetual Peace…an entirely new game has begun. One I'll wager the Scottish varlet will need all his wits to win.'

Ned held out two fists and then punched one of them into the air in a show of victory. 'I know upon which of you I'd wager.'

HOUSE OF STEWART

Chapter Forty

The same day. Holyrood Palace, Edinburgh.

Why won't my brother listen to you? Instead of trying to break the Treaty of Perpetual Peace between our two lands?'

Not liking the high colour in his wife's cheeks, James reached out and placed his right hand on her stomach. 'Calm yourself, hinny. Ye know it's no' good for ye to get so tetchy when the birthing chamber is no' so far off.'

Snatching his hand away, Margaret glared at him. 'Stop treating me as though I'm still a child. I'll be twenty-three in nigh on a month.'

'Forgive me. I was only thinking of the bairn.'

Margaret's voice was bitter. 'Of course you were. Of this one and the three others lying useless beneath the sod. Instead of in the nursery at Stirling Castle. Replacing your precious royal bastards.'

James was becoming fearful for his wife's wellbeing. Unfortunately, Margaret spoke the truth; their only bairn to have survived so far was the wee one named for him. James had hoped for a good breeder like Margaret's mother and maternal grandmother before her, but she seemed to be favouring her paternal grandmother who'd produced only one son at the tender age of thirteen, and then no more. This one was coming too soon after the April birth, not giving her sufficient time to recover.

Somehow he had to lead his heavily pregnant wife's mind away from this dark place. 'I was hoping to take ye to see my new Lion House before ye take to your chamber.'

Normally, Margaret's dark blue eyes would have shone with excitement but today they were dull with exhaustion and discontent. 'I don't need to see it,' she snapped. 'I'm already kept from my sleep by the earth-vexing thing roaring. Not to mention the civet you've put with it to rob your poor wife of any peace.'

James inwardly sighed. By sweet Saint Ninian, five pregnancies in as many years were beginning to take their toll on the fresh-faced lass he'd lifted from his saddle nine years ago in the Castle courtyard below. Carrying her eagerly across the threshold to a life of hope and promise. The presence of healthy male bastards was proof enough that the blame for breeding sickly bairns lay with her. It made him feel guilty this pregnancy had added an extra chin and unappealing rolls of flesh across Margaret's ribs. Best she didna know she looked more like a matron of thirty-five than a maid of twenty-three. Some women, like his own sweet Janet, strong and robust, were made to bear a man's sons; such a woman rose from the birthing bed with all the ease of one awaking from a good night's rest and stretching her arms in pleasure. For a fleeting moment, an image came to mind of a ravishing young girl (with hair as black as a mid-winter night, streaming down her back, past her tiny waist) who never rose from her birthing bed - before being swiftly banished again.

He decided that fulfilling Margaret's wishes and treating her like an equal as she demanded would be the best course of action. He leant back in his chair and put his arms behind his head. 'You're right about your brother, Maggie. He might represent the Tudor rose as do ye but he's a thorn in my flesh. Perhaps I should have entertained his toady, Wolsey, with more enthusiasm when he came up here four years ago, sent by the old King, your father. Afforded him the same courtesy I extended to the Earl of Surrey when ye and I were first wed. But Wolsey and I couldna see eye to eye, I'm afraid. He wouldna listen to my complaints and thought I was intent on pushing ahead with the "Auld Alliance".'

'If only Arthur hadn't succumbed to the sickness. He was calm where Harry was wild. He would have listened to you. And to me.'

'And kept in place the peace the Howards brokered.'

'Surely you mean the Earl. Not his sons. Edward Howard seems to be doing his best to persuade Harry to break it.'

'That's verra true, my love. I dislike the eldest son and Edward might be a favourite of your brother's but he's no friend of ours. Encouraging your brother to wantonly spend money on provisions for war with me, telling him I'm opposed to peace. I understand why Henry had a mind to make him Vice-Admiral of England but that didna give him the right to kill my man.'

'Harry said Andrew Barton was nothing but a pirate and a thief.'

'He also refused to let me bring the Howard brothers to justice at a Warden's Court. Believe me, Maggie, I've tried my level best with your brother, I really have. But he refuses to meet me halfway. He's probably still smarting at his treatment by his father-in-law. Making him into an ass for his own ends. Your Harry seems to want war at any cost.'

'He's still the annoying little brother who used to steal Arthur's wooden soldiers, knowing he was too kind to give him the beating he deserved. I remember him clenching his fists with rage when he found out that as a future Queen of Scotland, I would take precedence over him as the Duke of York. So I can well imagine how much he resents you for having the biggest ship in Christendom.'

'Aye.'

'You built "The Great Michael" long before he even thought of the "Great Harry".'

'Well, he certainly thinks the worst of me. Treating me as though I were a common robber on the Great North Road, dirk in hand, evil deeds in his heart. Even though I agreed to the renewal of the "Auld Alliance" with the French in July, it doesna mean I agreed to be their ally against England. Or that I have any intention of invading your brother's land.'

'You've brought all of Scotland together as one, my lord. Gained recognition of your kingdom as an independent force, and kept strong diplomatic ties with France.'

'Your Father understood I did that to maintain my independence. Your brother does no'. He deliberately sees it as an alliance against him.'

'Edward Howard seems to be getting worse—'

'Och, that's true. Howard's been stirring up trouble wherever he goes, using his fleet to menace everyone on the Narrow Sea. I heard he captured one merchant, had him taken back to Southampton and tortured. And all because he spoke French.'

'In that case, he might need to torture every noble man and woman in the whole of Europe.'

James laughed. 'He even dared to burn down the house of a French naval captain. It's as if he bears a grudge against the French. Perhaps there's something personal about it.'

'He's truly got the devil in him.'

'It seems he took it verra hard when his brother-in-law, Tom Knyvett, died in battle over at Brest. I heard he swore no' to look your brother in the face until he'd avenged his favourite's death.'

'I had a letter from Kate last week, telling me that Knyvett's widow, Muriel, Edward Howard's sister, has vowed to follow her husband to heaven. Exactly five months to the day from when he was killed. Kate said Muriel is desperately ill now. How onion-eyed I was by the time I'd finished reading it. Imagining those two sons and two little girls being left motherless.'

'The Queen is kind to keep ye up-to-date.'

'I only wish she had more influence with my brother.'

'It would help if she gave him a living son.' James dropped a kiss on the top of his wife's head. 'You've bested your brother in that, hinny.'

James was relieved to see a small smile of triumph on his wife's lips. Turning the tables away from himself and onto her troublesome brother seemed to be doing the trick. At least, the worrying scarlet had left her cheeks and she was looking more composed.

Keep her calm, keep her happy…and keep her off the subject of the jewels and plate left to her (by her brother, Arthur, and her grandam - for whom she was named), and still not delivered into her keeping by the choleric Harry.

PART SIX

THE CHRISTMAS CASTLES

"Green groweth the holly"
by King Henry VIII

From BL Additional Ms. 31922

'Green groweth the holly, so doth the ivy.
Though winter blasts blow never so high,
Green groweth the holly.
As the holly groweth green
And never changeth hue,
So I am, and ever hath been,
Unto my lady true.'

HOUSE OF STEWART

Chapter Forty-One

December 15ᵗʰ, 1512.
Darnaway Castle, near Forres, Scotland.

ome away from the window back to bed, my love. You'll catch your death standing there like that. In only your velvet robe. As ye and I both ken, the King of Scotland canna be found dead in his paramour's bedchamber.'

James turned to look at his dishevelled mistress, fresh from their very vigorous lovemaking on a soft feather mattress, beneath a red canopy. She was enveloped in the expensive sable furs he'd recently bought from a Russian trader. Her lips were swollen and her bright hair tumbled over her creamy breasts, reddened from his hard kisses. It amused him that she'd had the wooden ceiling painted with nymphs and cherubs, surrounding a reclining Venus, naked as the day she was born. It was no coincidence that her facial features and wickedly sensual body were unmistakably those of the lady of the Castle.

"Now I can experience heaven from above and below," he'd teased her.

He found the falling snow outside oddly comforting, creating a world within a world, except for the fact it meant he would soon have to leave this place to be back at court by Christmas. Not that there would be much cheer, given what had just happened, coupled with the deteriorating relations with his pignut of a brother-in-law.

Officially, he was here to visit the shrine of Saint Duthac in Tain and give thanks that the Scottish baby prince still lived…especially as the new princess, born at the end of November, hadn't survived beyond her baptism. Although he'd felt a pang of guilt deserting Maggie when she needed him most, he thought he'd go mad if he had to visit her bedchamber once more to find her lying pale and listless in her bed, railing against everyone and everything.

When he'd announced he was going on his usual pilgrimage to the shrine up here, she threw such a tantrum that she was left fighting for breath, and a doctor had to be fetched. It was only when he reassured her over and over that he wouldna be seeking comfort in Janet's bed (because her former lover, Archibald Douglas, had been released from prison and reclaimed his place) that she finally turned her face away from him and fell into a deep sleep.

And yet here he was, accompanied by his favourite poet, falconers, Italian minstrels, and this time, a Moorish drummer. In Darnaway Castle, hawking in the short December days, and whiling away the long evenings playing cards. Then making love with the only woman who could save him from the demons that pursued him, and make him feel whole again. Reuniting him with the three children they had together, including their first-born, also a James. Petting and pampering him and telling him he was the best king Scotland had ever known. Janet Kennedy was so different from the Tudor wife he'd left behind, too often a termagant for his tastes. With all the cares of the kingdom falling on his shoulders, he needed a woman who'd draw him into her soft depths, and afterwards, hold him in her arms, either in blissful silence, or listen to his woes if he felt the need to unburden himself.

Janet was the only woman in whom he'd confided his secrets…well, almost all of them. She knew how guilty he felt about the undignified death of his father, slaughtered by an unknown hand. Yet she'd managed to reassure him:

"Ye were just a wee boy, barely fifteen, and your father, King James, a bad king, already imprisoned in the past by his own family. The fault lies with him for abandoning ye, his son and heir, in favour of your younger brother, forcing ye to flee for your life and look to others for your safety. It's no' your fault his army was defeated at Sauchieburn, nor did ye ken of the dagger to be used at Bannockburn Mill by an assassin wearing a priest's robes. Ye ken how I feel about that heavy iron chain ye insist on wearing as penance every Lent."

'Come back to bed, my love,' she repeated now, her voice seductive, and as soft and mellow as the famous mead stored below in the Castle kitchens, produced by the Benedictine monks in the Priory on the Holy Island of Lindisfarne. 'Let me warm ye.'

This time, he did not resist.

∞

Janet ran her hands up and down his icy thighs, restoring warmth both to his groin and the rest of his body. She paused for a moment and pulled a fur rug over the two of them. 'Has Maggie been making your life a torment, again? I thought she might have grown up a little by now. I'm sorry she lost the bairn. No woman should have to go through that.'

'It was too soon after the birth of wee James. I should ken better than that. After all, I'm turning forty in March.'

'It canna be helped. Ye are a King and need strong healthy sons—'

'Like *our* James.'

She smiled and planted a kiss on the smooth skin of his cheek. 'Aye, like our James.'

Picking up some strands of her hair as if they were threads of red and gold in one of his tapestries back in Edinburgh, James sighed. 'Would that ye could have been my Queen, sweetheart. We would have had a veritable brood of bonny bairns by now. No' just our three. And Bell the Cat could never have taken ye to his bed. Or come back to it now.'

Janet reached out and took his hand. 'Ye should have been a shepherd and I, your loving wife. Preparing a feast of oatmeal bannocks, baked on an iron girdle on the hearth, for our brood. Me…nursing a hungry babe, and ye soothing it with: "*The Frog cam to the mill door*".'

'A verra pretty picture. And Bell the Cat?'

She sighed. 'While I'm flattered you're so jealous of Angus who…to be fair…met me before ye did, dinna deny ye didna have other loves before me.'

'No one like ye.'

For a moment, she didn't answer and all that could be heard in the small winter chamber was the sound of blazing faggots spitting in the fireplace at the end of the bed. When she did speak, her voice was very low. 'That's no' true. What about the fair Madeleine?'

It was as if a score of shards of ice were sliding down James's spine. He shot up in the bed in the manner of a scalded cat and turned to stare at his mistress. 'What did ye say?'

Even though she couldn't have missed the violence of his response, Janet remained as unperturbed as ever. 'Ye heard me, James.'

He hesitated; he'd only ever discussed his lost love with one other person in all the long years since she'd died of childbed fever, after the birth of their child. 'She was my first love,' he said at length.

'French.'

Startled, he was harsher than he intended. 'Who told ye?'

Janet reached out to stroke his back. 'Ye did, my love. Many times in your sleep. Ye'd call out her name and then whisper endearments in French.'

James suddenly relaxed when it was clear he'd betrayed his own trust. 'You're a remarkable woman, Janet. No' to be seized by the green-eyed monster. Like my Maggie would be, for example.'

'Then it's just as well ye dinna share a bedchamber with your Queen.'

'How long have ye known?'

'For as long as I've been with ye.'

'And yet, you've never said a word.'

'Why would I?'

'And ye weren't jealous?'

'Of a ghost? I hope I'm a better woman than that.' She pulled him back down next to her. 'At least I didna imprison past loves like ye did Angus.'

'No more than he deserved.'

Janet put her head on James's chest and began stroking the dark hair. 'I decided she must be dead or it would have been her in your bed...no' me.'

'Again, my hinny. You're a remarkable woman.'

'Tell me about her.'

James let out a long sigh. 'Her name was Madeleine de Louviers. She was from a high-born family in Normandy and came to Edinburgh with her parents to visit some relatives there. We met at Holyrood House when they came to dine. From the first moment we met, I was smitten.'

'And already King.'

'Yes, but a verra young and uncertain one, back then. I wasn't even a proper king, preferring others to do my work until I was past twenty-one. So I had plenty of time to hunt, hawk—'

'And make love.'

'Precisely.'

'What I had with Madeleine with akin to taking the first few sips of the sweetest wine you've ever had in your life.'

'And what do ye have with me?'

'My beautiful bold Janet, ye are the elixir of life itself. My *aqua vitae, par excellence.*'

Janet buried her head in his shoulder. 'Did anyone else ken about the affair?'

'Apart from the various servants, ye mean? No. Just Patrick Hepburn. The new Earl of Bothwell. He was the only one I told. With no father of my own, and a mother some said had been poisoned, I was totally alone. He encouraged me to enjoy myself while he managed the various factions in the country. So I did.'

'How did your Madeleine die?'

'After the birth of our child,' said James flatly, as he watched the pile of faggots burst into hearty flames. 'My first-born bairn,' he corrected himself. 'The Earl had arranged for Madeleine to be tended to by the nuns of Iona and promised me I could be with her when the time came. He kept his word and on a warm July evening in 1491, I mounted my horse and travelled back to the island with the man who'd come to deliver the message.'

'And?'

'By the time I arrived at the nunnery, crossing over from the Isle of Mull, it was too late. Madeleine was laid out on a slab, as cold as a marble statue, her perfect features already turned to stone. Although I begged her to come back to me, drenching her with all the tears one young lad could possibly shed, all my pleas were for nothing.'

'And the bairn?'

'A wee lad. She'd named him Nicolas after the patron saint of sailors, in honour of the ones who rowed her to the island.'

'What happened to him?'

'He left Berwick in September with a wet nurse and Patrick Hepburn on "The Katherine", bound for France, across the North Sea. The Earl was part of a mission *en route* to King Charles to renew the "Auld Alliance".'

'Was it sorrowful for ye to say goodbye?'

'I held him until the very last moment. Patrick almost had to tear him from my arms. Such a bonny wee fellow with eyes and hair as black as a starless Scottish night. It was almost as if he knew I was his father.'

'Have ye kept in touch?'

'Patrick said it was for the best if we said "*adieu*" rather than "*au revoir*". "*After all*," he told me, "*you're the king of a country on the other side of the North Sea who canna own him for your son. No' at the risk of jeopardising the good relations between our two nations. Taking advantage of a young French noblewoman wouldna be viewed with anything else but contempt by Charles's betrothed, Anne of Brittany, well-known for her piety.*"'

'So do ye ken, at least, where the wee laddie went?'

'No. All Patrick would tell me was that he'd made discreet enquiries through a contact in France. It seems Madeleine had some distant relations in another part of France with no children of their own. They were only too willing to have a son and heir to continue the family name. All that they were told was that he was the son of a high-born Scot.'

'Patrick sent a little money but the only thing I had to pass on was a ring just like this one,' he said, pointing to a turquoise ring on the finger of his right hand. 'It belonged to my mother. The bairn's grandam, Queen Margaret of Denmark. I had a copy made so whenever I wore it I would think of my son. I also sent a locket with him containing a portrait of his mother. I decided it was better that he should have it than me. I felt I didna deserve it because she would still be alive if it hadna been for me.'

'Hush, my love. It wasna your fault. Do ye ever wonder where he is now?'

'More often than ye could ken. I keep him in my prayers, hoping he's still alive and is safe and well. And if so, that he's a lad to make his poor dead mother proud.'

Janet smiled. 'And his father too. If he's anything like ye, she'd be verra proud. You're a good man, James Stewart. Your people ken that. They love ye like a father, son, brother and uncle. Pope Julius knew that. That's why he sent ye a purple cap and a sword of state, encrusted with jewels, five years ago. Ye should be proud, my love, no' self-doubting. You're the first Scottish king in three hundred long years to have received such gifts. Look how ye set sail to win over the Western Isles where no Scottish king had been since the time of Robbie the Bruce. Just yesterday, I heard a tale of how ye saw a man overcome with grief next to his dead horse, and straight away, gave him fourteen shillings.'

James nodded. 'I recall him well.'

'And look how ye helped that poor wee lass who was weeping for the loss of her babe. As well as the man whose corn was trampled to nought by your horses.'

'Stop it, I beseech ye. This head is no' fit to wear a burnished halo.'

'Your subjects would disagree. A king who takes the time to travel the length and breadth of his kingdom, distributing justice and alms, meeting no' just his nobles but common folk? Trust me, his head deserves that halo.'

❧

James threw off the fur rugs and walked back over to the fireplace, crouching down in front of it to place some more logs on the fire.

'I still find it strange,' he said, lifting the largest one out of the wooden basket, 'that I told Thomas Howard about Madeleine all those years ago when he brought Maggie up to wed me. Do ye recall meeting him? With that auld nurse of yours. The wise woman.'

Janet fell back on the satin pillows, laughing. 'Oh, sweet Jesus, I remember it so well. How could I forget his encounter with Mairghread?'

'God rest her kind auld soul. Do ye recall how she wouldna stop babbling at him. Calling him some name or other.'

'"*An ruadh diùc*".'

'Of course. "The Red Duke".'

Picking up an iron poker, James began jabbing at the fire. 'Who knows,' he said, shaking his head, 'if anything she said ever came true.'

'I never knew her to be wrong. Ye liked the Earl didn't ye?'

'Aye. I remember envying the Howard boys for their father. And talking to him about his and my first loves.' He stood up and turned around to face Janet. 'Who was your first love, my lovely lady?'

'Ye were,' she said without a moment's hesitation.

'No' Bell the Cat?'

'No, not him. Why don't ye come here and I'll prove it to ye.'

Leaping back onto the bed and taking his mistress in his arms, James threw off her furs, making her shiver. 'Are ye sure it's no' him?' he growled, thrusting a hand between her legs. 'I've heard he's verra skilled in the bedchamber.'

Janet began to squirm but he held her fast. Using his fingers to play her as if he were in the great hall, strumming on a lute, James chuckled to himself when he felt her melting beneath his touch.

'No' as skilled as ye, my heart,' she eventually gasped.

Briefly kissing either nipple in greeting, his tongue began to trace a winding path down towards her curved belly. 'The whole of Scotland thinks I've come to pray at a shrine. So I think it's only fit I do what they expect. Think of it as my early Hogmanay gift to ye.'

HOUSE OF HOWARD

Chapter Forty-Two

16th December, 1512. Hever Castle.

I don't understand why you have to have Lizzie,' I said, blowing hard on my reddened hands to warm them while pulling my cloak more tightly around me. Thank goodness Dame Fortune had made me rich enough again to be able to afford the lynx lining within. 'Why can't you have one of her younger sisters? All three girls are comely enough. Take it from me, Thomas. One untouched quinny is as good as the next.'

Listening to this, the angry look in my eldest son's eyes reminded me of the mean little red ones of the blood-soaked boar being carried aloft on poles by the huntsmen, following us back up the path to the Castle.

'Because I'm a Howard!' he exploded. 'Your eldest child. Your heir. And I don't want a younger daughter. I want Lizzie Stafford.'

<<If only Thomas knew he was my eldest child by a mere few weeks, not years, would that dampen his infernal pride?>> I somehow doubted it.

'You mean, you want her dowry of two thousand marks,' grinned Edward, thumping his sulky looking older brother on the back. 'What do you think, Pater? Surely it can't hurt that young Lizzie's father is the only duke in the country.'

I let out a chuckle, as much amused by the thunderous expression on Thomas's face as the teasing one his brother wore.

'We all know there should be two dukes…not one,' said Thomas, venom in his voice.

<<Aha! You'd like me to be a duke, would you? So you can be an earl awaiting my death. And my title. Well, there's scant chance of that happening, my boy, not with my seventieth birthday fast approaching. Unfortunately for you, my time for royal rewards for heroics of any kind is long past…as is the time a duke is made>>

269

 familiar

'I thought the Stafford girl had turned you down,' said Edmund, bringing up the rear and obviously guessing what we were discussing. 'Because she's in love with a boy her own age. I don't know why you're complaining. I would be content with any wife at all.'

My youngest son by Bess Tilney never ceased to irritate me. Even his appearance made me want to give him a hard clout. If my strong features had transferred themselves to something more than acceptable in Thomas, and to something quite remarkable in Edward, by the time they reached Edmund, they'd become as watered down as a small beer. What business did a man of only thirty-four have losing most of his hair? Not while his father still had a mane as thick as a badger's and could give him nearly two score in years. As it was, Edmund was forced to comb the few remaining strands across a scalp almost as woefully bare as a new-born babe's bottom. Even his brown eyes were the colour of a pail of pigswill. He didn't have the first notion of diplomacy: a vital commodity at the Tudor court where we had a king who could be offended if you so much as blinked when you shouldn't. Let alone humiliate him at a joust held to celebrate the birth of a royal boy whose breath left his body before he even reached eight weeks. Knowing Henry as I did, the five times Edmund knocked him to the ground on Saint Valentine's Eve would forever be linked to his grief at the death of the precious Duke of Cornwall, not ten days later. My third son put me in mind of an uncouth guest tramping over freshly laid rushes in the great hall, releasing great clods of earth from mud-spattered boots…but not noticing a thing.

Of course, being told that Lizzie Stafford favoured the twenty-five years younger Neville boy made Thomas gave him Edmund a well-placed (and arguably, well-deserved) punch on the upper arm, so hard I winced watching him do it.

'If you haven't got anything useful to say, brother,' growled Thomas, as ominously as a bear who has just encountered interlopers in his lair, 'just keep that pribbling trap of yours shut!'

'I didn't m-mean any h-harm, Tom,' stammered Edmund, another irritating habit of his that should have disappeared with childhood but made an unwelcome appearance whenever he was wrong-footed. Why didn't he stand up to the man who'd given the qualling infliction to him in the first place, as surely as he'd given him the enormous bruise on his arm (that must be beginning to turn livid). If only Edmund possessed a fraction of Edward's charm and *joie de vivre*, I would forgive him anything. But from what I'd heard, once away from the rest of us, all the arrogance and posturing that should have been there in our presence, came to the fore in a thoroughly unpleasant manner. <<*In my eyes, making him both a coward and, quite frankly, someone who brings the Howard good name into disrepute*>>

Edward and I looked at one another and rolled our eyes at the way things were progressing. How many times had we seen it before? Though, to be fair, Edward always had much more time for his younger brother than I did. It was as if he acknowledged that the gifts Dame Fortune had bestowed on him in abundance should have been more fairly distributed. Edward's big infectious laugh, so beloved by the King, came out as a mere squeak in my third born; his enthusiasm for everything he encountered became a lacklustre, half-arsed mockery of the same in Edmund; his success with women didn't even begin to compare. <<*The man is a disaster waiting to happen to him around the next corner*>>

Women had a nose for failure and, from what I'd seen, wanted none of him. I dreaded to think what the stars had in store for this ill-favoured runt of my first litter. Even Edward's tendency to jump in before he looked (my one criticism of him) showed a bravery and zest for life, totally lacking in his younger brother.

I glared at Edmund. 'I've already told you. The Culpepper girl is back on the market but I can't do anything until after Epiphany. You know very well that everything stops for the Christmas festivities at court.' I turned to Thomas. 'The same goes for you. Nothing is going to happen during the twelve days of Christmas. But, I promise, once it's over I'll have a word with the King…on behalf of the pair of you.'

৶

Ever the peacemaker, Edward flung his arms around the shoulders of his brothers. '*Pax vobiscum*, the pair of you! Don't we have enough worries in this family with Muriel being so ill? Spare a thought for our poor father and how he must be feeling. Christmas at court will be a sad affair this year, knowing Tom's gone and she's here and not there with us.'

When he said this, I glanced up at an upper window of the Castle, knowing full well my beloved girl was lying there, a shadow of her former sparkling self, dark shadows under her eyes, hollowed out cheeks and a skin so pale you could see the blue veins beneath. Beneath her robe, the skin was stretched over her swollen belly, scarcely any bigger than a cabbage, below her protruding ribs. How could any baby survive a pregnancy without nourishment? It was as if it was already encased its own little coffin within my daughter. Whenever I beseeched her to take some food, almost getting down on bended knees, she always repeated the same thing, turning her face towards the wall:

"*All I want is for Tom to come back to me. My life isn't worth living without him.*"

I felt so hopeless as I held her frail hand, desperately trying to give her some of my strength. *Shake* some of my strength into her, if need be. *All* of my strength…if that's what it took to make her better. Rather God took me than her, a young woman of twenty-six. Leaving behind two little boys and two girls. Even though I knew the thought was very wicked, it came to me that Edmund could be better spared than me. Perhaps I'd done the wrong thing by giving her a vital young husband with whom she'd fallen in love. After all, what place did love have in a marriage? I hadn't loved Bess Tilney, and although I still desired Agnes, and was grateful for the children she continued to bear me, I didn't love her. As I once told James of Scotland, I'd only loved one woman in my life and look where that had got me. Besides, that one had gone now and all the pink roses in the world wouldn't bring her back to me.

It was as if Edward knew my thoughts were turned towards death. Leaving his brothers to walk in a silence that almost crackled it was so hostile, he came to my side and linked his arm through mine.

'Muriel will recover, Pater. Lizzie and Tom brought her to Hever to make her better. You know Lizzie is taking good care of her.'

I smiled up at Edward, my golden son. He saw the world differently to the rest of us, finding good whenever he could. It was only when he didn't that he was a force to be reckoned with. I'd heard some hair-raising tales of his exploits at sea that made me both proud and glad that the young king saw in him what I did. It worried me that he'd sworn to avenge the death of Muriel's husband, lost to us in Brest in August. When his blood was up, and he had an appetite for revenge, there was no one on earth that could stop my boy. Not the King. Not even God Himself. With this in mind, I tried to temper my reply.

'If it is God's will to take her, my boy, then there's nothing we can do. Sadly, heaven is the one place we can never win a battle.'

I was distracted from my morbid thoughts by the sight of Ferdinand and Katherine, two of Tom and Muriel's young children, dashing down to meet us. Their little cheeks were rosy red from the cold wind, and their faces shone with excitement when they caught sight of the enormous boar. Thank goodness they had no idea their mother was clinging to life by a thin strand of gossamer. Perhaps Muriel could be persuaded to have a mouthful of roast boar, I found myself hoping. Right behind her little ones came Tom Bullen's two girls, together with their younger brother, George, all wrapped up warmly to face the cruel elements. As always, Tom Bullen was a perfect host, entertaining us and trying to keep our spirits up in the present difficult circumstances. We'd been such a tight family unit before the summer. Thomas's cruel streak and Edmund's lily-livered behaviour were almost forgotten next to the ebullience of Tom Knyvett and my Edward.

Meanwhile, Tom Bullen continued to find favour at court, while Muriel and Lizzie were well-liked by the Queen, enough to find coveted positions in her entourage. The two of them, like all Howard girls, were pretty and pleasing which was all that could be asked of a female. Looking at young Mary and Nan now, laughing as they chased after their baby cousins (the black-haired younger girl losing a red velvet mitten in the process), I could see the part they would play in the future of our House. Such a fine pair of girls would easily catch themselves good husbands with the right name. Although Tom Bullen, with his strong desire to rise up in the world, no doubt saw them as 'Bullen girls', they were nothing of the sort. The Howards could knock the Bullens into oblivion any day of the week, if they so chose. <<*If I have anything to do with it, we Howards will live forever*>>

'Lift me up, please, Uncle Ned!' cried little Ferdinand, raising up his pudgy baby hands to my son. I noticed that there was no such plea from his sister to her other two sullen looking uncles, and it was left to Tom Bullen to swing Katherine, giggling loudly, onto his shoulders.

Now, Kitty,' said Tom, 'We're going to have a race back to the Castle against your brother and Uncle Ned. What do you think of that?'

My granddaughter, so like her mother in looks, clapped her hands together. 'Oh, yes please, Uncle Thomas.'

On the other side, my son was adjusting his nephew into a more comfortable position. 'We're not going to let them beat us, are we, Ferdie?'

Ferdinand, an achingly small copy of his dead father, clenched his fists together. 'No, no, we're not.'

Edward turned to me. 'All right, Pater, on the count of three.'

Filled with hope that this happy family game might be the first of many that once again included the children's mother, I began counting. 'One. Two. *Three!*' I shouted, swinging my right down as hard as I could.

Accompanied by shrieks of laughter and cries of joy from the two lively riders, bouncing up and down on their trusted steeds, and whoops of encouragement from my other grandchildren, I watched Edward begin to pull ahead. I glanced across at Thomas and Edmund, the first of whom was grim-faced, the second, stifling a yawn, and then back at Edward. A born father, if ever I saw one.

Right then and there, I swore to find him a young wife who would bear him many sons. It would have to wait until after this confounded war had finished. But I knew young Henry would refuse Edward nothing; besides, the King, above anyone, was beginning to discover how frustrating it was to be tied to a wife who couldn't give you a child every year. Only once a woman had produced a son or two could she relax enough to give a man pretty daughters.

Of course, it would be better if Alice Parker were to die, leaving Edward free to marry again, but if that didn't happen, an annulment wouldn't be hard to secure. Not for a war hero. As I watched Edward and Ferdinand reach victory at the other end, an image of his first-born son came into my head. <<*What a pair he and Edward would have made*>> I only hoped Guy d'Ardres had changed his mind about forcing young Tristan into the church.

TRISTAN

Chapter Forty-Three

Christmas Eve, 1512. The library, Ardres Castle.

acrébleu! There's been an Ardres bishop in Avranches for the last five hundred years! And there'll be one for the next five hundred,' stormed my father, banging his fist down hard on the oak table.

I watched as the pile of books in front of him seemed to jump at least six inches into the air, instantly producing a cloud of fine dust motes that shimmered in a shaft of sunlight. It was as if he believed such anger would somehow convince me a career in the Church was written in stone. Why couldn't he see it was tantamount to passing a death sentence? It didn't help that today was a fast day, guaranteed to worsen anyone's mood.

'But *Père*—'

'I don't want to hear another word. I've had enough of your ridiculous outbursts. And I don't want you running to your mother again, like a small child. You're fifteen years old. Old enough to be thinking of taking a wife. And certainly old enough to respect your father's wishes.'

I was outraged. 'You talk of a wife. Isn't that the one thing you're making sure I never have in your bid to make me *"respect your wishes"*.'

Clearly, Father didn't trust himself to reply; instead, he marched over to the lattice window adorned with mistletoe, and stood looking out, his hands on his hips, his face turned to stone.

I sighed. <<*How many times have we had this same argument?*>> I could see it was useless to protest any further; I had a volatile enough relationship with my father at the best of times. Happily, with my mother, it was the complete opposite. I knew I was a great disappointment to him as he never lost an opportunity to compare me unfavourably with Gilles. Life was so unfair: a mere accident of birth had made me the younger and not the older sibling, thereby irrevocably changing my destiny. Not for me: a path strewn with military glory, amorous conquests, and finally, marriage and children. Instead, the Church was to be both master and mistress, condemning me to a life of sacrifice and unfulfilled ambitions. Yes, Father was right. I *had* asked my gentle mother to intercede on my behalf - except I'd ended up comforting her when she failed.

I suddenly thought about the Englishman, Edward Howard, whose path in life sounded more winding…and definitely more riotous than the one Father led or had planned for me. Since I'd first heard about the Vice-Admiral of England, he'd often played a part in my wistful imaginings of a different kind of life for myself. One thing was for sure: <<*I'd rather be the bastard offspring of an exciting man like that, an adventurer and a buccaneer, than the dutiful, true-born son of the cold-hearted Governor of Picar—*>>

'As you know, we have an honoured guest arriving for New Year. The Dutch scholar. I want you to personally look after him.'

Standing by his desk again, at least, Father seemed calmer…as if he wanted no further conflict today. For a moment, his face softened. Moving aside a sprig of holly, he picked up the top book from the pile in front of him. 'Here,' he said, handing it to me. 'These were meant to be your New Year's gifts but as you've already seen them, I'll give them to you now. Monsieur Erasmus penned them all.'

I looked down at the first volume entitled '*A handbook on manners for children*', and then glared at my father, repeating the title out loud. 'I thought you said I wasn't a child!'

Looking confused until he saw the title of the book, Father snatched it up and set it to one side. 'That's not what I wanted to give you. Perhaps Desiderius intended it for me.' He laid aside the second book in the pile, a copy of the New Testament in Greek, and lifted up another one. 'Here it is. "*In Praise of Folly*". Desiderius told me he wrote it to try and right the wrongs in the church today. And the world, in general. I think you should read it so you have plenty to talk about. Now, I must go and help your mother with arrangements for the New Year's banquet....'

❧

Left alone in the library, fury began welling up in me, searing my innards and threatening to envelop my entire being. My throat was dry. Hot tears of frustration were blurring my vision and I could feel my hands trembling.

I so wished my best friend, Jean, was here. As the younger brother of Claude, Duke of Lorraine, like me, he was destined for the church. And like me, he wanted none of it. How absurd to think he'd succeeded to the bishopric of Metz when he was barely seven years old.

'*Morbleu!*' I swore out loud. 'Why does Father always manage to ruin everything, watching my every move with spur-galled humour and then swooping down on me like some circling puttock?' My gaze fell upon his New Year's gift: the hell-hated books with their thin layer of dust: the very same dust with which he was attempting to enshroud me. <<*Locking me in an accursed monastery and snatching away my young life and all its pleasures*>>

'I hate him! I hate him to his very marrow. A pox on him!'

With one swift movement, I swept all but one of the brand new books onto the floor, taking great satisfaction in watching them peel apart. Normally, I loved books but not these. Sheaves of paper flew up into the air like so many wounded soldiers, before coming to rest in a pathetic pile on the wooden boards below: useless corpses on a battlefield.

But even this solid layer of paper wasn't enough to satisfy me. There was one book remaining: '"*A handbook on manners for children*",' I said aloud. 'Well, Father,' I sneered, 'this is what I think of your droning handbook!'

And with that, I launched the offending volume across the room with all my might, sending the missile high up in the air, aiming for the nearby balcony where more of Father's vast collection of books was kept.

There was a satisfying thud…immediately followed by a male voice of protest.

❧

'*Nom de Dieu!* Can't a man read in peace? You nearly took my head off. Surely flinging Monsieur Erasmus's advice about manners for children against the nearest wall isn't recommended by the great scholar.'

<<*Nicolas!*>> After recovering from the shock of knowing someone else had witnessed the argument with my father, I could feel my hackles rising. Of all the people it could have been, it had to be him. I decided attack was the only way forward.

'Haven't you got anything better to do than spy on others?'

'Not when it proves to be so entertaining.'

I inwardly groaned. Nicolas never missed an opportunity to bate me, just as he was doing now. At the beginning of November, he'd been setting off on a hunt with Father and several other older men. Seeing me hanging forlornly around the courtyard, he'd called out (in deliberate earshot of the others): "*What a shame you can't join us.*" The huge smile on his face belied this statement and proved he knew I was being forced to stay behind and do extra Latin, as a punishment for some petty crime or other.

The fact he was a good six years older didn't matter a jot. We were deadly rivals in everything: hunting, riding, jousting and archery, to name but a few. However, our greatest battle was vying to win the respect of my father. For me, it was no easy task when my future lay in being a pathetic milksop, fit only for the Church. Knowing this, Nicolas made it all the harder for me, gloating at every opportunity at being outwardly able to achieve all the things to which I aspired, but without any of the constraints of a future religious calling. It had made the two of us bitter enemies and, if anything, our relationship had only deteriorated with time.

"*Just think. One day I might have to make my confession to you,*" Nicolas had jested one morning recently as we were breaking our fast, the flirtatious looks passing between him and a pretty serving maid making it quite clear where he hoped to spend the night.

He leapt down from the balcony, landing in one graceful bound in front of me, still clutching a copy of '*Tristan and Iseult*'. 'I was reading about your namesake,' he smiled. 'Things certainly didn't end well for him.'

I could never work out why my enemy spent so many hours poring over the romances on the balcony of the library. Books about the art of warfare, the lives of Roman generals, or the rules of jousting, were of far more interest to me. As far as I was concerned, Nicolas had the tastes of a lovelorn, dismal-dreaming minstrel, haplessly strumming a lute; perhaps it had something to do with his current infatuation with the young wife of a local nobleman, a renowned flirt-gill. Ysabeau de Sapincourt. Nicolas had no idea I knew but I'd seen his looks of longing whenever she came to the Castle with her ageing husband: a conquest so far without success, of that I was certain.

'Searching for inspiration, Nicolas? Not enough ideas of your own.'

A look of annoyance crossed his face but he quickly recovered and glanced down at the paper on the floor. 'Well, *you've* just destroyed the only reading material you're going to need in that monastery of yours. I'm guessing that "*In Praise of Folly*" is somewhere amongst that lot. As it seems you're to be seated next to the great man at a banquet, I understand why your father wanted you to know something about the book.' He kicked up a snowstorm of paper sheets with a couple of measured strikes of his favourite shoes, made from Spanish leather. 'I know it's not New Year yet but let me make a gift of my knowledge to you. To help you when you meet Monsieur Erasmus. He wrote it at Thomas More's hous—'

'You can keep your beetle-headed gift to yourself!'

I was piqued the qualling Nicolas had actually read the worthless thing and would do better seated next to the fusty old scholar than me. 'I don't need your help. In fact you're the last person on earth—'

'I know I am. But I want to help. As I was saying, he dedicated it to his great friend, More, with "Folly", a harlot, as the narrator, empty compliments and love of self as her clients. She attacks all in her sight: idle friars, greedy princes, lawyers and theologian—'

'Enough!'

Nicolas reached for the brass door handle. 'I'm going. But you'll thank me when you meet him, I promise. Now, hadn't you better see if you can piece back together your father's "*Handbook on manners for children*". Who knows, you might learn something from it.'

CECILY

Chapter Forty-Four

Christmas Eve, 1512.
Saint Senara chapel, near Zennor Castle.

'*I*'ve got a secret!' cried Lizzie Stafford, closing the chapel door firmly in George Bullen's disappointed face. She pointed to the path beyond. 'Go and find the others. They're with Henry and Tom.'

I was glad for the six of us to have some time to ourselves: to escape the horde of little children swarming around the Castle. The Bullens had arrived the day before with four young Knyvett children in tow; Lizzie had arrived shortly after with her two younger sisters and older brother, Henry. And, of course, my Pendeen cousins were always eager to come and join in the fun whenever we had company at the Castle. Lizzie had managed to persuade Henry and Tom to act as nursemaids for the morning. I'd noticed Nan's older brother giving her sheep's eyes on more than one occasion; sadly for Tom, he didn't stand a chance as every word she uttered and all her thoughts were totally taken up with one person alone: Ralph Neville.

My cousin, Margery, Nan, and I, being the youngest of the six, were only tolerated if we didn't ask any foolish questions. On the other hand, Nan's older sister, Mary, and Lizzie's sister, Kat, were both thirteen and deemed worthy confidantes for Lizzie who, at fifteen, was practically a grown-up woman.

The chapel was looking beautiful; the villagers always took great pride in it and had adorned it with garlands of holly and ivy. Lizzie marched over to the mermaid chair and sat in it as if she were a queen, carefully re-arranging the skirts of her green velvet dress, beneath her fur-lined cloak. Caught up in the moment, Margery rushed over to help her. Lizzie's dark blue eyes were dancing with excitement and I could tell her cupid bow mouth was itching to tell us her secret. Her small hands fidgeted ceaselessly as she waited for us all to gather around Neptune's throne.

❧

'You look like a queen today, Lizzie,' I said.

She gave a delighted laugh and tossed back her long fair hair. 'I feel like one.' I watched a stream of vapour follow her words in the chilly air of the chapel and I hugged my arms around myself to stay warm.

'Well, Queen Lizzie, are you going to tell us your secret or not?' asked Mary Bullen, clearly tired of waiting.

'Only if you all promise not to tell a living soul. Cross your hearts and hope to die.'

I don't know which of us crossed our heart first. There was the longest pause in the world while Neptune's queen decided whether or not she could trust us. Eventually, she got to her feet and gave us all an imperious look.

'Very well. I shall tell you but none of you must break your promise. Especially you two,' she said, looking at the Bullen girls.

'Oh, just get on with it,' said Mary. 'It can't be that thrilling. Besides, it's freezing in here and we'll all turn to blocks of ice if we stand around much longer.'

Forgetting she was supposed to be a queen, Lizzie started jumping up and down, clapping her hands. 'Oh, it is thrilling. It is. It's the most thrilling news ever. Cecy, can you guess what it is?'

I thought for a moment. 'Your father's decided to get you that puppy you wanted, after all.'

She gave a laugh that had a hint of disappointed scorn. 'No. That's not it.' She turned to her sister. 'Kat?'

'The Queen has asked for me to join you at court.'

'Don't be crook-pated! Why would that be a secret? Margery, Mary. Can either of you do better?'

My cousin's eyes grew large with fear; at only ten, she didn't want to make a mistake. Taking pity on her, I had another guess. 'You've kissed Ralph.'

'Oh, la! We've been doing that for years.'

'I know!' cried Mary, looking triumphant. She looked around the chapel to check she couldn't be overheard before saying in a loud whisper: 'You've done "*it*"!'

Lizzie gave her a withering look. 'No, we haven't…yet. But…' she said, as she started marching up and down the aisle, 'we will very soon. Because—' She turned to stare at all of us, a radiant expression on her pretty face. 'Ralph and I are to be wed.'

⤫

Mary let out a whoop of delight and planted two kisses on her best friend's cheeks before wrapping her up in her arms.

'When?' gasped Kat, obviously as much in the dark as the rest of us.

'Soon. On Twelfth Night.'

'Where?' asked Mary, clutching Lizzie's hands and swinging her around.

Lizzie looked at me. 'Here. Well, not here. Over at Saint Michael's Mount. Your father and mine asked the Archpriest and he agreed.'

I was stunned; my parents had said nothing. Lizzie must have seen my mouth in the shape of an O because she came over and took me by the arm. 'I'm sorry, Cecy. I wanted to tell you before but it was too dangerous.'

'Dangerous?' I repeated.

'She means our Uncle Thomas has asked for her hand,' said Nan, coming to stand by us.

'Thank goodness Father said no.' Lizzie pulled a disgusted face. 'Or at least, told him he could have one of my other sisters.'

Kat let out a squeal. 'Not me! I don't want him. He's old. At least forty. Five years older than Father. And looks like a bad-tempered bear.'

Mary laughed. 'Nan and I know how vicious he can be if crossed, don't we, sister?'

'We do.'

I wasn't surprised to hear these things about the man I'd once been introduced to at Hever Castle. Next to me, Kat started to snivel.

'Don't worry,' said Lizzie kindly. 'You're too young for him. You haven't even started your courses yet. Sir Thomas needs sons to replace the ones he lost. Father told me he'll be forced to look elsewhere.'

I glanced over at Margery who'd gone bright red, obviously glad that this excluded her from marriage to this man.

'What did my father say?' I asked.

'He wanted to help,' said Lizzie. 'He told Father no man should stand in the way of true love as it's likely to weigh very heavily on his conscience.'

'But what will happen when Uncle Thomas finds out?' asked Nan. 'He'll be like an eagle that discovers its nest has been disturbed. And its chicks stolen.'

Mary put one hand to her cheek. 'Or a wild boar maddened by rage when it's been stuck with a spear. At least, that's how he looked when I last saw him. I can still feel that hard slap he gave me for being impertinent.'

'What did you say?' I asked.

'That Nan and I weren't Howard girls but Bullens.'

'That's why you and Nan mustn't tell your parents,' said Lizzie, urgency in her tone. 'Your mother's a Howard.'

'We would never do a thing to hurt you,' soothed Mary. 'Or push you in the direction of such a prickly hedge-pig.'

'Our other uncle is kind, though' said Nan. 'I heard Father telling Mother he found our grandsire sobbing his heart out in the chapel at Hever. He didn't know what to do so he called for Uncle Ned to come.'

'Why was your grandsire crying?' asked Margery.

'Because our Aunt Muriel is so ill.' Nan looked sad. 'That's why our cousins are here with us and not at Hever with their mother or ours. My grandsire said a house of sickness is no place for the young at Christmas.'

'What's wrong with her?' Kat asked.

'Her heart is broken,' said Mary.

Margery looked distressed. 'That's terrible! How did it break?'

'It's not really broken, silly,' said Lizzie. 'Her husband was killed in the summer and she doesn't want to live without him. I understand that. It's how I would be if anything happened to Ralph.'

'I pity the poor baby she's carrying,' said Mary. 'I heard Mother telling one of her friends that Muriel is no more than a bag of bones.'

'That makes me want to cry,' said Margery, looking as though she was about to do just that.

❧

I decided to change the conversation from this dismal topic we could do nothing to alter and back to Lizzie's happy news. 'You're going to be like Lady Catherine Gordon,' I told her. 'Wedding your great love.'

'Yes,' murmured Lizzie. 'In secret. Not even the King must find out. Father will be at court for Christmas, as usual.'

'Our father's leaving for Greenwich the day after tomorrow,' said Mary. 'He told King Henry he had to bring our little cousins down here first.'

'What did you tell the Queen, Lizzie?' asked Nan. 'After all, you're one of her ladies. And are supposed to be spending Christmas with her at court.'

'That I have to be with my mother who's been suffering from the ague. It's not true, of course.'

'What's the Queen like?' asked Margery.

Lizzie thought for a moment. 'She's very kind most of the time. Except when she thinks about babies. And then she becomes anxious.'

Nan rolled her eyes heavenwards. 'Our grandsire says it's because she's Spanish. She put one hand in front of her stomach, as if great with child. 'He says a Howard bride would have put, "*two or three fat little boy brats in the royal cradle by now.*"' She deepened her voice to imitate her grandsire. '"*Not puny Spanish ones too feeble to catch their breath.*"'

Her sister's brown eyes were glinting with mischief. 'He also says,' Mary continued, following her sister's lead by mimicking the formidable Earl of Surrey: "*that when a Howard girl strikes the fire of full of fourteen, she's ripe for a husband.*" So 1513 could be a very important year for me.' Mary stuck out her chest and stroked the rounded bodice of her gown. 'Look! Soon I'll be as big as Lizzie. Bigger even.'

Lizzie gave a little smile and folded her arms over her chest. 'Ralph says he can't wait for our wedding night.' She leant forward and whispered something in Mary's ear that made them both burst out laughing.

Nan looked at me and I instantly knew she was thinking of that game we'd once played. '*Mine will be a gentleman and yours a soldier,*' she mouthed.

Looking around at my friends, and thinking of Lizzie's secret wedding, I suddenly felt entirely happy. <<*This is going to be a Christmas to remember*>>

CECILY

Chapter Forty-Five

Christmas Day, 1512. Zennor Castle.

'I pray you, my masters, be merry,
Quod estes in convivio
Caput apri defero
Reddens laudes Domino.'

{'As many as are at the feast
The Boar's Head I offer
Giving praise to the Lord.'}

*T*he great hall was filled to the rafters with the familiar strains of my favourite carol, *'The Boar's Head'*. Heartily joining in the chorus with my family, friends and all our guests, at the far end, I could see four Castle servants entering, bearing aloft a glazed, roasted boar's head on a platter. It was set in a circle of red and yellow jelly, and decorated with gilded bay leaves, lemons and oranges. The music from the minstrel's gallery above, accompanied this impressive procession across the floor.

Glancing past Nan (whom I'd asked to be placed next to me), beyond my Pendeen cousins, I was pleased to see all the other children were equally impressed by the colourful display. A short while before, I'd noticed Lizzie Stafford and Mary deep in conversation…probably about the wedding night again. It was gratifying to see the rapt expressions on the faces of the two Bullen boys beside them, watching the progress of the boar around the hall. Although it was a Tredavoe family tradition and the centrepiece of the

Christmas festivities, the entrance of the boar's head never lost its appeal. Thanks to a double-wicked wax candle that had been wrapped in cotton and soaked in *aqua vitae*, before being placed in the roasted boar's mouth, our cook was able to produce a particularly fearsome, fire-breathing effect.

Christmas was my best-loved time of the year; without exception, the Castle would be transformed into a riot of colour. Yesterday, on our return from the chapel, nursing our great secret, we'd excitedly helped the servants hang the usual decorations. Green garlands with their bright red berries were strewn everywhere, including the famous Kissing Bough made of willow and covered in greenery, with its effigy of the child Jesus in the centre. We watched Father carefully place it above the front door.

"*Now Ralph can kiss you beneath it,*" Mary whispered to Lizzie, earning herself a fierce glare in case anyone was listening.

There were oranges, dried fruit, and candles in every nook and cranny, and the famed Lord of Misrule (in this case, Hugh, our family steward) had replaced Father for a day of mischief and merriment. Beyond the diamond-paned windows, the December sea was grey and stormy, but inside there was a roaring fire, good cheer and much laughter. The only person missing from this idyllic scene was my cousin, Tristan. I glanced down at my posy ring and smiled, hoping his Christmas was as joyful as my own.

In front of me, Hugh was brazenly stealing some grapes and oranges from the enormous platter and throwing them to all the children (including the little Knyvetts), making it deliberately difficult for everyone to grab it with their hands.

'Well caught, Mistress Cecily!' he cried, smiling as I pressed a sweet smelling orange to my nose.

'Here, Mother,' I said, planting a tender kiss on her cheek, 'I know how you love oranges.'

Standing up on the dais, I eased myself past my parents' high-backed chairs to go and take some grapes to the Knyvett children. With so many friends, neighbours, relations, as well as many of the local gentry, gathered this year, no expense had been spared. As well as the boar, lavish helpings of swan and goose were being served to make up for the lack of meat, cheese, or eggs, yesterday. Hogsheads of ale, Gascon claret and white wine had been rolled out of the cellar for our guests, although of course I was only allowed to consume the weak ale intended for the sick and the young.

'I don't think I can eat another thing!' protested Nan in a loud voice, clutching her stomach and winning her a glare from her nearby father for showing such bad manners in company.

I smiled to myself, knowing full well that all the food we'd just eaten was shortly to be followed by the famous Zennor Castle mince pies. They were in the shape of a crib and made from thirteen ingredients to represent Jesus and his Apostles, including my favourites of fresh chopped coriander and saffron. This last had been bought in October from a travelling peddler who told me he was from a strange-sounding place in Essex called Chipping Walden.

'Don't worry, Nan, you'll find room for mince pies *and* warden pie,' I assured her, first checking that Thomas Bullen was no longer listening.

She playfully puffed out her cheeks and I made a face back, knowing no one could resist the delicious, piping hot pie, using Tredavoe pears and the peddler's saffron.

I put out a hand to tickle her neck but she stopped me, whispering: 'Don't, Cecy. You'll get me into trouble with Father again.'

I looked across at Thomas Bullen, seated next to my parents as a mark of his importance. He didn't have the face of an unkind man; the expression in his large brown eyes was rather gentle and the general impression was that of one of the over-eager Hever dogs, panting with effort and hoping for praise from their master - but equally expecting a kick. Although he had unattractively thin lips, he didn't have the cruel look of his brother-in-law so desperate to marry Lizzie. He didn't even have the more forbidding features of his father-in-law, the Bullens' grandsire, Thomas Howard. I remembered Nan telling us how he'd cried because his daughter was ill, making me wonder if he was kinder than his son.

Yet, I'd always felt Nan's father was unduly harsh with his children, and that beneath the friendly exterior lay a man of almost frightening ambition. Watching him in earnest conversation with my own father, I remembered a story my mother had once told me about how he saved Father's life when they were young boys, around the same age as I was now....

Thomas Bullen had been visiting my own father at Zennor Castle and the two of them decided to go riding together. Wanting to show off, my father took a somewhat skittish steed, far beyond his capabilities, and the outing would almost certainly have ended in disaster - had it not been for the bravery of the young Thomas. Unnerved by some kind of animal in the undergrowth, my father's horse reared up and took off at lightening speed, leaving Father hanging on for dear life. According to Mother, horse and boy had fast been approaching a nearby cliff, with a sheer drop and certain death when Thomas caught up and risked his own life to reach over and grab back the reins, pulling the terrified horse - carrying his equally terrified friend - to a standstill.

"And ever since that day, Cecy, your father has felt he owes his life to Thomas," Mother finished, her eyes filled with tears.

As evidence of the two men's close relationship, on a visit to Zennor one summer, Thomas had persuaded my then unmarried Uncle Stephen (with whom he also got on well) to purchase a pretty manor house with a moat, in the county of Kent, not far from his own castle at Hever. I knew that since the early days of old King Henry (or '*Goose*', as my father and Nan's called him), wary of rivals in his kingdom, no new castles had been built; licences to build battlements, loopholes, or do major refurbishments were no longer available. Instead, the King preferred to live in palaces himself, and his subjects to live in far more modern manor houses with windows and chimney stacks. Places where the nobility could spend their time in comfort, enjoying the peace and stability he'd brought to the kingdom - instead of plotting against him. With frequent visits back and forth between Hever and Zennor, and Uncle Stephen's house nearby, the connection between our two families remained extremely strong up until this very day.

All around me in the great hall, there was fevered activity as the servants rushed around, clearing away the tables and benches, making preparations for the dancing.

'Your family always has the best feasts, Cecy,' said Tom Bullen, the eldest son and heir to his father's rapidly growing kingdom, stretching out his legs in front of him and rubbing his belly in appreciation.

'And the most handsome men,' laughed Mary, not caring that at thirteen she was supposed to be too young to say such things.

'Have you met the King?' one of my Pendeen cousins asked Tom.

'Yes,' began Tom in a voice full of self-importance, before catching Mary's eye. 'Well, I didn't speak to him…but I was sitting much closer than my sisters at a joust in Greenwich. He's as tall as a giant and they say he's the handsomest king in Christendom.' He winked at me. 'I'm sure he'd be smitten if he met you. His sister has the same colour hair. But not your dimples.'

I reached out and tapped Tom's shoulder. 'Oh, save your compliments for Kitty Culpepper, Tom Bullen. Nan's told me all about you two.'

'Cecy! You've made our Tom blush,' said Nan.

'He'd better not live at court then,' said Mary, 'if all it takes is Cecy's teasing. I've heard there's far worse there.'

Nan took a bite of her warden pie. 'What about Mary and me, Tom? Are we pretty enough to go to court?'

Tom was still looking put out that his admiration for one of their distant cousins was no longer a secret. He pushed out his lower lip. 'No. Mary's too brown and Nan's too black.'

I burst out laughing. 'Whatever do you mean?'

Tom's expression was unrepentant. 'I mean Mary has brown eyes and brown hair when it's best to have yellow hair and blue, grey, or green eyes. As for Nan, all you see when you meet her is black and white. People might admire her very pale skin. But not the rest. Black hair. Black eyes. She'd have more success crossing the sea to our Irish cousins.'

Sensing trouble brewing between brother and sisters, I quickly said: 'Who wants to go to court, anyway? I certainly don't.'

'I'm going to dance,' a red-faced George Bullen suddenly announced, pushing back his chair and standing up a tad unsteadily, making me wonder if he'd sampled a sly glass of wine. 'It'll be more interesting than listening to your mammering.'

His moment of ill-temper quite forgotten now he'd exacted his revenge on his sisters, Tom tugged off his green doublet to reveal his frilled lawn shirt. 'Come and dance too, Cecy,' he smiled, holding out his hand to me.

'Soon,' I promised, preferring to return to my father for the time being.

As I reached him, he pulled me onto his lap and I happily snuggled up to him. He put one arm around my waist while he continued to chat to Tom Bullen's father.

'So you don't think there's the slightest chance the King will change his mind?'

Thomas the Elder shook his head. 'Not a chance. Living down here in the wilds of Cornwall, I know it's easy to forget what's happening in London. But let me tell you, with that butcher's upstart, Wolsey, and his clever mind behind the arrangements, in his own head, our King is already a general leading his army into France.'

My father sighed as he absent-mindedly placed one hand on my head and began stroking my hair while talking. 'I suppose that's what happens when you're twenty-one and there's no one to stop you plundering your father's coffers.'

'*Goose* should have thrown away the key before he went.'

I felt the deep rumble of laughter in my father's chest. 'Henry might be a young cub now but I fear what will happen in the future. None of us will be able to hold him back.'

'Men of the cloth such as Warham and Fox might oppose this war with France, wishing to keep *Goose's* peaceful policies. As does my father-in-law. The other two are virtuous men who haven't got a secret mistress and children hidden away like that wretch, Wolsey. With him at the helm, willing to do the young King's every bidding, the others are fighting a losing battle. There's only one possible outcome for all this.'

I bit my lip. <<*War with France*>>

<<How can that possibly affect us down here in the furthest corner of England?>> I preferred to turn my thoughts to what I'd wear to Lizzie Stafford's wedding. True, not so many years ago, certain Cornishmen (not my father who'd been very well rewarded for his loyalty) rose up against harsh taxes imposed upon them by *Goose* to fund a war with Scotland. But that was all forgotten now. We were living in peaceful times down here in my beloved Cornwall. Somehow, I didn't think Thomas Bullen had meant it kindly when he said we lived in *"the wilds"*.

Lulled by the warmth of my father's chest and a stomach full of good food, I could feel myself drifting off. As the two men continued to voice their opinions about the worsening state of affairs between England and the country across the Narrow Sea, my own thoughts gradually began to drown out their deep voices and the sounds of laughter and music beyond....

Rudely shaken out of my reverie by the loud noise of trumpets, I came to with a start, drowsily becoming aware of the riotous dancing in progress. By now, the younger Bullen brother definitely looked as though it was a sampling of a glass of the Castle wine - as much as his wild jig - that had given him such flushed cheeks. Seeing I was awake, Nan waved at me to come and join them.

'*I'm coming,*' I mouthed back.

Seated at the high table of Zennor Castle, next to its lord and lady, in the centre of all the celebrations, I knew how fortunate I was to have been born to a life of privilege. I felt as though I was leading a charmed life. Being an only child, doted upon by both parents, I'd grown up in untold luxury, showered with gifts and the most expensive clothes that money could buy: silks, satin, velvet, furs to keep out the winter winds, and even cloth of gold when the occasion arose. Mother and I would always have the most beautiful dresses at the May Day Zennor joust. It was held every year in the lists especially erected in the grounds beyond the central courtyard, and my parents and I would have prime viewing in the stands.

Although, as a leading member of the local gentry, Father's greatest source of wealth came from the land, not just in Cornwall, but in various parts of Devon, Hampshire, Dorset and Kent where he owned several properties, he also had interests in the nearby tin mine at Perran Sands; he owned his own sailing ship, '*The Morvoren*' which he'd just chartered to the young King in case of war; in addition, he held various offices from which he received a very satisfactory income. Even though it was sad to think of loss of life, Father benefitted from any ships that were wrecked on the cruel rocks below Zennor Castle. He was in possession of so-called 'wrecking rights' which allowed him to share the booty with the finders - unless an owner came forward and could prove the ship was his. As it was, servants would eagerly go up and down between our Castle and the beach below on a regular basis, staggering beneath the weight of barrels of wine, weapons, ell upon ell of still dry, discarded cloth, animal hides and spices. The ships carrying strong-smelling pilchards or herring as their major cargo were not nearly as attractive to me, but were equally lucrative for my family—

Someone was shaking my arm rather hard. It was Thomas Bullen staring at me in with disapproval. 'Now, Cecily,' he said in a tone that brooked no resistance, 'I have a matter I'd like to discuss with your father. So run along and join in the dancing with the others.'

Giving a couple of little yawns of protest, I reluctantly slid from the warmth of my father's lap and sleepily brushed the creases out of my dress. *<<I feel like lingering just to annoy Thomas Bullen but don't want to upset Father>>* Leaning over, I deliberately planted a kiss on my father's cheek to show how much I adored him.

'Watch me dance.'

Grabbing my hands and laughing, he showered them with kisses in return.

'Go, little mistress, and enjoy yourself.'

As I reached the end of the long table where my smiling mother was waiting to help me down the steps from the dais, I heard Thomas Bullen saying rather loudly: 'However much I enjoyed my time at Archduchess Margaret's court, it's always so good to be home. And I consider anywhere with you and your family to be home, Will. Which brings me to the proposition I've got for you....'

ZENNOR CASTLE MINCE PIE

Hot water pastry:
500g strong plain flour
150g lard (such as Trex)
Pinch of salt and white pepper
1 egg yolk
300ml water

For the filling:
280g ground beef, 200g ground pork,
200g ground lamb mixed
1 small onion chopped
1 carrot chopped
2 big cloves of garlic
2 tablespoons of mixed fruit
2 tablespoons of brown sugar
2 tablespoons of red wine
1 tablespoon of fresh chopped coriander
1 tablespoon of fresh grated ginger
1½ teaspoons of cumin
1½ teaspoons of cinnamon
Salt and pepper
1 egg

1) Place the lard in a saucepan and bring to the boil.
2) In a large mixing bowl, sieve flour, salt and pepper together.
3) Take an egg yolk and conceal it under the flour on one side so that the boiling liquid does not cook it immediately.
4) Pour the liquid into the bowl and rapidly stir with a wooden spoon.

5) Once cool enough to handle, shape it into a ball and place in the fridge for 30 minutes.

6) Divide into two halves and roll out onto a floured board, one half for the base and the other for the lid.

7) Grease a shallow oval dish (30cm x 21.5cm) and line with pastry.

8) Mix together the pork, beef and lamb. Add the chopped coriander, ginger and garlic and mix together thoroughly. Then, in another bowl combine the brown sugar, cumin, salt, pepper, cinnamon and red wine.

10) Layer the ingredients into the pastry case. Start with a layer of the meat mixture then add the mixed fruit, onion, carrot, wine and sugar mixture.

11) Brush the edges of the pastry with beaten egg and fit the top, gently pushing it into place, using a fork to flute the edges.

12) Cut four pieces of pastry into triangles and place in the middle of the pie in a star shape. Between each triangle, make a cut. Brush the lid with egg.

13) Bake in a preheated fan oven 150°C. After 20 minutes, cover the top with tin foil, lower the heat to 140°C and bake for a further 1 hour 30 minutes. Serve warm.

—⟨⟩⟨⟩⟨⟩—

TRISTAN

Chapter Forty-Six

New Year's Eve, 1512. Ardres Castle.

It is only because I'm aware of Maman's anxious eyes upon me that I am pretending to listen to the Dutchman with a rapt interest I am far from feeling. I know I'm not being entirely fair on the poor man>>

It had more to do with my quarrel with my father than the innocent scholar. In fact, Desiderius Erasmus, a man in his mid-forties with a pleasant face and a mouth that was created to smile, was proving to be charming. It was not his fault he had a passion for changing the world about him I didn't share. Smiling at my mother, I decided to show off a little for her sake. What was it Nicolas had said about *'In Praise of Folly'*? Something about a narrator complaining about the world in which they lived.

'I thoroughly enjoyed your latest work, Monsieur Erasmus,' I began. 'I liked the way you addressed all the ills that exist around us. But what made you choose a harlot as your narrator?'

Erasmus choked on his hyppocras and swivelled around in his chair to stare at me. 'My "Folly". A harlot? By the Rood! No, boy! Whatever gave you that idea?'

I only hoped my mother hadn't heard. Or even worse…my father. Cringing that my 'folly' had been to trust a single word that came out of the toad-spotted Nicolas's lying mouth, I managed a weak apology. 'Excuse me. I think I need to read it again.'

<<Damn Nicolas. Damn him to hell!>>

I decided the sole salvation of the evening was being able to steal as many glances as possible over at a visiting countess: the most beautiful woman I'd ever set eyes upon. I was glad her husband had been delayed and wouldn't be arriving until the New Year's banquet tomorrow; the Count's presence would have put pay to my untrammelled enjoyment of his wife. Somewhere in her twenties, she had fair hair so long it looked as though she could sit on it if she wished, delicate features, and eyes the colour of freshly produced honey from the comb—

'Mark my words, my boy,' the scholar next to me was thundering in his thick Dutch accent - in my opinion, as if he were in the pulpit. He was jabbing his finger into the air, accidentally spraying my face with his spittle, his words carrying across the long table to my parents. Certainly, from the amused expression on his face...to Nicolas, who'd probably heard my ridiculous comment about 'Folly'. Erasmus held up a long bony finger and pointed it up towards the wooden rafters of the great hall. 'War causes the shipwrecking of all that is good and from it the sea of all calamities pours forth.'

The Dutchman looked over at my mother. 'I am honoured, as you know, Grace, to have as my closest friend in the world, one of your countrymen, Master Thomas More. We are in complete agreement on the subject of war. As he put it: "*common folk do not go to war by themselves but are taken there by the madness of kings.*"'

Erasmus's gentle face took on an almost dreamy look. 'You know,' he said, with a flourish of his hands, 'in those first days after we first met, "*mellitissime*" Thoma and I talked of nothing else but letters until we fell asleep, our dreams were dreams of letters, and the promise of literature awoke us from our slumbers. Some men are roused by their stomachs, eager to break their fast, but we hardly had time to eat as every moment was precious. I told him he was a man "*omnium horarum*" and in my eyes, that's exactly what he is: "a good companion the whole day long". What joy it is to spend time with him and his family. It's as if his whole house breathes happiness. Just as yours does, I must say, Grace.'

My father took my mother's hand in his. 'And this young English King. Has Master More given you any indication of what kind of stuff he's made? My wife and I met the boy. But we don't know the man.'

'Ah, "*Le Roi d'Angleterre*," Erasmus said, drawing out the title of 'The King of England' - his accent, to my sensitive ears, giving the name an unpleasant harshness. 'Like yourselves, I had the pleasure of first meeting the boy prince a very long time ago in England, at Eltham Palace. Thomas and I have discussed his virtues many times since.'

My mother smiled. 'Dame Fortune was kind to bring us all together that day.'

Erasmus bowed his head. 'Indeed, she was. Now, of course, Henry is king. But, Guy, I'm guessing the real question you're asking me is: "Will he lead his country into war?"' He paused for a moment and then continued: 'Because we sit here in the final hours of the old year with hope in our hearts for what the future will bring us, I want to say no, but my head is telling me otherwise. However, for the moment, let us forget our woes and raise our glasses to health and prosperity.'

<<*Feeling as grim as a gravedigger, with the thought of my own empty future weighing heavily on my heart, I am in no mood to raise my glass to anything*>>

However, I was interested in the closeness of the friendship between Thomas More and Erasmus. It made me think of my own best friend, Jean de Lorraine, a boy with tastes and desires similar to my own. But I wisely decided to keep my counsel on that one and not mention my friend. No need to pour oil on already troubled waters, not with Father seated so near who knew exactly of what stuff the Duke of Lorraine's younger brother was made....

Doubtless made tired by his hours of talking, the scholar suddenly gave a little yawn and turned to me. 'And now, my boy, I hope you and I can converse a little longer on the way to my bedchamber. All this talk of war has exhausted me and I need to find the arms of Morpheus to refresh myself for the morrow.'

I looked over at the extraordinarily beautiful Countess who, in my dreams at least, seemed to be staring straight at me. At fifteen, I knew I had to make the most of every minute until that time when the unforgiving door would slam tight shut behind me, robbing me of all the light in my life: in order to become a bishop, I would have to be ordained as a priest. Looking at this vision of loveliness, not twenty feet from me, it suddenly came to me in a blinding flash what I was missing. Dating back to the time of Adam and Eve in the Garden of Eden, there was one thing I'd never experienced.

"I'm sure nothing ever tasted quite the same as that very first bite of the forbidden apple," my godfather once said.

Erasmus might be longing for the arms of Morpheus, but I knew only too well in whose arms I'd like to bid farewell to the old year. What a shame she already had a husband and, besides, would never give a green boy like me a second glance.

I led the way to the Dutchman's bedchamber which was only a few doors away from that of the Countess, holding up a flaming torch in my right hand. There was no doubt that Erasmus had one of the finest minds I'd ever encountered; crammed to the brim with every fascinating topic under the sun, it would flit from one to another with all the ease of one of the butterflies in the Castle gardens. One moment he'd be discussing his belief that life begins in the womb and that a foetus is capable of understanding, the very next, my future path in life in which he seemed to be taking an avid interest.

'So your father wants to put you into the Church.'

'Yes. But I would rather throw myself from the battlements of the Castle.'

Erasmus gave a polite cough. 'I'm sure that won't be necessary. I see you more as a diplomat myself. Not a churchman. Besides, from what I've observed this evening, you have a taste for the finer things of life. Of the flesh even.'

I felt myself flushing and was glad of the comparative darkness. Did Erasmus mean the Countess? Surely not.

'She's very lovely. You have excellent taste.' Erasmus winked at me, his words proving she was exactly who he meant. 'Oh, don't look so worried. Your secret is safe with me.'

Before I could stop myself, I blurted out: 'But I'm too young for her. And she's married.'

'Unfortunately, that hasn't stopped many a married woman I've met along the way, my boy.'

I decided I rather liked this revered scholar and felt pleased I'd made an impression on him. Nevertheless, as we came to a stop outside his door, I decided it was time for a swift change of subject.

⬦

I placed my torch in the bracket above our heads. 'What's it like being a diplomat, Monsieur Erasmus?'

'Your father was asking me about King Henry before so let me explain to you about the ways of kings. No amount of pomp and self-importance will help an ambitious courtier unless he learns the cardinal rule of diplomacy.'

'Which is?'

'That a king…or a queen, for that matter, especially an exceptionally vain one, must always be allowed to have the last word. My friend, Thomas, is writing a book he's going to call "*Utopia*". In it, one of the characters, Hythlodaeus, is greatly opposed to royal service. He claims it's impossible to counsel a king since only false words and duplicity will succeed.'

I was intrigued. 'But surely,' I pointed out, 'the counter-argument to that is a man in the royal service might work for the public good.'

His reply was a bark of laughter. 'You see, with your pleasing disposition and fine mind, I told you you'd make an excellent diplomat.'

'What kind of training would I need?'

Erasmus considered this for a moment. 'One that would show you when to pull an invisible cloak of wisdom about yourself.'

'I hope I'd be able to do that.'

'You would. You'd also require patience. Physical endurance. Setting out upon a long journey, any traveller knows he's about to face hunger and thirst, extremes of cold and heat, fatigue, sickness, and even death itself.'

I thought of the English Vice-Admiral, Edward Howard, and the courage he must possess to face the challenges he had and be so admired by young Henry of England. 'It sounds exciting.'

Erasmus let out a sigh. 'Spoken like a brave young man who has yet to experience life. It's the same with war. "*Dulce bellum inexpertio.*"'

300

I couldn't help feeling a little affronted. 'I'm not afraid of any of those things you mentioned.'

'That…I can well believe. If you do find yourself setting off on such a journey, it would be as well for you, as a first-time wayfarer to make a will beforehand so that masses may be said for your soul, food distributed to the poor, and care given to the sick. You must make peace with your enemies, appoint someone to take over your affairs while you're away, and prepare the necessary letters of introduction, money, and clothes for your journey.'

The only enemy I could think of was Nicolas and I could no more imagine making peace with him than agreeing to go into the Church.

Erasmus was staring at me intently. 'Finally, you must give up thanks to God and the saints in heaven to do all in their power to protect you. Once you arrive at your destination, you'll soon discover that any ambassador needs a razor-sharp mind in order to cope with every conceivable situation.'

'Even at a banquet?'

'*Especially* at a banquet. Many a slip of the tongue's been made after too many sips of the cup. You would do well to remember this advice from a man who has been on this earth for nearly half a century. If you do, I promise you, you won't go far wrong.'

'So a diplomat must watch his tongue at all times?'

'He must wear his words as he wears his clothes: for the purposes of show. The game of diplomacy constitutes a fine line between power and treachery.'

By now, we had been standing outside the door to Erasmus's bedchamber for the best part of an hour. I felt a little guilty for keeping a man of nearly fifty from his bed, especially when the Dutchman yawned and rubbed his eyes. 'Meeting you this evening, young Tristan, has given me great pleasure.'

'Me too. You've made me see things differently.'

'That's because you have a mind like a small spring high in the mountains, pure and unsullied. But I fear I have to close my eyes now or I might fall down on the spot.' As he held the door of his bedchamber ajar, Erasmus looked straight at me, a broad grin on his face. 'Promise me one day you'll read "*In Praise of Folly*". I think you'd like it. Good night to you.'

And, still chuckling, he closed the door behind him.

❧

As I picked up a torch to guide me down the darkened corridor, I recalled Nicolas's grinning face earlier, anticipating what kind of dreary evening I was in for. Thanks to meeting the erudite Dutchman, it hadn't turned out like that at all. I felt a lightness of spirit that hadn't been there before. As I approached the Countess's door, I paused, true longing surging through my entire body. Then, giving a little sigh, I continued, knowing this particular path was closed to me for the moment.

'*Tristan.*'

The whisper behind me nearly made me jump out of my skin. And turning, what I saw nearly made my heart stop still in my chest. Standing in a long white miniver stole, with her pale hair flowing around her like a veil, was the beautiful Countess. She reminded me of a statue of a Greek goddess in the Castle grounds. To my astonishment, she seemed to be giving me a smile of encouragement.

'*Moi?*' I mouthed, looking behind me, half-expecting to see another there, even though she'd just spoken my name.

'*Oui...toi,*' she whispered back, putting a finger up to her lips. With her other hand, she pushed open the door of her candlelit bedchamber and beckoned me in.

As if in a trance, I followed her....

VALENTINE

Chapter Forty-Seven

New Year's Day, 1513. La Colombe.

hy has the King given Papa a tapestry?' asked Charlotte, coming up to the top stair to stand next to Valentine. 'Because he likes Papa.'

The two sisters were staring at an enormous canvas, covered by a length of red cloth, while waiting for their parents and all the guests to come up the staircase from the great hall for the official unveiling. Valentine still couldn't quite believe that the funny old man she'd met in the kitchens last year was actually the King of France. Luckily, her father had seen the humour in the situation, even if her mother had not been amused: "*I don't care what you say, Charles. It was still disrespectful to call our monarch 'Old Louis'.*"

"*But Athénaïs, she's only a child. How can she be blamed if he didn't tell her who he was.*" He'd winked at Valentine to show her it could be their private little joke.

'Grandmère!' cried Charlotte. 'Come and stand next to me.'

Although she was awaiting the unveiling with equal anticipation, Valentine was mindful this was the first day of the year when she would be able to count her age in two figures, not one. Accordingly, she needed to behave with more decorum than yesterday.

Valentine felt her father's hand on her shoulders while her grandmère took Charlotte's hand. Meanwhile, all the guests took their places on the stairs leading up to the landing.

'I wonder what "Old Louis" has sent for your father,' Grandmère Symonne whispered to Valentine.

She'd found it highly entertaining when Valentine told her what happened with the King. "*Chérie,*" she said, "*for one so young, you've clearly discovered there's nothing quite like putting a man in his place, no matter if he's the king himself, or one in waiting. I applaud you."*

'*Mesdames et Messieurs,*' said her father, turning to face everyone. 'As you all know, I've already been honoured once by the King who gave me a title for my part in the Battle of Agnadello. And now he has seen fit to honour me further by this gift we're about to see.' With that, he made a signal for the red cloth to be lifted.

There was silence as four servants tugged at the cloth. With a grand flourish, and cries of admiration from the guests, the tapestry was unveiled in all its glory. Valentine's grandmère let out an exclamation of wonder, as did her father who moved closer for a better look. As for Valentine, she immediately decided the King's New Year's gift was the ugliest thing she'd ever seen in her whole life. Admittedly, when she walked right up to it, she was entranced by the opulence of the cloth of gold and silver, threaded through with green and white silk. However, the subject matter appalled her. So this was what war was like. King Louis' tapestry depicted a battleground with huge embroidered figures filling the canvas, clutching swords and battleaxes as they performed heroic deeds. One of the soldiers had her father's facial features beneath the closely cropped, fair hair, encased in a helmet. But, instead of her father's kindly expression, for the sake of realism, this had been replaced by a suitably warlike one and the normally twinkling blue eyes were ice-cold - the full mouth twisted into a hate-filled grimace. Shifting her gaze away from this unsettling image, Valentine suddenly noticed the bottom left-hand corner; here, a poor horse lay in agony on its back, its hind legs broken, its eyes rolling in sheer terror.

Unable to bear it a moment longer, and forgetting she was almost an adult now, Valentine pushed past her parents and ran along the corridor, great sobs tearing at her throat. Blinded by her tears, she rushed into her bedchamber and threw herself onto the bed, covering her head with her pillow. She remained like this for several long minutes, not caring that she'd probably caused a scene by bolting to her room like that.

'Why, *ma petite*, whatever is wrong?'

It was her mother's anxious voice coming from the doorway. 'Your father and I were worried about you.'

Brushing away the tears that were coursing down her cheeks, Valentine lifted her head to find both her parents standing there.

'Was it the poor horse that bothered you?' said her father, walking up to the bed and cradling her in his arms. 'Did it remind you of your little Cassandre?'

'Y-y-yes. And I don't like war. I don't want you ever to go to war again, Papa.'

'He won't,' said her mother, coming down to sit on her other side.

'He will if King Louis tells him to,' Valentine said, worry making her fierce. 'I thought he was a nice old man. But he's not. He's hateful. I wish I'd never met him!'

'Hush now, *mon ange*,' said her father, stroking her hair. 'I assure you King Louis wants peace just as much as you do. He told me as much himself. Kings, emperors and popes make truces all the time. There's no reason at all why 1513 should be any different. Now then, we should all be getting back to our guests. It's New Year's Day, a time for wonderful gifts. And you haven't had yours yet. Nobody knows so far but your mother's just given me the best gift I could ever wish for.'

In spite of still being upset about the tapestry, Valentine couldn't help being curious. She looked at her mother. 'Did you give Papa a subtlety?'

'*Non, non*,' her mother replied, laughing. 'Not a subtlety.'

Her father used his thumb to wipe away her tears. 'Well, not exactly a subtlety. Even better than that, in fact.'

Valentine couldn't imagine anything better than one of Phélix's creations. She looked at her father expectantly and watched as he placed his hand on her mother's belly.

'Your mother's going to bake me something that will take many months to prepare. But when it's finished it will be well worth the effort, won't it, *chérie*?'

Valentine watched as he bent down to kiss her mother on the cheek. 'God willing, little Valentine, 1513 will bring us our heart's desire.'

Her mother smiled. 'Yes, I have a feeling Dame Fortune has got something very special planned for all of us.'

HOUSE OF TUDOR

Chapter Forty-Eight

New Year's Day, 1513. Greenwich Palace.

*W*ed, I want this to be the biggest and best Twelfth Night ever! Louis of France will discover I'm not some pinch-spotted, twenty-one-year-old, not long finished playing with his wooden soldiers. I want him to know who I am.'

'The grandson of the mighty Edwar—'

'Yes. And keeper of the flame of that great torchbearer, Henry Plantagenet.'

'Who took Agincour—'

'As we will again.' Henry grabbed his friend about the shoulder. 'God's Teeth! We'll take Louis' France from him like a mother pulling a suckling babe from the teat.'

Edward Howard laughed. 'I like the image.'

'I want word to get back to the French. To leave them in no doubt there'll be a war this year.'

Henry leapt onto a table in the antechamber. 'So, tell me what's planned so far. I know six of us are going to be Lords of the Mount, dressed in crimson velvet.'

'I went to the Revels office to see Henry Guildford yesterday. He's made a mountain decorated with green and gold silk flowers that's going to be wheeled into the great hall. With you on top, of course. And the rest of us below.'

'Kate will love that.' Henry reached behind him and produced a small black velvet bag. 'It's one of my New Year's gifts for her. A lucky charm.'

'What is it?'

'A rabbit's foot. Charles Brandon got it for me.'

'What's it supposed to do?'

'Make a woman as fertile as a female rabbit. Able to produce children like you wouldn't believe. Someone Charles knows swore it gave him three sons in three years. Do you think she'll like it?'

'Hal, knowing how much Kate wants to give you another son, of course she will.'

Henry lay down on the table, adopting the pose of a marble statue, and closing his eyes. 'I couldn't wish for a better wife, you know.'

'I know.'

'She's the mistress of my heart, my help-mate. By Saint George! I'll even leave her in charge of the country when we go off to war. If only she could give me a son, my world would be complete.'

Edward put one hand on Henry's shoulder. 'May the stars be looking down favourably on the two of us this year.'

Henry sat up and ran one hand through his hair. 'And Dame Fortune grant us both our heart's delight. What's yours?'

'To serve you well.'

'That's very commendable. But what of women and love? Surely those old women of yours don't give you what you need. I know you already have two boys from past dalliances.'

'*Rich* old women, I'll have you remember. And yes, I have my boys. But not full Howard sons I can parade about the place.'

'Ned, you have so many pretty young women panting after you, wouldn't you like to have one to yourself? All the time. Then you can have your Howard boys.'

'I tried it once. And she broke my heart into a thousand pieces. I've often wondered how it might have been if we'd had a son of our own.'

'Ah, the trials and tribulations of Cupid. What happened?'

'I thought she loved me. But she changed her mind.'

'So Venus's blindfolded boy came calling, did he? Beating his wings, as flighty as any lover, and bearing two arrows: a golden one to inflame you, and another of lead to chase your love away.'

'He certainly chased her away. She married another and forgot all about me.'

'Have you seen her since?'

'Once. With him. Eleven or twelve years had passed but I knew it was her the moment I set eyes on her, even though she was standing quite far away.'

'Did you speak to her?'

'Only as you would greet a passing acquaintance.'

Henry was sympathetic, not asking Ned the name of his true love lest it cause him more pain to say her name out loud. 'And how did you feel when you met her again?'

'Oh, Hal. She was still so beautiful…and so…so…her, I thought I would die of love all over again.'

'But you didn't. Which is just as well because then you wouldn't be able to enjoy the gift I've got you.'

❧

As he said this, Henry reached behind him again and pulled out another black velvet bag, this time with a large letter 'N' sewn on the front with gold thread.

He watched Ned open it and pull out a gleaming gold whistle.

'Surely this isn't an—'

'Admiral's whistle. Yes. That's exactly what it is. I had it especially made for you.'

'But John de Vere is—'

'An old man of seventy who might not see another New Year's Day. You and I both know we need someone young and vigorous. John has served me well, but once he's gone, the post is yours. And here's the whistle to prove it.'

'Thank you. Though my father might not like to hear you talk like that. He and Sir John are of an age.'

Henry sprang down from the table. 'Let's face it. Your father's immortal. He'll probably still be raising hell at ninety.'

'And producing boys.'

'To make me spit. Yes, I'm sure of it. I think he does it just to irk me.'

'He's not laughing at the moment.'

'Your sister?'

'Yes.'

'How is she?'

'To be frank, every morning she awakes to see a new dawn is a blessing.'

'We'll ask Warham to say a prayer for her later.'

'Thank you. I'll—'

'Hal. Hal. Ned, come quickly.'

Just then, Kate came rushing into the ante chamber from the great hall, her eyes bright and her cheeks flushed. Looking at her now, Henry couldn't help hoping they wouldn't have to use the rabbit's foot, after all. And that their dawn lovemaking would finally bear fruit and put a boy in the Tudor cradle in the coming year.

'Come on, you two, stop dilly-dallying. Everyone's calling for you to sing. You know you've got the best voices at court.'

TRISTAN

Chapter Forty-Nine

New Year's Day, 1513. Ardres Castle.

ood Heavens, Tristan!' exclaimed Guillaume Gouffier. 'The Comtesse de Saint-Séverin. Do you realize that woman's admired by every man in the kingdom of France...including the King himself. Are you sure you're your father's son and not mine?'

'Not unless you fathered me when you were nine. And even for someone with your reputation, that might prove difficult.'

The two of us were in the middle of an exciting game of chess. I'd woken up back in my own bed after stealing back to it just before dawn, feeling as high as one of the kites in the summer skies, brought back by the explorer, Marco Polo. <<*I never wanted the night to end: it was one of discovery, of unending wonder and untold pleasure. How could I have known a woman's body would be so sweet, so silken? Mysterious...yet willing to yield up its secrets at the touch of a man's hand...or his lips>>* Even though the night had begun with Annette de Saint-Séverin gently leading me into the unknown, I'd quickly found my way without her help. One thing it had done was make me even more determined than ever to defy my father's wishes.

I'd told my godfather about my recent quarrel with Father, and Erasmus's suggestion of being a diplomat. 'After all,' I protested, 'why did my parents bother naming me for a grand marshal of France, Tristan L'Hermite, or a Cornish knight of King Arthur's round table, if they meant to lock me away in a monastery.'

'Much as I'd like to help you, I'm afraid the only way I can ignore your father's wishes is if he were to die. And as he is still young and vigorous - and very dear to both of us, I might add - it looks as if you might have to get used to the idea of a mitre on top of that handsome head of yours. Unfortunately, last night doesn't change a thing.'

My godfather must have seen the expression on my face. 'I'm sure there are compensations to being a bishop such as…such as having a beautiful woman making her confession to you. Or having all those pretty nuns pining for the touch of a man's hand.' Seeing this didn't have the desired effect either, he picked up a painted wooden bishop from the chessboard and tossed it playfully into the air. 'All right, try being as bad as you can and maybe that'll change his mind. You could start off by letting him see that mark of Venus on your neck. And perhaps, if you're lucky, he'll send you off to be a mercenary. Either that or he'll toss you into the darkest dungeon and throw away the key!'

Brushing my fingers over where Annette de Saint-Séverin must have nipped me with her teeth, I could feel myself coming down to earth with a bump. What a shame Guillaume couldn't do more to aid me. I recalled a conversation from not too long ago when I'd threatened to run away and live with him:

"You're more stubborn than the most wayward mule," Father had yelled at me in the middle of the heated family argument. *"I don't know where you get it from. I know you get your charm from your mother. She could charm the very birds down from the trees."*

"Guy, mon amour, please don't be so hard on the boy," my mother pleaded, a reproachful look on her face. Defending me was the only time I ever heard her raise her voice to Father. *"He's got the Tredavoe family charm. My brother, William, is renowned for it the entire length of Cornwall."*

Of course that hadn't pleased my father one jot. *"Tristan doesn't need 'charm' to be a bishop. One day he'll find himself putting the Tredavoe charm to a far worthier use."*

Unfortunately, mentioning I wanted to live with my godfather had only stirred things up further: *"Over my dead body!"* Father exploded. *"Asking Guillaume Gouffier to be your godfather was possibly the worst decision I've ever made in my entire life. I can't believe I let Artus convince me it would be better for you to have someone nearer your own age instead of him. Artus Gouffier is probably the most sensible man in the entire kingdom of France. While his younger brother…at times…the least!"*

❧

Not even the brand-new longsword Guillaume presented me with a couple of moments later could lift my spirits again. His voice was apologetic. 'I'm afraid it has to be our secret. Can you imagine what your father would say if he knew I'd given a future bishop of Ardres a weapon as a New Year's gift, rather than a work of God.'

I slid my fingers over the shining steel, feeling frustrated I couldn't march out of there right now to show off the magnificent specimen to the entire Castle.

'With its shorter blade and long narrow handle, it'll be easier to handle,' said Guillaume. 'For now, hide it in your bedchamber, away from prying eyes.'

'You mean, the ones belonging to my horn-mad father?'

All of a sudden, I thought of a very different man...across the Narrow Sea. Although I had no idea what Edward Howard looked like, I had an image of a dark-haired nobleman, proud and fierce, dressed in the costume of a Vice-Admiral, aboard one of the King of England's ships. In his hand, he was holding an identical longsword to mine, slightly larger, of course. All around him, Frenchmen were rushing at him but no one could even come close to felling him. He was shouting orders and swinging his sword with such force and speed that sparks flew in the air every time he made contact with another weapon. In my head, it was as if King Arthur himself was slicing the air with precise strokes, his fabled sword, *Excalibur*, living up to the legend—

'Tristan!'

I was so deep in thought it took me a few seconds to realize my godfather was staring at me, an amused look on his face. 'What...or whom were you thinking about? As if I couldn't guess.'

<<*How can I tell him I've been thinking about a man I've never met... but very much hope to one day*>> 'I was thinking about how I'm going to call my new sword "*Excalibur*".'

Guillaume laughed. 'You weren't thinking of the lovely Countess? No matter! Let's hope naming it that brings you as much luck as the original.'

❧

313

Once outside my bedchamber, the disappointment of not being able to show off my new gift, especially to my father, affected my mood again. There wasn't even a chance of a repeat performance with Annette to cheer me up. It was typical of my bad luck that I'd just seen her greet her husband in the great hall. Dame Fortune seemed to be rewarding me one moment and punishing me the next these days. Playing a frustrating game of '*Peek-a-boo*', where she would suddenly appear at my side to do her worst when I least expected it.

Wandering gloomily to the entrance, I was about to step foot into the courtyard when I found myself rooted to the spot by the sight that greeted me. There, a few yards away, was my father handing my arch enemy the reins to the most achingly beautiful black stallion I'd ever seen. I thought I'd die on the spot of jealousy and hurt. How *could* he have given such a magnificent gift to an outsider, and a few paltry books to his own flesh and blood?

Nicolas was fairly jumping up and down with gratitude and joy, thanking Father over and over again. Looking at the pair of them was like looking in a mirror - except it was one that had been turned upside down. After a few minutes of this mutual rejoicing, Nicolas caught sight of me loitering.

'Tristan, come and look at my New Year's gift.' He held up one hand and stroked the horse's shaggy black mane. 'I've decided to call him *Minuit*. Isn't he magnificent?'

'Magnificent,' I repeated dully, unable to meet my father's eyes as I approached the pair of them with feet made of lead, and a heart turned to stone.

A look of malice suddenly appeared on Nicolas's face. 'Of course, your present from your father was every bit as special. In fact, Monsieur Guy, Tristan was saying to me before how he's going to read us an extract from "*In Praise of Folly*". Isn't that right, Tristan?'

Was it possible to smite an enemy dead with a mere thought? I was certainly going to try. Instead of gracing the flap-mouthed Nicolas with an answer, I mumbled something and rushed back inside.

<<*I'll get my own back for this*>> I vowed, as I stormed back through the great hall. <<*I swear it on the sword of Sir Edward Howard!*>>

HOUSE OF STEWART

Chapter Fifty

6ᵗʰ January, 1513. Twelfth Night. Uphaliday.
The nursery, Stirling Castle.

*J*ames looked down at the sleeping infant in his arms and smiled. Transferring his precious bundle to his left arm, he pulled his queen to him with the other. Outside, the snow was falling more thickly now, almost completely covering the four towers at the entrance, as well as the gilded stone lions and unicorns, perched beneath the turrets. The arched gateway had taken on the appearance of an exotic subtlety. Layer upon layer of white concealed the bright red lion on James's coat-of-arms and the golden-yellow limewash beneath, aptly known as 'king's gold'. Unlike the summer scene of inviting orchards and vast gardens, this wintry one was akin to a magnificent dessert, fit for a king - with the myriad snowflakes, the final culinary flourish of the royal pastry cook, dusting his masterpiece with icing sugar.

Stirling was very close to his heart. He always felt so regal seated on a raised dais in the great hall, beneath a golden canopy, the light streaming through the glass windows illuminating him in a way that made him almost seem divine. He had no difficulty believing this hilltop fortress had once housed King Arthur's court. That was why he'd willingly spent three thousand pounds on its upkeep. Soon they would be cut off from the rest of the world. But what did he care? He had everything he wanted right here, including a blazing fire in the open stone hearth behind them. The firelight gave a rosy hue to the entire chamber: from the escutcheons placed high in the timber roof, to the windows above, and down to the silver plate, goblets, bowls and platters on the table, brought in for his and his queen's pleasure. James smiled as he thought of his cook constantly beseeching him to eat more, sending across from the kitchens a new recipe, such as venison, pilfered from the court of King Henry in the south. Even Janet Kennedy's undoubted charms wouldn't be enough to pull him away from this window. Besides, he knew Bell the Cat was firmly ensconced back in her bed again; he could hardly blame her; a lonely bedchamber was no state of affairs for a vital young woman like Janet.

His Maggie had colour back in her cheeks and her old sparkle in her eyes. She'd even let him take her to bed again on New Year's Eve, after a rousing, indisputably bawdy tale by a wandering story teller, followed by a particularly hilarious display by his fool, Currie, and his wife, Daft Ann. James enjoyed giving Maggie pleasure, accepting that the passion she often showed on a daily basis was part of her nature and could be put to far better use naked in his arms. When he'd initially raised an eyebrow at her invitation during supper, fretting she still wasn't well enough after the loss of their baby girl in November, she put her arm around his neck and whispered in his ear:

"*I want you. Let it be my New Year's gift to you, my lord.*"

Later, in the huge four-poster bed, she'd smiled at him as he tugged at the strings of her nightgown. "*May the stars be smiling down on us tonight, my King.*"

Who knows, James thought now as he hugged his baby son to him, if Maggie was right about the stars, he might well have a second son in his arms this time next year. What a yuletide that would be. It was always a time when the Castle attracted a variety of entertainers: dancers, singers, tumblers, fiddlers and harpists, all eager to join in the merriment and earn a pretty wage.

In order to signal his wish to God, he'd silently mouthed a special prayer at that morning's mass, offering up gold, frankincense and myrrh.

In the distance, came the silvery tones of a harp. James grinned when he recognized what Andrew, his blind harpist, was playing on his clarsach. It was a song about a man going down to England to steal King Henry's finest horse. One that never ceased to amuse James and his courtiers.

'Are you content, my love?' asked Maggie, reaching out to stroke the smooth skin of their baby son's face.

'More than ye ken, my bonny lass. Anyone can see wee Jamie here is thriving.'

Maggie put a finger to his lips. 'Hush! You'll anger Dame Fortune with such words. After all, she took our first little James…and then Arthur, after only a year on this earth. And James is but ten months yet.'

'Och, it's verra true about the Dame taking the others. But trust me, this one is different. I can feel it in my bones.'

'I hope you're right.'

'I am right. Dame Fortune is pleased with us. Look at me. I am the luckiest man in Christendom. Certainly, the happiest king in Europe.'

'Happier than Harry?'

'Aye. Far happier. Your brother can brawl and boast all he likes, prancing and posturing, raising two fists up to me and Louis of France. He can even throw a magnificent Twelfth Night feast for his court this evening, worthy of an emperor from ancient Rome. There's to be another masque in the Italian style this year. Or so I've heard.'

'Acting and dancing suit Harry's character perfectly. He always liked dressing up when we were children. I once teased him he should have been born an actor in a travelling company. I remember the two of us dancing at Kate and Arthur's wedding and him flinging off his heavy gown to dance in his jacket like a gypsy boy.'

'Your brother can have all the fun he wishes. But ye and I both know that after all the festivities have ended and he and his queen are creeping past the empty nursery in his palace at Greenwich, they'll find it as quiet as a graveyard in mid-winter. Remember how he spent the equivalent of sixteen ships of war on the celebrations of their New Year's boy two years ago. That's how much your brother wants a son and heir.'

'You could say the same about King Louis and his nursery at Blois.'

'At least his queen has given him two girls. And reason to hope there might be a boy. Speaking of Twelfth Night, the French Ambassador was explaining to me earlier how they celebrate it over there. It's called the Feast of Epiphany or "*La Fête des Rois*" and, just as we do, they choose a King and Queen of the Bean to reign over it.'

'Do they hide a bean in a cake too?'

'Aye. The man who finds the bean in his slice is made king.'

'Then he chooses his Queen?'

'Ah, they do that a little differently. All the names of the bonniest young lasses at court are put in a hat. Then the newly created King of the Bean pulls out the name of his queen to cries of: "*La reine est faite!*" The pair are then set to make as much mischief as they like.'

'You speak excellent French, James. As good as any Frenchman, Monsieur de La Motte says.'

'That is a compliment indeed. The French Ambassador can come and visit us again any time he pleases. Only next time, he should take care not to scare the people of Edinburgh witless.'

'You're talking about Saint Andrew's Eve when there was a huge gale battering the Forth—'

'Aye. That one. My subjects in Leith swore blind they heard guns when the wind stopped howling. I couldna blame them for ringing the alarm for three hours because they thought Edward Howard was coming after them.'

'It doesn't help that people are terrified of the pest here in Stirling.'

James reached down and stroked his baby son's head. 'Dinna fret, Maggie, I've given orders for anyone sick with it to stay away from both kirk and market, on pain of death.'

'As for the French Ambassador, after receiving thirty tuns of wine and as much gunpowder and weapons as I need, I have nothing but good will towards him and his master. Your brother has left me no choice but to join forces with the French, nominally at least. Ye ken I have no wish to go to war with England. But I would be a fool no' to protect myself and my country against the land and sea might Henry is preparing.'

'You know I'm glad of the "Auld Alliance" Scotland has with France—'

'And of the eight rolls of cloth of gold La Motte brought ye,' James teased.

'Of that too. But I don't want French gifts if it means war ahead. If only Harry could be glad of the alliance too. And want peace for himself. Like Father did.'

James bent down to kiss the baby's forehead. 'If your brother and Louis had fine sons like this one here, perhaps they would no' be so bent on making mischief outside their kingdoms.'

Maggie leant into him. 'The stillborn son Queen Anne lost last January must have iced both their hearts. After our own losses, I can well imagine their pain.'

'So can I.' He gave Maggie a gentle squeeze. 'Ye see, you're the cleverest queen of all of them. The only one to produce a son and heir.'

'I know how proud and willful my brother is. The fact that - through me - you're heir to the English throne, must be like having a flea bite he needs to scratch all day and all night long.'

James laughed and pulled her closer. 'Verra true, my sweet Maggie.'

✍

Without warning, she went stiff in his arms and when she spoke, her voice was no longer tender but the querulous one he knew only too well. 'But he's not your only son, is he?' Her words came out in an accusatory hiss.

James stepped back from the window. 'Maggie, look at me.'

For a moment, she remained turned away from him, stubbornly still. But then he pulled her back to him quite sharply and she reluctantly turned her face up to his.

'How can those others,' he said, fire in his belly, 'mean the same to me as this little one here. They were already in my life before we met. Ye, Maggie Stewart, are forgetting ye are a queen and one day your son will be a king.'

In reply, Maggie jabbed a finger around the nursery as if invoking all the cradles from years past that had caused her such pain. 'What of your bastard sons?'

James let out a sigh. 'What can I say? I hope they grow to be strong fine men to make their mothers proud of them. But they're no' true born princes. And never will be.'

'But you've made your son, Alexander, Archbishop of Saint Andrews—'

'The last time I looked at the laws of this land, hinny, an archbishop was a man of God, no' an anointed king. So dinna let me hear ye say such a thing again. Ye are a queen amongst queens. Make no mistake of it.'

To his relief, he was rewarded by a smile from his wife, followed by a commotion outside. The two of them watched as the door to the nursery inched open to the sound of loud chattering.

'Jock!' exclaimed James, as Maggie's new pet monkey, his Hogmanay gift to her, burst into the nursery, a harassed maid in hot pursuit.

'Forgive me, Your Majesties, but the wee beastie bit the cook's finger and then ran off.'

As she said this, she tried to catch the offending animal but Jock was far too agile for her. Leaping onto baby James's wooden cradle, he began to rock it at a dizzying speed.

'Come, Jock,' said Maggie, scooping him up in her arms and heading for the door, 'let you and I go for a little walk before you wake the baby.' She turned to James. 'My lord, the morrice dancers will be waiting for us.'

'I'll be with you verra soon, my sweet love.'

Left alone with his infant son, James watched the snowflakes land on the window pane with a soft thud before settling there. They seemed to be falling in tune with Blind Andrew's harp strings, and the distant sound of singing:

> '*A wager he made, with two knights he laid*
> *To steal King Henry's Wanton Brown.*'

James cradled the babe to him. '*Mon cher fils,*' he whispered in French, before switching back to English. 'Your mother was right. Ye do have brothers ye'll meet one day. That is, all of them but one. I dinna ken where your eldest brother is, more's the pity. He must be twenty-one now. Almost a full-grown man. Let's hope, shall we, that he's content. Wherever he is....'

STIRLING CASTLE
TWELFTH NIGHT CAKE

170g (6 oz) butter

170g (6 oz) sugar

170g (6oz) flour

½ teaspoon each of:

Ground allspice, ground cinnamon, mace, ground ginger, ground coriander, ground nutmeg

2 grinds of pepper

3 tablespoons of brandy

3 eggs

340g (12 oz) currants

42g (1½ ounces) flaked almonds

One orange and one lemon grated

1 tablespoon of honey

1) Preheat the oven to 150°C. Grease and line a 15cm round cake tin. For the outside of the tin, prepare two strips of greaseproof paper and one long strip of silver foil. For the top, cut a sheet of greaseproof paper and one of silver foil. A piece of string will be needed to hold it all in place.

2) Soften the butter in a mixing bowl. Add the sugar and cream together with the butter until the mixture appears light and fluffy.

3) Add the eggs one at a time, beating well and also adding one tablespoon of flour to prevent curdling. Once all the eggs are mixed in, add the brandy, then the flour and spices, folding them in to keep air in the mixture.

4) Finally stir in the currants, almonds, lemon and orange peel and honey.

5) Pour the mixture into the prepared cake tin. At this point, you could also add a dried pea or a dried bean to the cake. Do <u>not</u> use a kidney bean.

6) Cook for half an hour at 150°C and then cover the top with a sheet of greaseproof paper beneath one of silver foil. Turn the oven down to 140°C and bake for a further one hour fifteen minutes. For the last ten/fifteen minutes, remove the foil to brown the top more. When a warm rounded knife is placed inside, it should come out clean.

NICOLAS

Chapter Fifty-One

6th January, 1513. La Fête des Rois. Ardres Castle.

ou shouldn't even have a horse! You're not part of this family. You don't deserve it.'

Nicolas was clutching his side where Tristan had punched him.

'At least,' he panted, 'I didn't destroy your father's New Year's present the second I got it.' The next moment, they were upon each other again, wrestling to the ground, cheered on by Gilles and a large group of stableboys, and Castle servants.

It was hard to know who was punching harder as they rolled over and over in the straw. At one point, Tristan deliberately grabbed Nicolas's locket so hard that the chain almost broke. That was when Nicolas hit his opponent very hard just under his right eye, to the sound of applause and wild cries of encouragement. Nicolas slowly became aware the cheering had stopped and a large shadow was blotting out the light filtering through the small window. But it was only when a hand grabbed him roughly by the left shoulder that he realized—

'Get up, you useless pair of jack-a-napes!' a furious voice yelled. 'You're a disgrace to the family name. You're no better, Gilles. Taking bets from everyone. Get out of my sight all of you. Now!'

Seeing that Nicolas and Tristan were too stunned to respond, Guy d'Ardres bent down and physically dragged them to their feet, shaking them as he did so. 'How dare you behave like this! Walking away from mass to damn your souls, without a thought for our family.'

Nicolas was winded, a couple of his ribs hurt, and he could taste blood in his mouth from a cut on his lower lip. He was glad to see Tristan hadn't come off any better; there was a bright red swelling below his right eye that would be purple by this evening's banquet. Nicolas longed for the privacy and comfort of his bedchamber where he could at least escape the look of disappointment on Monsieur Guy's face. <<*One I've helped put there*>>

The Count was glaring at him. 'Perhaps you'd like to explain your behaviour. What were you two fighting about this time?'

Although Nicolas would have liked nothing better than to reveal the real reason for the fight, he was no loose-tongued blabber, not even where the whoreson Tristan was involved. He would rather face the rack than reveal that Monsieur Guy's son had stolen his horse and ridden it to near exhaustion the day before. It was only when Nicolas exploded with rage at the state of Minuit that one of the flustered stableboys had pointed the finger of guilt at Tristan (in case it was pointed at him instead).

Nicolas knew he had to come up with a reason. 'It was all over nothing,' he croaked, his voice still a little hoarse from where Tristan had grabbed him around the throat. 'Please forgive me.'

Monsieur Guy narrowed his eyes and sucked in his breath. 'By God's Nails! How can you possibly ask for forgiveness when you won't even tell the truth? That's not how things work in the world.'

Feeling no better than a pinch-spotted clotpole who'd been caught filching from the collection box in the church of Notre Dame de Grâce, Nicolas hung his head in shame.

'With the threat of a war hanging over our heads, it would be foolhardy of me to forbid you to ride your horse, or join in the training. However, every other waking moment for the next two weeks, you are to spend in here, cleaning every single piece of brass in the entire place. I want these stables to sparkle like the Castle kitchens, is that clear?'

Cringing at Monsieur Guy's stream of invective, Nicolas wished the ground below him would open up and swallow him. 'Yes, Monsieur Guy.' As he stroked his swollen lip, he vaguely wondered what Tristan's punishment would be.

෨

Monsieur Guy strode to the far end of the stables where his surly younger son was lounging on a plank of wood. When he spoke, his voice was clipped and Nicolas could see his dark eyes were blazing. 'Tristan, I know what happened. No man ever takes another man's horse without permission. I've a mind to ban you from the banquet this evening but as that would only distress your mother, I won't. But, believe me, celebrating Epiphany will be the very last time you enjoy yourself for a long time. At least a month. You will neither ride nor tilt at the quintain; instead, *you* will spend every waking hour split between the Castle kitchens and the church of Notre Dame de Grâce. I will personally inform Père Alphonse you are to help him clean every single candlestick until it gleams. After that, you will go to the kitchens and relieve the spit turners.'

The Count's expression was grim. 'Perhaps that will teach you not to act so dishonourably in the future.'

Nicolas watched Tristan stand up and take a step towards his departing father's back, defiance written all over his face. 'Perhaps if you'd bought *me* a horse in the first place—'

There was a moment when Nicolas thought, from the expression on Monsieur Guy's face, that he was going to strike his son. <<*I so hope he does*>> Instead, he turned and began approaching Tristan with slow graceful steps…every one of them deliberate. When he spoke his voice was dangerously quiet. 'You've just earned yourself a second month. Nicolas is as much a part of this family as you and Gilles. As for the books you destroyed, you will personally write to Monsieur Erasmus and explain why we need some replacements. You can start your punishment by accompanying me to see Père Alphonse.

'And you, Nicolas, you can stay here and get to work—'

Once the Count and Tristan had left the stables, the place fell silent apart from the occasional sound from Nicolas's four-legged companions: the stamping of a pair of hoofs on the straw, the thud of flanks bumping against a wooden stall, the swish of a tail, or the noise of satisfied munching. Nicolas lifted the locket over his head to check that Tristan hadn't damaged it during the fight. Expertly, as he'd done so many times before, he pressed on the small gold clasp and the locket flew open. As usual, the girl seemed to be smiling at him...not mocking him...but looking at him in a gentle loving way. Her huge dark eyes were brimming with compassion, and her full lips seemed to be quivering.

'I don't deserve any pity,' he told her, sadly closing the locket and carefully placing it back around his neck.

Picking up a saddle and a brush while trying to ignore Minuit's friendly whinnying from the far end of the stables, urging him to place a saddle on his back and ride across the frost-gilded fields together, a despondent Nicolas set to work. He shouldn't have let his temper get the better of him, especially where Tristan was concerned. Look what it had brought him: punishment and loss of favour with a man who was the closest thing he'd ever had to a loving father. Nicolas began polishing the saddle in front of him with great vigour, as if trying to make reparation for the folly-fallen fight, finding comfort in the slightly nutty aroma of flaxseed and how such work helped him forget the biting cold. <<*What a way to repay two people who have opened their home and their hearts to me*>> Feeling wretched, he picked up a tin of beeswax and a dry cloth....

At least, putting his heart and soul into Monsieur Guy's tasks compensated for the pain in his now reddened hands. Time passed very quickly and, taking pleasure in how every icy breath he exhaled was worthy of the most fearsome dragon, he picked up his third saddle. Nicolas suddenly felt more carefree and turned his mind to the Epiphany Eve banquet in a few hours. And who was coming. Well, he was thinking of one guest alone.

<<*Ysabeau de Sapincourt*>>

She was an exquisite little thing, good enough to eat with her luscious curves, innocent blue eyes, and sinful smile. She was barely twenty years of age, married off to a wealthy husband nudging forty-five, making her ripe for the plucking. Nicolas wanted nothing more than to entwine himself in her long silky hair that looked as if it had taken a hundred bees to reproduce its hue. He was so sure of a successful conquest that he hadn't bothered to make any particular overtures. *<<So no one else knows of my intentions towards Ysabeau. That's always the best way>>* He crossed the stables and bent down to retrieve a large curb bit belonging to Monsieur Guy's most prized horse.

When Tristan had nearly taken his head off on Christmas Eve with that poxy handbook about childhood manners, Nicolas was engaged in something far more pressing. How irksome that Tristan hadn't been too far from the truth when he accused Nicolas of trying to find inspiration between the covers of the romances. He had no intention of making a proper move on Ysabeau this evening, no matter how curious he was to discover whether she was as appealing inside the bedchamber - as out of it. Like a skilled hunter setting a trap, he was prepared to be patient, knowing this course of action brought the richest rewards....

He stooped down to get a pair of stirrups, noticing how dirty they were, guessing Tristan must have used them yesterday. Although he was tempted to leave them where they were, he thought of Monsieur Guy's pained expression before. Making a noise of exasperation, he cleaned them vigorously until they shone. Then he tossed them disdainfully to one side. *<<How little Guy d'Ardres' fly-bitten son deserves my help>>*

Before long, Nicolas had cleaned and polished every single saddle in sight. Standing up, he stretched, immediately wincing from the pain in his ribs where Tristan had punched him. He decided to go off to the kitchens in search of a drink, on the way idly wondering how many candlesticks Tristan had polished in the church. Reflecting back the well-deserved black eye he'd received a few hours earlier.

There was a tiny part of Nicolas that almost - but not quite - pitied Tristan for the miserable life that lay ahead of him. *<<Not for him the feel of a woman's hand caressing his face and body, but instead the hard stone floor of a monastery, rewarding a life of prayer and abstinence with aching joints>>* Although the vision didn't come easily, he somehow managed to picture

Tristan as a portly, heavy-jowled bishop, sporting a monk's tonsure, his chubby fingers clutching his crucifix to a protruding belly. He would never know the paradise to which a desirable woman like Ysabeau de Sapincourt could transport a man. Instead, it was to be his fate to remain a puny virgin to the end of his days, never knowing the ecstasy of release.

'Oh, Tristan,' he said aloud as he reached the door to the kitchens, 'you have no idea what you're missing. None at all.'

NICOLAS

Chapter Fifty-Two

That evening. Ardres Castle.

*Y*sabeau de Sapincourt was even more beautiful than Nicolas remembered. He'd had almost no appetite to enjoy the sumptuous fare being served, apart from a slice of the traditional Epiphany cake. He hoped to discover a bean amongst the dried fruit and be chosen as King of the Bean. That would provide him with extra opportunity to carry out his mission. To his annoyance, Tristan had been the one to find the bean…although the circumstances were somewhat suspicious. Nicolas could have sworn he saw a knowing look pass between Tristan and the Castle pastry cook. Seated next to Tristan on the high table was his best friend, Jean de Lorraine. He'd turned up in the afternoon for the festivities, in the company of Guillaume Gouffier <<*like two bad copper dizains*>> From the way he was openly laughing at his friend's supposed triumph (and Nicolas's defeat), it was obvious he knew about this morning's fight. Staring pointedly over in Nicolas's direction, his very blue slanted eyes were dancing with mischief while his lips were twitching with malice.

Although it pained Nicolas to admit it, the younger boy was a good-looking little varlet; he had an attractive slender face with high cheekbones, a narrow chiselled nose, hair the colour of burnished gold, and beautiful hands which he was constantly using to illustrate some point or other. He and Tristan were clearly having the time of their lives, the fight and subsequent punishment forgotten. No doubt the pair of them had bribed the pastry cook to let Tristan win so they could cause havoc. Jean certainly didn't look like a future churchman (any more than Tristan did), evident from his obvious appreciation of Ysabeau's charms. Nicolas narrowed his eyes as he watched Jean point her out to Guillaume.

Staring over at the blue-eyed beauty who'd haunted his dreams these past couple of months, Nicolas told himself it didn't matter he'd lost to Tristan. He only had an appetite for one thing. This evening, Ysabeau was wearing a sprig of honeysuckle in her yellow hair, the delicate white buds with their golden stems giving off a seductive fragrance he could almost smell from where he was sitting.

Tristan could have his fun as King of the Bean. Nicolas had something far more interesting planned. He couldn't wait for the dancing to begin as this was the opportunity he'd been waiting for. After all, there was no way Ysabeau's old husband would be able to keep up with them on the dance floor. He watched the servants clear away the last trestle tables and benches and was about to get to his feet to cross the room to Ysabeau when Tristan, sporting a dramatic black patch over his right eye (that hadn't been there before), stood up. In his new role as King of the Bean, he marched purposefully over to the centre of the great hall. With his patch and a scratch down one cheek, Nicolas thought he resembled a brigand from the Mattois area of Paris - except that he was carrying a lute rather than a dagger in his right hand. All around the great hall, guests were calling out for him to select his Queen of the Bean.

'Choose her yourself, Tristan!' shouted Guillaume. 'We trust you to pick the prettiest here. We don't want a name out of a hat today.'

Nicolas could hardly hear himself think because of the noise Guillaume and Jean were making, whistling and banging their goblets on the wooden table. 'Patience, good folk,' said a smiling Tristan. 'All will be revealed in good time. I promise you, you'll have your queen.'

Hoping for much rougher treatment of Tristan, preferably a rebellion, Nicolas was disappointed when a hush quickly fell over the assembled company. Tristan had them spellbound as he bowed his head slightly in the manner of a king acknowledging obedient subjects. Then he pointed at a large painting in a heavy gilt frame, hanging on the opposite wall.

'This evening, as your new King,' he announced, 'I'm going to tell you a tale of days gone by. The lady who appears to enjoy it the most will be the one I select to be my Queen.'

This brought forth cheers and the sound of approving thumps upon tables around the great hall. Feeling disgruntled that Tristan was not only proving popular but had also delayed the dancing, Nicolas scowled at the painting. He knew it well. It was particularly well-lit this evening due to all the candles placed beneath it, ones blessed in that morning's mass. The painting had been a wedding gift to Guy and Grace d'Ardres from a visiting Count of Toulouse. It depicted a slender woman, dressed in a scarlet dress, edged with gold, standing on a rock in what were clearly the red scorched hills of the South. Her beautiful upturned face was filled with pride, and her long dark hair fanned out behind her. She was gazing out into the distance, one hand on her heart. Beneath her lay the sprawling countryside of Provence while behind her were enormous white clouds containing images of men with their swords drawn. Nicolas could see they were guarding the woman in their midst by the way their weapons were pointed downwards, and their fierce handsome faces turned away from her. At the bottom of the portrait were some lines of verse, written in the old language of Occitan.

'Once there was a minstrel,' began Tristan, strumming softly on his lute. 'Who was in love with Etiennette de Pennautier. Commonly known as "Loba, the She-Wolf". She was a woman of almost unearthly beauty. Three hundred years ago, she lured countless men to her mountain hideaway of the Castle of Cabaret.'

As he said this, the lutenist's gaze travelled around the room, taking in all the women, until it very pointedly came to rest on one woman alone.

Nicolas's quarry.

He swallowed hard as he watched Tristan's eyes linger on Ysabeau, before coaxing a smile from those delectable lips. Nicolas became aware of something resembling a low...almost wolflike...snarl coming from his own throat. He could hardly believe how Tristan was every inch the courtly lover with his feigned earnestness and adoring looks. His voice grew lower and more seductive as he plucked at his lute:

'Etiennette lived at a time when certain of the populace in southern France were inspired to embrace a new religion. But this caused consternation elsewhere and culminated in a vengeful crusade, led by both King and Church. Yet, high up in her retreat, the fearless She-Wolf of Cabaret still openly entertained admiring troubadours and warriors of the Cathar faith with perfect ease.'

Nicolas wanted to cry out to Ysabeau that it was only an act: a cheap imitation of the behaviour to be found at the long-ago Aquitaine court of the fabled Eleanor. But instead he was forced to suffer in silence. To do anything else would look shabby and mean-spirited; besides, his rival for Ysabeau's affections hardly gave him the chance as he confidently held forth. He was looking at Ysabeau as if he were speaking to her alone…and as if the story was solely for her ears. Nicolas could see 'Tristan the courtly lover' was leaving no one in the great hall in any doubt he'd found *his* Lady to worship: his Queen of the Bean.

'One of these, a minstrel called Peire Vidal, forever immortalized Loba, the She-Wolf, in his verse. He even dressed up as a wolf—'

'Whatever for?' cried Ysabeau, clapping her hands together in excitement, obviously forgetting where she was, or that a courtly lady was supposed to behave with restraint and dignity.

'As I told you, the nickname of the woman he wanted to visit was Loba which means "she-wolf". Peire pranced around the hillside below her castle on all fours, half-hoping wild dogs would savage him.'

'But why would he do something so crook-pated?'

'I really have no idea, Dame Ysabeau,' replied Tristan, putting one hand to his heart, playing the part of a lovesick minstrel to perfection - as if he'd been born to it. 'But I am told men do all kinds of "clay-brained" things in the name of love. I even know one man who has the nickname of "Wolf"', he said, shooting Nicolas a sly look and earning a loud laugh from Guillaume Gouffier. Turning back to Ysabeau, he became serious again. 'Our troubadour obviously thought if he had some physical wounds to show, his lady would take pity on him and favour him over his rival, the Comte de Foix.'

'You look as though you've got some physical wounds, Monsieur Tristan,' simpered Ysabeau, to the sound of laughter ringing all around the great hall.

Furious that Guillaume Gouffier had told Tristan François d'Angoulême's name for him, Nicolas wanted to jump up and blacken Tristan's other eye. But all he could do was grit his teeth as he watched his rival produce a golden crown seemingly from thin air and place it on Ysabeau's head.

'You see, I promised you I'd find my Queen of the Bean,' he told his audience.

Judging from the cheers and clapping, Ysabeau was a popular choice. Nicolas guessed that not only Tristan, Guillaume, and Jean, shared his longing, but most of the males in the great hall. He also noticed that some of the females looked as though they'd sipped on vinegar rather than wine. It didn't take the cheers from Tristan's friends to tell Nicolas where Ysabeau's favours lay now. He knew his own cause was hopeless. At that moment, Tristan looked across the hall and shot Nicolas a triumphant look as if to say:

...I know you wanted her. Well, I've got her!...

All the breath left Nicolas's body as if he'd been punched in the ribs again. The awful truth came to him in a blinding flash: <<*the venomed canker-blossom is deliberately wooing Ysabeau to spite me*>> It was the most exquisite act of revenge Nicolas could have imagined. Yet all he could do was watch helplessly while Tristan gave his prize a winning smile. He knew he might as well go to bed. It was pointless to wait for the dancing, especially when Tristan began to sing in a melodious voice that even a thwarted Nicolas had to admit was made for seduction:

> *'Et ab joie li er mos treus*
> *Entre gel e vent e neus.*
> *La Loba ditz que seus so,*
> *Et an be dreg e razo,*
> *Que, per ma fe, melhs sui seus*
> *Que no sui d'autrui ni meus.'*

{'I go to her with joy
Through wind and snow and sleet
The She-Wolf says I am hers
And by God she's right:
I belong to her
More than to any other, even to myself.'}

∽

Ysabeau returned Tristan's smouldering look as he held out his hand to lead her out into the middle of the floor.

'My Queen and I will now dance *"Le Branle des chevaux"*,' declared Tristan, signalling to several young people, including Jean and Guillaume, to come and join him in the circle. Even though Nicolas enjoyed the lively dance that usually ended up with at least one person left lying on the floor helpless with laughter because of its speed, all he felt tonight was despair.

'Not joining us, Nicolas?' said Jean as he leapt over the table.

'I'm not sure Tristan invited him, did he?' laughed Guillaume, grabbing the hand of a pretty girl and pulling her along with him, his hapless wife, Bonaventure, totally forgotten. Knowing him, she was probably languishing in some distant château or other.

It quickly became obvious that the whole thing had been pre-planned. A man entered the great hall, dressed in the costume of a minstrel and carrying a wheel fiddle known as a *vielle à roue* under his arm. Did the pair have no shame? To a roar of appreciation, the man began to play, turning the handle on the side of the long wooden box, slowly at first, and then gradually faster. Inside, the four strings began to vibrate and produce the distinctive music of the often frowned-upon Branle.

Deliberately ignoring the fact he would have had no qualms about being in Tristan's red velvet shoes this evening, Nicolas glanced over at Ysabeau's husband who was being made a public cuckold: in sentiment, if not in deed. All in the name of the King and Queen of the Bean. Happily for Tristan, Robert de Sapincourt was slumped over the table, deep in his cups, not far from Guy d'Ardres. Most conveniently for his fobbing son, Monsieur Guy was in earnest conversation with the French Ambassador to England. No doubt the Abbot of Fécamp had brought further disturbing news to Ardres Castle from the Tudor court.

Even Dame Grace didn't seem to mind Tristan's outrageous antics. She was in a particularly good mood this evening because it was her birthday. What delight she'd shown when Nicolas gave her a brand new saddle for her dappled grey mare, the one he'd been saving up for since May. Feeling a pang of envy and disappointment, he watched her smiling indulgently at her son, clapping in time to the music, and occasionally exchanging what was clearly a humorous remark with the Baroness de Fleury and her mother-in-law, Symonne. Looking at all of them, seemingly oblivious to the sensual dance of love being performed right under their noses, a disgusted Nicolas tried to distract himself with thoughts of the country across the Narrow Sea.

<<*I wonder how the English celebrate La Fête des Rois*>>

CECILY

Chapter Fifty-Three

Twelfth Night. Saint Michael's Mount.

*J*ust think. By thish time tomorrow, I'll no longer be Lady Lizzie Stafford, eldest daughter of the Duke of Buckingham, but Lady Lizzie Neville. Countessh of Weshtmoreland.'

As she said this, Lizzie spun around, her cheeks flushed and her eyes glittering. In her hand, she held the wassailing bowl of which she'd just drunk deep and long. Perhaps too deep and long. I'd noticed her taking a swig outside when we took the bowl to wish the trees good health. The remaining contents of the bowl - after it had been passed from mouth to mouth - should have been poured onto the roots of a tree. Instead, I'd watched Lizzie drain the bowl. Perhaps she was more nervous about the wedding night than she was letting on.

'By this time tomorrow, you'll no longer be a maid!' smirked Mary Bullen, as if reading my thoughts.

Lizzie tried hard to look offended but didn't quite manage it. Swaying slightly, she pointed an accusing finger at her friend. 'As Lady of Mishrule for the day,' she said, slurring her words slightly, 'I pronounce that as punishment, you must sing a solo verse from the "Glosh...the Gloucestershire Wash... Wassail".' She passed the bowl to Nan and held up one hand to her eyes as if she were seeking someone. 'Where ish my Abbot of Unreason?' she asked, blinking several times. 'Ah, there he is.'

Across the great hall, handsome Ralph Neville, dressed in his finest clothes (and considerably more sober than his future bride), was deep in conversation with his future in-laws, Edward and Alianore, the Duke and Duchess of Buckingham; his own mother, Edith, and his step-father, Thomas. Already bound to the family by the wardship that had been granted to Lizzie's father a couple of years ago, that bond was about to get much stronger.

ॐ

<<I feel so happy standing in the hall, amongst all my friends and family>> We'd arrived at the Mount by boat yesterday, together with servants transporting everything we needed for the wedding. My mother surprised me with a brand new dress of yellow velvet, bordered with cloth of gold, and furred with ermine. Lizzie was to wear a gown of silver satin, lined with white taffeta, and a cape of scarlet velvet around her shoulders.

I could see my parents, standing next to their friend, John Arscott, the Archpriest, all of them smiling at us indulgently, knowing they'd played their part in the wedding plans. We'd had such fun since Thomas Bullen left to go back to court: no overbearing adult telling us what to do from dawn to dusk. The Knyvett children soon learned that life at Zennor Castle was much freer than at Hever and made the most of it. Nan told me her brother, Tom, was sweet on me (after realizing his cause with Lizzie was lost forever), and wouldn't stop talking about my dimples. I liked Tom well enough but when I saw Lizzie and Ralph gazing adoringly at one another, or stealing a kiss when they thought no one was looking, I knew I'd never feel that way about him.

Nan came up to me and wound her arm around my waist. 'What do you think 1513 holds for us, Cecy?'

'I don't know. It's going to begin with a wedding....'

'A love match.'

I smiled at her. 'Well, surely that's a good sign. It means the stars are in our favour.'

'I don't want to wait for my palace the cherry stones once promised me. I want it soon.'

'You already live in a castle. So why do you have to live in a palace?'

She gave a shrug. 'Because it's not *my* castle. It belongs to my father. And I have to obey him.'

'If you lived in a palace, you'd still have to obey whoever owned it.'

'Well, let's hope my royal husband will be so old he'll do whatever I tell him.'

We both laughed, not truly believing in the predictions of our game of cherries.

◌

'Hush,' a far more sober Lizzie called out a little later. Within a few minutes, she managed to bring her subjects to heel and arrange for her Abbot of Unreason to accompany us on a lute.

'Nan and Mary Bullen, Cecy Tredavoe and I, will now sing "The Gloucestershire Wassail",' our Lady of Misrule announced to the hall in a clear voice. 'And Mary Bullen will sing a solo for the fourth verse. Let the fun commence.'

As she said these last words, the heat made me feel momentarily faint and I thought I was going to fall. The entire hall seemed to sway before my eyes as if it had been built on quicksand, not on stone. But then Nan grasped me under the elbow and thankfully, the moment passed.

I looked over at Ralph who was seated on a small wooden stool, holding his lute. He still looked like a boy with his tousled brown hair and grin that seemed to stretch from ear to ear. But he was certainly man enough to know he wanted to take our Lizzie to wife, with all this entailed.

◌

'*Wassail, wassail all over the town,*' we began to sing, with Lizzie indicating that everyone in the hall should join in the chorus which they did with gusto:

'*Our toast it is white, and our ale, it is brown*
Our bowl it is made of the white maple tree
With the wassailing bowl, we'll drink to thee.'

As promised, after the third verse, Lizzie beckoned to Mary to step forward for her solo.

'*So here is to Broad Mary and to her broad horn,*' Mary began to sing to a big round of applause.

'May God send our master a good crop of corn
And a good crop of corn that may we all see
With the wassailing bowl, we'll drink t – '

All of a sudden, she faltered and I realized she must have forgotten the words. Next to me, Nan let out a gasp and I noticed Lizzie had gone deathly pale. Expecting her to fall to the floor at any moment, I held out my hands to catch her. But then I saw Ralph had dropped his lute and total silence descended upon the great hall. For some reason, all heads were turned towards the door at the far end.

And then I saw them.

Four men, dressed in grey and black, with long fur capes draped around their shoulders, were standing at the entrance to the hall. Lizzie hadn't mentioned anything about mummers coming to play. Perhaps they were supposed to be Jesus and the Three Wise Men come to celebrate Twelfth Night with us. Except that they bore far more of a resemblance to the Devil and his henchmen come to do mischief. Outside, the chapel bell started to ring out six chimes. But inside there was only silence.

<<*It's so quiet in here I can hear a pin drop*>>

I took a deep breath to calm myself as they began to walk towards us.

'*No!*' I muttered. <<*Surely it can't be…can it?*>>

Nan and I looked at one another, her dark eyes fearful. I felt my knees go weak beneath me.

'God save us all!' she whispered, taking my hand and squeezing it as tightly as she could. 'It's the Howards!'

GLOSSARY OF SIXTEENTH CENTURY WORDS AND TERMS

A

A las visperas se conoce la fiest	at vespers is the feast at its best.
Ague	from the middle French aiguë, an intermittent fever, with fits of hot and cold: a malarial type ailment.
Almoner	official distributor of alms (money or food) for the royal household; office requiring personal attendance on the King, and involvement, on a junior level, to the royal council.
Aqua vitae	a strong alcoholic drink such as brandy.
Astrolabe	an ancient instrument used to solve problems relating to time, and the position of the sun and stars in the sky.

B

Bat-fowling	cheating.
Beef-witted	stupid, dull.
Beslubbering	smeared with something thick and oily.
Beetle-headed	a stupid person, a blockhead.
Black Redstart	a small robin-sized bird. The greyish-black male has a red tail.
Blockhead	a stupid person.
Boar-pig	named after the Bartholomew boar-pig, sold at the annual London fair, held on Saint Bartholomew's Day.
Boil-brained	hot-headed.
Bower	a lady's private apartment in a medieval manor or castle.
Bum-bailey	sheriff's officer who catches people by sneaking up behind them.
Bustard	the world's heaviest flying bird.
By-blow	an illegitimate child.

C

Canker-blossom a grub that destroys the blossom of love.

Cameline sauce a medieval sauce made in large quantities, usually containing bread, vinegar (or verjuice) and spices such as cinnamon.

Cateran a warrior or raider from the Scottish Highlands.

Chevalier of Saint-Michel a French chivalric order begun by Louis XI, 'the Spider King'. Its aim was to confirm the loyalty of its members to the King. At first, there were only thirty-six members, but these were amongst the most powerful nobles in France.

Churlish rude, boorish.

Civet an animal with a cat-like appearance, native to Africa or tropical Asia, from which a musky scent used in perfume, was obtained.

Clack-dish a begging bowl that could be clacked to attract attention.

Clapper-clawed thrashed, reviled.

Clareshaw a harp with strings.

Clarsach a Gaelic triangular harp.

Clay-brained stupid.

Clotpole blockhead, dolt.

Corbie a raven or crow.

Close-stool a covered chamber pot enclosed in a wooden stool.

Comfort happiness, joy.

Confiture de noix walnut and honey conserve.

Coxcomb a fool's cap with a crest like a cock's comb; a simpleton.

Craven a cock that shows no fighting spirit; a coward.

To be in one's cups be very drunk.

Crookbacked hunchbacked.

Crook-pated having a deformed head; not in one's right mind.

Crowstepped a gable with a staircase kind of design.

Culpae poenae let the punishment fit the crime.

D

Dalliance flirtation, coquetry.

Damask rose thought to have been brought to Europe from Syria by the Crusaders in the thirteenth century.

Devil-monk a mischievous monk.

Dewberry a sweet deep purplish berry, closely related to a blackberry.

Dismal-dreaming full of ill-boding dreams.

Dissembling   deceitful, false.

Dog-hearted   cruel, callous.

Doxy   a beggar's mistress; a whore.

Dread-bolted   armed with frightening thunderbolts; terrifying.

Droning   to talk for a long time in a boring way.

E

Earth-vexing   extremely annoying.

Effeuiller la marguerite   the Daisy Oracle.

Ell   a unit of measurement equivalent to six hand-breaths from a man's elbow to the end of his middle finger.

Escutcheon   a shield on which a coat-of-arms is shown.

F

Fat-kidneyed   very overweight and clumsy.

Fen-sucked   rising from the marshes.

Filbert   a hazelnut, named after the French saint, Philbert.

Flap-mouthed   having broad, hanging lips; talkative.

Flirt-gill   a pert or wanton woman.

Fly-bitten   attacked by flies, unattractive.

Folly-fallen   acting stupidly or rashly.

Footlicker   a sycophant; a toady.

Fripperies   ornate or showy clothing or adornments.

Full-gorged   fed until satiated.

G

Gable   a triangular shaped part of a roof, over a window or door.

Galopin   a kitchen helper.

Gleeking   to make fun of; foolish.

Goodly   excellent.

Gorbellied   having a large belly; a paunch.

Gourd   a vegetable such as a pumpkin or cucumber.

Greybeard   an old man.

Groat   an English silver coin worth four pennies.

Grudge   begrudge.

H

Harquebus	an early type of portable gun.
Hautboy	from the French 'haut bois' 'high wood'. A woodwind instrument. An oboe.
Hedge-born	born under a hedge; of lowly birth.
Hedge-pig	a hedgehog.
Hell-hated	hated as hell is hated.
Henbane	a poisonous plant.
Hennin	a headdress in the shape of a cone or steeple.
Hobby horse	a child's toy made from a stick with a horse's head at one end.
Put horns on a man	cuckold him.
Hornbook	a page to teach children the alphabet, for example, covered by a transparent piece of horn and attached to a frame by a handle.
Horn-mad	mad like a savage bull.
Hugger-mugger	one who keeps secrets.
Hurdy-Gurdy	a medieval stringed instrument that produces sound by turning a wheel (using a crank) with one hand, and operating a keyboard with the other to change pitch.
Hyppocras	a wine mixed with sugar and spices.

I

Ille	ill.

J

Jack-a-nape	an impertinent person; ape.
Jointure	a provision made by a husband for his wife in the event of his death.
Jolthead	a stupid or foolish person; a large or heavy head.

K

Kirk	a church in the north of England and Scotland.
Kingdom of Castile	a large powerful state on the Iberian Peninsula during the Middle Ages.
Kissing comfit	a perfumed sugar-plum or thin sugared lozenge to sweeten the breath, with musk, civet, ambergris, and white orris, set with gum dragon.

Knave	a dishonest or unscrupulous man.
Knotty-pated	block-headed, dull-witted.

L

Lamprey	an eel-like vertebrate with a round sucking mouth to feed off the blood of other animals.
Le Branle des chevaux	the Horses' Brawl.
Le Val Doré	the Golden Vale.
Let	hinder, prevent.
Lichen	a combination of algae and fungus.
List	desires.
Lyare	a rich carpet.

M

Maggot-pie	a magpie; a pie made out of maggots.
Malmsey wine	a sweet wine, imported from Greece.
Malt-worm	drinker of malt liquor; a drunkard.
Mammering	hesitating, stammering.
Manchet loaf	a small flat, circular loaf of very high quality.
Marchpane	marzipan.
Master Falconer	a position in the King's household in France from the Middle Ages onwards. He was responsible for organizing the royal falcon hunt and looking after the monarch's hunting birds.
Master of the Hunt	was the most important office dealing with the royal hunt and carried great prestige.
Mattois area of Paris	an area of Paris famous for thieves.
Megrim	a headache, a migraine.
Milk-livered	cowardly, timorous.
Milksop	a man or boy who is indecisive and lacks courage.
Minnow	a small European freshwater fish; an insignificant person.
Miracolo del marito geleso	the miracle of the jealous husband.
Miscreant	one who behaves badly, often breaking the rules.
Moldwarp	a mole; an old man.
Motley-minded	having the mind of a jester, foolish.
Muddy-mettled	dull-spirited.
Mummer	an actor in a masked mime or a traditional mummer's play, often on feast days.

O

Occitan	a Romance language spoken mainly in southern France, but also in Italy and Spain.
Onion-eyed	eyes filled with tears.

P

Pastance	pastime.
Pignut	a small umbellifer (member of the carrot family) with fine leaves and delicate stems. Tubers used to feed hogs.
Pinch-spotted	a spotty complexion.
Popinjay	a conceited, foolish person.
Pottage	a thick soup or stew made by boiling vegetables and grains, and if available, meat or fish.
Poulaille farcie	stuffed poultry.
Pribbling	argumentative.
Pumpion	a pumpkin, hence a fat person.
Purgatory	in Catholic theology, an intermediate stage after death, a place to atone for sins before being considered pure enough to enter heaven.
Puttock	any of several birds of prey.

Q

Qualling	insufferable.
Quintain	a practice target such as a board on a pole or a shield, used by knights to hone their skills or train new knights.
Quinny	female genitalia.

R

Rebeck	a pear-shaped, two or three-stringed medieval instrument.
Reeling-ripe	so drunk that ripe for reeling or staggering.
Ring-dove	a ringed turtle dove.
Rood	a crucifix, especially one placed above the rood screen of a church.
Roup	a croak.
Roynish	base, vulgar.
Rump-fed	fattened in the rump, pampered.
Running at the ring	a crosspiece from which a ring was dangled, intended to

be plucked by a knight, galloping at full speed, using his lance.

S

Sample	a piece of embroidery to keep stitches and patterns as a reference.
Scullion	a servant employed to work in a kitchen.
Scurvy-valiant	supremely worthless.
Set	set upon it.
Shard-borne	born in dung.
Sheep-biting	giving to snapping at defenceless people.
Shooting at the butts	target practice using a longbow, aimed at a butt: a seven-foot tall, wedge-shaped mound of earth, covered by a cloth or pasteboard.
Shrill-gorged	displeasing to the ear.
Small beer	the third use of the malt in brewing to produce a bitter, very weak beer, given to servants, invalids, the elderly and small children. Or to anyone to quench a thirst as water was considered too unhealthy to drink.
Smettila!	stop that!
Snipper-snapper	a small insignificant fellow.
Sola virtus invicta	virtue alone invincible.
Soringue	a cereal grain plant of the grass family.
Sot	a drunkard; an idiot.
Spur-galled	to be wounded by a spur; galled.
Stew	a brothel.
Stock(e)	the trunk or main stem of a plant or tree.
Stomacher	a triangular panel, often decorated with jewels, on the front of a woman's gown.
Swag-bellied	having a prominent, overhanging belly.
Swain	a male lover or admirer.

T

Tallow candle	a wick of flax, cotton or hemp, placed in animal fat such as from a cow or a sheep.
Termagant	a harsh-tempered or overbearing woman.
Tiziano Vecelli	an Italian painter known as 'Titian' (1490-1576).
Tragacanth	gum from a small shrub, imported from Turkey or Syria, used as an emulsifier.

Tétons	breasts.
Tickle-brained	dim-witted, under the influence of strong drink.
Toad-spotted	foully blemished, most evil.

U

Un seul coeur en trois corps	one heart in three bodies.
Usquebaugh	from Scottish Gaelic, '*uisge beatha*', 'water of life'; whisky.

V

Varlet	a base unprincipled man.
Verjus	a pungent acidic liquid.
Vielle à roue	hurdy gurdy.
Void	the dessert course of a meal, consisting of spiced wine, wafers and spices, eaten in a separate chamber, by invitation only.

W

Wassail	from Old Norse, a drink of spiced ale, served at Christmas, calling out a salutation, meaning: 'Be healthful!'.
Wastrel	a wasteful or good-for-nothing person.
Waterfly	a dragonfly; a flighty or troublesome person.
Wayward	wilful, erratic.
Weevil	a type of beetle, often found in nuts, seeds, cereal and grain.
Wherryman	a man in charge of a light rowing boat/barge, mainly used for carrying passengers.
Whey-face	a very pale face; milk-face.
Whoreson	a bastard, a coarse fellow.
Will-o'-the-wisp	a flame-like ghostly light (caused by gases from decaying plants), seen at night over bogs, fens and marshes; something that is impossible to obtain or achieve.

—◆◇◆—

Recipes...

'*Zennor Castle Mince Pie*', adapted from '*A Medieval Christmas Pie*', and reproduced with kind permission of Sophie Jackson, author of '*The Medieval Christmas*'. Sutton Publishing. 2005.

'*Stirling Castle Twelfth Night Cake*', copied from a recipe of the same name, also very gratefully received from Sophie Jackson.

All other recipes have been personally tried and tested by the author and adapted from original recipe books of the time.

—◆◇◆—

ACKNOWLEDGEMENTS...

First of all, I would like to thank the following historians (as well as others) for taking time out of their busy schedules to answer my questions on the finer details of French law and society:

- Professor Emeritus Frederic J. Baumgartner (University of Virginia). Author of 'France in the sixteenth century'.
- Professor Barbara B. Diefendorf (University of Boston). Author of 'Paris City Councillors in the sixteenth century'.
- Professor Mark Greengrass (University of Sheffield). Author of 'Christendom Destroyed. A History of Europe (1517-1648).

Next, I'd like to thank my father for his thoughtfulness and generosity in giving me gifts of books from the period. My mother for always believing in me. And my sister for her suggestions. Then, of course, there is my extremely supportive husband and sons who have lived and breathed all things Tudor for a very long time. Our eldest son even decided to arrive in the world on the same day of the month as Henry VIII!

I have to say a big thank you to all my lovely friends who've helped me on this journey, especially Jan for all our cosy chats about history and ancestry by the fire, and for your constant support and encouragement, telling me never to give up. And Nancy, for your positive feedback which meant so much, your thought-provoking comments - and, of course, the magnificent Henry VIII mug you gave me. Flick, Lin and Neilian for your enthusiasm. Clare and Eszter for loving Nicolas from the outset. Agnès, for kindly checking my French. And Ingrid, for your help and ideas.

Last but definitely not least, I'd like to thank my coffee-loving writing group on Twitter. Your help, humour and support means the world to me.

ONE LAST THING....

If you enjoyed this book, I'd be grateful if you could post a short review on Amazon, Goodreads, Facebook etc.... Or kindly spread the word. Your support really does make a difference.
Thank you.

Vivienne Brereton *
October 2018
www.viviennebrereton.com

* Brereton is an old Cheshire, Staffordshire, and West Yorkshire name. A mixture of 'briar' and 'tun' (settlement), together meaning 'from where the briars grow', one of the most famous bearers of the Brereton name was Sir William Brereton, (1487- May 17th, 1536). One of Anne Boleyn's supposed lovers and a Groom of Henry VIII's Privy Chamber, his downfall and execution probably came about because of a previous falling out with Thomas Cromwell. His last words came closer to maintaining his innocence than any of the other four men, executed alongside him: '*I have deserved to die if it were a thousand deaths. But the cause whereof I die, judge not. But if ye judge, judge the best.*' He repeated this phrase over and over, as a final attempt to proclaim his innocence.

COMING IN 2021...

Book Two: Beware the Lizard Lurking

Find out what happens next....

Made in the USA
Las Vegas, NV
16 January 2023

65733996R00218